Please turn the page for more reviews. . . .

BODYGUARD

SUZANNE BROCKMANN

BALLANTINE BOOKS • NEW YORK

A Ballantine Book
Published by The Random House Publishing Group
Copyright © 1999 by Suzanne Brockmann
Excerpt from *Flashpoint* copyright © 2004 by Suzanne Brockmann

All rights reserved under International and Pan-American Copyright Conventions. Published in the United States by The Random House Publishing Group, a division of Random House, Inc., New York.

Ballantine and colophon are registered trademarks of Random House, Inc.

www.ballantinebooks.com

This book contains an excerpt from the forthcoming book *Flashpoint* by Suzanne Brockmann. This excerpt has been set for this edition only and may not reflect the final content of the forthcoming edition.

ISBN 0-345-46620-9

Manufactured in the United States of America

First Fawcett Books Mass Market Edition: December 1999
First Ballantine Books Mass Market Edition: February 2004

OPM 10 9 8 7 6 5 4 3 2 1

For Ed, Eric, Bill, and Scott, the survivors of the "Small or Large" incident, and brave Kathy who stayed in orbit with V'ger Snacktray. Thanks for Katonah.

One

〜〜〜〜

"Okay," George Faulkner said, quieting the group of men around the VCR in the coffee room, "any second now he'll see what's going on through the window and come in."

The video they were watching wasn't a typical blurry security tape. It was from a state-of-the-art surveillance setup, complete with audio track—designed to stop the sale of drugs among the broccoli and cantaloupes—paid for by the owner of a chain of New York City markets.

Just hours ago, the camera hadn't caught an illegal drug transaction on video but rather a robbery attempt that easily could have escalated into a multiple homicide.

Three perps, strung out beyond belief, had just shot the young store clerk. A very young teenage girl cowered by the front counter, weeping silently. One of the robbers—a short Hispanic kid with a bandanna around his head—had gone back behind the counter and was trying to open the cash register.

The second perp, the man who'd shot the clerk, was so high he couldn't stand still. He danced around nervously near the door, a .38 clutched in his hand. The third was a tall, painfully gaunt man who stood threateningly close to the girl, watching intently as Bandanna wrestled with the cash register.

"Here he comes," George murmured.

1

The door opened.

All three men looked up.

Harry O'Dell, George's partner in the Bureau for the past eight months, walked into the market as if their guns didn't exist. In fact, he was moving a lot like the dancer, as if he, too, had just shot something toxic into his veins. It wasn't until he was all the way up to the checkout counter that the overhead light glinted off the gun he held in his own hand.

The bandanna-wearer and the skinny man saw it at the exact same second, but it was already too late. Harry had aimed it directly between Bandanna's eyes at close to point-blank range. "Empty the cash register!" he shouted. "Nobody moves fast, nobody gets hurt!"

"Holy God." The precinct's lieutenant was standing next to George, watching the tape. "He's pretending to rob the store. Is he completely insane?"

George nodded. "Watch. It gets better."

The dancer's indignation was off the scale. "You can't fucking hit this place, man, we're hitting this place."

Harry turned and looked around the room, as if taking in the other guns and the cowering teenager for the very first time. "What do you mean, I can't hit this place? You got some kind of agreement with the owner says you're the only ones can rip him off?"

He leaned over the counter to look down at the clerk who was out cold on the floor, bleeding. Harry's sharp gaze quickly assessed how badly the kid was hurt. George knew Harry saw the blood staining the clerk's pants, and that he could tell the worst of his injuries were from hitting his head when he fell.

"Damn, you shot this guy in the ass. What, were you afraid he was going to sit on you?" Harry laughed uproariously at his own joke.

"He is insane," murmured one of the detectives watching the tape.

On the tape, the dancer wasn't happy. "Go away, man. I'm warning you!"

Harry snorted. "You go away. I've been planning this job for days. Weeks."

"Yo, we was here first!" Bandanna joined the shouting match.

"Screw you. I'm here now! What gives you the right to come in here ten minutes too early and screw up my job, anyway? Go the fuck home and leave this to a professional."

Bandanna laughed in disbelief. "A professional? Look at you, man! Who the hell does a holdup in a freaking suit? Not just a suit—a shitty suit that you've been sleeping in for three weeks."

"Oh," Harry said quietly. "Perfect. Now you're slamming me for getting caught in the rain." He began to shout again. "When I planned this job, I didn't plan for it to rain, all right? Can you give me a fucking break here—"

Skinny found his voice. "Yo, asshole, this is our territory."

Harry turned and looked more closely at him. "Hey, Fat Jimmy, is that you?" he asked, his tone changing abruptly again, softer now, as if his sudden anger were instantly forgotten.

The skinny man looked behind him. "Fat who?"

Harry shouted with laughter. "You wily old son of a bitch, it is you! We were in Walpole, up near Boston, in '87 and '88, remember? How the hell are you, Fatman?"

The look on Skinny's face was incredulous as Harry grabbed him in a bear hug. He struggled to get away. "I'm not Jimmy, and I'm not fat."

"Christ, you lost a lot of weight since prison, didn't you? That fattening food up there really made it tough to keep those pounds off, huh, Jim? Hey—how the hell is Bennie Tessitada? You and the Benster were like blood brothers."

"Is this guy completely fearless, or what?" the lieutenant asked.

"Or what," George answered even though he knew the question was mostly rhetorical. "This is how he spends his first night off in seventeen weeks. Don't misunderstand me, he doesn't look for trouble. But somehow trouble always manages to find Harry."

On the tape, the dancer looked as if he wanted to use his gun. "Get the hell outta here, man! You're messing things up."

"I'm messing things up?" Harry laughed. "I'm messing things up? You're the geniuses shot the clerk in the ass before Einstein here realized he doesn't know how to get the register drawer open. And you're doing this in front of an audience, to boot." He focused on the girl. "What the hell are you looking at? Get out of here. Go home!"

She was as terrified of Harry as she was of the three perps, but she tossed her blonde hair defiantly even as tears streamed down her face. "I'm not leaving Bobby."

"What the fuck you doing, man?" The dancer was even more upset. "You can't let her go. She's our hostage!"

"Wait a minute," Harry said, lifting the girl's chin and looking at her from both sides. "Oh, man. Of all your stupid choices tonight, guys, holding her hostage's got to win the stupid award. Don't you know who this girl is?" He didn't wait for them to answer. "She's Tina Marie D'Angelo. She's Antonio D'Angelo's daughter. He runs most of Newark, and while Jersey might seem like very far away to you, D'Angelo has very, very long arms. If you don't want him to reach out and touch you with a couple of bullets in the back of the head, you might want to help me show Tina here to the door."

Skinny and the bandanna were properly taken aback, but the girl was not cooperating. "I'm not—"

Harry yanked her toward him and she shrieked with alarm. "I've got a message for your father, Tina." He pulled her away from the perps, scowling. "It's private—do you mind?"

He leaned close to the girl, whispering into her ear. And just like that, visibly, she calmed.

"He's telling her he's FBI, and he needs her out of there before he can help the clerk," George said. "He's promising her that he'll die himself before he lets anything else happen to Bobby."

And the girl believed him. Or at least she did after she looked up into Harry's eyes. His back was to the perps, and as he gave the girl a reassuring smile, all the craziness left his face. "I promise," he whispered.

She decided to trust him and she nodded.

"Go," he said, and she bolted for the door.

Harry moved with her, blocking her in case one of the perps got startled. He already knew they were trigger-happy sons of bitches.

"Good job clearing the room," the police lieutenant said.

"You shouldn'ta let her go, man." Dancer was pissed. "Now, something goes wrong, we don't have a hostage."

"No way do we want Tony D'Angelo's kid for a hostage," the bandanna said earnestly.

"That was bullshit." The dancer spat on the floor. "She don't look Italian." He had to use two hands to level his gun at Harry. "You're fucking this up, man. I oughta fucking shoot you!"

For the first time since he'd come in, Harry stood

absolutely still, looking directly down the barrel of that gun, looking straight into the man's eyes.

"You wanna shoot me?" he asked. His voice was so quiet the police lieutenant had to lean forward, straining to hear. "Go ahead and shoot me. I don't care. But you can bet your life, you shoot me—even in the head—I'll shoot you before I hit the floor."

No one moved, not in the market, not in the coffee room. No one so much as breathed. Except George, who shook his head and laughed. "He does this all the time. He really doesn't care—which can be a little disconcerting. I've got to admit, when we're in a car together, I no longer let him drive."

On the tape, the dancer lowered his gun.

Harry burst into sudden laughter, moving back behind the counter. Skinny and the dancer exchanged uneasy looks. George knew they were thinking that whoever this guy was, he was definitely crazed. They were probably right.

"Outta my way, kid," Harry pushed the bandanna-wearer aside, effectively putting himself between the clerk and the perps. "I can get this thing open." He reached down underneath the counter with his free hand. "What you've gotta do is find the secret release button, and it's right . . . here."

Around them, a piercing alarm went off.

"You dumb shit!" the skinny man shouted. "That's the alarm. Now the police are definitely gonna come."

Harry smiled and raised his gun. "No, friend, the police are already here. Hands up, no one move—you stupid motherfuckers are under arrest."

That was when the shooting started.

But Harry being Harry, it was over almost before it began.

*   *   *

Every light was on in the house.

Alessandra Lamont pulled into her driveway and just sat, looking at the Tudor-style monster she'd called her home for the past seven years.

When she'd gone out to visit Jane at the Northshore Children's Hospital not quite three hours ago, she'd only left the hall light burning.

Now every light was on. And every window was broken.

Less than three hours ago, the last of the cleaning teams had left. Less than three hours ago, the house had been pristine and perfect, ready for Sunday morning's real estate open house showing.

She leaned forward slightly to get a better look out the windshield. Yes, indeed, every window—including the round stained-glass antique over the front door—had been shattered.

It had been a very bad year, and it obviously wasn't over yet.

In January, Griffin Lamont had rung out the old and ushered in the new. And at twenty-seven years of age, Alessandra had joined the washed-out ranks of the legendary first wives' club. At twenty-seven years of age, she'd been traded in for a newer, shinier model. At twenty-seven, after being the center of attention at every party she'd ever attended, after being the Heisman of all trophy wives, she'd been all but put down to die.

In February, she'd sat down at a table with Griffin and their lawyers and worked out a divorce agreement. He'd sat across from her, his blond hair perfect, his blue eyes expressionless behind his glasses, his handsome face showing no regret, no remorse, no sign that the past seven years had even existed. He'd given her everything she'd asked for, though. The house. All three cars. A substantial percentage of his liquid assets. Apparently, the only thing he wanted was the azalea bush that had belonged to his mother—the one just outside the kitchen door.

Alessandra had thought she'd won a major victory, particularly when she'd set the paperwork in motion to adopt Jane. Eight months old, severely handicapped, and born with a heart defect, Jane was labeled unadoptable by Social Services and the nurses at the hospital where Alessandra did fund-raising volunteer work. She'd taken to stopping in the nursery several times a week, helping to give bottles and warm arms to the unwanted babies.

Most babies didn't stay unwanted for long, but Jane's physical problems were daunting. Still, her smile was pure sunshine, and Alessandra had applied to adopt as a single parent. Months earlier, she had gathered her courage and approached Griffin about the possibility of adopting the baby, but he'd flatly refused: "No way. Was she crazy?"

Maybe.

And in February, she thought she'd won.

Until March.

In March, she'd discovered that the house was triple mortgaged to the hilt, the cars were leased, and Griffin had filed for bankruptcy. He was broke. There were no liquid assets. And as a result, she was broke.

In March, Alessandra had received word that she had been turned down by the state. She wouldn't be allowed to adopt Jane. With her finances in disarray, with the sheer amount of her debt, she no longer had the ways or means to care for the baby, particularly since she would be a single mother.

Griffin's leaving had hurt, but this broke her heart. No one else wanted the baby who had been named Jane Doe. What would become of her?

Just tonight, Alessandra had found out that Jane

would be placed in an institution as soon as she was strong enough to leave the hospital.

January had been awful, February was bad, but March really took the cake.

In March, Alessandra had found out that Griffin was wanted by the police in connection to a drug deal that had gone wrong. And later in March, the police had come to her door again, this time bringing her the news that her soon-to-be ex-husband had finally been found, his body washed up in the East River, near LaGuardia Airport. His hands had been tied, and the autopsy report revealed he'd been shot twice in the back of the head. He'd been the victim of a classic gangland slaying.

It was terrible. She'd been angry with him, sure, but she hadn't wished him dead.

When the police questioned Alessandra, she'd told them she didn't know who or what Griffin had been involved with.

She didn't know, but she sure had her suspicions.

Michael Trotta. Alleged mob boss. Griffin had met him nearly ten years ago, playing golf at some local charity tournament. She herself had been to barbecues and cocktail parties at his Mineola home.

As she gazed expressionlessly at the broken windows in her house, her car phone rang. She picked it up, years of training and elocution lessons enabling her to sound cool and detached despite this latest disaster. "Hello?"

The voice was harsh, wasting no time on pleasantries. "Where's the money?"

"I'm sorry," Alessandra said. "What did you—"

"Find it," the voice rasped. "Fast. Or you're next."

The call was disconnected.

Apparently, March wasn't over yet.

* * *

Harry had put his head down on the table in the interview room and had fallen asleep. He was out cold, a cup of coffee still clutched in his hand. He slept exactly the way George expected him to sleep—with his teeth gritted and his eyes tightly, fiercely shut. There was absolutely none of that boyish-angel, relaxed serenity stuff happening when Harry slept, that was for certain.

George gazed at the precinct lieutenant over Harry's head and shrugged. "It's been a tough couple of months. We were working nonstop with a task force over in Jersey City, looking to indict Thomas Huang."

The beefy lieutenant sat tiredly at the table, across from Harry, as he shook his head. "You take out one mob boss, two weeks later his replacement's got the show up and running again."

"Not this time. We got the whole top half of Huang's organization. Harry made sure of it. He's a stickler for things like that."

The lieutenant looked at Harry. "He doesn't look like a stickler. Or a fed."

George adjusted his tie and brushed nonexistent lint from the sleeves of his own impeccable jacket. "He hasn't been my partner for long. We're still working on the suit thing."

"You want me to get a couple of the boys from the squad room to help you carry him out to your car?"

"No, thanks. He'll walk."

"Are you sure? One of the detectives wanted this room, shook him, but couldn't wake him."

George smiled. "I can get him on his feet." He leaned closer to Harry and whispered, "Michael Trotta."

Harry lifted his head. "What? Where?"

George spread his hands, gesturing See? "The task force worked so well, we're keeping it intact but moving it out onto the Island. Our next target's out near

Mineola. A gentleman named Michael Trotta. He's allegedly hip deep in illegal drug sales, prostitution, and graft. To name but a few potential charges—leaving out little things like murder one."

"So it is true. You're actually going for Trotta," the lieutenant mused. "And apparently you don't care who knows about it, huh?"

"We like to make 'em nervous," George said.

Harry took a slug of his coffee then spit it back into the cup. "God!" He looked up at George accusingly. "How long did you let me sleep?"

"I'm not exactly sure." George looked at his watch. "Two, maybe three hours, tops."

Harry rubbed the back of his neck with one hand. "What's the medical status on the clerk from the market? He all right?"

"He's gonna be okay," the lieutenant told him. "It was just a flesh wound. The blow to his head's nothing major either. He'll be released in the morning."

"What about the perps?"

"All have lived to waste precious taxpayer dollars," George said.

"What were you saying about Trotta?" Harry asked, rubbing his eyes with one hand.

"Just gossiping with the lieutenant."

"You know, something came in about Trotta only an hour ago," the lieutenant told them. "Some B&E report from the Island. Guy who recently showed up dead— word's out he made Trotta unhappy. No proof tying him to the murder, though." He snorted. "Of course not. Anyway, this guy's house was just trashed. Somewhere in . . . Farmingville, I think it was."

"Farmingdale?" Harry stood up. "Is the dead guy Griffin Lamont? 'Cause Griffin Lamont lives in Farmingdale. Lived."

"Yeah, Lamont, I think that's the name," the lieutenant stood up, too. "I can check if you want."

"Yeah," Harry said. "Please. Check the name. And the address, while you're at it."

"Oh, shit," George said. "I knew I shouldn't have let you sleep."

Harry rolled his head, trying to work a crick out of his neck. "Farmingdale's not that far. We could get out there in about an hour, this time of night."

"No," George said. "I'm not driving out to Long Island tonight. Absolutely, positively, definitely not."

Alessandra stood in the kitchen, shaking.

Whoever had done this had been thorough. As far as she could tell, there was little left intact in the entire house. Her couches and draperies had been knifed and torn, the wooden furniture splintered. Every piece of clothing in her closet had been shredded, her cosmetics crushed. Drying paint coated the once-expensive wall-to-wall carpeting and stained the walls. Here in the kitchen, her china had been smashed and ground into the Mexican tile floor along with broken jars of food from the pantry and refrigerator.

The devastation was complete. The quiet old house that had once been her sanctuary had been overrun by violence and chaos.

She closed her eyes as she bent over the sink, afraid she was going to vomit, silently cursing Griffin's immortal soul to hell. In life, he'd treated her as little more than a possession. In death, his grip on her was still as tight as ever.

Where's the money?

Alessandra couldn't begin to guess.

"Mrs. Lamont?"

She quickly straightened up, automatically checking

her hair in the broken glass of a photo of Cold Spring Harbor that still hung crookedly on the wall. "In the kitchen."

The police detective pushed open the door, wincing apologetically as he crunched on the remains of her Waterford crystal. He held out the phone. "Call waiting beeped while I was on with the captain. It's a Brandon Wright for you . . . ?"

Her lawyer. Finally. She took the phone. "Brandon, thank God. The house has been completely ransacked. Can you get over here right—"

"Alessandra, it's nearly two A.M."

"But the entire house is—"

"No, I'm sorry, I can't come out there now." He sighed heavily. "And I know this is not the right time, but I've been meaning to talk to you about this. You're broke. You can't afford me anymore."

She kept her voice calm as she went into the living room, searching desperately for some place, any place to sit down. "I see." There was no longer anywhere to sit in the entire house. She was going to have to take this latest blow standing up.

"I'm sorry. I hate to desert you at a time like this, but if I come out there at two hundred and fifty dollars an hour the drive time alone will—"

"Of course. You're right." The front door was ajar, and as Alessandra watched, two men pushed it even farther open and stepped into the entryway. "Seven years of friendship is worth far less than two hundred and fifty dollars an hour."

Her acerbic comment had completely taken Brandon aback. It was unlike her to speak out. Years of living with Griffin had taught her to murmur her agreement, even when she didn't agree. But Griffin was dead now, and over the past few months her life had taken a rather drastic turn. "Brandon, please. Can't you come out here as my friend?"

Brandon hesitated. In the silence Alessandra watched the two men who had just come in.

One of them was dark and compact. He was probably only an inch or two taller than her own not-quite-statuesque five feet eight, but he was powerfully, muscularly built. The other man was tall and elegantly slender, the perfect example of high fashion, his suit clearly brand-new—this minute's style, in fact. The shorter man wore a raincoat that looked as if it hadn't been to the dry cleaner's in the better part of a decade. Underneath, she caught glimpses of a rumpled dark suit, a white shirt with the collar unbuttoned, tie loosened.

The taller man was a walking ad for the Hair Club for Men, every strand perfectly in place, inventoried and accounted for. The other had thick, dark hair that had to be completely his own, arranged in a style that could only be described as permanent "bed head."

They were cops. Detectives, most likely. She could tell from the way they looked around as they came inside. The shorter one's dark gaze flickered over her, identifying and processing her as completely as he'd taken in and filed the torn sofa cushions and the bloodred paint splattered on the walls.

"I can't," Brandon finally said, just as she'd known he would. "It was different when you were married to Griffin, but now, especially with him dead . . . I don't think Jeanie would understand."

His wife wouldn't understand that Alessandra could use a little support after her ex-husband was killed by mobsters and her house was completely destroyed? He read her silence correctly.

"I'm sorry, Alessandra," he continued. "But I know what she would think if I went out there at this time of night. I can't help you. In fact, I've got to get off the line. I am sorry."

"I'm sorry, too." Alessandra cut the connection. She was alone. She was completely alone. For the first time in her entire life, she didn't have someone to call, someone to take care of things for her.

Where's the money? Find it. Fast. Or you're next.

For several long seconds, Alessandra couldn't breathe.

"Mrs. Lamont?"

She looked up, directly into the eyes of the cop with the messy hair. His eyes were dark brown and meltingly warm. With eyes like that, a man could get away with a rumpled suit and a grungy raincoat. With eyes like that, a man could get away with just about anything.

His face wasn't particularly handsome, but then again, he wasn't not handsome, either. His nose was a little too big and slightly rounded at the end, his lips too thin, his cheekbones a little too lost in the fullness of his face. He was pushing forty and the stubble on his much-too-stubborn chin was flecked with gray.

"You all right?" he asked.

For half a second, all of the grief and desperation and fear she was feeling almost escaped. But instead of bursting into tears and hurling herself into this stranger's arms, she reminded herself that he was a cop, not a friend, and delicately cleared her throat instead. She didn't have any friends. She had to remember that.

One by one, she'd let her own friends slip away during the seven long years of her marriage. She'd kept her distance from the other volunteers at the hospital, and she'd socialized only with Griffin's business associates. That was the way he'd wanted it. But when Griffin had left, most of his acquaintances had gone with him. And when he'd turned up wanted by the police and then dead, the phone had stopped ringing completely.

"I'll be fine," she told the dark-eyed man. And she would be. She might not have someone to hold her, but somehow she was going to get through this. Somehow she would survive. She had to believe that. It was Jane Doe she was worried to death about.

"I'm Harry O'Dell, Mrs. Lamont." He held out his hand, and she took it hesitantly, afraid it would be as warm as his eyes. She managed to shake while hardly touching him, giving him a Ladies' Club smile. Polite yet distancing.

"I'm with the FBI," he added. The smile he gave her in return was crooked, as if she'd somehow amused him and he was trying not to laugh. The gentle warmth in his eyes had been replaced by something much edgier. "And this is my partner, George Faulkner."

"FBI?" She kept her voice low and managed to sound only mildly interested, hiding the fact that her pulse had just kicked into double time, sending icy rockets of fear down to her fingers and toes.

Where's the money?

Was it possible the police knew about the threatening phone call? Why else would they have sent in federal agents? She held the phone tightly with both hands, praying she wouldn't start shaking again.

He didn't offer an explanation for why they were there. He just looked at her.

She could feel him taking in the details of her face, of her hair, of the silk blouse that was neatly tucked into the waistband of her soft wool pants. Like most men, he wasn't just looking at her clothes. He was assessing the body underneath.

She knew what he saw, knew he liked what he saw. With her movie-star-perfect features and softly lidded blue eyes, with her thick blonde hair and perfectly proportioned body, with her elegant clothes and perfectly applied makeup, she was a fifteen on a scale from one to ten. She was drop-dead beautiful.

Too beautiful to have any friends.

"We'd like to ask you some questions, Mrs. Lamont," Harry O'Dell finally said. There was a trace of blue-collar New York City in his voice as well as his face. Brooklyn maybe. Or the Bronx. He wasn't from the Island, though. Alessandra herself had worked hard to eliminate that particular accent from her own speech, and she knew it well.

"We're sorry about the recent loss of your husband," the other man cut in. He was definitely from Connecticut, just as Griffin had been.

"Ex-husband," Alessandra corrected him quickly. A little too quickly.

They exchanged a look and she continued, "The divorce hadn't gone through, but he moved out in January. I considered our marriage over at that time."

Harry nodded. "That's fair. So I guess you weren't too broken up when he showed up facedown in the East River?"

"I didn't kill him, Mr. O'Dell, if that's what you're implying."

"I wasn't implying anything, but I'm glad to hear that." He was silently laughing at her again, despite the fact that the icy look she was giving him would've sent another man running. "Do you know who did this to your house?"

She gave him the same short answer she'd given the local police hours earlier. "No."

He was watching her closely. "No ideas at all?"

"I have ideas, of course. But that's not what you asked. You asked if I knew who did this."

"Who do you think did this?" he asked.

She chose her words very carefully. "If I had to guess,

I'd say it was probably the same people who killed Griffin."

"Any ideas why?"

Where's the money? Find it. Fast.

Alessandra gripped the cordless phone more tightly. "The police seemed to think Griffin was involved in something having to do with drugs."

"And you know nothing about that?"

"Whatever he was doing, he didn't mention it to me. He rarely discussed business with me. He rarely discussed anything with me at all."

Harry gestured to the room around them. "Whoever did this was searching for something. This isn't just random destruction, Mrs. Lamont."

Where's the money? Where's the money?

"I'm afraid I can't help you," Alessandra said.

He didn't say anything for many long seconds. He just watched her, a trace of amusement curling the corners of his mouth. He didn't trust her, didn't believe her, didn't like her.

But he wanted her. Yes, if she had held out her hand, he would've taken it and followed her right upstairs. No further questions.

"Thanks for your time," he finally said.

He started to walk away but then turned back. "Do you have a place to stay tonight?"

"I'll be fine," she said again, hoping that this time she'd believe it, too.

"She's smarter than she looks."

George checked his side mirror as he moved into the left lane on the Long Island Expressway. "That's not uncommon among most members of the human race. You're smarter than you look, too."

Harry shifted in his seat, watching Queens speed past

him through the side window of George's car, trying to get comfortable. His shoulder hurt like hell.

"Of course, as long as we're making comparisons, she definitely smells better than you," George added.

Harry glanced at him. "I didn't particularly notice."

George smiled.

"All right, so I did notice. Jesus." Alessandra Lamont had smelled elegant and freshly, sweetly female. She'd smelled like the expensive shops in Paris, like that one tense vacation he'd taken with Sonya two months before they'd split up for good.

He briefly closed his eyes. "What is it about blondes? Why is it I start talking to a blonde, and my vocabulary is reduced to a few dozen words, most of 'em unspeakable in polite company?" He shook his head. "Talking about polite company—that high society crap totally maxes out my bullshit meter. Did she think she was the Duchess of Nassau County or what? And did she seriously think we believed for one second she didn't know that fancy house had been bought and paid for with mob money?" He imitated Alessandra's cultured voice. "Griffin rarely discussed business with me. He rarely discussed anything with me at all." He snorted. "That's because ol' Griff was no fool. You get a woman like that alone in a room, you don't let her use her mouth for talking. Christ."

The silence in the car stretched on for a half, and then a whole, mile. "Are you done?" George finally asked.

Harry let out a burst of air as he rubbed the back of his neck with one hand. "No," he said. "No, I'm not done." He had the feeling Alessandra Lamont was going to show up again and again and again in this investigation. And if that was the case, he wasn't going to be done for many, many weeks.

Damn, he hurt all over. He'd hit his shoulder hard, diving to cover the store clerk tonight in that bodega, after the taller of the three perps had opened fire. The gunplay hadn't lasted more than fifteen seconds, but he probably had a new bruise for every one of those seconds.

Still, it had been sleeping with his head on the table in the police station interview room that had done him the most damage. He was getting too old for that. Of course, he couldn't remember the last time he'd actually slept stretched out in his own bed over the past few months.

He also couldn't remember the last time he'd slept in the bed of a woman like Alessandra Lamont.

Yes he could. That would have been four years ago, before his divorce. Before—

He interrupted himself. "So what do you think she knows?"

George turned on the windshield wipers to clear away the light rain that had begun to fall. "I think there's definitely something she's not telling us." He glanced at Harry. "And I think despite her Ice Queen routine, she gave you one very serious once-over. I don't know why, but the phrase 'pillow talk' keeps popping into my mind."

"Oh, no," Harry said. "Nuh-uh. No way."

"You've got to admit, it would be a less life-threatening way to blow off steam on your nights off than taking down three armed robbers without any backup."

"I'm not so sure about that." Harry tried to stretch out his legs and hit his already bruised knee on the dash. "Ow. Besides, she's not my type."

"She's beautiful and she's blonde. She's exactly your type. You just said so yourself."

"She's more your type," Harry countered. "She's not real broken up over the husband's death—obviously she married the guy for his cash. She's nothing but a high-priced hooker."

"There's a big difference between exotic dancers and hookers, thank you very much."

"Sorry," Harry said.

"Hookers would be going too far. The dancers I can actually bring to office parties, and God, does that make Nicole squirm." George grinned.

"How is Nicki? I only caught a glimpse of her yesterday. She was moving too fast even to say hello."

"That about describes her." George had been divorced from Nicole Fenster since before Harry had met him, but not a single day passed in which her name didn't come up. "Isn't it convenient, now that we're no longer married, policy allows us to work in the same area, out of the same building? That's why I've stayed partners with you, you know. Because if I did what everyone else has done and asked for a transfer, I'd probably be hooked up with Nic again."

The tires made a shushing sound against the wet pavement as they rode for several long moments in silence.

"Have you had a chance to check out Griffin Lamont's file?" George asked. "Did you look at his picture?"

They'd both seen his body after he'd spent a few days in the river. That was not the same thing as seeing his photograph. "Yeah." Pale hair, pale eyes, pale face. Relatively handsome if you were into mushrooms who never saw the light of day. Of course, most women wouldn't look further than the dollar-sign motif the guy was practically wearing on his tie.

"Can you believe Lamont dumped her?" George laughed. "What was he thinking?"

"Irreconcilable differences," Harry said flatly. "According to the divorce papers, he wanted children, she didn't. Guess she didn't want to ruin her figure."

"Wait—when did you see the divorce papers?"

"This afternoon. While you were shaving for the

second time today. I left the file on your desk. See what you miss by being fastidious?"

"I thought I'd be spending the evening with Kim." George glanced at him again. "You know, I bet if you went back to Farmingdale tomorrow and offered Mrs. Lamont a strong shoulder to cry on—"

Harry shook his head. "Don't start with that again. I don't need that kind of trouble."

"Where's the trouble? Two consenting adults who get together for a little dinner, a little intellectual conversation, a little—"

"Intellectual conversation?" Harry laughed. "She's not exactly a Harvard grad. In fact, I'd bet my paycheck she had trouble getting through her Mavis Beacon Typing Tutor software."

"You just said you thought she was smart," George pointed out.

"Smarter than she looks. Which sure as hell isn't saying much. I bet if you dig underneath those designer clothes, the step-aerobic-toned body, and the five tons of makeup and hairspray she wears, there's nobody home."

"Why the hell would you want to dig deeper than her body?" George laughed. "For God's sake, Harry, get your priorities straight."

By four A.M., the twenty-four-hour emergency service had finished boarding up all of the windows in Alessandra's house. By five minutes after four, both the repair truck and the patrol car that had been idling out front finally pulled away.

Alessandra went into the garage then, searching for the charcoal barbecue grill Griffin had stored there for the winter, all the way back in October. Nearly six months ago. Only six months ago. It seemed like an entirely different lifetime now.

She'd tried so hard, and for so long, first to please her parents and then the husband she'd married much too young. She'd tried to make herself exactly what they'd wanted, with no regard to her own wants and needs.

And now, with her parents long since passed on, and Griffin dead, she was adrift, clinging to her old life out of fear and this awful sense of uncertainty.

It was going to take getting used to—no one telling her what to do. There were no expectations. No rules. And for the first time in her life, a life that might have been viewed as very pampered by some but was in truth smotheringly restricted, she was going to do exactly what she wanted, simply because she wanted to.

She found the grill, found the bag of charcoal Griffin had neatly sealed. And beside it, she found what she was really looking for.

She took the lighter fluid into the kitchen, turned on the back-porch light, and stepped out into the night. She took a deep breath, filling her lungs with the cold spring air.

The garden was starting to bloom. The trees had young, fresh leaves and they seemed to glisten and shine.

The azalea, Griffin's azalea, right by the steps leading up to the porch, was covered with small, pink buds.

Alessandra squeezed the plastic container, lit a match.

And then she stood in the predawn darkness and watched Griffin's azalea burn.

Two

ALESSANDRA HAD JUST picked up her clothing from the dry cleaners and was glancing at her watch, wondering if she had time to visit Jane, when the limousine pulled up behind her car.

It was following closely, too closely, and it stayed behind her as she approached the street that led to home.

She didn't turn, heading instead toward the grocery store. Maybe the limo wasn't following her. Maybe . . .

Her car phone rang.

She pulled up to a red light before she answered, taking a deep breath to calm herself. This was just a coincidence. It was the Realtor calling. Or the man from the insurance company. "Hello?"

"Mrs. Lamont." The voice was heavily accented, but soft, cultured. "Pull into the shopping area across the street to your right and park there, please, in the front of the bakery."

"Excuse me?" The light changed, but she had to put on her brakes right away as an oncoming car turned left, crossing in front of her. "You don't really think I'm just going to "

"Mr. Trotta wants to see you," the man told her. "We can do this nicely. Friendly. Or we can do this not so nicely. Not so friendly."

24

Alessandra pulled into the lot and parked in front of the bakery.

It was four o'clock in the afternoon, but inside the windowless Fantasy Club, time had no meaning. Four P.M. or four A.M., or any other time of day or night, a woman was onstage, dancing, and men were in the audience, watching.

George took a seat at the bar in the back of the room, smiling a greeting as Carol, the bartender, gave him his usual—a vodka and tonic with a twist of lime.

"Will you tell Kim I'm here?" he asked, and she moved to the phone.

He took a sip of his drink and lit a cigarette as he looked around the room. He recognized quite a number of the faces in the audience. And of course, he knew all the girls by name. Monique had the stage. She was rolling and gyrating in ways that defied description, doing what George liked to think of as her floor routine. He smiled, imagining an entirely new adults-only category for the Olympic gymnastics competition filled with competitors named Trixie Devine and Bunny LeFleur.

"Kim's up next, Mr. Faulkner," Carol came over to tell him. "She says she'll be out to see you after."

"Thanks, Carol." He took another pull on his cigarette, reaching for an ashtray as he watched Monique dance.

The limousine pulled up outside a warehouse. They were in a part of Queens that Alessandra had never seen before, down near the river, by the docks.

The man with the accent, the one who'd spoken to her on her car phone, opened the door, gesturing for her to get out. He was tall and broad, with sandy blond hair and a distinctly Eastern European face. Flat, Slavic cheekbones, slightly flattened nose, broad forehead, pale blue eyes.

"Where are we?" Alessandra asked.

He looked at her with complete dispassion in his eyes. There was absolutely nothing there. No registering of her beauty, no interest, no humanity. It was as if she were invisible.

Or as if she were already dead.

"It's best if you don't ask many questions," he said in that voice that so reminded her of Arnold Schwarzen-egger playing a high-class art dealer.

Taking a deep breath, she gathered all her nerve. "I thought you said Michael Trotta wanted to talk to me. I don't know why you dragged me all the way down here when he lives not too far from—"

"You will follow me, please."

This was ridiculous. She had no real reason to feel so utterly afraid. She'd known Michael and his wife, Olivia, for seven years. And even if the rumors she'd heard for all those years were true, and some of the business Michael did was illegal, that still didn't mean she had to be afraid of him. He liked her.

Just last Christmas, she'd attended a holiday party at his house. He'd fixed her a drink himself, telling her a very corny joke about a rabbi, a priest, and an alligator.

Yes, Michael Trotta liked her, but then again, Alessandra had always thought he'd liked Griffin a whole lot, too.

The man with the accent opened the warehouse door, and she followed him inside. The space had been subdivided and partitioned. Instead of one vast area, she was in a long corridor that stretched all the way to the end of the building. Her heels echoed on the cheap tile floor.

There were no doors off this part of the corridor and only one other dimly lit hallway that led to the right.

It was spooky and silent and not at all where she wanted to be.

God, what if she were wrong? What if Michael Trotta were behind the destruction to her home and that frightening phone call she'd received last night? Where's the money? Find it. Fast. Or you're next.

What if he was responsible for Griffin's death?

The accented man paused outside a door—the only door in the entire expanse of the hallway. He knocked, and it opened a crack. A man peeked out, but no one spoke, and the door closed again.

"What—" Alessandra started.

"We wait. Quietly."

"I knew I'd find you here."

George closed his eyes. That wasn't his ex-wife's voice. He refused to let it be his ex-wife's voice. But when he opened his eyes, Nicole was slipping onto the bar stool next to him. "I called you at home, and when you weren't there, I figured you'd be here." She fanned the air between them. "God, when did you start smoking again?"

He took another drag on his cigarette, then put it out in the ashtray. "About four months before we split up."

Nicole was wearing khaki slacks and a sweater, but despite the fact that she was dressed down in Saturday clothes, she still looked every inch the efficient federal agent. Her short brown hair was neatly pulled back behind her ears, and she wore just a touch of makeup. A little bit of lip gloss, something on her cheeks to give her face a little color.

George focused his attention on Monique. "This is my first day off in weeks. There better be a really good reason this couldn't wait until Monday."

Onstage, on her knees, Monique released the front

catch of her bra, slipping it off. She threw back her head and arched her back, letting the stage lights catch the full glory of her naked breasts, her absurdly large nipples standing at full attention.

"Whoa," Nicole said. "Is that all real?"

George nodded. "Real enough for me."

"Is this Kim?" she asked.

He turned to find her watching him as intently as he'd been watching Monique, her light brown eyes tinged with just a hint of sadness. He turned back to Monique, refusing to acknowledge it, refusing to think about the way their still-too-recent divorce might've affected Nicole.

Because it hadn't affected Nicole. She was as heartless as she always accused him of being. Whatever he'd just thought he'd glimpsed in her eyes was nothing but an act.

"No," he said flatly. "Kim's up next. You'll be gone by then."

Monique was moving now, her breasts nearly perfectly shaped, two firm hemispheres of flesh. Nicole's skepticism was well-grounded. The dancer had to be surgically assisted. Had to be.

"I'm going to be working with the Trotta team," Nicole told him.

"In the field?" George's voice cracked, and he couldn't keep the horror from his eyes. "With me and Harry?"

Her smile was tight. "Relax. I'll be working out of the office most of the time. But you'll be answering to me."

"Oh, that'll be fun."

"Actually, one of the things I wanted to discuss with you is Harry O'Dell. How much of a liability is he?"

"He's the best partner I've ever worked with." George met her eyes, daring her to bring up the fact that they'd been partners once. A billion years and a christload of aggravation ago.

Nicole didn't take the bait. "The psych department thinks he's on the verge of becoming unreliable. He's got a pretty serious rep as a wild man. There's talk his obsession with Trotta is personal."

"It's all personal to Harry. He's completely insane," George agreed. "But he's the best. I'm serious about this, Nic. Don't pull him off the team."

She held his gaze for several long moments, then nodded. "All right. He stays. For now."

"Mrs. Lamont. What a pleasure it is to see you again."

Michael Trotta sat behind an enormous oak desk. The first glimpse Alessandra had of his office was a surprising one. She'd imagined all dark wood and black leather, but the walls were light, and despite the lack of windows, the room was bright and airy. There were fresh flowers and plants everywhere.

But then she didn't see anything but the huge dog, teeth bared in a snarl, straining against its chain, held by a silent man standing beside Trotta's desk.

Alessandra moved behind the man with the accent.

"I'm sorry," Michael said. "Down, Pinky. Sit."

The dog sat, but his ears were up, lips still pulled back, his eyes watching her relentlessly.

Alessandra's heart was beating so hard she could barely breathe. Still, she forced a smile. "It's one of those childhood fears I never quite grew out of. Even friendly dogs scare me a little."

"I know," Michael said. "But Pinky's not friendly. In fact, he's been trained to kill." He smiled. "Won't you have a seat?"

The only chair in the room was within a few feet of the dog. Pinky. What a ridiculous name for an attack dog.

"I'll stand, thank you," she told him.

"Please sit," he said. "I insist." He turned to the man with the accent. "Ivo?"

Ivo took her arm, but she pulled free, stepping forward herself. She took the chair and dragged it several feet farther from Pinky's still-bared teeth.

Amusement and something not quite as funny gleamed in Michael Trotta's brown eyes. "Do you know why you're here?" he asked.

There were times in life when a woman might get further by playing dumb, but this was not one of them. "I assume it has something to do with Griffin's death."

"There's a connection," Michael admitted. He sat back in his chair. "My dear Mrs. Lamont, you have something that belongs to me."

Nicole glanced at the Fantasy Club stage, at Monique, who was coming to the end of her dance routine, legs spread, hips gyrating wildly.

"She's good, isn't she?" George asked.

Nicole laughed. "You're such an asshole."

He slid down off the bar stool. "Come on, I'll walk you to the door."

"My oh my, you're in a hurry to get rid of me. But I'm not done. We've got a little more to discuss."

George glanced toward the stage as Monique exited to the sparse applause. He sat back down with a sigh. "Nicole. Darling. It's my day off."

"It's my day off, too, but this couldn't wait." She reached for his drink and took a sip. "You and O'Dell went to Long Island last night, right? Checking into that B&E and vandalism report called in by Alessandra Lamont?"

He took the glass away from her. "My report will be on your desk on Monday. No sooner."

She waved that away. "I got a call this morning from a reliable informant," she told him. "According to him, the word on the street is that Alessandra has something that belongs to Trotta. A substantial sum of money, to be exact. The story goes Trotta found out Griffin was double-crossing him by doing business with a competitor. He had him snuffed as a punishment, you know, as a 'this could happen to you' visual aid for the rest of his people. It was only after Griffin had two bullets in his head that Trotta found out there was a million dollars missing."

As awful and macabre as that was, George had to laugh. "Oops. Kind of hard to get a dead man to tell where he hid a million dollars."

Nicole's mouth curved up into a smile, too. "Yeah. The stupidity factor here is off the scale."

"And that's why Lamont's house was trashed?" George asked. "Trotta's men were searching for the million?"

"That's what we think. My informant told me Trotta's either going to get the money back from the wife, or take her out, too—reinforce that message he sent by killing Lamont. Rumor has it this time it won't be a clean kill. According to my source, if he doesn't get the money, Trotta's going to make sure everyone knows that the wife suffered for her husband's sins."

George shook his head. "This is a technique that wasn't touched on in The One Minute Manager. Control through fear of hideous death."

He glanced at the stage. It was still empty. There was usually a ten-minute break between dancers, which gave him about seven minutes before Kim came on.

"My plan is to pull Alessandra in," Nicole told him. "Have Trotta think she's gone into the Witness Protection Program, then let slip her location. We've got enough leaks in the local police department—we can make it look unintentional. And when Trotta sends his men to hit her, we'll be ready for 'em. With luck, we'll have him on conspiracy and attempted murder in just a few short weeks."

"And you think Alessandra Lamont's going to go along with this?" George asked.

Nicole shook her head. "No. We can't tell her what's going on. We don't know the extent of her connection to Trotta. We don't want her thinking she might have a better shot at surviving by trying to prove her loyalty to him and then blowing our setup."

George nodded. "And the reason you couldn't wait until Monday to tell me all this . . . ?"

"Word on the street is that Trotta's given Mrs. Lamont a deadline. My guy wasn't clear on exactly how long, but I'm guessing it's only a matter of days. I need you to go out to her house, tell her what we know about Trotta, and scare her to death."

Alessandra was scared to death. Her heart was pounding so loudly, it seemed impossible that Michael Trotta couldn't hear it. A million dollars. Griffin had stolen a million dollars.

The dog, Pinky, was back on his feet.

"But I don't know where the money is," she said. "Griffin and I were getting divorced. He wasn't even living at home. For all I know, he already spent it."

Michael looked at Ivo. "Did I say I was looking for excuses and complaints?"

"No, sir. You are looking for the money Griffin Lamont stole."

"As far as we can tell, Griffin took the money almost an entire year ago," Michael told her. "Early last April. At that time, he was still quite happily married to you."

He stood up. "You've got forty-eight hours to find that money, Mrs. Lamont. I suggest you go straight home and get to work."

"But—"

Ivo's hand came down on her shoulder. She looked up, and he shook his head at her. It was just a slight movement. Right, then left, then back again. She closed her mouth.

Michael took the dog's chain leash from the man who was holding it. "Do you know how long it would take for a dog like Pinky to tear apart a person who's about your height and weight?" he asked.

Fear caught in Alessandra's throat and she shook her head, soundlessly. No, she didn't know. A million dollars. If Griffin had spent all or even some of it, she'd never be able to repay it. Not a chance.

Michael smiled, the same smile he'd given her after handing her a drink at his Christmas party. "Neither do I," he said. "But if you don't return my money within forty-eight hours, we're all going to find out."

The music started to play, loud and pulsating, and George looked at his watch. It was four minutes early. Kim was starting her dance four minutes early. Shit. He slid down off the bar stool. "Maybe we should go find Harry, so you can tell him everything you just told me."

But then the stage lights came on, and George knew just from looking at Nicole that Kim had come out onstage. She looked at Kim, looked at him, looked back at Kim.

"Jesus," his ex-wife said. "She looks just like me."

George snorted in disbelief the way Harry always did, successfully putting just the right amount of disdain into his voice. "She does not."

"She most certainly does, too."

He turned and watched Kim, squinting slightly as if trying to see the resemblance between the stripper and his ex-wife. On stage, Kim wriggled out of her skirt, revealing a very, very small thong bikini. She turned to give the audience a better view of her rear end as she danced.

"No, she doesn't," he lied. "Well, aside from the fact that you're both women, and you're both about the same height . . ."

"We both have short brown hair, cut almost exactly the same way, and virtually the same facial features. God, George, she could be my twin."

Kim moved closer to the edge of the stage and let one of the men slip a dollar bill underneath the string of her panties. She smiled and ran her tongue across her teeth.

Nicole punched him on the arm, hard.

"Hey! What's that for?"

"It's for being a sick son of a bitch. It's for getting off on watching someone you can pretend is me act like some kind of bimbo sex toy." She was madder than hell. Her lips were so tight, her mouth was ringed with white. "Because that's what this is about, isn't it?"

"You are so completely paranoid—"

"You really are threatened by the fact that a woman could be as successful as I am at the game you want to win, aren't you?"

George rolled his eyes. "Oh, that's just dandy. Let's drag this topic back to life."

"Does this girl know you're only using her for some kind of twisted revenge?"

"Everything always has to do with you, doesn't it?" he countered. "Has it occurred to you that the vague similarities—which I still don't really see—might be a coincidence?"

"No."

"FYI, although it's none of your damned business, I'm

dating Kim purely for the sex, and she's well aware of that. The feelings are quite mutual. She happens to really enjoy getting it on with an FBI agent—I don't know why. In my experience, sex with a federal agent sucks."

As soon as the words left his mouth, he knew he'd struck her hard below the belt. And for one dreadful second, he thought he'd done the impossible. For one dreadful second, he thought he'd made Nicole Fenster cry.

His words weren't even true. It wasn't the sex that had sucked. It was the fact that she was so wrapped up in her job, so intent upon breaking through the glass ceiling, that she didn't have time for him, for them.

But she didn't cry. As he watched, she grabbed hold of her composure, the way she always did. God forbid she should ever be mistaken for a real, live, flesh-and-blood woman. Her voice was cool, one eyebrow slightly cocked as she asked, "Did you ever have a heart, George? Or did you simply manage to fool me right from the start?"

"You're the hotshot agent-in-charge—you figure it out. A good mystery like this is right up your alley."

"Go to hell," Nicole said and walked away.

George watched until she went out the door but she didn't look back.

Onstage, Kim had taken off her bikini top. She'd oiled her body, oiled her perfect breasts, and the lights gleamed off them enticingly. George turned away, heading for the pay phones. He had to call Harry.

The walk back down the corridor was just as endlessly long as it had been going toward Michael Trotta's office.

Forty-eight hours. A million dollars. Forty-eight hours. A million dollars. The singsong in Alessandra's head repeated over and over and over and . . .

A man appeared from around the corner. There was

only one turn off the warehouse corridor, and a dark-haired man staggered out of it, crashing into her and pushing her up against the wall.

Alessandra screamed at the sight of the face that was only inches from hers. It was scraped and bloody, battered and scratched, one eye almost completely swollen shut.

He was young and Hispanic, with a pencil-thin mustache beneath his nose and full, high cheekbones. His chin-length hair was parted in the middle. It was dirty and matted with sweat and blood. His clothes were torn and filthy.

"Help me," he breathed through swollen lips. "Please. I am Enrique Montoy—"

Ivo grabbed him, smashing his head hard into the wall mere inches from Alessandra. She was close enough to hear his grunt of pain, close enough to see his eyes roll up in his head, close enough to smell the stench of fear and blood and urine.

The man's hands were cuffed behind his back and he was bleeding from more than the scrapes on his face, she realized with horror. The entire side of his shirt was drenched with bright red blood—blood that now stained her own blouse as well.

Ivo thrust the man toward the two other goons who'd been escorting them back to the limousine. He took Alessandra by the arm and hustled her toward the door.

She couldn't help but look back.

The guards dragged the beaten man just as quickly in the other direction down the corridor, and as she watched, they opened Michael Trotta's office door and pulled him inside.

Who was that man?

She looked at the grim set to Ivo's usually impassive face and didn't dare ask.

He pulled her out the door and pushed her into the waiting limo, this time following her into the back. He closed the door behind them and tapped on the glass, signaling the driver to go.

As she struggled to catch her breath, as she fought to bring her pulse back down to merely heart-stopping as opposed to sheer mindless fear, Ivo took out a crisp white handkerchief and held it out to her.

"There is blood on your face," he informed her, pointing to his own cheek.

There was blood on her hands, too, and she wiped herself clean as best she could. Her blouse was ruined, her pants as well. She felt numb and faint. This couldn't be happening.

Help me, please . . .

She didn't want to think about that man, didn't want to think that someone else might be wiping her blood from their hands in forty-eight hours, after Michael Trotta's deadline had passed.

She forced herself to stay alert, stay in control. She forced back the tears that were threatening to escape, refusing to give Ivo the satisfaction of seeing her completely crumble. She was all alone, completely on her own. No one was going to save her. If she wanted to be saved, she was going to have to save herself.

She took a deep breath, trying to slow herself down, trying to think. Think.

Okay. Okay. Her options were pretty limited. She could look for the money, and she could either find it or not. And if she didn't find it, if Griffin had spent it, wasted it, she could die. She would die.

She took another breath.

She could run and hide.

And live the rest of her life looking over her shoulder,

afraid that someday Michael Trotta would find her, certain that she'd never see Jane again.

Of course, another option would be to go to the police.

Or she could call the FBI.

She sat back against the leather upholstery. She would definitely set aside her mistrust of law enforcement officials and call the FBI. Harry O'Dell had looked like a man who would know what to do. She'd call him. As soon as she got home.

Maybe she wasn't as completely alone as she'd thought.

Ivo was watching her, his pale blue eyes intent, as if he were reading her mind. "That man," he said. "Do you know who he was?"

Alessandra shook her head no, surprised he would talk about it.

"He, too, owes Mr. Trotta a great deal of money," Ivo told her. "But he made the very big mistake of going to the authorities. You will be smarter than he was, yes?"

Alessandra nodded, her fear tightly lodged once again in her throat. Yes.

Her options had just been reduced to one. She would search for the money and pray that when she found it, it would all be there.

She had no choice.

Three

ALESSANDRA STOOD IN her living room, filled with a rising sense of dread, uncertain where to begin.

She'd arrived home to find the police, warrant in hand, searching her house.

They hadn't found anything, but she knew that somehow they'd found out about the missing money.

Michael Trotta's men hadn't found it. The cops hadn't found it. How on earth was she supposed to find it? Assuming Griffin hadn't spent it all. Dear Lord.

She'd had to carry the dry cleaning she'd picked up earlier against her body as she'd come inside the house, hiding the drying blood that had stained her clothes.

If the danger that loomed hadn't been quite so deadly, she might've started laughing. Every piece of clothing she owned had been shredded or stained with blood, except for the few articles she'd had at the dry cleaners: an evening gown, a turquoise silk sheath dress, four blouses, and her floor-length black velvet Christmas skirt.

Out of all of those outfits, the silk sheath seemed least inappropriate for searching a house from top to bottom.

She'd changed out of her bloodstained clothes in the bathroom and wrapped them in plastic, intending to take them to the dry cleaners as soon as possible. They would be permanently stained, but at least she could wear them around the house.

Finally the last of the police had left—empty-handed, thank goodness—and once again she was alone in the house. Work crews had replaced the windows in the first floor, but they'd gone home as the sun began to set.

Forty-eight hours. Forty-two hours now. Dear God.

Alessandra sat in the shambles of the living room and tried to think like Griffin. He had just stolen an exorbitant amount of money from the mob: Where would he hide it?

She'd rearranged the room he'd used as his home office back in December, on the day after he'd moved out. She'd packed up all his books and papers and taken his big wooden bookshelves down to the basement, transforming the room into another guest bedroom.

She now had four guest bedrooms and exactly zero friends.

Forcing those thoughts away, she squared her shoulders and got to work.

"How are you, kitten?"

Kim Monahan closed her eyes and let herself hate Michael Trotta. Over the phone, talking to him was easy. She didn't have to smile, didn't have to look at him as if she were dying to unzip his pants. She could seethe with anger if she wanted to—as long as it didn't ring in her voice. "I'm fine."

"What have you got for me?"

"Nothing much, but you asked me to call, so—"

"Just tell me what you've got, and I'll decide whether or not it's nothing much." There was a trace of that nasty edge Trotta sometimes got in his voice. Kim was glad she was separated from him by forty miles of telephone wire. Although, there were times when forty thousand miles wouldn't seem far enough.

"All right," she said evenly. "He made a single phone

call last night, got a machine, left a message for Harry. That's his partner. He was brief, simply said to call him at home. But nobody called back. He called again this morning, connected with Harry, told him he was going to swing by and pick him up, take another trip out to the Island. After he hung up I asked him which island he was going to, and why he had to go there on a Sunday. He didn't give me an answer."

George had looked down at her, still naked in his bed, as if he somehow knew she was only there because she was working for Trotta. But he couldn't possibly know. There was no way he could know.

He wasn't particularly attractive—not according to her standards. She liked hockey players, football players. Big beefy bruisers with broad shoulders and arms the size of her thighs. George Faulkner was a far cry from that.

His face was handsome enough, in a sort of elegant way—if you liked pretty men. He was tall and graceful, with long tapered fingers and nails that were better manicured than hers.

She should've hated him, the way she hated Michael Trotta, the way she often hated herself.

But he had a certain gentleness about him. A kindness. And when he laughed, when his eyes lit up with amusement, she didn't think about the fact that his shoulders weren't particularly wide or that his biceps weren't the biggest she'd ever seen in her life.

And no, he didn't know she was working for Trotta. That had been her own guilt she'd seen reflected in his eyes.

"What time did he leave his apartment?"

"A little after nine."

"Stay close and keep in touch. Don't go anywhere," Trotta told her and hung up.

"Where would I go that you couldn't find me?" Kim asked the empty line.

"If you light that cigarette," Harry said, getting into the car, "I'll kill you."

George reached for the car lighter. "You know, you'd get a lot further if you started using words like please and thank you."

"Please don't make me fucking kill you. Thank you."

George put the lighter back. "Much better." He pulled out into the Sunday morning traffic, slipping the unlit cigarette into his shirt pocket. "Is there a reason you look as if you haven't slept since I dropped you home Friday night?"

Harry closed his eyes, slumped in his seat. "I don't want to talk about it."

"If it has to do with a woman, it's okay—you can look as tired as you want."

Harry kept his eyes tightly shut. "Take the Cross Island down to the Southern State. The L.I.E.'s already backed up."

"I take it that's a no—no woman is involved."

"Please just shut the fuck up. Thank you."

"You've been working the street for far too long," George said cheerfully. "You need to buy a thesaurus and find yourself a new favorite word."

Harry didn't answer.

"Either that," George hypothesized, "or you've got to get laid—get your mind off the subject. I happen to know that Kim has a friend who—"

Harry gave up. "I got to my room night before last," he interrupted, "to find my answering machine completely filled with messages from Shaun." The first of the messages had been old—dated back almost two months ago. His first thought had been God, had it really been that long since he'd called his kids? But he knew it had. He dreaded calling home. It was too hard, even now, two years later. "He didn't say what was up, just 'It's Shaun again, call me.' It was late, but I thought someone would be up in the house, so I called." The time difference made it earlier for them. "No answer. Machine wasn't on, nothing."

"That's odd."

"Yeah, it gets even worse." Harry rubbed his forehead. God, his head ached. He'd slept maybe three hours last night, and no more than two the night before. "The landlady's been collecting my mail, bringing it inside—there's an enormous pile right on the bed. It's mostly junk mail, but I go through it because there might be credit-card bills mixed in, and what do I find?"

George wisely didn't try to guess.

"A notification that the equivalent of adoption proceedings have been started. A petition has been made to the county court about some freaking name change crap. And there's some bullshit paper I'm supposed to sign, giving up all legal rights to custody. My stepsister's trying to steal my kids."

Even as he said the words aloud, Harry couldn't believe it. Why would Marge do that? What the hell was going on?

"So I call back—by then it's at least one A.M. And they're still not home. Emily is only a baby. What the hell is she doing out at one A.M.? I called at two and three and four, and they still weren't home. I called all yesterday, too, and last night. They're gone."

"Maybe they're out of town. Maybe it's no big deal—"

"And what? Maybe the letter I received from the legal firm of Peckerhead Backstabber and Jones was just a mistake?"

George opened his mouth to speak but then closed it, saying nothing.

"What?" Harry asked.

George glanced at him then shook his head. "No."

"No, Faulkner, what? Tell me what you were going to say."

"I don't think we've known each other long enough."

"Are you kidding? You can say anything to me." Harry smiled ruefully. "You usually do. I don't know why you're being so f—" He stopped himself. George was right. His language needed some serious self-editing. Funny, he never used to let the foulness of the street extend into his personal life. Of course, back then he'd had a family. Two impressionable boys and a toddler girl. It was Emily, his daughter, who was the living tape recorder. Anything that slipped out of his mouth would be played back—at high volume—usually at some inopportune moment. "I don't know why you're being so . . ." He cleared his throat. "Uncharacteristically restrained."

Traffic on the Southern State was heavy but still moving at about ten miles an hour faster than the posted speed limit. George finessed his way into the left lane, letting several quick miles slip past before he glanced up.

"Promise you won't shout at me?"

Harry tried to look hurt. "When do I shout at you?"

George just smiled.

"Okay," Harry said. "All right. I won't shout at you. I promise."

"Maybe," George said, slowly, carefully, "you should just sign the paper."

"What?"

"You promised you wouldn't shout!"

"I'm not fucking shouting!" Harry shouted. He took a

deep breath and tried again, more softly. "I'm not shouting. Gosh darnit."

"I know this isn't what you want to hear, but think about it, Harry," George said. "You've seen those kids, what? Two times in the past two years? For a half a day at Christmas? That's not being a father. That's being Santa Claus."

"No," Harry said. "No. They're my kids. They're not orphans. They don't need to be f— They don't need to be adopted."

"Maybe you should take some time off, go out to wherever it is you've got them hidden," George suggested. "And stay for at least a week this time. Emily's what? Five now? After two years, she probably doesn't even remember you."

"Emily's four and a half. Shaun's fourteen," Harry said. And Kevin . . . Kevin was dead. He would've been just about to turn seventeen.

Harry closed his eyes, fighting the waves of sickness that accompanied all thoughts of his oldest son. Even after two years, it still hurt too much. Even after two years, the wounds were too fresh. He was okay as long as he didn't think about Kev. Problem was, he couldn't look into Shaun and Emily's faces without thinking of their older brother.

Was it really any wonder that he never went to visit?

He pushed all thoughts away, keeping his eyes closed, effectively ending his conversation with George. "Wake me when we get to Farmingdale."

Alessandra was frantic. Twenty-four hours had passed since Michael Trotta's ultimatum. That left only twenty-four more to go. Her time was half up, and she was no closer to finding the money than she'd been when she started.

She'd slept only a few hours last night. She hadn't meant to sleep at all. But fatigue had overcome her while sorting through several boxes of Griffin's papers that had been hidden in the garage, searching for something, anything that might be a clue. She'd woken up in a panic, dreaming of an attack dog leaping at her, razor-sharp teeth going for her face.

She'd gone out to the twenty-four-hour Dunkin' Donuts and bought five large cups of coffee, cursing herself soundly for falling asleep. She had only forty-eight hours, total, and every minute counted.

By mid-morning the workers were back, replacing the rest of her broken windows. By mid-afternoon, Alessandra had finished the last of her coffee, long stone cold.

Her turquoise dress was streaked with dirt and dust as she stood in the room that had been Griffin's office and slowly turned in a circle. She'd torn up the carpeting and found nothing. She'd searched and removed all that was left of the furniture and books.

She'd brought the pickax in from the garage, prepared to tear open the walls if necessary. But it seemed so improbable. If Griffin had hidden something in the walls, she would have known about it. Wouldn't she?

She sat down on the floor, slumping with fatigue, trying desperately to think.

Michael Trotta had said that Griffin stole the money last year. Last April. She tried to think back, tried to remember what they'd been doing, tried to think of something that would set that particular time apart from all of the endless, similar, blurred months of her marriage.

They'd gone on vacation, spent a week in Cozumel, Mexico. God, if Griffin had spent the money gambling or even hidden it down there . . .

Alessandra forced herself not to think of disaster scenarios. April. April. Spring. Spring would have been in full bloom. Flowers and . . .

She sat up.

Griffin. Out in the backyard. Working with a shovel and a rake. Planting that azalea.

She'd come home early from another of the endless baby showers she'd received invitations to as Griffin's wife. She'd left before dessert was served, before the presents were opened, feigning illness. In truth, she couldn't take it. She couldn't bear the sight of even one more disgustingly adorable tiny pink or blue outfit, she couldn't stand to listen to one more endless conversation about breast-feeding.

She'd been surprised to see Griffin home in the middle of the day—almost as surprised as she was to see him actually doing yard work. They paid an enormous amount for a landscaper to come in once a week and maintain the grounds. Griffin had allergies—and an aversion to getting his hands dirty, too.

Yet there he was, out in the back, planting that azalea. The same azalea he'd made a point to ask for in the divorce settlement. The azalea he was supposed to pick up this month, as soon as the ground thawed enough to dig it free. The azalea she'd set on fire just two nights ago.

With a burst of renewed energy, Alessandra pulled herself to her feet and went out to the garage, searching for a shovel.

"Where's Emily?"

Shaun looked up from his book, shading his eyes to see his aunt in the glaring sunlight. Her words didn't make sense, because Emily was right in front of him. She was building a sand castle down at the edge of the water. She was . . .

Gone.

Her red bucket lay on its side next to a small mound of sand, but Emily was gone.

Shit.

Shaun stood up, his heart pounding. The Pacific Ocean was calm today, but even calm, the waves were strong enough to knock over a four-year-old—even one as tough as Em.

Marge was already purposely striding toward a man and a woman on a blanket nearby, and Shaun could hear her clear voice asking if they'd seen which way the little girl had gone.

Em's bathing suit was a bright, cheery yellow that made her hair and eyes seem an even darker shade of brown. Shaun scanned the waves but saw no flash of color. Shading his eyes again, he gazed down the beach, spinning first one way and then the next. And there, through the mist rising off the water, he could see it.

A very small spark of yellow, way, way down the beach, heading north toward Carmel.

He dropped his book and ran.

Heart pounding, legs and stomach churning, he prayed that yellow spot was Emily, not some empty sand pail or lost beach towel. He was supposed to have been watching her. He was responsible for her safety. How could he have let this happen? What if she'd gotten too close to the punishing force of the ocean, been knocked over and drowned? What if she was already dead?

It happened. He knew it happened. People died. People he loved could go into the city, or down to the beach, or even just around the corner and they might never come back. He'd learned that the hard way.

But Emily . . .

He wasn't sure he could live if Emily was dead.

And, God, how would he ever face his father?

His stomach hurt, but he kept running, his eyes fixed

on the bit of yellow. It was growing larger, growing a head with stringy dark hair, two arms, two legs.

It was Emily.

She was crouching in the sand, poking at a shell as he skidded to a stop. Thank God. Relief flooded through him, turning instantly to a cramping wave of nausea. He dropped to his knees and threw up, right there, in the sand.

A trio of high school girls hurried past him, giggling and making noises of disgust, and the mortification nearly made him throw up again.

One of them turned back to him. A pretty one, with long red hair tied back into a ponytail. Her eyes were blue and wide. "Are you all right?"

Shaun wiped at the tears that had flooded his eyes. Perfect. He was crying. Could this get any worse? He checked with one hand to make sure his bathing suit hadn't slipped down to expose his bare butt as he swept sand over his former breakfast with the other.

"You should slow down and walk it off after doing sprints," she told him. "Particularly in this heat."

God, he'd managed to puke on his glasses. He was looking at the prettiest girl in the world through dots of vomit. What a complete and total loser. He took them off and wiped them on the bottom edge of his shorts, and the world became fuzzy. Safer. Emily was a yellow blob, and the girl was like something one of those dead French guys painted. Still nice to look at, but hazy, undefined.

"You were running really fast." She laughed. Her laughter was like magic. "I was watching you for a while."

She had been watching him? Shaun put his glasses back on. She was wearing a black two-piece bathing suit that clung to a perfect body that screamed to be watched. She was probably around sixteen, a couple years older than he was. A couple years older than the girls in his eighth grade class at school, and unlike many of them, she had sixteen-year-old breasts. She had very, very nice breasts. Oh, God. Shaun felt himself blush a deeper shade of red.

"I'm a runner, too," she told him. "I've almost lost my lunch more than a few times when it gets hot like this, so I know exactly how you're feeling. Are you sure you're all right?"

Shaun opened his mouth and squeaked. Oh, God. He cleared his throat and started again. "I'm okay," he said, his voice managing not to break. "I just . . . I was . . ."

"You know, sometimes when marathon runners have intestinal distress, they just go to the bathroom in their shorts," she told him. "They just keep running."

"You've got to be kidding."

She laughed. "It's true. At least you had the decency to stop."

Emily had seen him and had come to stand nearby, her eyes wide as she stared at the girl.

He gave the girl a weak smile. "I'm sorry I grossed out your friends."

"They're babies. You know, you should run in the morning, around seven-thirty or eight, before it gets too hot. That's when I run." The red-haired girl smiled back at him. "Maybe I'll see you around, huh?"

She turned, breaking into an easy trot to catch up with her friends.

What just happened here? He blows chunks, and the prettiest girl on the beach starts to flirt with him?

"Do you got the throw-up flu?" Emily asked as he crawled toward the surf and rinsed his face in the salt water.

"No," he said tersely. "I puked because . . ."

She didn't have a clue. Em was standing there, frowning slightly, concerned because he'd gotten sick, but other than that, she didn't have the slightest idea that she'd been the cause of his distress.

"Where were you going?" he asked her far more gently than he would have had the red-haired girl not stopped. "You know you're supposed to stay where you can see me on the beach, or Marge won't let us come down here alone."

Em gazed at him calmly, still without a speck of remorse in her eyes. "I was following Daddy."

Shaun froze. "What?"

"I saw Daddy, and I followed him, but he goed too fast for me to catch him."

The elation that had come with the pretty redhead's smile wore off, leaving complete exhaustion in its place. "Em, you know Dad's not in California. He lives in—"

"Washin'ton, D.C.," she recited. " 'Tecting the president from bad guys." She sat down next to him in the sand. "But we're on vacation, maybe Daddy's on vacation, too."

Shaun put his arm around her. She was sturdy but so small. "Daddy doesn't take vacations," he told her gently. "His job's too important, remember?"

Em nodded, content with that explanation. "The president needs him."

"Yeah," Shaun said, wishing he was still young enough to believe the stories he'd started making up two years ago. He hugged his sister more tightly. "Next time you wander off, you're gonna be in big trouble, you got that?"

Emily nodded. "Shaun?"

"Yeah, Em."

"What does Daddy look like?"

Shaun closed his eyes. "Like you, Em, remember? Just like you, only a whole lot bigger."

* * *

"What the . . . ?"

Harry stopped short as he went around the side of the house, and George had to tap-dance to keep from crashing into him.

Alessandra Lamont hadn't seen them yet.

George opened his mouth to complain again, but Harry shook his head, holding one finger up to his lips and then pointing at Alessandra.

She was digging in the garden. Her hair had fallen almost completely loose from an elegant knot at the back of her head. Her face and arms were streaked with dirt.

She was working hard, digging around the roots of the skeleton of a bush. Only three or four branches remained, covered with soot, blackened fingers reaching pathetically toward the sky. It was weird, as if that bush, and only that bush, had been completely consumed by a miniature forest fire.

But that wasn't the odd part. It made sense she'd want to remove the dead plant. It was ugly, and she was trying to sell her house. And it made sense she'd be covered with dirt. Harry knew a little about gardening, knew that people could get dirty when the richness of the earth mixed with the sweat of hard work.

But the odd part was that Mrs. Griffin Lamont was doing her gardening while wearing a dress more appropriate for a cocktail party.

"That's an Armani," George murmured. At Harry's blank look, he explained. "A designer dress. Probably cost upward of seven hundred fifty bucks. What is she doing?"

"Searching for buried treasure?"

As Harry watched, Alessandra stood up. Her legs were long and slender, very nicely shaped despite the streaks of dirt running from her knees down her shins. She hooked one ridiculous-looking high-heeled shoe on top of the shovel and, using her body weight, dug in. The muscles in her arms and legs strained, and her dress tightened across her rear end.

"It would kind of be a shame to offer to help," George said quietly.

Harry nodded, perfectly content just to watch for a while—to see exactly what it was she was digging up.

But she spotted them and dropped the shovel, spraying herself with dirt.

"Lord!" she said. "You scared me!"

"Sorry." Up closer, she was even dirtier. She had cobwebs in her hair and an angry-looking scrape on her shoulder. Her dress was ripped, too. It had pockets on the front, and one of them looked as if it had caught on something and torn partly free. It had ripped right through the dress, leaving a little triangular-shaped hole through which he could see her underpants. Her bright red underpants. God. "Whatcha up to today, Mrs. Lamont?"

She made an attempt to push several loose strands of hair behind her ear—as if that would improve her disheveled appearance. Her hands were shaking. Caffeine jitters, Harry guessed. Hell, if he were her, given a too-short deadline by Michael Trotta, he'd keep himself wired with coffee, too.

She seemed exhausted. And terrified. Her blue eyes looked bruised, her mascara smeared, most of her other makeup long since worn off. She looked like complete hell, yet somehow even more attractive than she had two nights ago when they'd first met. She looked more like a real woman and less like a posable Barbie doll. And Harry found himself wanting to help her.

"Look," he said quietly. "We know what's going on. We know about the missing money. We know Michael Trotta's threatened to kill you if you don't give it back."

She turned away, all but putting her hands over her

ears to block his words. "I don't know what you're talking about."

"I can help you," he told her. "Mrs. Lamont—Alessandra—look at me." He took her arm and looked into her eyes. "I can help you."

He saw her uncertainty, saw her waver, and for a moment, he actually thought he had a chance. But then she pulled away, and he knew he'd lost her.

He kept going anyway. "It's in your best interest for us to take you into protective custody. It's the only way we can guarantee your safety."

It was also currently their best route to catching Trotta, but no one was going to tell Alessandra that. Harry felt a twinge of guilt, which he ruthlessly stomped down. "From there we can get you into the Witness Protection Program. You'll be given a new name, a new identity, a new life. In return, you'll testify against—"

"I didn't ask you to come here today. Do you have a warrant to be here?"

She was scared to death. Beneath her heavy ice-princess attitude, she was nearly shaking with fear. Harry looked closer, eyes narrowing.

"Is that blood on you?" he asked. "Just beneath your ear?"

It was dried, but it was definitely blood. He felt a rush of anger, a wave of disgust.

She reached up, as if to rub it away, or maybe to cover it from his view. "My shoulder," she said lamely. "I scratched myself and . . ."

"What did they do?" He couldn't keep his hatred of Trotta and everyone connected to organized crime from ringing in his voice.

"I don't know what you're talking about." She didn't sound so convincing this time. Harry had to put his hands in his pockets to keep from reaching for her. What was it about this woman?

"They gave you a sneak preview of what was going to happen to you, and told you not to go to the police," Harry guessed. She tried to pretend she didn't know what he meant, but he could tell he was right. "Alessandra, please, don't you understand that by listening to them, you're doing exactly what they hope you'll do? You stand no chance of winning on your own."

"I've heard Trotta's planning to use you as an example," George added. "He will kill you, and he'll make it hurt."

They weren't getting through to her. She straightened her narrow shoulders and lifted her chin. "This is private property. Please remove yourselves from my yard. You're welcome, of course, to stand out at the curb for as long as you like."

Frustration made him grit his teeth, but Harry knew when it was time to beat a retreat. He also knew that he wouldn't win any points by laughing aloud at her haughtiness. He took out his card and held it out to Alessandra Lamont instead. "Call if you change your mind."

She didn't take the card, didn't move. She just stood there, shaking slightly, but otherwise firm in her belief that her way was the only way.

Harry dropped his card and it fluttered to her feet. "In case you decide you want some help," he added.

"I won't," she told him.

"That's too bad. Because if you don't, you're probably going to die," he told her tightly, and walked away.

When Alessandra got home from the mall, the money was gone.

She'd found it, all of it, exactly where she'd expected—

buried in a locked metal box underneath Griffin's double-damned azalea.

She'd called the number on the card Michael Trotta had given her, and Ivo's frighteningly familiar voice answered the phone. He'd told her to wait for him—he'd be right over to pick up the money. But she'd left it on the dining-room table and gone out. If she never saw Ivo again, it would be too soon. And she didn't doubt his ability to get through a locked door.

Besides, she'd had to go to the mall. Right after she found the money, she'd gotten a call from a Mrs. Wong in the foster-care division of Social Services. She wanted to know if Alessandra would consider providing foster care for baby Jane Doe.

Just like that, her luck was changing. A meeting was set up for tomorrow morning.

It was the kind of meeting to which she couldn't wear her floor-length Christmas skirt. She needed to look good. She needed to look capable.

Alessandra went into the bathroom and filled the tub with warm water. She'd allowed herself no more than a quick shower after she'd found the money. But now that it was over, she deserved a long, leisurely soak, a chance to gather herself before the morning's meeting.

She left her blouse and the black velvet skirt she'd worn to the mall on the bed in the room she'd been sleeping in since Griffin moved out. The plastic bags with the purchases she'd charged to her last usable credit card were on the floor. New underwear from the sale table at Victoria's Secret. A plain yet fashionable skirt in a neutral beige, also on sale. A white sweater. A pair of spring-weight wool pants.

It wasn't much, but it would get her through two or even more meetings. And there would be more than just one, she was sure of that.

She was going to pack her new clothes in one of Griffin's gym bags and carry them around with her, if she had to. No way was she going to let them get shredded or bled on or . . .

But she wasn't going to have to carry them around. This was over. She'd given back the money.

She'd won.

The tub was nearly full as she slipped into it, sighing her pleasure. She turned off the water with one foot and closed her eyes, letting herself truly relax for the first time in more than two days.

Harry sat alone in his car outside the Lamont's Farmingdale estate, pondering his next move.

He and George had flipped a coin to see who would return to Long Island and keep an eye on Alessandra Lamont.

Harry had lost.

He hadn't expected her to leave her house as Trotta's deadline drew closer, and she'd surprised him by pulling out of the three-car garage in a nifty little sports car. He'd followed, expecting her only to be making a coffee run, but she'd surprised him again by making a quick stop at the dry cleaners on Main Street, and then heading over to the Sunrise Mall.

He'd left his car near hers in the parking lot and followed on foot while she shopped. She went into four or five different stores, making a purchase from each one.

It was weird. She had a death threat hanging over her head, and she was blithely buying underwear from Victoria's Secret.

He'd followed her home, still without her catching sight of him, and she'd pulled her car back into the oversize garage.

She'd gone inside, and as he'd watched from the street,

she'd turned on a few lights in the house, most of them upstairs.

Harry made up his mind. He was going to do it. He was going to get out of the car and ring her doorbell and talk to her again. Maybe this time he'd get lucky and get through to her.

Get lucky . . .

He shook his head to clear it of unruly thoughts. He was not George. He was not even going to consider the possibility of her modeling that fancy lingerie she'd just bought. There wasn't a chance in hell of that happening, and he'd be far better off not letting his thoughts stray in that direction.

He got out of his car, habit making him check that the dome light was off before he opened the door. He closed the door gently, also out of habit, glad he'd finally made the decision to take action.

He'd decided to take action with that mess he was in with Marge and his kids, too. As soon as Alessandra Lamont was safely in the hands of the specialists from the Witness Protection Program, he was going to catch the next flight to Colorado and find out what the hell was going on, find out where the hell they'd all gone.

But right now he had to give his full attention to her royal highness, Alessandra, Queen of Long Island. He truly hoped he wouldn't catch her fresh out of the shower, with a towel wrapped around her head and a bathrobe on. He'd be damned distracted the entire time they spoke— with a serious slice of his attention focused on whether she was wearing anything underneath that bathrobe.

Silently cursing all beautiful blonde women, Harry started for the front door.

But before he even reached the front path, the house exploded.

Four

DAZED, ALESSANDRA PULLED herself up and out of the tub, uncertain of where she was in the darkness. The shower curtain had fallen down on top of her, and she yanked it free from the pole, wrapping it around herself.

An emergency light sputtered to life, illuminating the thick smoke that was everywhere. The smoke detectors screamed. It didn't make any sense. She wasn't upstairs anymore. She was down in the kitchen. Somehow the bathtub had fallen through the ceiling and . . .

Glass was everywhere. The brand-new windows were shattered. Every one she could see in the dim light had been destroyed.

An explosion.

She'd fallen asleep upstairs in the tub and had awakened down in the kitchen from the sudden deafening sound and force of a tremendous explosion.

Her mother had always warned her not to fall asleep in the tub.

The house was on fire. Alessandra coughed, choking on the smoke, unable to breathe.

Whatever exploded had ignited the house, and it was burning. She could see the flames from the west wing and . . .

Her clothes! Her new clothes were still upstairs, up in

her bedroom. She needed them for that meeting tomorrow! She leapt over the broken glass, scrambling
toward the entryway, toward the staircase. The smoke
was chokingly thick, and she dropped to her hands and
knees, crawling up what was left of the stairs.

"What the fuck are you doing?"

The hoarse male voice came from out of nowhere, and
she jerked back in surprise as hands came down on her
shoulders, dragging her down the stairs.

She wriggled away. She didn't want to go that way.
Her new clothes were upstairs. Without them, she didn't
stand a chance of getting Jane.

Whoever he was—he of the foul mouth and large
hands—he was bigger than she was. And he wasn't about
to take no for an answer. He reached for her again, but
this time she was ready for him. She fought back in
earnest, flailing and hitting and kicking. Her leg connected with him solidly, strategically, and she heard the
breath leave his lungs, heard him squeeze out another
hair-curling curse.

He grabbed for her, catching the shower curtain, and
she slipped out of it, leaving it behind. She wouldn't need
it, anyway, once she reached her new clothes—her new
clothes that she would not let burn.

But she hadn't gone more than three steps farther before his hand closed around her leg. He dragged her
toward him, roughly pinning her legs before picking her
up and throwing her over his shoulder. He was coughing from the smoke that burned her lungs as well, and
he staggered slightly as he carried her down and out of
the house.

She was naked. She was completely naked, and he
must've realized that right before he carried her out the
door. Because once outside, he didn't stop to catch his

breath before peeling off his overcoat and wrapping it around her.

He carried her away from the house, set her down on the lawn, then sank to his knees beside her.

And a second explosion rocked the house.

He threw himself on top of her, shielding her as soot, ashes, and debris rained down upon them.

"What the hell," he asked, gasping for breath as he pulled himself off her, "is in there that's so important you've got to die trying to get it out?"

Alessandra gazed at the flames leaping from the entire west side of her house and couldn't stop her tears.

"Is the money still in there?" FBI Agent Harry O'Dell asked. For it was O'Dell who had pulled her out of the house. The man with the melting chocolate-brown eyes who could glance around a room and instantly see all the details that mere mortals missed. "Is that what you were after? Or is there someone else still inside?"

Alessandra couldn't answer. After days—no, weeks, months—of keeping her composure, she couldn't do anything but cry.

Fire engines were coming. Alessandra could hear the sirens in the distance. But it was too late. Too late. All she had left in the world was already burning. No one would ever let her have Jane now.

She couldn't keep from sobbing.

"Is someone else inside?" Harry O'Dell all but picked her up by the lapels of his raincoat and shook her. "Come on, Alessandra, don't lose it on me now!"

"My clothes . . ."

"What?"

"My new clothes . . ."

"Just tell me—yes or no—is someone else in the house?"

She shook her head. "No—"

Realization dawned in his eyes. "You were risking your life for some goddamn new clothes? I don't fucking believe it." Harry O'Dell shook his head. "You are one amazing piece of work, lady. One amazing piece of work."

As the first of the fire trucks and police cars squealed to a stop in front of the house, he yanked his raincoat more securely around her, tying it closed with the belt, then rose to meet the fire chief.

Alessandra sat in the Farmingdale Police Station, still wearing only Harry's raincoat.

She looked utterly defeated. Her face and hair were streaked with soot, and her eyes were dull with fatigue and shock.

It seemed impossible she'd survived a blast of that magnitude completely unscathed.

Either luck or the angels were with this lady, all right. She'd been in the bathtub, and the heavy enamel had shielded her against the force of the explosion, protecting her from flying debris. She'd actually fallen—inside the tub—from the second to the first floor of her house without getting hurt.

It didn't seem fair that someone like Alessandra Lamont, who could be moved to tears over the loss of a new bag of underwear, could have such stupendous good luck. Talk about shallow. Talk about completely skewed priorities.

Talk about gorgeous.

Harry sat down across from her, trying not to think about the fact that beneath that raincoat—his raincoat—she was absolutely naked.

He should know. He'd had his hands all over her tonight. Her skin was silky smooth, her body damn near perfect. Soft where it should be soft. Firm in just the right places.

The light from the fire had made her skin seem to gleam through the smoke. And try as he might, even all these hours later, he couldn't shake the image of her, scrambling up the stairs, trying to get away from him. Her breasts were small but perfect, well proportioned to her small-boned slenderness. Her legs were four miles long, her hips softly curved, her butt thong quality, her stomach enticingly soft.

She was also definitely a natural blonde.

At the time, his body hadn't reacted to the sight of her. After all, the house was on fire, and she'd just kneed him hard in the balls—two factors which always put something of a damper on his ability to become aroused.

But now he ached. It might've been an aftereffect of that knee to the groin—of having his very fragile package handled completely without care. If he were the sort who could get away with lying to himself, he would've willingly gone with that excuse. But the hard fact was, something about Alessandra Lamont got his hormones dancing and squawking.

But it sure as hell wasn't her unswerving honesty, her unshakable morals, or her superior intellect—all of which were nonexistent.

That left only her world-class body and perfect, beautiful face, with her perfect, beautiful, empty blue eyes.

Alessandra Lamont might be nothing more than a bimbo, but as bad as that was, Harry was worse.

Because if she were a bimbo, that made him a man who lusted after a bimbo.

He was a complete hypocrite. He scorned her for who she was, what she was, yet the mere sight of her gave him a major hard-on.

He didn't want to have to sit and talk to her, didn't

want to deal with her shallowness and stupidity. But he was dying to get down with her.

Yeah, he was a fine, upstanding human being.

Harry cleared his throat, but she didn't look up. She was sitting with her arms wrapped tightly around herself, as if holding herself together. She looked completely vulnerable and very young. And underneath his raincoat, she was wearing nothing.

"Mrs. Lamont?" Harry purposely used the formal name, hoping it would remind him that she'd willingly married some mob-connected scumbag for his money, hoping it would make her seem that much more despicable, hoping it would reduce his relentless attraction.

It didn't work.

She looked at him then, and he could see fear in her eyes. Fear and something else. Something that looked an awful lot like hope. "Have they discovered what caused the explosion?" she asked. "Was it a problem with the gas line?"

Harry didn't answer right away. He just looked at her for a moment then shook his head. "Mrs. Lamont. Do you really think it was a coincidental gas explosion that took out half your house? Your husband—"

"Ex-husband," she corrected him.

He watched her. "—stole five million dollars from the mob."

"Five million dollars!" There was real surprise in her voice, in her eyes. "Five million?"

Harry leaned even farther forward. "Am I wrong? Was it less?" He knew it was only a million.

The animated expression on her face instantly disappeared as she realized she'd nearly given herself away. She was now expressionless, her eyes devoid of the life that had glistened in them just moments before. "I don't know what you're talking about."

"Car bomb," Harry told her.

Uncertainty sparked in her eyes, along with a flare of disbelief, and he knew she was much smarter than she let on.

"Yeah, you heard me right," he said. "The arson squad's still looking the place over, but from what they can tell right now, the blast was caused by a faulty trigger device in a bomb that was planted in your Jeep Cherokee. The bomb wasn't supposed to blow until after you backed the car out of the garage and put the sucker into drive. There was a second bomb in the sedan, just in case you took that car when you went to the mall in the morning. That second explosion—that was the second bomb going off, triggered by the fire." He paused. "I guess they were gambling on the fact you wouldn't drive the Miata two days in a row."

Her eyes were wide and she was starting to shake. He knew he could stand up and walk around the table and sit down next to her and she wouldn't move away. He knew he could put his arm around her, gently pull her close for a little comfort, and she wouldn't complain. In fact, she would probably lean in to him, trembling, and he'd reach up and soothingly stroke her hair.

She wanted someone to take care of her—she probably didn't particularly care who. He'd bet she'd even trade sex for his protection.

The possibilities loomed above him for a moment as he sat gazing at her. He could stand up and set the process in motion. And within a matter of days, maybe even hours, he'd find himself in bed with this beautiful woman.

But Harry didn't stand up. He didn't move. He'd never paid for sex, and he wasn't about to start now. Even if the payment was in protection, not U.S. currency.

"Maybe you can give me a list of names—people who

might want to see you dead," he said to her. "Irate neighbors who object to your lighting the shrubbery on fire, perhaps?"

She glanced up quickly at him, and he knew he'd been right about the fire. "Or maybe you want to start by explaining why the word on the street has your name at the top of a very short list of people with contracts out on their lives. You're marked for death, sweetheart. Someone wants you cold and dead. I'm not a gambling man, but I'd put my paycheck on the fact that it's Michael Trotta who's behind that."

"I gave the money back," Alessandra whispered. "I don't understand. I did what he wanted. I found the money—all of it. One million dollars. And I gave it back."

She gave the money back. "Jesus, lady, you are without a doubt the Queen of Bad Judgment. That million dollars was evidence we could have used—"

"They told me they'd kill me if I went to the police!"

"Yeah? Well, it looks as if killing you is on their agenda regardless."

"It doesn't make sense!"

"What doesn't make sense is you giving the money back."

"I saw what they did to a man who'd gone to the police," Alessandra told him, her voice shaking. She was scared to death, but her pretty blue eyes were dry. Apparently the only thing that made her weep was the thought of all those great bargains she'd picked up at Saks Fifth Avenue and Victoria's Secret going up in smoke.

"So why'd you wait so long?" Harry asked harshly. "Why not just return the money when Trotta first approached you?"

"I didn't know where it was. I had to find it first."

"You found it." Harry let his skepticism ring in his voice.

"It was under the azalea."

"You found it," Harry repeated. "All by yourself? Under the azalea?"

"It was the only thing Griffin asked for in our divorce settlement," Alessandra told him. "That, and the fact that he planted it himself got me thinking. I didn't have to be a rocket scientist to know that I should dig under the azalea."

She may not have been a rocket scientist, but she had stopped to think during her search for the missing money. Most people never bothered to stop and think. Most people just let themselves be swept along by the chaos, acting and reacting.

Yeah, Alessandra Lamont was definitely smarter—and stronger—than he'd first thought.

In fact, as she sat there, across from him, chin lifted in pitiful defense against his skepticism, Harry almost found himself liking her.

Almost.

But regardless of his newfound admiration, he still didn't trust her. There was something else she'd left out, something she wasn't telling him. Had to be. Why else would Trotta want to kill her? The mob boss had to know he'd scared her enough for her to stay silent about the money. So why the car bomb? Why the contract on her life?

"What happens now?" Alessandra asked softly.

Harry gazed at the streaks of soot on her delicately featured face. "We take you into protective custody." He gave it to her as if she had no choice in the matter, steeling himself against the guilt of his deceit. "We keep you safe, and in return, you testify after we get enough evidence to bring down Trotta."

It wasn't really as simple as that. George's ex, Nicole Fenster, had set up a plan to take Alessandra into custody then leak her whereabouts to Trotta. According to the plan, Trotta would attempt a hit that the task force would intercept. They'd have Trotta on charges of attempted murder and everyone would be happy.

Of course, Alessandra probably wasn't going to be happy to find she'd been used as bait. But by the time she did find out, it would be over and done with.

"Is there any chance . . ." She hesitated, glancing up at him and blushing slightly. "I don't have any clothes. I know you . . . know that. And I . . . thank you for giving me your coat, but, I was wondering how . . ."

"We'll get you something to wear first thing in the morning," Harry reassured her. "Your needs will be taken care of—as part of the deal we make with the DA and the Witness Protection Program."

She nodded, obviously embarrassed but determined to get it said. "I'm sorry if I . . . hurt you. When you were trying to pull me out of the house."

"You don't have to apologize," Harry said quietly. He refused to feel bad about using Alessandra as unsuspecting bait to catch Trotta. After all, she'd married Griffin Lamont. She'd had to know at least some of what was going on. She was no innocent bystander, despite her attempt to play that part.

"Yes, I do. You saved my life," she told him. "If you hadn't pulled me out of there . . . When the second car exploded . . ."

"Luck," Harry told her. "It was all dumb luck." He smiled, and she managed a very small, very shaky smile back.

But it quickly faded, and she looked away.

Harry knew despite his promises, she didn't trust him any more than he trusted her.

And rightly so.

Five

A PAIR OF pajamas were out on the bed, waiting for her, after Alessandra got out of the shower.

They were men's pajamas, made of stiff new flannel, boxy and oversize, in a green plaid print.

She looked about twelve years old in the bathroom mirror, wearing those pajamas, her pale face scrubbed completely clean of makeup. She went out into the other room of the suite still combing her hair, self-consciously aware that she was by no means looking her best. But she had no makeup, no hair gel, no perfume, no clothes besides these green plaid pajamas.

And that raincoat, which hung on the back of a chair.

This whole wretched scene had to be a mistake.

The sight of FBI agents Harry O'Dell and George Faulkner sitting in her hotel suite made this entire situation seem even more absurd.

There had to be some kind of mistake. A misunderstanding. She'd returned the stolen money, but somehow the wires had gotten crossed. Someone hadn't gotten the word and her name had been put on the "still owes a million dollars or her life" list instead of the one marked "paid in full."

Maybe all she'd need to do was make a simple phone call to Michael Trotta, explain about the confusion, and let him straighten everything out.

Because why would Michael order her to be killed? It didn't make sense.

Harry O'Dell was on the phone again. He'd made a beeline to the telephone to make a call the moment they'd stepped into this hotel room. Then, as now, he hung up in frustration, as if his call hadn't been answered.

He turned, hesitating only very slightly as he saw her standing there. But then he forced a smile, choosing to pretend he didn't notice the magnetic pull of attraction she, too, felt every time she so much as looked at him.

"Feeling any better?" he asked.

She was exhausted. It had been nearly forty-eight hours since she'd last slept, longer than that since she'd last eaten, and she was barely standing. She'd completely missed the morning meeting with Social Services—not that she had any hope of getting care of Jane now. Her home had been burned to the ground, and according to Harry O'Dell, there was a contract out on her life. Was she feeling better?

Could it get any worse?

Still, she nodded politely. "Yes. Thank you."

What was it about Harry, anyway?

He may have been solidly, muscularly built, but he was short. If she wore her usual three-inch heels, she'd be at least an inch taller. Even under the best of circumstances, she'd be hard-pressed to call him handsome. And with his rumpled, ill-fitting suit, permanent five-o'clock shadow, the puffy bags underneath his eyes, and his lawn-mower-styled hair, this could hardly be considered the best of circumstances.

Still there was something about him . . .

As she watched, he shrugged out of his jacket. His button-down dress shirt had short sleeves. Dear Lord, Harry was definitely one of the top ten most-wanted fugitives on the run from the fashion police.

"Did you get a chance to look at the room service menu?" he asked.

She was holding both the menu and the list she'd made of things she'd need. Clothes, underwear, shoes, moisturizing lotion, a notebook to write in, something to read, a jacket. Her stomach growled and she glanced at the menu again. Unfortunately, it hadn't changed while she was in the shower. "Isn't there somewhere else we can order from?"

Harry laughed aloud. "Look, princess, I know it's not gourmet food, but it's here in the hotel and it's what we're going to eat. So suck it up and order a burger."

"I don't eat red meat," she said coolly.

"Now, there's a surprise."

"The fish chowder's pretty good here," George suggested, glancing up from the TV, where he was watching a basketball game with the volume muted.

"Perfect," Harry said. "Have the chowder. If George says it's good, it's good. Are you going to get all bothered if I have a burger?"

"No—"

"Great. Then we're set."

Alessandra shook her head. "The chowder won't work. I know it's not on the menu, but maybe they could grill some chicken, plain. That and a salad—"

"This isn't luncheon at the country club," Harry interrupted. "You're on the run from Michael Trotta. It's in your best interest to keep a low profile—and that includes reducing the pain-in-the-ass factor for the kitchen staff. The menu's not that short. Pick something from the menu."

"But everything has cheese in it, or some kind of heavy cream or—"

"Go crazy. Have an extra thousand calories. After surviving that blast, you deserve to celebrate."

"I can't—"

"Sure, you can."

"No," Alessandra said. "You don't understand. I'm allergic to milk—to all dairy. Does the word anaphylactic mean anything to you?"

"Oh, shit," Harry said.

"Anna-what?" George asked.

"Phylactic," Harry said. "It means the princess here is so allergic to milk that if she accidentally has any, her body starts to shut down. My ex's cousin had an anaphylactic reaction to peanuts. If there was so much as a quarter of a teaspoon of peanut oil in something she ate, she'd be dead within a matter of minutes. She carried around this special little injection thing filled with adrenaline that she'd shoot into herself if she felt a reaction coming on. It would supposedly give her enough time to be rushed to the hospital."

"An Epi-pen," Alessandra said. "Mine was in my purse." Her purse and its entire contents had no doubt gone up in flames. "I thought it would be a good idea to have one, so I put it on the list of things I need for tomorrow morning."

Harry took the list from her, glancing at it quickly. "Christ," he said. He turned the paper over, but there was nothing written on the back. "Is this all? I mean, it looks like you forgot to include the plane tickets to Paris and the pet ferret. And what about that autographed poster of John Travolta you always wanted?"

Alessandra felt herself flush. Her list was long. But he'd told her to write the things she needed, and she needed every one of the items on that list.

"If there's a problem . . ." she started to say.

"Nope," Harry said, handing the list to George. "No problem. The FBI has plenty of money for three new pairs of shoes. We don't need to buy silly little things like bullets."

Alessandra's temper flared. Instead of quietly burying it, the way she'd done for years with Griffin, she let it snap loose. "I don't know the rules," she told him hotly. "Don't expect me to be able to play this game without telling me the rules. I've got nothing. My feet are bare. I need sneakers, something to wear with a dress, and boots for when it rains. You told me to make a list—"

"I imagined it would be necessities. Things like a toothbrush and maybe a stick of deodorant." He took the list back from George. "What the hell is Neutragena soap? Can't you use the stuff from the hotel? And what the hell do you need with three different kinds of lotion?"

"One's for night, one's for day—it's got a sunblock— and the third is a hand lotion. Not that it's any of your business." Being mad—and showing it—felt good.

Except Harry didn't seem to care that she was mad.

"From now on," he told her, "and until you get settled in the Witness Protection Program, everything you do, every molecule of air you breathe is my business. It has to be, if I'm going to keep you safe."

Harry sat down, rubbing his forehead as if it ached. "I don't suppose it's too much to hope that you kept your milk allergy secret from everyone you knew—including your ex-husband?"

His question was absurd. Alessandra didn't answer.

He glanced at her, his dark brown eyes glinting with self-mockery. "Yeah, sorry. Stupid question." He sighed. "So we've got to assume Michael Trotta knows. And all he'll have to do to find you is have his men make some discreet inquiries, find out if any of the local hotels have been asked to prepare any special meals with no milk, no butter, no cheese." He shook his head. "Shit. Why couldn't this be easy? Just for once."

"If it were easy," George stood up, "you'd go find something hard to do. From now on, no room service—at least not for Alessandra. I'll go find a deli—pick us up some sandwiches. You want your usual?"

Alessandra looked up to find Harry staring at her, something unreadable in his eyes. His gaze was probably meant to intimidate. After all, her pain-in-the-ass factor, as he'd called it, was off the scale. She was making things difficult with her long list of needs and her dietary restrictions, and he was giving her the evil eye to make sure she knew it.

But she was done apologizing. That part of her life was over. She held his gaze pointedly, defensively, daring him to speak aloud any of his less-than-polite thoughts.

She realized too late that the something in his eyes wasn't hostility. It was more complicated than that.

He was beyond tired. He was bone weary. It was etched into his face in the lines around his mouth and his eyes. They had once been laughter lines, Alessandra realized. Once upon a time, his eyes had crinkled at the edges from smiles and laughter. Those same lines that made his face look tired and old had no doubt made him a vital, handsome man. Those same lines had helped bring him to life.

But not anymore.

Now he was too tired even to hide the attraction he felt for her. She could see a reflection of her own body in his eyes, naked in the flickering light from the burning house. She could see the unmistakable glint of his hunger as he remembered all that he'd seen and touched.

It was completely hypnotizing.

It was the way Little Red Riding Hood must've felt looking into the eyes of the big bad wolf.

But it was accompanied by contempt. He was attracted to her, and he despised both himself and Alessandra because of it.

"Harry," George said impatiently. "Tuna salad on rye?"

Harry pulled his gaze away from her, looking up at his partner as if surprised he was there. "Yeah," he said. "Sure." He glanced back at Alessandra and stood up. "I think I should probably be the one to go."

He didn't want to be here, alone with her.

"Why don't you find out what she wants," Harry said, "while I try to make that call again."

As Alessandra watched, he picked up the phone and dialed a series of numbers. Long distance.

"So what'll it be?" George asked. "What you said—plain grilled chicken and a salad?"

"That's fine," Alessandra said absently. Harry's shoulders were tense as he stood with the phone receiver to his ear, a living picture of intensity. "Is there a problem I should know about?"

George shook his head. "Harry's making a personal call. He's having some kind of hassle with his kids."

Kids. Harry had kids. Alessandra turned away, careful not to let her surprise show. If he had kids, he probably had a wife. She never would have guessed in a million years that Harry O'Dell was a family man. She tried to picture him at home, tried to picture his kids.

She tried to picture his wife.

No wonder he didn't want to be alone with Alessandra. He was married, and she—she was only a temptation. Forget about the possibility of forming a simple friendship. She was too beautiful for that. Men—even married men—either wanted to possess her or to keep their distance. There was no in-between.

It was too bad, because she could've really used a friend.

Even one like Harry O'Dell.

Maybe especially one like Harry O'Dell.

Wiping the steam from the bathroom mirror in the beach house, Shaun leaned closer to study his face.

Even with his blond hair dark from the shower, he didn't look much like Harry. Emily had their father's coloring, while Shaun looked like a masculine version of their mother.

Not masculine enough, though. He was nearly as pretty as she had been. He'd always been pretty—and been teased mercilessly about it by the kids at school. And after they'd moved to Colorado, Kevin hadn't been around to stand up for him.

The kids had called him "Leprechaun," and still did even though he was no longer as short as he'd been back in sixth grade.

Being called a leprechaun was better than his other nickname.

Fag.

He had blond hair, green eyes, and soft, pale skin that burned instead of tanned, while both Harry and Em turned a deep nut brown in the sun.

He was going to be taller than his father, too. At fourteen, it was clear he'd inherited his mother's Northern European stature. Over the past two years, he'd gone from being the smallest kid in his class to being one of the tallest. In fact, at five feet eleven, he looked old enough to pass for a high school student.

Apparently that's what that red-haired girl had thought when she'd stopped to talk to him.

Shaun put on his glasses and stepped back slightly. The muscles in his chest and legs were strong and well devel-

oped from two solid years of dance class. He'd played
Little League baseball before he and Em had moved to
Marge's house in Colorado. He'd been good at it; he was
coordinated and a fast runner, but his heart hadn't been
in it. He'd merely gone along with it because Kevin and
Harry liked it so much. And he'd adored them.

He would have gone swimming in shark-infested wa-
ters just to be near them, if that's what they had wanted
to do. Baseball hadn't been quite that bad, of course.
Still, it didn't get him excited.

But dancing . . . Ballet, jazz, or tap—he didn't care
which, he loved it all. And he was getting good. Good
enough to have gotten the part of the Artful Dodger in
the middle school musical. Dozens of kids had tried for
the part, but he'd seen Mrs. Janson's face when he'd
started to dance.

All of the teachers had been impressed with his
performance.

All of the kids still called him "fag."

His aunt had urged him to call Harry, to tell him about
getting the part in the show, but Shaun hadn't done it. He
couldn't bear to leave another message on his father's answering machine.

He hadn't told his dad about the musical, so he hadn't
been disappointed when Harry hadn't shown up.

And Harry wouldn't have come, even if Shaun had
called.

He was certain of that.

"Can I pick my new name?" Alessandra asked.

"You can definitely have some input," George told
her. "Do you have a name in mind?"

"I've always wanted to be called Friday," Alessandra
said almost shyly.

Harry nearly choked on his tuna-salad sandwich.

"She was a character in a book I really liked," she continued.

Friday. He looked at George and rolled his eyes. "Perfect," he said sarcastically, after he swallowed. "You'll blend right in with the fifty-eight other Fridays in whatever small town in Ohio you end up being placed in."

"Ohio?" She sounded horrified.

Christ, she was clueless. He steeled himself as he looked back at her, refusing to acknowledge the zing of physical response he felt each time he forced himself to meet the pure blue of her gaze.

"Ohio," he repeated. "Or Indiana. Or maybe even Illinois. You have a better chance blending in in the Midwest than you would in the South. Unless you want to learn to speak with a southern accent."

"I can do that," she said, meeting his gaze in a way that was almost challenging.

Harry had to smile. Yeah, sure, she could. And his mother was the pope. "It's harder than you think, Mrs. Lamont."

"I know exactly how hard it is," she told him quietly. "I learned to speak without a New York accent. I grew up out on the Island. Massapequa Park. I took elocution lessons for nearly half a year to lose my accent."

That surprised him. According to her file, she'd been born in Connecticut. He'd been so certain she'd lived in Fairfield County nearly all her life, attending private school and taking tennis lessons, and speaking with perfect, round, very wealthy-sounding vowels from birth.

Massapequa Park was pretty solidly middle class.

Why hadn't that been in her file? Harry made a mental note to find out who'd fucked up. Screwed up. Sheesh.

"We'll need to talk to the people at the Witness Protection Program before we know exactly where they'll end up sending you," George told Alessandra. "And as far as the name goes . . ." He shook his head with an apologetic smile. "Friday's not going to fly."

Harry was more blunt. "They'll choose something absolutely white-bread bland. Ordinary. Barbara Conway. There's a perfect name for you."

Her extremely nonordinary blue eyes were filled with dismay.

"They'll make you cut your hair," he continued ruthlessly. It was going to happen; she was going to have to get used to the idea. "And probably dye it a real average shade of brown. And they'll get you clothes more suitable for a Barbara Conway, too. Probably lots of knee-length skirts in olive drab and navy blue. Sturdy shoes. Cotton blouses that button to the neck. That sort of thing."

She was looking at him as if he were describing the horrors of Armageddon.

George delicately wiped his mouth with a napkin. "Come on, Harry, make it sound worse than it is, why don't you?"

Alessandra looked to George hopefully. "I won't really have to do that, will I? Dye my hair?"

"You will if you want to be safe," Harry told her. "You'll say good-bye to Alessandra Lamont and become Barbara Conway."

"But what good is being safe if I have to turn into someone I don't want to be? I mean, what's the point?"

Harry shrugged. "Your choice. Although, it seems pretty clear to me that if it's a choice between short brown hair, ugly shoes, or a bullet in the head . . . Brown hair and ugly shoes win, hands down."

She didn't look convinced. But she didn't argue any further. They ate in silence for several minutes before she spoke again.

"So tomorrow someone from the Witness Protection

Program will arrive," she said to George. "Will you and Mr. O'Dell go home at that time?"

Mr. O'Dell. Jesus. "We won't leave you until you're set up in your new town, and we know you're safe. And call me Harry," he said. "Mr. O'Dell gives me a rash."

"You call me Mrs. Lamont," she countered.

Damn, she was right. He took a deep breath. "Okay," he said. "You call me Harry, I'll call you . . . Allie."

She looked pained. "My name is Alessandra."

"Not anymore it's not. Consider Allie a temporary stop between your old and your new name—whatever it's gonna be."

"Who actually gets to decide that?" she asked.

George finished the last of his 7UP. "Probably some computer somewhere."

"How long will it be before I'm actually allowed to start living my life again?" she asked.

Harry looked at George. This was a tricky question. If this were a normal Witness Protection Program deal, they would say good-bye to her tomorrow. They'd pass her off, put her in someone else's capable hands. But this wasn't normal. They were using her as bait, to lure Trotta into a trap. Because of that, he and George were going to be beside Alessandra, 24/7, for a week or two. Maybe even longer. Certainly as long as it took for Trotta to take the bait and attempt a hit.

There was that twinge of guilt again. God, he had to get over it. Yes, they were using Alessandra as bait. Yes, that was a shitty thing to do. It was unfortunate, but necessary. Why couldn't he accept that and move on?

George cleared his throat. "That really depends," he said. "It'll probably be at least a week, maybe more."

"That long?" Alessandra's gaze flicked in Harry's direction, and he knew what she was thinking.

He didn't like it, either. He forced a smile. "Just until

we know you're safe," he said. "We're pretty thorough. And you know, after awhile, you won't even know we're around." He reached for his soda, but his fingers fumbled and the can slipped free, spilling the cold liquid directly on his crotch. "Shit!" he shouted, grabbing the can and then a pile of napkins to mop himself off. His pants were soaked. It looked as if he'd wet himself. Or worse. "Fucking unbelievable!"

He looked up, directly into Alessandra's cool blue eyes.

"I beg your pardon," he said, feeling the cold of his cola saturate his boxer shorts.

She looked at George, as if choosing to pretend Harry didn't exist. "When do you get to go home and spend time with your families? How do your wives feel about you spending the night here—in my hotel room?"

"I'm divorced. And we didn't have kids, so . . ." George shrugged. "And Harry—"

"I don't have a family either," he interrupted. "Not anymore."

Alessandra turned to look at him. "But George said you had kids."

Harry stood up, wishing he had a clean pair of pants to change into, wishing he'd brought his bag with his jeans, wishing he were anywhere but here. "George needs to work on his compulsive lying."

"Harry's got a son and a daughter," George told her.

"If you're here with me all day and all night, when do you get a chance to see them?" Alessandra asked.

His pants were cold and sticky—never a good combination, even on the best of days. And this one was definitely out of the running for the best. "Never," he said flatly, heading for the bathroom. "I try to see them as close to never as possible. Maybe that way they'll live to see their sixteenth birthdays."

"I don't understand." Alessandra looked to George

for an explanation as Harry closed the bathroom door behind him.

"Harry had another son," he told her quietly. "Kevin. He was killed two years ago when—"

Alessandra jumped as the bathroom door swung open and hit the side of the tub with a crash.

"What the fuck is wrong with you?" Harry came back out of the bathroom with a towel and a dangerous light in his eyes. Luckily for her, his death glare was aimed at George.

George shrugged, unperturbed. "I thought—"

"Don't!" Harry shouted at him. "Don't talk about me as if I'm not here. And don't talk about me when I'm not here. Just keep it the fuck to yourself."

Alessandra felt responsible. "I asked, and he was just—"

He turned toward her. "I'm not sure why George seems to think it's important you know that my son Kevin was virtually decapitated when the car he was riding in slid underneath a truck. What do you say George? Were you also going to tell her that the crash that killed my kid and my ex was the result of the mob trying to scare me off a case? The bullets were supposed to be fired only in warning, but someone screwed up and a truck driver was hit. He lost control of his rig, and Sonya and Kevin didn't stand a chance."

Alessandra closed her eyes, dizzy from lack of sleep, dizzy from the harshness of Harry's words. Dear Lord.

"But hey, you know, if Allie here needs to know that, maybe she should know all my deeply personal and private shit, too." Harry's voice was softer now but no less intense. "Like the fact that I haven't had sex since 1996. I really think she better know that. Or how about sometimes the only way I can fall asleep at night is to stay awake for seventy-two hours and then collapse. Oh, I know. This is a good one, Al, you're going to like this: I was too much of a coward to face my surviving son and daughter and tell them that both Kevin and their mother were never coming home again. And let's not forget how I still can't look my kids in the eye, so I just never go home. Does that give you the fucking insight you needed to psychoanalyze me?"

Alessandra couldn't look at him, couldn't move. He'd lost a child. She couldn't begin to imagine his pain.

He slammed back into the bathroom, locking the door behind him.

George cleared his throat and gave her a weak smile. "I think we'll let Harry go out to get dessert."

Six

❧ ❧

ALESSANDRA SAT IN the darkened bedroom of the hotel suite. The small amount of grilled chicken she'd managed to choke down an hour ago now made her stomach churn ominously as she stared at the telephone.

The glowing red numbers of the clock beside the phone calmly changed from 2:13 to 2:14. Despite the fact that she was nauseous from fatigue and more than ready to sink into bed and sleep until morning, it wasn't the middle of the night. It was only mid-afternoon.

It was smack in the middle of the workday.

In fact, Michael Trotta was probably back from lunch, probably in his office right this very minute.

Just a phone call away.

The grilled chicken made a slow circle in its unending dance of horror, and she reached out to touch the phone with one finger.

She didn't want to be here. She didn't want to spend another minute playing this frightening game. She wanted to call a time out and find the road that led back to her real life. She wanted to push her way behind the curtains and remove herself from this alternative reality in which she'd found herself trapped.

She wanted to pick up that phone and call Michael Trotta. She wanted the destruction of her cars and her house to be a giant mistake. She wanted to find out that some not-too-bright thug named Lenny or Frank or Vince had misheard Trotta's instructions and set those bombs.

She wanted her life back.

She'd prefer the evil she knew over this horribly frightening uncertainty.

She didn't want to live in Ohio. She wanted to stay here, where maybe someday she'd have a prayer of a chance of adopting Jane.

She couldn't give up hope. It was close to hopeless, she knew, but she couldn't give up.

She wouldn't.

Alessandra glanced at the door to the main room of the suite. It was open a crack and dim light streamed in. She'd wanted to close it, but Harry had told her not to. Even when she showered, even when she used the facilities, she was supposed to leave the door unlocked.

Welcome to privacy hell.

When Harry had informed her of the open-door rule, she'd glanced up and for the briefest of moments their eyes had met and locked. His were probably the darkest, blackest shade of brown she'd ever seen, filled with a weariness that seemed at least a million years old, permanently shadowed from the loss of a child and the death of a woman he probably still loved. Her heart had twisted, imagining the open rawness of his pain, and in that instant, time had seemed to twist and turn, too. For the slightest fraction of seconds, for a segment of time too small to measure, she was back inside her house, just out of the bath, flames and smoke around her, Harry's rock-solid body pressed against hers, his callused hands warm against her still-damp skin.

His touch had felt sinfully good.

She stood up abruptly, banishing that memory to the

farthest reaches of her mind. She didn't want to feel anything for Harry O'Dell, particularly not this odd compasssion. Compassion and . . . lust? No, she was tired. She was still in shock. He'd lost a child and she felt sorry for him. That was all this was. Compassion. Period.

Lord, she hated this. She didn't want to be here.

And one phone call—just one—could clear up this entire misunderstanding.

She picked up the phone.

"Calling anyone I know?"

Alessandra jumped, and the phone handset rattled in its cradle.

Harry pushed the door open even farther and stepped into the room. His face was harsh and grim, his eyes as cold and devoid of life as the farthest reaches of outer space.

"I was just . . ." She didn't know what to say. He knew exactly what she was just about to do.

He stared at her, nearly boring an ice-encrusted hole into her with his zero-degree gaze, waiting for her to continue.

And she could only think about the way he'd looked at her before, the heat in his eyes, the way he'd touched her.

Alessandra knew she looked good. Not great, but passably good. George had made a quick run to the drugstore and had picked up a number of things from her list, including some cheap makeup. She'd put it on immediately and had instantly felt a little bit better. A little bit more in control.

She shifted back very slightly on the bed, pulling her legs out from beneath her. She moved just a little bit so that the stream of light from the open door fell on her carefully made-up face, on the shining gold of her hair, on the deep V-neck of the pajamas she wore, giving him a flash of skin, a clear shot of her delicately boned ankles, a hint of gracefully shaped legs.

It was a calculated movement, a subtle invitation to look, meant to distract and befuddle. A nonverbal change of subject.

And although Harry did look, his gaze lingered insolently on her breasts before he practically scraped his way down her legs. He wasn't at all distracted. And certainly not befuddled.

"Did you try this on Michael Trotta?" he murmured, his gaze intimately tracing the curve of her hips and thighs before moving back to meet her eyes.

Alessandra pulled her knees in to her chest, holding them tightly, instantly embarrassed. This was her fault. She'd done it automatically. All her life she'd used her looks as a bargaining chip. But she should have known not to play with fire. It was all she could do not to burst into tears. "I don't know what—"

"Yes," he said. "You do. You know damn well what you look like. You didn't want to admit to me that you were thinking about calling Trotta, so you figured you'd change the subject by giving me a hard-on. Well, guess what, Al. Didn't work."

Alessandra felt a flare of anger at the crassness of his words. "You really are—" She stopped herself.

"What?"

She turned away. "No. I refuse to be dragged down to your level."

"A fucking bastard. That's what you want to say, isn't it?"

Alessandra stood up and began pulling the covers back from the pillow. "You said it, I didn't."

He sat on the end of the bed before she could pull the bedspread all the way off. "I really am curious, though. What was Trotta's response?"

She tugged at the spread. "Excuse me. I'm very tired and—"

"He could buy and sell you." Harry didn't move. "In a way, he already has. Think about it. He pays a price—and not even a particularly high price for a guy with as much money as he has—and someone snuffs out your life."

She gave up on that bed and moved to the other one.

"Oh, but wait," Harry said, feigning a sudden realization. "You don't think he's really put out a contract on you. That's why you were going to call him, right? You think two car bombs in your garage is the result of some kind of clerical error."

She stiffly kept her back to him as she turned down the sheets of the second bed.

"So, tell me, Allie," he continued. "What were you planning to say to him when you got him on the line?" He did a poor imitation of a female voice. " 'Please, Mikey, tell me it's all been just a big mistake.' And what do you think he's gonna say to you when you say that? I'll give you a few extra seconds to think that one over—I don't want you to strain yourself."

Alessandra turned to face him, letting herself hate him. "I'd like you to get out of here."

He moved then, but it was only to sit in another position, his back against the headboard, his legs stretched out comfortably on the bed. "He's gonna say, 'Why, of course, Mrs. Lamont.' " This time he did a rather chillingly accurate imitation of Trotta's dulcet tones. " 'It is indeed a mistake, Mrs. Lamont. Please come into my office, Mrs. Lamont, and I'll take care of everything.' "

"Maybe he will say that. I gave back the money."

Harry laughed, arranging the pillows more comfortably behind him. "Oh, yeah. He'll say it. But you know what happens next? You know how he'll 'take care of everything'? You can go in there and flash him the goods all you want, sweetheart. You can even go further, put your mouth where your money is, so to speak. Yeah, I'm betting Michael Trotta won't have any problem at all with you giving him a blow job before he kills you."

She flinched. "You're disgusting."

"The truth is disgusting. Don't confuse the messenger with the message."

Alessandra pulled herself up to her full height and gazed at him with as much haughtiness as she could muster. "Please. I'm exhausted."

Harry smiled. "The ice bitch thing doesn't work with me either, Al."

"Stop calling me that."

"What? Ice bitch or Al?"

She held herself tightly to keep from shaking. She wasn't sure if what she felt was anger or fear or just sheer desperation. All she knew for certain was that the thought of losing her identity scared her to death, and that she missed baby Jane so much she ached. "My name is Alessandra."

"Not for long." Harry stood up in one smooth motion. "Here's the deal, Allie." His voice was harsh. "I know you don't believe your dear friend Michael really wanted to blow you into a million little pieces, but if you so much as dial his phone number, you'll be out on the street, on your ass, faster than you can spit. Because if you call Trotta, he'll know exactly where you are within minutes. And then not only will you be dead, but George and I will also probably die attempting to protect you.

"If you really have a death wish, I can get you a T-shirt with a great big target on it, and you can wear it as you walk out of this hotel. It'll be a short walk, though. You'll only get a few blocks before you're spotted and taken down."

She didn't believe him. She couldn't believe him. And he knew that just from looking at her.

He picked up the phone and with one swift, effortless yank pulled the wire right out of the wall. "Maybe this will reduce the temptation, huh?"

"Are you intending to lock me up in here, too?" Her voice shook.

"You're free to leave whenever you want. My advice, though, would be to get your personal effects in order first." Harry turned toward the door but then turned back. "Oh, and Al? If you get in touch with Trotta, either by calling on the other hotel line or any other way, and he finds out where you are, you're toast. Even if his hitmen somehow manage to miss you, you'll be dead. Believe it. Because I'll shoot you myself."

"Hello?" Kim's breathless voice sounded impossibly young and innocent. Nicole had never sounded that young. Not even when she'd first come up from the Academy.

"Hi, babe. It's me—George."

"Who?"

He had to laugh. "Jeez, it's been that memorable, huh? George. Remember? George Faulkner?"

"Omigod, George! I'm sorry, I couldn't hear you. It's noisy in here and . . . God, of course I remember. Where have you been? Wait a minute, let me move to another phone."

There was a thud then only bar sounds—loud music, laughter. Then a click and Kim's voice was back. "Hang up, Carol." Louder. "I said, hang up." Then deafeningly, shrilly, "I said, hang the motherfucking phone up! Now!"

The bar sounds disappeared and Kim was back, as sweet and breathlessly innocent as ever. "Baby, I'm so glad you called. I was starting to think you'd forgotten about me. Where have you been for the past three days? Can I see you tonight?"

Cold and hot. Psycho and sweet. Kim was an actor—George knew that. He was something of an actor himself.

"I'm on assignment," he told her. "I can't get free. Not tonight, anyway."

"Where are you now? If you can come over here right this minute . . ." Her voice trailed off, leaving George's imagination to fill in the blank.

He was too tall for the so-called privacy shields built around the pay phone to make any kind of difference. Still, he ducked awkwardly closer to the phone, wishing he could crawl through the line, wishing he could steal half an hour. He had a very good imagination. "I thought the club had a rule about what goes on in your dressing room."

"Are you in town?" Her voice was even more breathless now. Whispery, intimate. "Because if you are, I'd like to show you just what I think about the rules when it comes to me and you."

George sighed. "I'm here—for the moment anyway, but I can't get away," he told her. "I'm breaking every rule in the book just calling you."

"I don't suppose you can tell me what you're doing."

"Not a chance."

"Not even if I beg and make all kinds of promises?"

The images that called up were heart-stopping. Kim could do things with her lips and tongue that could win her a place in the Guinness Book of World Records. "Nope."

"Is it terribly dangerous?"

"Incredibly dangerous," he teased.

There was a pause, and when she spoke again, her

voice was different. Quieter. "You're being careful, right?"

For several seconds, George was silent. She actually sounded as if she cared. "Yeah," he finally said. Damn, maybe she did care. Wouldn't that be an ironic twist? He finally finds the perfect sexual relationship, one based purely on twisted psychological needs—both his and hers—and she begins to develop a warm spot in her heart. "Of course I am."

"When am I going to see you?" she asked, still in that quiet voice. It frightened him, that voice. But at the same time, he liked it. Too much. God knows Nicki had never spoken to him in a voice like that.

"I don't know," he admitted. "It could be another week. Maybe longer." He glanced at his watch, wishing he could talk longer, desperately glad he couldn't. "Look, babe, I've got to go."

"George."

"Kim, I'm sorry, I've really got to—"

"Call me as soon as you can. I've got a surprise for you." She then completely blew any chance of surprise by telling him, in exact detail, exactly what she was going to do to him when she saw him next.

By the time George hung up the phone, he was gripping the privacy divider so hard his knuckles were white. He took a deep, shaky breath and let the air out all in one whoosh.

He lit a cigarette and took his time walking back to the hotel, feeling the fresh spring air cool against his face. This next week was going to pass far too slowly. But it would pass. And then he would see Kim.

And he would close his eyes and pretend he was with Nicki again.

* * *

"Gentlemen and ladies," Nicole said as she opened the car door and stepped back to let the passenger out, "may I introduce Mrs. Barbara Conway."

Harry coughed to hide his laughter as Alessandra gracefully emerged from the backseat of the town car.

She should have had her long hair dyed a nondescript shade of brown and cut into as unflattering a style as possible. She should have been wearing ill-fitting department store clothing and little to no makeup at all.

Instead, she looked like some kind of movie star. Dressed in a curve-hugging black turtleneck and slim-fitting black pants, with a funky pair of heels that made her a solid inch taller than he was, she was about as unnoticeable as a parade of elephants marching through the Holland Tunnel. Her hair was long and dyed sleekly black. The new hair color made her eyes stand out, making them seem brighter and even more startlingly blue. It framed her pale face, accenting her carefully made-up features, her long elegant nose and full, graceful, very red lips. It was pretty damned remarkable. The new hair color actually made her even easier to identify.

Harry glanced at George, who was having a sudden coughing fit, too. The other agents, Christine McFall and Ed Bach, looked embarrassed. This entire operation would succeed only if they did their jobs badly, and Alessandra was living proof that they'd done just that.

If Trotta were looking—and Harry knew he would be looking, particularly since they were about to drop some not-too-subtle hints about this location in his lap—he'd have absolutely no problem finding Alessandra Lamont in this hick-town haystack.

Alessandra slipped a pair of sunglasses on over her pretty eyes as she took a look at her new home.

Paul's River, New York.

It was upstate, along the Connecticut border, about

twenty miles north of the end of Route 684. It was rural, with plenty of houses like this one, which sat separated by two very wide acres of land from its nearest neighbors. Farmland dotted the gently rolling hills, making for extremely picturesque landscape—and plenty of room to ward off a mob hit while only risking the lives of a few stray cows. And the big bonus: It was within a two-hour drive of New York City—a manageable commute for hitmen and agents alike.

As Harry watched, Alessandra took in the postage stamp–size white Cape Cod cottage, from the peeling paint on the twin dormers to the peeling paint on the faded red door. It wasn't much of a house—at least not compared to the palace she'd lived in in Farmingdale. But to her credit, she didn't gasp in horror or exclaim in dismay. She didn't even curl her lip in disgust.

She simply looked.

The front flower beds were overrun by weeds, the lawn—if you could call it that—was knee-high in places, barren and dusty in others. There were no trees at all on the half acre of land surrounding the house, and the spring sun shone glaringly down. In the summer the house and yard would be as hot as hell. The backyard was surrounded by an ugly high chain-link fence. It was the kind of fence you might put up after installing a swimming pool, but there was no pool in sight.

One of the front windows was broken, the glass taped. The garage—a stand-alone structure—looked as if it would collapse in the next mild gust of wind. Compared to Alessandra's house in Farmingdale, this was a big—a very, very big—step down, indeed.

She turned to watch as the town car pulled away.

"We should go inside," Nicole told her. "For the first few weeks, you'll need to keep a low profile."

Alessandra looked away from the dust being kicked

up by the disappearing car, her eyes hidden by her sun-glasses. "I thought I'd be safe here." Her voice was low and controlled. "Are you telling me I'm going to have to hide inside the house?"

"It's just a precaution," George said smoothly. "Just for these first few days."

"Days?" Alessandra asked. She looked at Nicki. "Or weeks?"

"I've got the key to the back door." Nicole sidestepped both Alessandra and her question, heading down the long driveway, toward the gate in the chain-link fence.

Bach and McFall both turned away, too, uncomfort-able with the part they were playing in this task-force op-eration. George had already followed Nicole.

That left Harry.

Alessandra didn't look at him for more than half a second before she turned, clearly believing that he, too, would dodge her question.

"Weeks," he told her, and she turned back, surprise temporarily breaking through the nearly expressionless Imperial Princess face she'd been wearing since she stepped from the limo.

He gestured for her to precede him down the cracked tarmac of the drive. Your Majesty. "It'll probably be weeks."

She didn't like his answer, but she liked it better than not getting any answer at all, so she nodded. "Thanks." Her smile was very small and slightly crooked, and not at all part of the princess act. It was quite possibly sincere.

Harry caught a whiff of her perfume as she went past. It was sweetly fragrant, deliciously fresh, and very fa-miliar. It was the same fragrance she'd been wearing when he'd first gone to her Farmingdale house, the night of the break-in and vandalism.

If Trotta's team of hitmen didn't see her coming from a mile away, they could always sniff her out.

God, this setup made him nervous. Harry didn't know what it was—if it was the situation, or the timing, or the target.

The target. Alessandra Lamont made him nervous in more ways than one.

But he'd worked protecting beautiful women before. What was it about this one that had gotten under his skin?

Nicole had been fumbling with the lock on the fence, but she finally got it open and pulled back the gate, gesturing for Alessandra to go in first.

Harry saw the dog before Alessandra did, before any of them did.

It had been standing silently, menacingly, in the fenced-in yard, in the shade of the garage, but now it lunged, an enormous German shepherd with sharp-looking teeth and a very convincing snarl.

Harry threw himself forward, pushing Alessandra back and out of the way as he kicked the gate shut just in time.

Even Nicole squeaked in alarm as the dog hit the fence with a crash, shock waves rattling it against the posts as Harry wrestled with the latch.

Alessandra had fallen down, onto the driveway, and George and the two other agents helped her back to her feet as the dog began to bark and snap viciously at Harry's fingers. The noise was deafening—nearly as loud as any burglar alarm he'd ever heard.

Finally, finally, with Nicole's help, he got the latch secured with all his fingers still attached.

George had pulled Alessandra out of immediate ear-splitting range. She clung to him now, her face buried against his jacket, her body trembling. She'd torn her pants and skinned at least one of her knees, but she didn't seem to notice. She just hung onto George as if she'd fall thirty thousand feet to the earth below if she let go.

Damnit, that could have been him with her arms around his neck.

Harry pushed that thought away as quickly as it had arrived. Stupid. It was completely stupid to think about this woman that way. And although he was no genius, he sure as hell wasn't stupid.

"Who put in an order for a guard dog?" he barked even louder than the dog in question.

Nicole's face was flushed with anger, but Harry bet she was more pissed at making that decidedly female shriek when the dog first attacked than the fact that an unauthorized guard dog had shown up on the premises.

Bach rustled through the paperwork on his clipboard, frantically looking for someone to blame. He didn't have to look far because McFall stepped forward.

"I did," she said, calmly ready to face both Nicole and Harry's wrath. "We knew Mrs. La— Mrs. Conway had a problem with dogs. It was part of the information in her file. We thought a watchdog would provide a good cover, simply because of that. Anyone looking for her wouldn't expect her to have a dog. I put in the order before . . ." She glanced at Alessandra, aware she was about to say just a little too much.

She'd put in the order before she knew this entire assignment was going to be a setup, before she knew that the task force wanted Michael Trotta to find Alessandra Lamont.

"The dog's name is Schnaps." To Harry's surprise, George spoke up, raising his voice to be heard over the racket. "Joe Harris is her trainer. I worked with them both about three years ago." He tried to pass Alessandra off to Bach, but the flustered agent could barely juggle both his clipboard and his pen, so she was thrust in Harry's direction instead.

Harry tried. He really did. He first tried to step aside and then to push Alessandra toward Nicole, but Nicki was busy being the irate boss.

That meant that Alessandra was all his. She seemed to be okay standing on her own, so he held on to her arm with only one hand, touching her with as few fingers as possible.

"Take her around to the front," Nicole ordered him sharply before glaring at George. "Can you make this dog shut up?"

Alessandra was all too eager to go toward the front of the house, and she broke free from Harry and headed for the cars at a near run. He had to jog to keep up. As he turned back, he saw George make some kind of hand signal and, as if by magic, as if he'd flipped a switch, the dog stopped barking.

George Faulkner had worked with dogs. Go figure. Harry would've thought his partner would be completely adverse to getting dog hair on his designer suits.

"I'm especially good with bitches," Harry heard George say with his usual, soft-spoken, deadpan delivery.

Harry had to laugh, picturing Nicole's slow burn, knowing she'd be unable to respond to her ex-husband's subtle barbed remark in front of the two other agents. But she'd want to. Man, would Nic want to blast him.

Alessandra was holding on to herself, arms tightly folded across her chest, as if she'd fall apart if she let go. "You think this is funny?"

Harry instantly sobered up, well aware that the last thing she needed was to think he was laughing at her. "No," he said. "No, I was just . . . It was just George. I didn't know he'd ever worked with dogs."

She was shaking. She had to sit down on the cracked concrete of the front steps, she was shaking so hard. Her left knee was definitely skinned and bleeding through the hole in her pants. Her hair was rumpled and her sunglasses had broken. Sitting there, she looked forlorn—nothing like the cool, confident woman who'd stepped out of the limo just minutes earlier. It was as if that woman had deflated like a balloon the instant her elegant facade had been torn.

"You all right?" Harry sat down beside her, feeling sorry for her despite the fact he'd vowed not to. She wasn't a victim. She'd gotten herself into this as surely as she'd given her wedding vows to Griffin Lamont.

"That depends on whether you define someone who's about to throw up on your shoes as 'all right.' "

Harry looked down at his shoes. "These are old. Do what you gotta do."

Alessandra laughed, but then, almost instantly, her eyes filled with tears and her lower lip trembled. Just his luck. She was going to cry.

But she fought it, trying to blink back the tears. He had to give her credit for that. "I hate this," she told him. "I hate this house, I hate my hair, I hate you."

"I know," Harry told her. She hated him. It shouldn't have mattered, but it did. "And I know you're not going to believe this, but I am sorry."

Sonya had been one of those women who looked even more beautiful when she cried. Harry'd expected—and hoped for—the same from Alessandra. Perfectly shed tears no longer had the power to move him.

But Alessandra's tears came in a flood, in an unchoreographed rush, complete with swollen eyes and a drippy red nose. She savagely swiped at them, fighting them, even though it was obviously a losing battle.

Harry's battle was a losing one, too. Cursing, he put

his arm around her. He half expected her to stiffen and pull away, but she was completely overwhelmed. She grabbed on to him, clutching his jacket, her face pressed tightly against his neck.

She was warm—much warmer than she looked when playing the Imperial Princess. She was soft, too. And she smelled so damn good his throat ached.

He cursed again, softly, gently this time, as he couldn't keep himself from touching her hair. As he ran his fingers through its baby-fine softness, he knew he wasn't doing this merely to provide comfort. He'd been dying to touch her hair from the first moment he'd laid eyes on her.

"Is this dog going to stay here forever?" she asked, her voice muffled.

Forever. It was a relative term, considering that contrary to what Alessandra believed, she wasn't going to be in Paul's River for very long.

Besides, after Trotta attempted to kill her, after they got all they needed to put the bastard away for a good long time, she'd be moved again. Even then, there'd be no guarantee she'd stay in that new place for long. There were never any guarantees. Forever was an unrealistic concept—except when it came to death. Being dead, or grieving someone who had died, those were the only things Harry knew would last forever. Relentlessly, endlessly forever.

"If you want," he told her, "the dog'll go."

"I want."

"The dog really scares you that much?"

She held out her hand, tried to hold it steady but couldn't. "No, I always shake like this."

Harry smiled. He liked her attitude, her bitchiness, if you will, better than the emotionless chill of the Imperial Princess. "I've read the file Chris McFall mentioned. You told the agents you had a problem with dogs, that this was something that was well known by both your husband and his friends—presumably also Michael Trotta."

"Michael Trotta knew," she said flatly.

"So okay," Harry said. "That's why Chris thought it would be a good idea to have a dog here, why it's in your best interest for Schnaps to stay. If you really don't want Trotta to find you, you've got to look and act completely different from Alessandra Lamont. You've got to become Barbara Conway in every possible way. And if Barbara is more securely hidden because she has an enormous dog, well . . ."

She lifted her head. Her mascara was smudged around her swollen eyes and her nose was running. She looked almost human. "You probably think I should have let them keep my hair that ugly brown, right?"

He had to smile. "Is that what happened? You didn't like the color, so you talked them into dying your hair this darker shade?"

She wiped her face with her hands. "It was really bad. It looked realistic, but who would ever actually want hair that drab?"

"Someone trying to hide from a mob hitman?" he suggested.

"Do you have a handkerchief?"

"Do I look like a guy who carries a handkerchief?"

She shook her head and, giving up, wiped her nose with the back of her hand.

He still had his arm around her shoulders, and he gave her a reassuring squeeze before he pulled away. "Why don't you give yourself a few days to get used to the dog and—"

"I'll never get used to it. Little dogs terrify me." She drew in a deep, ragged breath and drooped dejectedly, her chin in her hands, elbows just above the torn spots of her pants. "I'm so tired."

"It's been a tough couple of days. I'm pretty tired, too."

They just sat for a moment. As Harry gazed out at the unkempt yard, she stared down as if fascinated by an anthill being pushed out of the hard-packed dirt at the bottom of the stairs.

But then she spoke. "I didn't get a chance to say this yesterday." She glanced up. "But I'm really sorry about your son. I can't imagine what it must feel like to lose a child that way." She laughed, but there was no humor in it as she went back to her perusal of the industrious ants. "I know all about what it's like to want one and not be able to have one, and I know what it's like to try to adopt and get turned down, but that's hardly the same thing."

"Wait a minute." Harry turned toward her. "You wanted kids?"

"Griffin and I tried to have a baby for two years." She shrugged expansively but her lip trembled again, and he knew she felt far from matter-of-fact about what she was telling him. "I went through just about every test in the book before being declared sterile. God, I hate that word. The doctors think a case of scarlet fever I had when I was in sixth grade might've done the trick."

Well, there was a new spin on the story. Griffin Lamont hadn't started divorce proceedings against his wife because she refused to have his child. Lamont had left her because she couldn't have his child. The son of a bitch.

"Christ," Harry said. "I'm sorry. I can't believe you and Lamont tried to adopt and were turned down."

"Griffin refused to adopt. I only tried after we split up. There's this baby named Jane Doe—can you believe someone in the hospital actually named her that? Nobody wanted her because she would probably never be able to walk, and she had to have all these operations on her heart. But I love her, and they still thought she'd be better off in an institution than with me. That's why I got so crazy at the thought of losing my new clothes."

He didn't understand.

"When the car bomb went off," she explained, "and I, you know, kneed you . . . ?"

"Yeah," he said. "I remember that pretty well."

"There was a meeting I was supposed to go to—an interview to see if maybe I would be acceptable as Jane's foster mother." Her lip trembled. "I thought if I looked good, they'd like me and let me have her. It didn't occur to me at the time I was risking my life for those new clothes, that I no longer had a house to bring Jane home to."

"I thought you were crazy," he told her.

"Yeah, maybe I am," she said. "If loving that baby makes me crazy, then I definitely am." She looked at him, her eyes brimming with tears again. "I'll never get her now."

He couldn't stand it. He reached out hesitantly, knowing that touching her was a major mistake. Still, he awkwardly placed the palm of his hand on her back. "I'm sorry," he said.

She sat up and turned toward him, throwing herself into his arms as if she were starved for any kind of human contact—even from a man she professed to hate. "I want to go home," she whispered. "Please, can't you just take me home?"

Her home was a pile of rubble and ashes, cordoned off by yellow crime-scene tape.

He patted her back awkwardly, ineffectively, afraid to hold her too tightly. "I can't do that, Barbara."

"God, don't call me that!"

"It's your name now. You've got to get used to it."

"I don't want to get used to it! I want to go home! I

want to be able to visit Jane." She lifted her head. "Please, Harry! She must wonder where I've gone. I just want to go back to Long Island."

His heart twisted. "I can't take you there."

"Can't or won't?" Her mascara ran down her cheeks in smudgy black rivers. "I don't have to be here, do I? You can't make me stay. Can you?"

Oh, damn. He could not let her leave. "It is your choice, but—"

"Maybe I should just go and take my chances with Michael Trotta."

Harry gripped her more tightly. "Do you want to die? Is that what you want?"

"No! But I don't believe Michael really wants to kill me. I find it hard to . . . After I returned the money . . . ?" She wiped her eyes, tried to explain. "If I stay here, I'm going only on what the FBI is telling me. How do I know you're not wrong?"

He held on to her shoulders, afraid if he let go, she'd realize that she could leave. And she could leave. At any given time, she could just get up and walk away from all of them. Straight back to Trotta. Who would kill her.

Harry did not want her to die. "We're not wrong."

"But if you are . . . Don't you see? I could have my life back."

He pulled her even closer, holding her tightly against him, pressing her head against his chest, knowing what she wanted, knowing how she felt. It wasn't fair. Her life had been taken from her. The injustice was profound. "You can't, Allie. It's gone. The house is gone. Everything's gone."

She shook her head as if blocking out his words. "I want my life back." She made a noise that was half sob, half laughter. "God, sometimes I think I'd even take Griffin back if I could."

"You can't," Harry said flatly. "He's dead. Go back to Long Island, and you're dead, too."

She gripped his jacket. "If I stay, I'm Barbara Conway. Alessandra Lamont will be just as dead."

"Yeah, well, maybe it's about time you got rid of her anyway, huh?"

She lifted her head at that, her eyes wide, tears clinging to her eyelashes. His nose was inches from hers, her mouth close enough to kiss.

Close enough to kiss.

Harry saw the exact moment she, too, realized she was in his arms. And just like that, their embrace wasn't only about comfort anymore.

She felt like a woman—no longer just another human body against him, but a female body with soft, full breasts. He felt the tautness of her thigh, the curve of her hips. He felt the promise of something incredible.

And his arms no longer felt awkward around her. His hands settled comfortably, one against the small of her back, the other tucked up against her neck, beneath her hair. She was a perfect fit. And he was holding her so easily, as if he'd been practicing for this moment for most of his life.

It wouldn't take much effort for him to lower his head and cover her mouth with his. Her breath smelled like coffee and chocolate, and he knew she would taste just as sweet.

But he didn't move, and she didn't either. He didn't speak, and she, too, was silent. They just hung there, suspended, hardly even daring to breathe.

Seconds ticked by, more and more of them. Why the hell didn't she pull away? Did she want him to kiss her? Dammit, what was he doing? Kissing her would be completely insane.

Harry slowly lowered his head and she still didn't pull away. In fact, she lifted her face and—

The front door opened behind them, and Alessandra sprang up and away from him.

George pushed open the screen, giving Harry a look that told him he hadn't missed the implications of Alessandra's rushed movement—her imitation of teenagers getting too friendly on the playroom couch, startled by mom or dad. "All clear. Nic wants you inside."

Alessandra was wiping her face again and trying futilely to fix her hair. She adjusted the holes in the knees of her pants, but it was hopeless. Until she washed her face and changed her clothes, she was going to look bedraggled, not chic.

"You got a handkerchief?" Harry asked George.

Of course George had one. He silently handed it to Harry, who passed it to Alessandra, who kept her tear-streaked face carefully averted.

"We'll be in in a sec," Harry told his partner.

George discreetly faded back, closing the door almost all the way behind him as Alessandra wiped her eyes and blew her nose with an indelicate honk.

What was he supposed to say? Should he apologize for almost kissing her? Or apologize for not taking the opportunity to kiss her when he could have? It would probably be good to address this attraction thing point-blank. Acknowledge it, get it out on the table between them, and deal with it accordingly. When Alessandra took a breath, about to speak, Harry steeled himself for the words to come. She'd been caught up in the emotion of the moment. She didn't even like him. She'd appreciate it if he could keep his wandering hands to himself from now on.

She said none of those things. "I don't want them to

know I've been crying," she admitted, her back still toward him. "Don't tell them I was crying—please?"

Or . . . she could completely ignore the almost-kiss. Simply pretend it didn't happen. That was definitely an option.

He cleared his throat. "I won't."

Alessandra turned to face him. "Do you think they'll be able to tell I was crying?"

Harry gazed at her mascara-smeared raccoon eyes, still puffy with emotion, at her red nose, at the tear-streak lines visible on her cheeks where her makeup had been washed away. He wondered if he had kissed her, would she still have pretended it hadn't happened? "Yep."

"That definite, huh?"

He took his sunglasses from his jacket pocket and handed them to her. "These'll help."

She gave him another of those funny little smiles as she put them on, and they went inside.

Seven

Harry pushed the door to Alessandra's bedroom open with a crash, the sound of her scream still echoing in his head.

He took everything in at once. Allie, still in bed, sitting up but cowering, still breathing, no blood, still alive, thank you Jesus. An empty room. No furniture except for the metal-framed double bed and a bargain-basement dresser. No hitmen. No mobsters. No other people.

The closet door—double sliders—shut. Shades pulled down tight over the two windows—one a dormer, the other on the west side of the house.

He realized in an instant that Alessandra was cowering because of him, bursting into her room the way he had, half dressed, gun drawn. He watched her out of the corner of his eye as he did a quick check of the room. Closet—empty but for a few shirts hanging there, a pair of shoes and sneakers on the floor. Windows—tightly locked. Bed . . . He went into a quick squat as he scanned beneath the bed. Not even a dust bunny in sight.

George stood in the doorway, his gun held at ready.

"False alarm," Harry told him. He rose quickly, crossing to the windows and lifting the shades one more time, giving a quick signal to the agents watching the house. All this op needed was twenty agents rushing in to save the day. Allie was sharper than he'd first thought. She would realize instantly that this was no standard Witness Protection Program operation. She'd know it was a setup.

God, he hated that this was a setup.

"I had a nightmare," she said, her voice shaking. "I'm sorry, did I scream very loudly?"

Did she scream very loudly?

Harry still had about twelve quarts of adrenaline raging through his system from the power and intensity of that scream. He'd never heard a scream so filled with terror, and he'd heard his share of screams, that was damn sure. One moment he'd been sound asleep, the next he'd been taking the stairs to the second floor three at a time.

He slipped the safety back on his weapon then bent over, resting his hands on his knees. Thank God he was still too young and in too good shape to have a heart attack.

"It was that dog." Alessandra's dark hair was rumpled, her face slick with perspiration. She held on to her knees as if she were afraid her entire body would fly apart if she let go. "I used to have this same nightmare all the time when I was little."

"You look like you've got this under control," George said, vanishing back down the hallway.

"Wait." Harry straightened up, but George was already gone.

Damn. He'd done his best to avoid being alone with Alessandra all afternoon and evening. And now here he was, alone with her in her bedroom, for christsake, with only the dim light from the hall shining into the room. It was warm, it was dark, and it was cozy as hell.

Alessandra was wearing the same pajamas she'd had on back at the hotel. They covered her completely. There was nothing sexy about them—except for the fact that she was wearing them.

And right now, that was enough.

"I'll be downstairs if you need me." That was a stupid thing to say. Why on earth would she need him?

But she nodded, as if the fact that she might need him was completely reasonable and even likely.

"Can you check the back door for me?" Alessandra asked. "Make sure the dog can't get in?"

He turned back from the door to look at her. "The dog really bothers you that much?"

Alessandra couldn't see Harry's face. He was completely backlit, just a shadowy shape standing there. She couldn't see his eyes, but she could feel him watching her.

"I was attacked by a Doberman when I was five," she told him. "A neighbor's dog got loose. I saw it out in our yard, and I ran toward it—I wanted to pet it. Grandma Carp had a poodle named Mitzi and . . . But this was no lapdog. I must've startled it, because it went for me."

She closed her eyes, shutting out the nightmare image of bared teeth and those terrible dark eyes. She'd carry the memory of those awful eyes to her grave.

"I don't know how I got away," she continued, her story coming out in a rush, now that she'd started to tell it. "I guess I must've been right next to the fence that separated my yard from my friend Janey's. It was like the one in this yard, and I was small enough so that my feet fit in the chain links. I climbed up, but when I was at the top, the dog crashed into it and I fell. I fell into Janey's yard, thank goodness, but I hurt my leg really badly. I couldn't move. I remember just lying there with that dog barking and snarling at me. I knew it was just a matter of time until that dog found the hole in the fence I used as a shortcut to Janey's. And I just lay there and waited to die."

Harry had stepped farther into the room, and now the light from the hallway fell across half of his face. His chin was dark with even more stubble than usual. His hair stood straight up in places, a thick lock falling down over his forehead.

Alessandra managed a weak smile. "Of course, I didn't die."

"But to go through that at five years old? You had to be traumatized. No wonder you have nightmares."

"I haven't been able to get near a dog since. After it happened, I couldn't even be in the same room with Mitzi. And she was about the size of your fist. Not exactly dangerous. My mother made my grandmother lock Mitzi in the bathroom whenever we came over."

Harry must've been sleeping with his gun very close at hand, because he wasn't wearing a shoulder holster. He had on a pair of navy blue sweatpants and a white tank-style undershirt that hugged his muscular chest. It made his shoulders look about a mile wide and his arms strong enough to carry nearly anything.

Alessandra looked away, unable to keep herself from thinking about how strong and warm his arms had felt around her this afternoon. About how close she'd come to kissing him. It was crazy. She didn't even like him. He was rude, crude—but quite possibly the only person out of all the multitudes of agents she'd dealt with these past few days who was completely straightforward with her.

She trusted him.

At least as much as she could trust anybody.

Harry was so different from any other man she'd ever met. He seemed completely detached and removed, totally unaffected by her physical beauty—until she looked like complete hell. This afternoon, sitting out on the steps, she'd probably looked about as bad as she'd ever looked in her entire life, yet that was when he'd wanted to kiss her.

And he would've kissed her, too, if the door hadn't opened, interrupting them.

None of it made sense.

Alessandra pushed her hair back with hands that were still shaking, mopping her forehead with her sleeve. Her face was glistening, her hair and her pajamas were soaked with sweat. She knew she looked awful.

She wondered if he wanted to kiss her now.

"Sometimes the best way to get over a phobia like that is to get tough and climb back on the dog—so to speak," he said. "Your mother probably would've done you more good to make you face Mitzi. Instead, every time you see a dog, you're five years old again and completely defenseless." He shifted his weight. "You know, there are ways to defend yourself against an attacking dog."

She gestured to the gun he was still carrying. "Having one of those would do the trick. But there'd be a lot of irate dog owners in the neighborhood if I started shooting every dog that came within a hundred feet of me."

He smiled and instantly looked ten years younger. "There are other ways to defend yourself against an attacking dog. The most powerful weapon is knowledge. If you can learn to identify a dog that might be dangerous, and if you can learn what to do if you come face to face with one of them . . . You know, George worked with dogs. I bet he'd be glad to talk to you about 'em in the morning."

He shifted his weight again, and Alessandra knew that any minute he was going to walk through that door and leave her alone up here in the dark.

"Do you ever have nightmares?" she asked, wanting him to stay just a little bit longer.

She realized instantly how ridiculous and inane her

question was. His son had been killed, violently, terribly. She could hear an echo of Harry's voice: ". . . sometimes the only way I can fall asleep at night is to stay awake for seventy-two hours . . ." Of course he had nightmares.

But Harry didn't berate her for her stupidity. He didn't tell her to butt out and mind her own f—ing business, either. He just gazed at her, his smile long since faded.

Finally he sighed, a quiet exhale that echoed the lines of fatigue he perpetually wore on his face. "You wanna sandwich?"

Her stomach churned. "No, but I'd love some tea."

"Tea." His smile briefly reappeared. "Well, lah-di-dah," he said. "Let's have some tea."

"Drowning," Harry said, his mouth full of pastrami on Jewish rye. "God, this is good." He held up his sandwich. "You sure you don't want some of this?"

Alessandra shook her head, her hands cupped around her mug of tea as if she were cold. With her hair up in a ponytail, wearing those oversize pajamas, she looked about fourteen. Clean of makeup, her face was pale, her skin smooth and unlined.

"I was never a strong swimmer," Harry continued. "I mean, I took lessons and I learned how to move my arms and legs, but I'm not exactly ready to swim across the English Channel. I have this dream where the street is flooding, and I'm on top of my car, and I know I'm going to have to swim for it. I go into the water, but the current's too strong, or I trip or something, but anyway, I get knocked off my feet. And I wake up just as the water's going over my head." He took another bite of his sandwich. "Nightmares suck. And that's what I dream about on a good night."

On a bad night, he'd dream about Kevin's last few moments on earth. Sometimes he'd even dream he was

Sonya, at the wheel of the car. He'd see that truck go into a skid, the way she must have. He'd know he and Kevin were both going to die, there was nothing he could do to stop it, to prevent his precious child's death. He'd reach for Kevin, wanting at least to hold him close, but the boy was always just out of range, just beyond the tips of his fingers. Harry could never reach him. He was completely powerless.

Personally, Harry preferred the smothering sensation of water going over his head.

He took another bite of his sandwich, but the pastrami now tasted like shit mixed with ashes. He put it down, and Alessandra briefly glanced up from her tea to look at him.

He would've bet big money that she knew exactly where his thoughts had gone. A few days ago, Harry wouldn't have thought her capable, but now he knew otherwise. Alessandra Lamont was no dummy. She was far more perceptive and definitely more sensitive than he would have believed.

He wasn't surprised when she spoke. "Do you think Michael Trotta had something to do with your son's death?"

"Yes."

She glanced up again, and this time he was ready for her. He met her gaze, holding it. "There was no proof, though. Nothing we could bring to court. At the time, he was tightly connected to the boss I was investigating. The one who was trying to scare me off. It's likely Trotta was in the room when the deal went down, when the gunmen were hired to fire those shots into Sonya's car." He pushed his sandwich away from him. "Your nice Michael Trotta, the real friendly guy whose Christmas parties you went to—he conspired to commit a crime that resulted in the death of my son."

Alessandra couldn't look at him.

"It was meant to be a warning," he continued. "A few well-placed bullets in the windshield of Sonya's car. No one was supposed to get hurt—just shaken up enough so I'd back down with my investigation. But someone fucked up, one of the shots went wild and the truck driver got hit.

"It happened on the highway, where everyone was driving much too fast. The trucker lost control of his semi and jackknifed. Sonya hit the brakes, but she and Kevin never even had a chance." Funny, he could tell the story like a news reporter. He could relate the facts emotionlessly, as if they'd happened to someone else's ex-wife, someone else's son.

Alessandra closed her eyes. "I'm so sorry."

"Yeah," Harry said. "I am, too. But Trotta's not. Trotta probably doesn't care." He pushed the plate with his half-eaten sandwich away from him and glanced up to find her watching him. "He's not going to go to jail for killing my kid," he continued, watching her just as steadily. "But he is going to jail. Sooner or later, he's going to screw up royally—and the FBI's gonna be there. I'm gonna be there."

"But that won't bring Kevin back."

Her quiet words stunned him, and he had to look away. No one, not even George, not even Marge, had ever dared to be so blunt. He knew they'd all been thinking it, but Alessandra was the first to come out and say it.

He thought of his dreams of Kevin, with the kid always just beyond his reach. "I'm aware of that," he said stiffly. "But sending Trotta to jail—or to hell, I'm not picky—is gonna go a long way toward making me feel better."

"Will it really?"

Harry studied her face. In the harsh fluorescent kitchen light she looked exhausted, her eyes nearly bruised from fatigue. She wasn't just playing devil's advocate. She honestly wanted to know.

She leaned forward slightly. "Did you feel better when what's his name—Riposa—died resisting arrest?"

"How the hell do you know Frank Riposa's name?" Harry knew the answer to that question the moment it left his lips. "You've been talking to George about me."

It was Alessandra's turn to look away, shrugging delicately. "There's not much else to do around here besides talk. So, yes, I did ask him some questions—"

"Out of the four hundred and sixty-eight trillion possible topics of discussion," he mused, "I'm number one on the list. I'm flattered."

She took a sip of her tea, completely nonchalant—except for the slight pink tinge that colored her cheeks, and the fact that she refused to meet his gaze. "Don't be. I was just trying to break this endless boredom."

She was lying. He knew it. And she knew that he knew it.

She took another sip. "So did you feel better knowing Riposa was dead?"

Harry stood up and put the mustard back in the refrigerator. "Yeah," he said.

They both knew he was lying, too.

Alessandra opened the door and tripped over Harry.

He was sitting in the hall, right outside her door, fast asleep.

He woke up though, as her foot connected with his ribs and she hit the opposite wall with a very loud thump.

He was beside her in an instant. "Are you all right?"

His eyes were heavy lidded and sleepy, his hands warm

through her pajamas. Alessandra knew his arms would be just as warm and wonderfully solid. It would be so easy to lean back against him, to let him take care of her.

In every possible way.

The awful truth was, she missed sex. Griffin may not have been the most reliable lover, but he had been imaginative—at least at the beginning of their marriage. Of course, all those years of trying to get pregnant had put a boatload of stress on their sexual relationship, taking all of the fun out of it. It had been years since Alessandra had had sex purely for the sake of sex.

Harry was standing much too close, his hand on her shoulder. He'd gone very still, very quiet, as if he somehow knew the decadent direction her thoughts had traveled. She could feel his body heat, smell his warmth. Lord, he smelled so good.

She cleared her throat but still her voice came out much too huskily. "Are you all right? I didn't see you there. I didn't mean to kick you."

He was looking at her, examining her, and he smiled crookedly. "You look good in the morning, Al."

Her hair was stringy, her eyes were tired and puffy, and she had on absolutely no makeup. "I look like hell."

"Whoa, that's pretty harsh language for you."

"You look like hell, too."

"Hell is an improvement for me," he told her. "In fact, I consider it a compliment. See, shit's my usual look. On really bad days, I look like total shit. So, yeah, hell is a big step up for me." His smile made his eyes crinkle. "So, thank you very much."

Alessandra couldn't keep from smiling back.

He stepped away from her then, his hand sliding intimately down her arm to her elbow before he moved out of reach.

She felt cold without him touching her. But while cold

was uncomfortable, it wasn't half as bad as she would feel if she let herself become involved with this man simply because she wanted to feel warm and safe.

There was no such thing as warm and safe, though, when the cold came from deep inside.

She'd learned that the hard way.

Harry had caught a glimpse of himself in the hall mirror and was futilely attempting to smooth down his hair. It was a losing battle. "Christ, would you look at me? I need a haircut."

"Were you guarding my door to keep dogs and villains out, or to keep me in?" she asked.

He gave up on his hair and turned to gaze at her for a long moment before he answered. "A little of each."

Alessandra nodded. "I like that you're honest with me."

"Yeah, well, I'd like for you to be honest with me, too."

"Even if I told you I still think there's been some kind of mistake?"

The muscles in the side of Harry's jaw jumped as he stood there, just watching her.

"I counted the money," she said softly. "It was all there. I'm sorry, I know you believe Michael Trotta killed your son, but . . ."

He nodded. "If you go back, Trotta will let his dog tear you apart." His voice was gentle, contrasting the harshness of his words.

Alessandra turned away.

"You want honest," he added softly. "That's what I honestly believe, Allie."

"What if you're wrong?" she asked tightly.

"What if I'm right?"

"I want to call him."

"Not from this house. Not from this town."

She spun to face him, ready to drop to her knees and

beg him if she had to. "Then let's take a ride. Please. We can drive over into Connecticut. I'll call from . . . I don't know, Hartford. From a pay phone."

Harry was silent again for a long time. Without his smile, the lines around his eyes made him look weary. But then he nodded. "I'll do what I can to set it up. You've got to be patient, though. It might take a few days to get approval from my boss."

"I promise I won't call from the phone in this house."

Harry nodded again. "Good."

She started toward the bathroom but then turned back. "Do you trust me?"

He didn't hesitate. "Not enough to leave you alone in a room with a phone."

Alessandra nodded. "Thank you again for your honesty."

Harry smiled. There was more than amusement, there was a hint of approval lighting his eyes. "You're welcome, I guess."

Shaun pretended he didn't see Ricky Morgan and Josh French following him as he left the middle school.

It was late, nearly four-thirty, and there were only a few other kids around, waiting for rides after rehearsal for the school talent show.

Shaun unlocked his bicycle from the stand by the front doors and slipped both of his arms into the straps of his backpack, carefully keeping his back to Ricky and Josh.

With any luck, he'd be on his bike and halfway down the drive before they approached him. With any luck . . .

"Yo, fairy boy, where you going so fast on your little silver wings?"

Shit.

Shaun didn't lift his head. He refused to respond unless they called him by name. His real name.

He staggered as Josh grabbed his backpack and spun him around. "Hey, we're talking to you, leprechaun. Show a little respect for your elders."

Josh was only two months older than he was. Nine years ago, he'd just squeaked past the cut-off for entry into kindergarten a year earlier than Shaun.

"Just leave me alone." This was really stupid. Although they were ninth graders, he was bigger than both of them. But he hated violence. He wasn't anything like his father, who entered into any altercation with a gleam in his eye, ready and willing to use fists and muscle to deal with whatever came his way.

But then again, Harry only used his fists as a last resort.

"In a hurry to go home and put on your auntie's undies, faggot?"

Shaun took off his backpack and set it down, balancing himself lightly on the balls of his feet, as if he were preparing for a strenuous jazz combination, drawing himself up to his full height. And then, as he looked down, way down into Ricky and Josh's inbred, squinty little eyes, he gave them Harry's best smile. "There've been studies done that prove most homophobes' problems stem from fear of their own latent homosexual urges."

Josh blinked. "Huh?"

Ricky was a little brighter. "I think he's calling us queer."

"Queer and faggot are derogatory terms," Shaun scolded them gently, just the way Harry would've. "You should love yourselves more. Be proud of who you are."

Ricky was already backing away in horror, but Josh wasn't going to let that one go. Shaun made himself into a rock and didn't sway more than an inch as the smaller boy shoved him. And when Josh reached for him again,

Shaun caught his wrist. "Look, I know you feel this need to touch me, but the truth is, I'm not gay. I'm sorry—I know how much you gay guys go for dancers, but I met this girl out in California, and we've been keeping in touch and—"

Josh charged him. Shaun thought he was ready for it, but the force pushed him backward, into the bike rack and over its top. He landed with a bone-jarring thud on the hard-packed dirt, grateful that Josh didn't fall with him, grateful for the thick metal of the bike rack that now separated them.

He was grateful, too, that Josh seemed content with the sight of Shaun sprawled in the dirt. Apparently that was enough to restore the ninth grader's threatened manhood.

Shaun watched the two boys swagger away as he straightened his glasses and checked to see how badly his elbow was bleeding.

It was only slightly scraped.

"Are you okay?" Mindy MacGregor, the tallest girl in the class, forty pounds overweight, with thick glasses that gave her the not-too-appealing look of a bubble-eyed fish, offered him a hand up.

"Yeah." Shaun let her haul him to his feet then dusted off the seat of his jeans. Funny, he was taller than giant Mindy MacGregor. When had that happened?

She flashed her braces at him in a weirdly shy space alien–like smile. "I was kind of hoping you would kill them."

"Yeah, well, I was hoping they weren't going to kill me."

"I'm sorry," Mindy told him.

"Why? I survived. I'm considering it a victory."

"I was too afraid to come stand next to you. I saw what they were doing, and I knew I should help, but . . ."

Ricky and Josh always called her "Fats MacBlubber"

or "Mindy the Mountain." Shaun had seen her more than once, rushing toward the girls' room in tears.

"It's okay." He forced a smile as he slipped on his backpack, wishing she would stop staring at him with those magnified eyes.

"I was so amazed that you could just stand there smiling at them like that."

Shaun had been amazed, too. He smiled ruefully. Maybe he wasn't as different from his father as he'd thought. Harry could talk his way out of anything.

Mindy giggled. "They didn't understand half of what you said."

"Good thing, or I probably would be dead."

"Together, you know, we could crush them." A pinkish hue tinged her cheeks and she was giving him another of those weird smiles and . . .

Oh, God, she liked him. Mindy the Mountain liked him. He froze, uncertain of what to say or do.

"You're really great, you know, your dance number. I'm in the talent show, too. I'm playing my French horn."

"Great," he said unenthusiastically. He raised the kickstand of his bike and climbed on. Mindy liked him. But whenever he imagined his fighting sidekick, he conjured up a girl who looked more like something out of the X-Men comics than Mindy MacGregor. He conjured up a girl with long red hair, a killer figure in a tiny black bikini, and normal-size eyes that sparkled when she smiled.

"Have you thought about getting contact lenses?" Mindy asked. "Mrs. Fisher told me not to wear glasses onstage, that the lights would reflect off them, so I'm going to the eye doctor as soon as my mom has the time and . . . Not that you look bad in glasses. You look . . . Well, I heard Heather Ullman say you would be one of the top ten cutest guys in the school if you didn't wear glasses and . . . I'm sorry, I didn't mean you look bad in glasses. Personally, I think they're . . . nice." Mindy closed her gigantic eyes. "Oh, God," she moaned. "I'm such a dweeb. Just kill me now."

Shaun knew he should tell her that she didn't stand a chance, that he would never like her the way she liked him, not in a million, billion years. He knew all about false hopes and dashed expectations. He knew the longer hope was left alive, the bleaker and emptier it felt when its light finally burned out.

But instead, he reached over and patted her awkwardly on her giant shoulder. "Thanks for helping me."

Her eyes flashed open and she smiled. She was almost pretty when she smiled. "I should've helped you crush 'em."

He forced another smile, cursing himself for being a coward. "Maybe next time."

Mindy nodded energetically, buoyant with hope. "Definitely next time."

Shaun slipped his feet into the pedal straps and rode away.

Instead of being honest, he ran away. Instead of confronting the issue, he hid from it.

Yeah, he was definitely more like his father than he'd thought.

Alessandra stood in the living room, holding the telephone.

Harry cleared his throat and she jumped.

"Oh," she said. "Harry. Hi."

He just looked at her.

"I thought you went out to the store."

He didn't say a word, didn't move a muscle.

She dropped the receiver into the cradle, and in one nervous motion, sat down on the couch, drawing up her knees and hugging them close to her chest. "I wasn't calling him."

She looked nice today. Her hair hung shiny and smooth around her shoulders, her face carefully made up, her lipstick a work of art. She was wearing a blue sweater that was almost a perfect match for the color of her eyes, and a pair of jeans that were more expensive than most of the suits he wore to work.

She looked like something you'd want to wrap in plastic—kind of the way his grandmother had covered the furniture in her living room because it was too good to actually use.

"I promised you," she told him earnestly. "And I . . . know you probably don't believe this, but I keep my promises."

Harry sighed. He took a step farther into the room. "So who were you calling?"

She bit her lip. "Look, I know I'm not supposed to make any phone calls—"

"Then what the hell were you doing? And don't tell me you couldn't stand another day not talking to your pals on the Psychic Friends Hotline."

She was holding her knees so tightly, her knuckles were almost white. "I was going to call the Northshore Children's Hospital."

He just waited for her to explain.

"Jane had her final heart operation this morning," Alessandra whispered. "I just . . . I need to know if she's okay."

Jane? Who the hell was Jane? The answer came to him in a flash. Northshore Children's Hospital. Jane was the baby that Alessandra had told him about. The one she'd wanted to adopt.

"She's had a . . . heart operation? Jesus, can babies have heart operations?"

Alessandra nodded. "She was born with some kind of hole in her heart. They have this new method of going in and creating some kind of patch and—" She shook her head. "I just . . . wanted to find out if she . . . you know, survived."

"Oh, shit." Harry started to pace.

If this was some kind of story she was handing him, this woman should be given an Oscar. He turned to look back at her.

Her face was so pale, her lips so tight.

No way was she that good of an actress.

"What was your connection with Northshore Children's?" he asked. "Was it just some place you went when you decided to try to adopt?"

"No. I did volunteer work there," she told him. "Fundraising. Why?"

"And this was something people knew about?"

"Yes."

Damn. "How about your connection to this baby? Did people know about that, too?"

"I didn't keep it a secret," she said. "Why?"

"I can't let you call them," Harry told her. "I'm sorry, but it's too risky."

"Isn't there any way we could find out?" Alessandra asked. "I just keep thinking of all the things that could've gone wrong, and . . . I just want to know if she's okay."

Harry picked up the phone and dialed the New York City Bureau office, punched in Nicole Fenster's extension.

"Fenster." Nicki sounded more and more like Joe Friday every day.

"Nicki, it's Harry O'Dell. I need you to call the Northshore Children's Hospital out on the Island and find out the status of one Baby Jane Doe, who had a heart operation this morning."

Nicole sighed, extremely exasperated. "Has it occurred to you that I might have better things to do with my time?"

"This is one call you definitely don't want us to make," Harry said. "We need this information like an hour ago. This baby is special to Barbara Conway. Call me right back."

He hung up without waiting for Nic's response.

Alessandra had such hope in her eyes. "Will she really call back?"

"Sure," he said. There was a notebook, its top page filled with incredibly sloppy handwriting next to the telephone. He picked it up and read a description of sunlight on the ocean, the feel of the sand, and the smell of the beach. It wasn't half bad. "What's this?"

Alessandra snatched it away from him. "That's private."

"Did you write that?"

She held it against her chest, obviously embarrassed.

"It was good, but Jesus, who taught you penmanship?"

"I have awful handwriting," she admitted. "I was never very good at school." She looked down at her notebook. "I don't know why I even bother."

"Do you like to write?" he asked.

She looked up at him, and he could see from her eyes that she was aware he was distracting her, trying to keep her from biting her nails to the quick until Nicole Fenster called back with news about Jane. "I don't know," she said. "Yeah. I guess. I mean . . . I've almost filled this entire notebook."

"Do you write stories?" he asked. "Or is it more stream of consciousness?"

"Harry, I can't stop thinking about how it might just be more merciful for Jane if she—" She couldn't say it. "I mean, what's her life going to be like? If they were considering me, that means they couldn't even find a foster home for her." Her eyes filled with tears. "But I don't want her to die. You should see her smile. She's got this great smile. But I can't stop thinking that maybe my wanting her to live is just being selfish and—"

"Shhh," he said, sitting next to her on the couch and pulling her into his arms. He knew it was trouble to touch her, but how could he not? "It's not being selfish, Al. Because as long as she's alive, there's a chance that someone will want her. Who knows? As long as she's alive, there's hope, you know?"

Alessandra nodded. She knew.

She was far too perfect to kiss. Harry didn't want to mess up her lipstick, yet he couldn't keep his gaze from dropping to her mouth.

She was looking at his mouth, too. Oh, Christ, she wanted him to kiss her.

Where the hell was George or Christine or Ed when Harry needed them? But the house was dead silent. Nothing moved. If any of the other agents were here, they were sound asleep.

Alessandra nervously moistened her lips with the tip of her tongue and . . .

The phone rang, and Harry let go of Alessandra as he nearly went through the roof.

On his way back down, he scooped up the phone. "Yeah," he said hoarsely. Sweet God, that had been close. He moved farther away from Alessandra, who was still on the couch. She was watching him intently, her focus on the phone call, the fact that she'd nearly kissed him again was completely forgotten.

"O'Dell?" It was Nicole. "The patient Jane Doe is in recovery, doing fine."

He repeated her words to Alessandra, who burst into tears. "Thank God," she whispered and ran from the room.

"Thanks, Nic," he said, watching Alessandra head up the stairs toward the privacy of her bedroom.

There was no way in hell he was following her.

No way.

Eight

"THIS DOESN'T MAKE me happy." Harry stood by the front door with George, waiting for Alessandra to do God knows what in the bathroom. She'd come downstairs after lunch with her makeup perfectly applied, her hair already gorgeous.

"It's a good setup," George reminded him. "The yard's completely clear. We know none of Trotta's men have gotten past us. If they're going to shoot, it's going to be from back beyond the tree line."

"They could be set up anywhere from here all the way into town." Harry adjusted his jacket over the heavy weight of his body armor. As if wearing a bullet-proof vest was going to do any good. If he were a mob hitman, he'd be perched in some church tower with a high-powered rifle and a scope. He'd wait until Alessandra's car approached, and he'd take 'em all out, aiming for their heads, right through the car roof.

"I'm hating this," Harry murmured to George as Alessandra finally emerged. "I want her in a vest, too."

"Believe me, it wouldn't work under that shirt."

Alessandra was wearing tight-fitting black jeans and a snug black T-shirt that showed off her perfect body. Her hair was pulled back from her face in some kind of fancy braid thing. Her made-up face was as flawless as fine porcelain, her lips were the color of wine, and her eyelashes were darkly, artistically enhanced.

He liked her better in baggy pajamas, with a faint smattering of freckles across her cheeks and nose.

She stopped directly in front of him. Her high heels made her exactly his height and put her eyes exactly on his level. They were cool, distant, detached. She was in Princess Alessandra mode.

Harry wanted to shake her, to bring her back to life. But on the other hand, he couldn't blame her. He was the one who'd spent the past few days avoiding her. Ever since she'd tripped over him in the hallway and he'd touched her arm, ever since she'd looked at him as if she wanted him to kiss her, he'd kept at least a room length between them. Ever since they'd sat in the living room and she'd told him about baby Jane, he'd only given yes/no responses to her questions. He didn't want her to tell him her secrets, didn't want to tell her his. He didn't want to see the heat from his touch reflected in her eyes.

But, Christ, he hated the way she was looking at him now. "Are we going to Hartford so I can call Michael Trotta today?" It was a yes/no question. She'd obviously been paying attention.

"No. I still haven't gotten approval for that." It wasn't a lie. He hadn't gotten approval. However, he knew he wasn't going to get approval. Nicole didn't want to give Trotta any false clues, and she'd nixed the idea completely, at least for the short term.

As for the long term . . .

Hopefully there wasn't going to be a long term. After four days, Harry was bouncing off the walls. He'd finally reached Marge, but she was uncommunicative and cool when he'd asked where the hell they'd been. She'd told him she'd taken Shaun and Emily to the beach, to California, the way she did every spring vacation. They'd had a lovely time, thank you very much.

She'd refused to talk about the letter from the lawyers requesting custody, only telling him that he needed to come out there. This could not be discussed over the phone. It had to be dealt with face to face. She'd gotten even more stiff on him then, telling him she'd thought he would at least have come for Shaun's performance.

Harry's kid had had a lead role in the school musical, and nobody had bothered to tell him about it. Of course, with his schedule, it would've been near impossible to fit in a trip west. Even now, with this personal crisis nearing an eruption point, best case scenario didn't have him catching a flight to Colorado for another few weeks.

George held the front door shut, keeping Alessandra from going out into the yard. "No trips to Hartford today. You'll have to be happy going only as far as the local library and the grocery store. Think you can handle the thrill?"

Alessandra granted him a small smile. "Actually, you can't imagine how excited I am at the thought of going to the library."

Every day for the past four days, Harry had sent either Chris McFall or Ed Bach to the library to pick up books for Alessandra to read. She wasn't a fan of daytime TV. In fact, she wasn't a fan of TV at all. But books . . . She was a voracious reader. She read constantly—when she wasn't scribbling in her notebook. She read or wrote during breakfast, lunch, and dinner. All day and quite possibly most of the night, too. She read anything and everything. Cover to cover. If it had words on a page, Alessandra read it.

George looked over at Harry. "Are we ready to go?"

No. He wasn't ready. And Alessandra wasn't ready either. She had absolutely no clue that bad guys might start shooting at her, hoping to kill her, the moment she stepped out into the yard.

"Do me a favor," he said to her, "and stay close to me at all times. If I tell you to get down or to run like hell, you do it. No questions, you just do it, you got that?"

A small furrow creased her perfect brow. "I thought I was safe in this town."

"You are." George shot Harry a what-are-you-doing look behind Alessandra's back.

Harry ignored him. "Humor me," he told her. "Please? I know you don't believe this, but Trotta's a son of a bitch, and he's known for his persistence."

George opened the door. "Harry just wants an excuse to put his arm around you."

Alessandra glanced quickly at Harry, surprise lighting her eyes. Surprise and something else. Something as hot and electric as lightning. It brought her to life so completely and made her exquisitely beautiful despite the heavy makeup.

But as instantly as it appeared, it was gone. Quaffed and shoved back inside. Somewhere down the line she'd learned to hide any excitement, any life, any passion. Someone hadn't wanted her to be anything more than a pretty bauble. A decorative but unobtrusive piece of art.

George closed the door. "If you want, I'll turn around and you two can kiss."

Harry eviscerated George with his eyes. "George imagines there's some kind of weird attraction thing between us, Al. But George is wrong. George is dead wrong." He muttered under his breath, "In fact, George is dead." He looked at Alessandra. "I'm sorry if he offended you."

"He didn't. I'm aware that you're not . . . that we're not . . . I'm aware."

"Still, that was completely inappropriate." Harry

looked at George again, who was totally amused. "Stu-pendously, asshole-ishly inappropriate."

"I think we're all a little punchy." The icy princess had been replaced by someone softer, someone less certain. Someone he had far more trouble resisting. Someone he did want to kiss.

And George knew it, too. The son of a bitch was grin-ning at him, damn him.

Harry would've turned away, but Allie stopped him with a hand on his arm.

Her perfectly manicured fingernails had been bitten and torn, some down all the way to the quick. She'd been playing it cool for the past few days, but in truth she was a seething bundle of anxiety. As he looked down at her, she quickly pulled her hand back, hiding it behind her.

"I didn't call Michael," she told him.

Her eyes were very, very blue. Michael. It took him a few extra seconds to realize she was talking about Trotta. "I know," he said. "Thank you."

He hated the perfume she was wearing. Whatever she wore to bed at night—he wasn't sure what it was exactly, she had so many different lotions and potions all lined up on a shelf in the bathroom—but whatever it was smelled so delicately sweet, it seemed a crime for her to cover it up with this other, fancier, stronger scent. He turned to George. "Let's get moving. Asshole."

George laughed and keyed his radio. "Okay, team, we're finally coming out."

The food market was a Super Stop and Shop. It seemed oddly out of place in the quaint little town that was filled with antique shops and farm stands. Standing inside of the mega-store, with its well-lit, wide aisles, its attached Blockbuster Video, bank, bookstore, flower shop, and goodness knows what all else, Alessandra might as well have been back on suburban Long Island instead of out here on the edge of nowhere.

It was something of a disappointment. If she was going to live in Cow's Bowels, New York, she wanted the complete small town package. She wanted a Fourth of July parade, a country fair with an oxen pull and a pie-eating contest, and she wanted a little, homey mom-and-pop supermarket, run by Mr. Whipple himself.

Instead, she had the isolation of living a million miles from her nearest neighbor, combined with the isolation of an efficient but completely impersonal supermarket chain. It was, without a doubt, the complete worst of both worlds.

It felt odd to be out here, under the bright fluorescent lights after spending so many days all but locked in her room. It was odd, too, doing her shopping while trailed by both George and Harry.

Harry was still on edge. Alessandra suspected he wouldn't begin to relax until they were back inside the little house. Her little house. Her ugly little house. It wouldn't be long until Harry and the other agents left, and she'd be on her own in her ugly little house, pretending to be Barbara Conway for the rest of her pathetic little life.

Of course, after the agents left, she could call Michael and get this mess straightened out. No one would be there to stop her. Not George, not Harry. Harry would have moved on to the next case. He would be focusing all his seething passion and intensity on some other mob boss, in his never-ending quest to find unattainable absolution.

He was standing at the end of the international foods aisle, his suit as rumpled as ever, his hair in dire need of a cut.

The odd attraction that she'd thought simmered between them wasn't real. It was completely her own, totally one-sided. Harry had made that more than clear.

She smiled at the irony. She was used to men falling around her, smitten, littering her path, as far as she could see. But the one man who was completely unaffected by her beauty was the one man she couldn't stop thinking about.

George held up a package of gourmet pasta. "Have you tried this?" he asked. "Lemon pepper linguine. It's wonderful."

She shook her head.

He began loading the cart with enough to feed a small army. "I'll make it tonight and—oh, shit!"

He grabbed her, pushing her down to the linoleum-tiled floor with one hand as he pulled over a display rack in front of them with the other.

There was a sound, sharp and deafeningly loud, and George swore again, falling hard against her.

Something had spilled. Alessandra could feel it, warm and wet against her.

But then she heard Harry shouting, heard more of those same deafening noises, and she realized what was happening. Guns were being fired. That was no jar of spaghetti sauce that had broken and spilled on the floor, soaking through the knees of her jeans. The wetness was from George's blood. He'd been shot.

She heard herself screaming, heard George cursing, heard more of those gunshots—a whole lot more, in rapid succession. The store seemed to explode around her and she screamed again and again as George fired back.

She was the target. The men who were shooting—and it sounded as if there were at least a dozen of them—were trying to hit her. She was in mortal danger, and it was very likely that she was going to die surrounded by a mound of gourmet pasta. Dear Lord, she didn't want to die!

The world was moving in fast motion. From the corner of her eye she could see Harry, both hands wrapped around his gun, firing at whoever was shooting at them. George was shooting, too, but he was distracted by his wound.

The bullet that had struck him in the thigh was bleeding unlike anything Alessandra had ever seen in her life. Blood was pulsing out of him with every beat of his heart, draining his life away right before her eyes. The bullet must've hit an artery.

He was still cursing, but his speech was starting to slur. When she looked into his eyes, she could see death reflected there. He didn't want to die, either.

She was shaking, tears of fear blurring her vision. She raised her head, looking for help, but a bullet smashed into the rack that shielded them, and she knew help wasn't coming. At least not soon enough for George.

Apply pressure to a wound. Pressure stopped the bleeding. She'd taken a first-aid class back in high school, and although she'd usually let schoolwork slide, she'd liked this class. She'd paid attention, thank goodness.

She had nothing to use as a bandage, nothing sterile, nothing to hold against the awful hole in George's leg, but she covered it with her hands anyway, praying this would help.

It didn't. His blood seeped between her fingers.

He was struggling with his tie, trying to get it off, and she remembered. Tourniquet. If she could tie off George's leg between the wound and his heart, that might keep him from bleeding to death.

She tried to help him with the tie. Her fingers left bright red smears on his crisp white collar as she fumbled in her haste to pull it free.

"Get out of the store! Get out of here!" Harry was shouting at her as he fired his gun, and she realized he was holding the gunmen off, pushing them toward the rear of the store and giving her a clear route to run to the front doors. "Go!" he shouted at her. "Goddamn it, Allie, go!"

She wanted to go. She wanted to run like a frightened rabbit to safety. But she couldn't do it. She couldn't just leave George to die.

And he would die without her. He was already too weak even to hold his gun. "Go," he whispered.

"No!" Sobbing, she wrapped the tie around his thigh. Knotting it, she pulled it tight—tight enough to make him cry out with pain.

"I'm sorry! I'm so sorry! But I've got to pull it even tighter!" George didn't answer and she yanked harder, chanting a litany beneath the sound of guns being fired, "I'm sorry, I'm so sorry . . ."

It still wasn't enough.

In the back of her mind, she'd thought she might be able to tie the tourniquet and then scramble to safety, but she wasn't strong enough to tie it tightly enough, and it had only slightly slowed his bleeding. She pulled her T-shirt over her head, wadded it up, and pressed it against the wound.

"Don't die," she ordered him. "Goddamn you, George, don't you die!"

"Allie!"

Harry's hoarse shout made her lift her head, and something else, some sixth sense made her look up toward the ceiling.

And there, way up on top of the shelf separating the aisle, at a vantage point that left her completely exposed, was Ivo.

Ivo, with the pale eyes and hair, with the Slavic features and lilting Eastern European accent. Ivo, Michael Trotta's right-hand man.

She could hear Harry shouting, but his words no longer had any meaning.

Ivo was holding one of those enormous Dirty Harry–style guns, the kind with a barrel the size of a cannon. That barrel was cold and blank and very, very deadly looking. Alessandra could see the same emptiness in Ivo's eyes, and she knew in that split second before he aimed the gun at her forehead, that he was going to kill her.

This was no mistake. There was no miscommunication here. Michael Trotta had told Ivo to kill her, and he was going to do just that, no questions asked.

There was nowhere to run, nothing to hide behind.

Alessandra could do nothing but sit there helplessly and wait to die.

Nine

❧ ❧

HARRY'S CLIP JAMMED.

Of all the fucking bad times for his clip to jam, this had to take the cake.

Some six and a half feet tall, six and a half feet wide gorilla had somehow gotten past him and was on top of the shelves about to permanently mess up Alessandra's makeup by putting a bullet hole in her forehead.

Moving at a dead run, Harry threw his gun—useless piece of crap—at the King of the Apes and it bounced off of Kong's arm, distracting him for several brief seconds.

But several seconds were all Harry needed. He launched into the air for a perfect intercept just as the gorilla fired a double burst.

Both rounds caught him square in the chest, hundreds of pounds of energy pushing him back and down, on top of Alessandra, on top of George, on top of George's semiautomatic.

He couldn't breathe, he could barely see, his ears were roaring from the tidal wave of pain, but his fingers closed around George's Beretta. He raised his arm and squeezed off a shot and King Kong disappeared.

And just like that, it was over.

At least for now.

Alessandra didn't know it, though. She was sobbing as she tore at his jacket, one hand still holding her T-shirt against George's leg. She was covered in blood, her nose bright red from crying, her makeup completely smeared. With her T-shirt off, she knelt above him now like a horror movie survivor, in tight black pants and a black bra made of lace that didn't quite conceal her lush dark nipples, blood streaking her smooth, pale skin like some kind of sick body paint.

She ripped the buttons off his shirt in her haste to see how badly he'd been injured and stopped short, confusion on her face, as she came up against his body armor.

Harry pushed himself onto his elbows. "Man down!" he wheezed as backup finally stormed into the supermarket. "I need an ambulance for my partner, and I need it now!"

Christ, George had lost more blood than Harry had thought humanly possible. It was slick on the floor around them and he winced as he skidded slightly in it. The pain in his chest was unmistakable. At least one of his ribs was broken. But he'd take a broken rib any day over the alternative—having to clean Alessandra's brains up off the floor.

He took over for her with George, keeping her already saturated T-shirt tight against his partner's wound.

"Come on, George," Harry muttered, lifting his eyelids, checking his eyes. He wasn't looking good. "Stay with me, buddy."

But then George stirred and his lips moved. "Tell Nic—"

"Tell her yourself," Harry rasped, refusing to perform any kind of last rites. "What do I look like, some kind of fucking messenger service?" He looked up at Alessandra. "Be ready to flag down the paramedics. And find me McFall."

She was shaking and crying, but she wiped her tears away with the backs of her arms as she looked around.

Over twenty agents were combing the place. The parking lot outside the big front windows was filled with cars parked at haphazard angles, some with lights still spinning in their front windshields.

Alessandra waved over Christine McFall, who took one look at George and started to shout, "Where's that ambulance?"

"Chris, there's still another shooter." A hoarse whisper was the loudest Harry could manage. His chest still felt squeezed, as if someone had thrown him a touchdown pass with an anvil. "He's built, dark blond hair, looks like Arnold Schwarzenegger's bigger brother. Check the next aisle over—carefully. I got off a shot, but I don't think I hit him."

Chris nodded, her clear voice ringing out over the chaos as she gave out orders.

And then the paramedics arrived. Harry moved aside, pulling Alessandra back and out of the way as they swarmed over George.

"His name's Ivo," she whispered.

Harry turned to look at her more closely. "That shooter?"

She nodded.

"You knew him?"

She nodded again, fresh tears flooding her eyes, her lower lip trembling like a child's. She was still shaking, her arms folded across her chest. She hugged herself as if she were cold.

No doubt she was cold—she wasn't wearing a shirt.

It hurt like hell to take off his jacket, but Harry did it anyway, draping it over her narrow shoulders. She pulled it more tightly around herself and sank down onto the floor as if her knees couldn't hold her up another minute longer.

She was crying again. And from the state of her mascara, it seemed pretty obvious that she'd started crying close to when the shooting had begun.

And yet, when push came to shove, she'd refused to leave George. Harry had seen big, strong men panic and knock aside women and children in their haste to get to cover when shots were fired. But Alessandra had stayed calm enough to tie a tourniquet around George's leg. She could have run away, but instead she risked her life for a man she barely even knew. She was either really stupid or really brave. And Harry had already discovered that she wasn't really stupid.

If George survived—Harry was praying hard that he would—it would be solely because of Alessandra.

Harry gingerly lowered himself to the floor next to her, leaning back against a shelf filled with bags of rice, as George was wheeled out of the store. "Tell me about your little friend Ivo. Do you know his last name?"

She shook her head. "He brought me to Michael Trotta's office. He rode in the back of the limousine with me on the way home. He answered the phone at the number Michael gave me to call when I found the money." She looked at Harry. "Why does he want to kill me? I gave it back. All of it."

She was trying not to cry, trying to keep her sobs from shaking her body. It was a losing battle.

Harry could sympathize. He was fighting a losing battle of his own. It seemed stupid as hell to fight, so he gave up completely and put his arm around her. She crumbled against him, holding him just a little too tightly. But he didn't mind the pain in his side. No, he didn't mind at all.

There were definitely worse things than losing this kind of battle.

"I hate to break it to you," he said, "but this time a

pair of sunglasses isn't going to cut it. People are probably going to know you've been crying."

"I thought you were dead," she told him, her voice muffled, her face buried in his shirt. "When those bullets hit you, I thought . . . I thought . . ."

"Yeah, I know," Harry said, stroking her hair. His heart was in his throat. Was it possible she really cared that much? "I know you pretty well by now, Al. You thought, 'Oh, fuck, the dumb son of a bitch is dead. Now who are they going to send to annoy the crap out of me?' "

She lifted her face to look up at him, laughing tremulously through her tears—and that was it. He was toast. Completely. Utterly. Charred to a crisp. It was the red nose that did him in. Must've been some wonderful yet long-forgotten childhood incident with a clown that had put its stamp upon him forever. Whatever its origin, he couldn't stop himself from leaning forward and covering her mouth with his own.

He'd meant to take no more than a gentle taste of her deliciously soft lips. But as soon as his mouth touched hers, he knew that wasn't going to be enough. Not for him. And not for Alessandra.

She kissed him hungrily and he deepened it, sweeping his tongue into her welcoming mouth. She tasted like salty tears and bitter fear, but beneath it, she was pure sweet fire. She took his breath away with her eagerness, with her need. With her desire.

He pulled her closer, the pleasure of her body next to his definitely worth the raw pain in his ribs, and his hand slipped beneath the edge of the jacket she wore draped around her shoulders. Her skin was as soft as he remembered, as silky and smooth as a baby's.

It was sheer perfection, and he came into contact with

sheer perfection so infrequently in his life, it jarred him back to earth.

What in God's name was he doing? It would have been insane enough to kiss her in the privacy of the house, let alone out here in freaking public.

He pulled away from her, but God, it was quite possibly one of the hardest things he'd ever done.

"I'm sorry," he managed to say. Sorry that he had to stop. Sorry that he couldn't take off her clothes and get it going with her right then and there. He wisely let her make her own interpretation.

"No," she said. "I . . . I'm . . ." She looked as confused as he felt. How could they both have had such bad lapses in judgment at exactly the same moment?

"Bad timing," he said. Bad timing, bad thinking, bad call, bad everything but sex. Good sex. If they had been able to keep going it would have been very, very, very good sex. Except afterward, all of the collective bads would've reared up and bit him on the ass. He was on the job, for christsake. He was supposed to protect Alessandra, and last time he checked, there was nothing in the rule book that talked about doing that with any amount of efficiency while in a horizontal position, without any clothes on.

She reached up to push her hair back with a shaking hand. "You probably want to go make sure George is okay."

"I want to get you to safety first. Get a vest on you. Get you into a room with a lot of guards near the doors and windows." Lots and lots of guards. So many that he wouldn't have to be alone with her again. Not that the crowd had stopped him two minutes ago.

"A vest?" she asked. His hand was still against the perfect smoothness of her back. He didn't want to move it, but he did. It felt like a caress, embarrassing them both all over again. And reinforcing this damned urge he was having to throw all caution to the wind and kiss her again.

Harry gestured down at his body armor instead. "A bullet-proof vest." He fingered the pair of bullets embedded there. "These things really work, you know."

"What made you wear it?" she asked. "I mean, a trip to the library and the grocery store . . . ?"

He wasn't sure what to say. He didn't want to lie, but she obviously hadn't caught on yet as to the real situation.

Christine McFall appeared, temporarily saving his ass. "We've got two perps, and they're both too dead to talk about who sent them. Both carried ID—Ed's running it now."

"Only two, huh?" Harry asked.

She nodded. "They were both medium to slight build. It looks like your bodybuilding shooter got away." She glanced at Alessandra. "We should get Mrs. Lamont back to the house, let her get cleaned up. And you should go to the hospital, sir, get yourself checked out. We've got enough manpower to handle this without you."

Enough manpower.

Harry could see realization dawning in Alessandra's eyes as she looked around once again at all the police and federal agents in the store, at all the official-looking cars in the parking lot.

She looked at him, looked again at his vest before gazing searchingly into his eyes. "How did so many federal agents get up here so quickly?"

She knew. A woman as smart as Alessandra had to have already figured it out. She just wanted to hear it from his traitorous lips.

Harry glanced at Christine. "Give us a minute, will you?"

Chris moved tactfully out of earshot as Harry cleared his throat. "This may be a time when you might want to opt not to hear the truth."

"You wore the bullet-proof vest because you knew this was going to happen," Alessandra guessed. She was furious. "Didn't you?"

"Allie, it sounds a whole lot worse than—"

"Didn't you? It's a simple question, Harry." The tears—angry ones this time—were back in her eyes, about to brim over. "You either answer it yes or no."

He touched the side of her face with one finger. He couldn't help himself. "Yes."

She nodded, pushing his hand away as she blinked furiously to keep her angry tears from falling. "All those agents—you were all just waiting for this to happen. You knew there would be a hit attempt, didn't you? You knew because you were using me as bait."

Jesus, when she put it that way, it sounded terrible. Had he really done that? He had to look away. "Yes."

She pulled violently away from him, put two solid feet of space between them. "Why didn't anyone tell me? Why didn't you tell me? Didn't it occur to you that this might be something I'd like to have a say in?"

"We had a better chance of getting Trotta if you didn't know anything about this. When we planned it . . . Allie, we didn't know you wouldn't try to warn him that this was a setup—you know, to get back on his list of friends rather than his list of people he wants dead."

"I could have been killed," she said. "But that wouldn't have been a big deal, would it, since then you'd have Michael Trotta on murder charges, instead of just attempted murder."

"As of right now, we don't have Michael Trotta at all." Christine was back, with Ed Bach at her side. "We've got nothing connecting the dead perps with

Trotta. They're not hired killers. They've both got rap sheets a mile long, filled with grocery store heists. As for your mysterious third man, you two are the only ones who saw him. Everyone both inside and outside the store only saw two shooters. We're still canvassing, but it doesn't look good. We can try going after Trotta based on your claim that you saw one of his men here today, but I don't think we're going to get very far with that in court, considering."

"I don't fucking believe it. George gets shot, maybe dies, and we've still got nothing on this bastard?"

Ed shook his head. "No one else saw this third shooter, Harry. We'll have whatever bullets we can find, but you know damn well this guy's gun is probably already long gone. We're looking for a solid conviction. You know as well as I do we can't get that with the two key witnesses being an agent bent on revenge and a woman who thinks Trotta's trying to kill her. Even a court-appointed lawyer would leave the jury thinking reasonable doubt. The one Trotta can afford will leave them thinking they should try to convict you."

"At last report, George was hanging on," Christine said quietly.

"Great. He's not dead. Yet. Did somebody call Nicole?"

"She had a meeting down in Washington," Christine said. "We haven't been able to reach her yet. But she's not going to be able to get a flight up here until tomorrow morning. I've already checked that out."

"She's not married to him anymore," Ed pointed out. "She may not want to come at all."

"Someone contact what's her name," Harry ordered. "Kim. That dancer George was seeing from the Fantasy Club."

Christine nodded. "Yes, sir."

Alessandra stood up. "Well, this was certainly educational. Can someone please drive me back to the house? I need to take a shower." She turned to Harry. "You're obviously needed at the hospital." She held out her hand and gave him one of those ridiculously cool royal smiles. "Good luck. I hope you enjoy your revenge—if and when you finally get it."

"I'm not going anywhere," Harry pulled himself painfully to his feet.

"You may not be, but I am. I'm going back to the house to shower and pack my things."

Harry laughed, but then stopped when he realized she was dead serious. "What are you going to do? Just walk out of there? Ivo's probably waiting for you. No, not probably. He is waiting for you. I can guarantee it."

"I'm well aware of that. But somehow I think I'll stay alive longer without the help of the FBI, thank you very much." She turned to Christine. "Please, will you take me back to the house?"

Christine looked at Harry. "Sir, you're looking a little pale. You should go to the hospital. If your rib's broken you'll need to get it X-rayed and taped and—"

"The only reason I'm pale is because you keep calling me sir."

"I'm sure Mrs. Lamont can be convinced to stay at least until you return from the hospital."

"Don't count on it," Alessandra muttered.

"Al, don't make me order Chris here to tie you up and sit on you until I get back. Because you know if I did, she'd say 'yes, sir,' and that would really give me a rash."

Alessandra didn't smile, she didn't so much as move a muscle in her face, and he played one of the only trump cards he was holding. Drawing her away from the others, he lowered his voice. "Alessandra, have I ever lied to you?"

"By omission. Yes, you have." She pulled her arm free from his grasp.

"Yeah, that." He waved it away. "But whenever you asked me something directly, I answered truthfully. Whenever you needed an honest answer, you knew I'd give it to you, straight."

She didn't say a word. She just stood there with her arms tightly crossed in front of her. She'd slipped her arms into the sleeves of his jacket. They were about three inches too long, not because her arms were shorter than his, but because her shoulders were so much more narrow.

"If you still want to leave after I get back from the hospital, I'll let you walk away," he continued. "I'm giving you my word on that, okay? Just stay until I get there."

Alessandra gazed at him for several very, very long moments.

In desperation, he pulled out his very last trump card. "Allie, I saved your life today. Do this, and we'll call it even."

"I'm not sure it counts as saving a life when you're the one responsible for putting that very same life in jeopardy."

What could he say to that? Particularly when she was giving him the royal evil eye. "If those bullets had hit me in the head, I'd be dead right now. If I'd let you go back to Trotta when you wanted to, you'd be dead right now. Maybe this wasn't the smartest scenario, maybe we should've told you what was up, but the fact is, by luck we've both been left with our hearts still warm and beating. Use that heart and show me a little mercy. Please."

She nodded grudgingly. Thank God. "I'll wait. But you won't convince me to stay."

* * *

"Call for you, Ms. Fenster, on line three."

Nicole didn't stop on her way to the ladies' room. She only had fifteen minutes to pee and grab a sandwich and a Coke and get back into the conference room. "Take a message please, Bonnie."

"They say it's urgent, ma'am."

Dammit, everything was urgent lately. "Take a message."

"One of the members of your task-force team has apparently been injured quite badly. A Christine McFall is on the line. She's insisting she speak directly to you."

Nicole's entire insides turned to ice as she stopped short. She turned back and took the telephone out of the receptionist's hand. "Chris? Who's been hurt?"

"Nicki, it was George."

George. Oh, God.

"We had a complete snafu," Christine continued. "Several of the local teams weren't where they were supposed to be and during the gunplay—"

"Is he dead?" George. Please God, not George. Nicole turned away from the receptionist, knowing she couldn't keep her anguish from showing on her face.

"No, but he's in surgery right now and—"

"Is he going to die?"

Chris was silent for a little too long. "No."

"Dammit, don't lie to me, McFall." Nicole kept her voice quiet and even despite the pounding of her heart.

"He was shot in the leg. I don't even think it's broken, but the bullet hit a major artery and he's lost a lot of blood. So, yes, there's a chance he may not make it." Chris paused. "I'm calling you as a friend, not as one of your staff. I think if you've got anything at all that's been left unsaid, you might want to get up here."

Nicole felt tears rush to her eyes and she blinked them back furiously. God help her if anyone in this office ever saw her cry. "That was part of the trouble, Chris. There was nothing left unsaid."

She took a deep breath, hating herself for being so practical but knowing if she dropped everything and went to him, it wouldn't make a bit of difference. He wouldn't not die just because she was there. And her reputation for being as reliable and emotionless as a machine would be severely compromised if she went running off to sit by the hospital bed of the man who had left her. "I'll be back in a few days. Earlier if I can manage it."

"Nicki, he needs you."

"He divorced me. That seems to imply that he doesn't need me. Please let me know if there's any change in his condition."

"Yeah, right," Chris said, frustration sharpening her voice. "I'll give you a ring if he dies."

The line went dead, and Nicole handed the phone back to the receptionist, managing to hide the fact that her hands were shaking.

"You gave me your word," Alessandra couldn't keep her voice from quivering with anger. "You said you'd let me walk away."

"I am letting you walk away. I just happen to be walking away with you."

Harry opened the front door to the car and all but pushed her inside. She opened it again as soon as he closed it. "I don't need your help."

The moon was only a sliver and his face was completely in shadow. "Can we argue about this after I get in the car and start driving? I've been banking on the fact that Ivo's following one of the decoys I sent out the front door, but just in case, I'd like to get out of here without a hole in my head. Or yours."

Alessandra pulled the door shut.

Harry tossed their bags in the back and climbed carefully behind the wheel. He started the car. "Thank you."

She stared straight ahead.

He laughed quietly, the sound as velvety and soft as the darkness that surrounded her. "The silent treatment. That's very original. No one's ever done that before."

He kept the lights off as he pulled onto a dirt road. It wasn't until he turned onto the state highway that he flipped them on.

This car was just too small. She was practically sitting on his lap. The two bucket seats were separated only by a parking brake. Their shoulders were so close, they were almost touching. And Harry drove with his hand resting on the gear shift, his fingers mere inches from her knee.

Alessandra couldn't believe she'd let him kiss her.

Let him? Dear Lord, she'd done more than simply sit back and let him kiss her. She'd nearly inhaled him.

Yes, she'd been seriously shaken by the violence, but that was no excuse. The sad truth was, she'd wanted to kiss him like that for days.

Of course, that was before she knew he was a complete and total liar. Before she knew he'd do anything—sacrifice anything and anyone—to get his twisted, pathetic revenge on Michael Trotta.

She'd kissed him thinking he was that rare animal, a completely honest and forthright human being. She'd kissed him thinking foolishly, childishly, that he was someone worth kissing.

He shifted in his seat, reaching up to touch the bandage that had been wrapped around his chest, and she knew he was uncomfortable.

"Were your ribs broken?" She couldn't keep from asking.

"Just one." He glanced at her. "But one's enough."

"I'm sorry," she said stiffly.

He'd come back from the hospital knowing she'd already made up her mind. She was out of there, out of the Witness Protection Program for good. He hadn't seemed surprised when she informed him of that.

He'd apologized again and asked her to reconsider several times. The fourth time she'd told him flatly that she was leaving Cow Pattie, New York, that very night, he'd made a few phone calls and changed into a pair of worn denim jeans and a plain black T-shirt.

It was a very different look for him, much more in sync with his personality and looks than the wrinkled suits. The jeans were loose fitting, yet they managed to show off his muscular body. He wore sneakers on his feet and a baseball cap over his untamable hair. The fashion statement was completed by a lightweight distressed-leather bomber jacket. It worked. As angry as she was at him, she had to admit that he looked about as good as she'd ever seen him.

Harry cleared his throat. "Here's the deal, Al. We're both on the same side. We've both got the same goal, although I know you're still mad at me, so you don't want to see that. But it's a fact. You want to stay alive, I want you to stay alive. What we need right now is for you to acknowledge the fact that I fucked up," he said flatly. "The whole agency fucked up. You're right and we were wrong. You should have been informed. You should have been allowed to decline the dubious honor of acting as bait to catch a scumbag." He glanced at her. "There's nothing I can do to change the past, but I can change the future. I'm going to take you to a place I guarantee will be safe, and I'm going to show you what you need to do so you don't stand out in the crowd once you get there."

"How can you guarantee that place is safe? And how do I know you're not just going to set me up again as soon as we're there?"

He took the ramp onto Route 84, heading west. He eased the car into fifth gear and then turned to look at her in the dim dashboard light. "Because my children live there. You better believe there's no way in hell I'd lead Trotta's men to the town where my children live."

"But what if someone else on your task force decides to let Michael know where I am?"

"No one else is going to know where you are," he told her. "I'm sure as hell not gonna tell them."

"But I thought you said your kids lived with your sister. She shouldn't be too hard for anyone to find."

"She's my stepsister," Harry said. "Actually, she's not even really my stepsister. She was almost my stepsister. Her father and my mother lived together for about eight months. They were supposed to get married, but it didn't work out. Marge was twelve and I was seven, and . . . she was good to me. We stayed friends even though our parents didn't. After Kevin . . . after . . . you know . . . I needed someplace safe for Shaun and Emily to go. Marge was living out in Colorado, and she came through for me. Nobody I worked with knew about her. I've been careful, and the kids have been safe since then. Not even George knows where they are."

Alessandra was silent for a moment. "And you don't feel compelled to report my whereabouts to your boss?"

"Hey, I'm on vacation for the next month. I don't have to report anything to anybody."

Vacation. He was spending his vacation helping her.

He glanced at her again, as if he could read her mind. "I figure I owe you one," he said quietly.

"I'm not sure I can trust you, Harry."

He nodded. "I know. Let me get you as far as Colorado," he said. "I'll show you how to disappear, and once we're there, if you want to vanish, you can just vanish." He looked over at her. "Do we have a deal?"

Outside the windows of the car, the night was dark. Alessandra could see Harry's blurred reflection, watching her. She didn't exactly have a lot of options. She sighed, wishing he had been the hero she was looking for, wishing that ambush had been as much of a surprise to him as it was to her.

"You still haven't tried to set the past behind us," he pointed out. "Why don't you go ahead and tell me what a sorry-assed son of a bitch loser I am, so we can start moving forward?"

She glanced at him.

"Come on," he said. "Let me have it. Full power."

"You're . . . such a jerk."

"What, are you kidding? Jerks cut you off when you're driving. They steal your parking space. They don't nearly get you killed. You can do better than that."

"You're a . . ." She couldn't say it.

"Start with bastard. I'm a bastard. Come on, Allie. The word's barely even offensive. Try it. Bastard."

"You . . ."

". . . stinking sack of shit." He laughed at the look on her face. "Yeah, you're so polite, but I know you want to say it."

"I . . ."

". . . hate you, you scum-sucking loser. Asshole. Dickhead. Multiple choice, Al. I'm making it even easier for you."

"I thought you might be special." She finally forced the words out. "I thought you were better than the others."

Silence.

Harry stared at the road, all laughter gone from his face. "Yeah, well. You were wrong, huh?"

She had been wrong. But he couldn't begin to guess how badly she wished she hadn't been.

Ten

❧ ❧

As HARRY GOT back into the car, Alessandra stirred. She'd been asleep for close to seven hours. He couldn't remember the last time he'd seen someone sleep that ferociously in a car. He'd had to pull over to the side of the road two different times to take a leak—he didn't dare leave her alone in the car at a rest stop and it seemed a shame to wake her.

But this phone call could no longer wait. He'd pulled the car as close as he could to the phone booth, so she'd be able to see him if she did wake up.

But it wasn't until he squeezed himself back into the subcompact, jarred his broken rib, and swallowed a curse of pain that her eyelashes began to flutter.

Harry put the car in gear and got back on the interstate, watching out the rearview mirror for many miles, still making sure Ivo wasn't following them.

But there was no one in the mirror. They were completely alone on the road.

Dawn was pushing up past the flat horizon behind them, and in the growing light, Harry let himself look at Alessandra. He'd been watching her off and on all night, in the light from the dashboard.

Watching her sleep.

Letting himself look at her—really look, without having to worry that she'd catch him staring.

Amazed that she had kissed him the way she did.

Listening to her snore.

He liked that she snored. Liked that beneath her facade was a real, flawed human being. A real woman with a deviated septum.

The motion of the car and the sound of the engine had put her back to sleep, but it wasn't a good, solid sleep. It was fitful, filled with movement and soft noises.

Harry had spent half the night trying not to think about that way she'd kissed him, and the other half trying not to think about the fact that she wasn't likely to kiss him again, any time in the near future.

But oh, God, her kiss had been seventeen million times better than his daydreams and fantasies. And he was no amateur when it came to fantasies.

The ice princess thing was just an act. Beneath the snazzy hairstyles, designer clothes, perfect makeup, fancy perfume, and cool, polite voice was a woman with molten hot lava running through her veins.

If he hadn't been part of the conspiracy that nearly got her killed, he knew he would've spent last night in her bed. He would've had sex again. He actually wanted, really, really wanted to have sex again. It wasn't that he hadn't wanted it before, he just hadn't really wanted it that badly, and it never seemed to be worth the effort.

Sex with Alessandra would be worth the effort. After that kiss, he knew that for a fact.

Sweet God, if this had played out differently, he could have been fast asleep right now, with his arms still around her, her perfect body tucked next to his, his face buried in her sweet-smelling hair. He could have been sated and truly relaxed for the first time in years.

But no, instead, she hated him. She was never going to smile at him again, let alone touch him, never mind get naked with him. It wasn't going to happen, and the sooner he stopped thinking about it, the better.

Alessandra made a sound that was a cross between a sigh and a cry, and Harry glanced at her. She made it again—it was a fearful sound. Harry put his hand on her knee and shook her slightly.

"Nightmare," he said. "It's just a nightmare. Wherever you think you are, you're not there. You're here, and you're safe."

He glanced up at her face, and her eyes were open. She was still breathing hard, but she was awake. He squeezed her knee before he released it. "You okay, Al?"

She looked around, looked at the car, at the endless flat highway stretching out in front of them forever, at the morning light streaking across the sky, at him. She drew in a deep breath and let it out very slowly.

"I can't believe any of this is real."

"It's not too late to go back."

"Yes, it is." She closed her eyes. "I was dreaming about the dog. You know, I did it again."

"Did what again?"

She opened her eyes. They were almost colorless in the pale light. She didn't look at him. She just stared up at the hole in the fabric that lined the car's roof. "I sat there and waited to die."

She was talking about yesterday. About when Ivo aimed his gun at her head.

"It was as if I were five years old again, staring up at that attack dog." She turned and looked squarely at him. "I've decided I'm never going to let myself be that helpless again. That's why I can't go back."

"And you're convinced you can hide yourself better than an organization that specializes in hiding people from bad guys?"

"From what I've seen, yes. The Witness Protection

Program didn't do a very good job of keeping me safe, did it?"

"Whereas you will, yourself?"

She lifted her chin defiantly. "There's obviously a lot I'll need to learn. But there's got to be some book in the library that will tell me what to do. How to hide."

A book from the library? Harry concealed his laughter with a cough. She was going to get a book.

"The setup was a complete goatfuck, I'll grant you that." He took a sip from a can of Pepsi he'd opened four hundred miles ago. It was warm and flat, but it contained caffeine. Christ, he was tired, and she was going to get a book. "Despite that, you're alive, right? Whatever we did wrong, we still managed to keep you alive. That's got to be worth something."

"I'm alive because of you, not your task force, not the Witness Protection Program," she pointed out. "If you, Harry O'Dell, hadn't been there, I'd be dead right now."

"Speaking of dead right now," Harry said, "George is out of intensive care. He's going to be okay. I just called New York."

"Thank God."

"Thank you," he said quietly. "You saved his life, Al."

"I saved his life, you saved my life." Alessandra held open her hands in frustration. "That still doesn't make any of it okay. No one should have been shooting at us in the first place. If I had died, your task force would have been as responsible for my death as Michael Trotta."

"Hey, as long we're slinging blame, you need to do a little inner soul-searching yourself, sweetheart. You made it pretty damned easy for Trotta to find you. We leaked your general whereabouts to him, but you did the rest. All he had to do was have Ivo ask around, see if any woman who looked like a supermodel had moved into the area."

"I don't look like a supermodel."

"A movie star, then." Harry shrugged. "You aren't the average, ordinary Paul's River farmer's wife, that's for sure."

"But I didn't even leave the house!"

"You didn't have to. All you had to do was drive through town, the way you did, and pick up the keys to the house at the real estate office. You were in the backseat of that car looking like you'd lost your way to a power lunch at Schazti's on Main with your agent. People noticed you."

Alessandra shook her head. "That's crazy. I was just sitting there."

"How many people do you think noticed you that day?"

Alessandra shrugged. "I have no idea."

"Guess."

She sighed, shaking her head. "I don't know—two or three?"

"Try twenty-five. At least. And of those twenty-five—and those twenty-five are the ones we know about, there may have been more—most of 'em mentioned you to some significant other or friend, who mentioned you to someone else. We found this out when we canvassed the area after the shooting at the Stop and Shop. The people in this town knew that someone incredibly beautiful had moved into the old Archer house on Devlin Road." Harry glanced at her. "And, for your information, even if only two or three people had noticed you, it still would have been too many. People in town still would have been talking about you." He gave her a moment to think about that. "Do you really want to stay alive?"

She didn't hesitate. "Yes."

"Then you have to become invisible, Allie. The clothes

you bought when you went shopping with Christine McFall . . ." He shook his head. "They don't make you invisible." He looked at her outfit, a form-fitting black blouse, a pair of silky, flowing black trousers, high-heeled shoes. Christ. She should look rumpled from sleeping all night in the car. Instead she looked ready for a high-fashion photo shoot. "Did you pack all those clothes?"

"Of course."

"Where are they?"

Alessandra blinked at him. "In my overnight bag. On the backseat."

"Open it, will you?" Harry finished the Pepsi. They were going to have to stop soon to get some coffee. He was exhausted. On the other hand, all he had to do to stay awake was breathe. Every time he inhaled, his side felt as if it were on fire. He took a deep breath. Ouch.

Alessandra didn't move. "You want me to . . . ?"

"Grab your bag and open it," he said patiently. "You have about three pairs of really tight pants somewhere in there. One black, one gray, and one navy blue, I think. Get 'em out. We need to talk about your clothes."

"They're leggings," she informed him, wrestling the cheap nylon bag George had bought for her up into the front seat.

"Whatever. And that black turtleneck," Harry said. "The tight one with the lines."

"It's a rib knit," she said, unzipping the bag and rummaging around.

"Rib knit. At last. My life is surely more complete now that I know that." Harry took the leggings and the sweater from her and held them up. "Tight," he said. "Too tight, too nice. You look too good in this stuff." He put them on his lap then reached directly into her bag and pulled out two very tiny T-shirts, one plain white, the other olive green. They were remarkably soft to the touch. That blue sweater she'd worn the other day. "These looked very nice on you, too. Very flattering to your figure. What else you got in there?"

"Not much. A few more shirts. A skirt. A pair of jeans."

"The same style as that black pair you wore yesterday?"

"Yes, but in blue."

"Let me see." Harry dropped the T-shirts into his lap with the other clothing as he took the jeans from her. Yes, they were definitely cut to be formfitting. "And the skirt?"

She held it up. It was black and very short. Very sexy. It would make her long legs seem even longer. He took it and put it in the growing pile then reached into the bag for the last two shirts. One was an oversize T-shirt. He tossed that back, along with several satin panties and a lacey bra. It didn't matter what she wore underneath her clothes. No one was going to see it.

Especially not him—a thought that hurt him worse than the pain in his ribs.

The last shirt was a tank top. He hadn't seen her wear it, but he didn't have to. He had a good imagination. Too good at times. He put the tank top in the pile.

"Those shoes you're wearing," he said. "Give one to me, will you?"

With an exasperated sigh, she slipped one of her shoes off and handed it to Harry. "Why?"

"High heel," he said. "Too high. Too sexy. You're going to want to stick to flats from now on, probably even just wear sneakers."

He moved into the left lane, rolled down his window, and tossed all of Alessandra's new clothes and her shoe out of the car.

"Oh, my God!" She spun in her seat, watching as her clothes hit the ground seventy-five miles an hour, getting caught in the brush. "Oh, my God!" She stared at him, aghast. "Why did you do that? Are you completely out of your mind?"

"You told me you want to stay alive."

"Stop this car!" She was furious. "Stop this car right now and back up and get me my clothes!"

"Can't do that. Backing up on the highway is against the law. And as a federal agent—"

She punched him. She actually hit him in the arm. "You idiot! That was everything I owned in the whole world! And you just threw it all away! Oh, God, how could you do that?"

"You couldn't have worn any of it, Al. It would've gotten you killed."

"I refuse to believe I can't wear nice clothes, that I can't just be quietly attractive—"

He raised his voice to talk above her. "Quietly attractive? Are you nuts?" He gestured to what she was wearing. "This isn't quietly attractive! This is full twenty-trumpet fanfare. Everybody look quick because here comes one of the ten most beautiful women on earth. This sets off alarms and bells and whistles. There's nothing even remotely quiet about this!"

"Okay, so maybe in your opinion, I need to tone it down a little, but—"

"No buts. No maybes."

"I tried not to go overboard with the makeup, but when I looked into the mirror, with my hair this color . . . I just couldn't stand looking so sallow." She shook her head. "It was the same thing when we went shopping. These clothes were all so cheap, I thought—"

"They don't look cheap on you."

"But—"

"What do you want, Allie? Do you want to be able to hide, to blend in with a crowd? Or do you want to keep on being the beauty queen, wearing clothes that will make people look at you? You can't have it both ways."

"You make it sound as if I'm Helen of Troy. I'm not that beautiful."

"Don't be coy. You know exactly what you look like. When you walk into a room, people turn to look at you. Men turn to look at you."

"But don't you see?" she burst out. "Being beautiful is all I've ever done. It's all I'm good at!"

Christ, she was serious. "If that's really the case, then it's definitely time for you to learn some new skills. You know, plumbers get paid a shitload—"

"Stop making this into some kind of joke!"

"You want dead serious? If you dress so that people notice you, sooner or later Trotta will find you. And if you're lucky, he'll have someone put a bullet in your head. If you're not, he'll bring you back to New York and let his dog tear you apart for an afternoon snack. How's that for dead serious?"

She had gone pale. "Now you're just trying to scare me."

"Bottom line, Al. Unless you agree that the best way for you to hide is by completely—and I mean completely—altering your appearance, I'm not taking you to Colorado. I'm not going to risk my kids getting caught in the cross fire when Trotta's men finally catch up with you. And they will catch up with you."

"I have altered my—"

"No, you haven't."

She pulled down the sun visor and flipped open the vanity mirror on the other side and looked at herself. "I look completely different with my hair this color. And I've never worn this style of clothing in my entire life!"

Again, she was serious. She actually believed she looked different enough to hide from Michael Trotta.

"Sorry." He gestured toward her again. "But this doesn't cut it. You're going to have to trust me on this one. From now on, you wear nothing tight, nothing that really fits, nothing even remotely fashionable."

"I can't believe—"

"Believe it. Think about the word hide. If you hide, no one can see you, right? You can do it by locking yourself away from the world. Or you can do it by making yourself invisible, making it so that no one gives you a second glance. Invisible. Think about what that means."

Alessandra started to speak but stopped herself. She sat silently, eyes closed and hands pressed against her forehead as the miles rolled past.

When she did speak, her voice was subdued. "There's no other option?"

"Plastic surgery." He glanced at her. "Completely change your face."

"No other viable option?"

"Not that I'm aware of, but next town we go through, we can stop and see if the library has a copy of Hiding from the Mob in Ten Easy Steps. Maybe there'll be some tip in there that I've missed."

She shot him a dark look. "Very funny."

He laughed. "Actually, it was pretty funny. George really would've liked it."

"I have no money." Her voice shook slightly, but she cleared her throat and when she spoke again, she sounded as cool as ever. "How am I supposed to buy these new ugly clothes that will render me magically invisible?"

"My treat," Harry told her. She shot him another look. "Sorry. Bad choice of expression. Look, Al, we'll be coming up on Louisville just about when the stores open. We'll find a Target or a Kmart or an Uglyland or whatever they have out here."

"Uglyland," Alessandra murmured. "That's just great."

"We'll take care of your hair, then, too."

She looked at him. "Mousy brown?"

He nodded. "Mousy brown."

She nodded, too, looking out the window so he wouldn't see that she was blinking back tears. "Do me one favor, Harry," she said. "Try to enjoy this just a little bit less."

"You have a visitor."

George opened his eyes to find the nurse standing over his bed. It was amazing. He'd survived being shot, survived surgery, survived an incredible loss of blood and all those transfusions. They finally pulled him out of ICU, giving him a permission slip to celebrate the fact that his life wasn't over yet, and what did they do?

Did they give him Felicity, the twenty-four-year-old bombshell of a nurse, just out of school, ready to be impressed by the brave and handsome FBI agent who'd been shot while on the job?

No.

No, they give him Stanley. The male nurse.

"A visitor?" George whispered. "Who?"

Stanley shrugged. "I didn't catch the name, dude." Stanley, the surfer nurse. Even better.

"Man or woman?"

"Woman," Stanley told him. "A most excellently bodacious woman."

Nicki. It had to be Nicki. He'd expected to see her when he was in ICU, expected her to push her way through the door and plant herself next to his bed.

He'd asked for her. He'd been in a haze of pain, light-headed from the loss of blood, afraid he was going to die, but he could remember asking for Nicki. He'd wanted to tell her he was sorry about everything. He'd wanted to hold on to her hand, certain that if anyone was strong enough and tough enough to pull him back from the dead, it was Nic.

But she'd never shown up. Not until now.

"Better late than never," George whispered to Stanley. "Dude."

The nurse checked the amount of painkiller going into his IV drip. "I'm going to assume that was a hearty yes."

"Yes." George closed his eyes, managing a wan smile. Nicole was finally here.

He heard Stanley leave, heard the door open and close and then open again. He heard her footsteps as she approached his bed.

"Omigod, you look awful!"

George opened his eyes.

Kim. It wasn't Nicki, it was Kim. She smiled at him tremulously. "I guess you must look pretty good considering you almost died, but . . ."

Kim. He fought the haze of stupidity caused by the painkillers. "How did you . . . ? What did you . . . ?"

She sat down next to the bed, looking oddly out of place in the sterile hospital room. She was wearing jeans and a T-shirt, but despite that, she still looked like a stripper. Her generous bustline seemed seriously disproportionate to the rest of her. Bodacious, Stan had said. He should have known.

"Your partner told me what happened," she said, "and gave me a ride up here."

His partner? "Harry?"

Kim shook her head. "Someone named Christine."

McFall. What was Chris McFall doing, giving Kim a

ride to be by his side? Chris was really tight with Nic, and . . .

And she'd probably called Nicki, who no doubt had let her know she didn't give a damn if George lived or died. And Chris, being a complete softy had brought someone here to sit by his bed.

He fought to blink back the tears that had rushed to his eyes, afraid that Kim might see, and know.

But he was too late. She did see. But she didn't know a thing. She took his hand and smiled sweetly, gently brushing his hair back from his forehead. "You really are glad to see me, aren't you?" she said. "Oh, honey, I'm so glad I came."

Eleven

ALICE PLOTKIN.

The woman in the motel-room mirror was definitely named Alice Plotkin.

Alessandra Lamont had vanished, perhaps forever, and in her place stood geeky Alice Plotkin, whose life was destined to be one bad hair day after another.

Her new bangs hung limply in her eyes. The short cut itself was exactly wrong for the shape of her face. And the color . . . There was almost no distinguishable color. Her hair was now simply drab. More mousy than brown.

Without any makeup on, she looked both older and younger. Her eyes looked naked and tired with unconcealed bags beneath them, yet the freckles on her face made her look like a fourteen-year-old.

And her clothes . . .

Nothing fit quite right. Her jeans were so baggy she had to wear a belt to hold them up. Her T-shirt was oversize. It swallowed up her breasts and hung down to her thighs, concealing the fact that she actually had a waist. It drooped off her shoulders, the short sleeves coming down past her elbows. The entire outfit—if you could even call it that—made her look skinny rather than slender, her arms and wrists bony instead of elegantly graceful.

169

The running shoes she wore weren't a name brand either. They were a hideously horrible mix of bright white and neon blue, made of plastic and fake leather.

No, Alice Plotkin would not be turning any heads in the near future. She looked like a rather unremarkable teenager.

And that had been Harry's idea. She would move into this still-nameless town in northern Colorado, pretending to be a very young woman. Gradually, over the next few years, as the people in the town came to know invisible Alice Plotkin, she would age a bit and graduate up to clothes that fit a little bit better and a haircut that actually made her look decent again. At best, she would be quietly pretty.

Alessandra sighed.

Harry was sleeping the sleep of the dead on one of the beds behind her, still wearing his jacket and baseball cap, the cap bent uncomfortably beneath his face.

He'd checked them into this room under false names, paid in cash, unlocked the door, tossed the bags with her new department-store clothes onto the dresser, and fallen facedown onto the nearest bed.

They were alone in a motel room, and Harry had fallen instantly asleep. Alessandra didn't know whether to be insulted or relieved.

She caught another glimpse of herself in the mirror as she gently pulled his cap free and set it down on the bedside table. Was it any wonder he hadn't tried to kiss her again, to reignite that fire they'd started back in the Stop and Shop nearly three whole days ago? She looked like a fourteen-year-old boy.

Not that she really wanted him to kiss her again. And, indeed, she wouldn't have kissed him again, not after the way he'd betrayed her. But she wanted him to regret the fact that he couldn't have her. She wanted him to lie awake, desperate from wanting her. She wasn't proud of that, but it was the truth. She wanted him to suffer.

But since about ten hours ago, since she'd had her "makeover," she didn't look like anything anyone would ever want. And Harry sure wasn't having trouble sleeping.

Alessandra sat down on the other bed, watching him. With his face slack, his mouth slightly open, his soulful eyes tightly closed, he shouldn't have been so good-looking. Shouldn't have been, but he was. What was it about him? He'd lied to her, nearly gotten her killed. And now he'd gone and forced her to conceal her beauty—the only thing she'd ever been 100 percent positive she had going for her.

"You bastard," she whispered.

She stared into the mirror at her reflection, and Alice Plotkin—Lord, even the name he'd given her was awful—stared expressionlessly back. Geeky and plain, unskilled and unwanted.

Completely unlovable.

But tough. Way tougher than Griffin ever imagined her to be, of that much she was certain. Tougher and stronger and smarter than Ivo and Michael Trotta—and even Harry—realized.

She may have lost everything she'd ever thought she'd cared about, but as long as her heart was still beating, as long as she could draw air into her lungs, she was winning.

She'd hit her low. Right here, right now was the absolute bottom. From now on, it could only get better.

She hoped.

"He wasn't exactly sure when he was going to arrive. He's driving out," Marge said, and Shaun looked away, carefully keeping his face expressionless.

It was stupid. He should know by now not to let his hopes rise when his aunt told him something like "Your father is coming to visit." Until Harry arrived, unless he had a plane ticket in his hand with the exact date and time of his arrival printed on it, it was more likely than not that he'd be calling back to apologize, to say that something important had come up, something he couldn't get out of.

To say that he wasn't coming.

"Do me a favor," Shaun told Marge. "Don't tell Em."

Emily was too little to temper her expectations. She would be horribly disappointed if Harry didn't show. If? Who was he kidding? When was more like it. His stomach twisted.

"He got the letter from the lawyers," Marge told him. "He's pretty upset."

Harry wasn't the only one. "Just don't tell her, all right?"

"All right." Marge sighed. "Shaun, about this custody thing . . ."

Shaun didn't want to talk about it. It made his stomach hurt too much, made him want to cry. He stood up and took his plate to the sink, rinsing it and putting it in the dishwasher. He forced a bright smile, forced it to touch his eyes, so Marge would know that he really didn't give a shit about Harry. "I've got a lot of homework."

Marge brought her own plate to the sink. "You're so much like him."

"No," Shaun said, escaping down the hall to his room. "I'm not."

Alessandra stirred, and Harry looked over to find her awake.

The early morning air was cool coming in the car windows, and she pulled her legs up under one of the enormous sweatshirts he'd bought her. Without any makeup on, her beauty was more delicate, more subtle. More. He couldn't believe it. She'd gotten the worst haircut in the world, and he now found her more attractive than ever.

He knew she didn't see it that way, though. She looked into the mirror and only saw what she was missing. As if the makeup, hair, and clothes had been the crucial elements in her beauty. It was completely absurd.

He was worried that she was still too beautiful. That too many people would still notice her. She was going to have to lose that regal manner of sitting and walking. Start ducking her head down, slouching her shoulders. Stop looking like a queen dressed down in her kid brother's clothes.

Of course, right now, the way she was sitting, she looked a lot like a gray beach ball with a head. Harry smiled. When he'd first met her, he never dreamed in a million years that he would ever describe Alessandra Lamont as a beach ball with a head.

"What's so funny?" she asked.

During the days they'd been on the road and the night they'd spent together in a motel, she'd initiated conversations maybe twice. Maybe. He'd lectured endlessly about the best ways to hide herself. She shouldn't wear perfume, especially not the scent she wore in the past. She should take care to keep her dairy allergies completely hidden, even to the point of occasionally going to the local ice-cream stand and getting a cone, throwing it out when no one was looking. She should get a job doing something completely alien to her past life. She should change her habits and her lifestyle. She should overcome her fears and get herself a dog. Something big with lots of teeth. She should take that dog everywhere she went.

She'd listened quietly, somberly agreeing to it all—except the part about getting a dog. She'd asked questions, but never personal ones, not even vaguely personal ones like "What's so funny?"

He was going to take the fact that she'd asked one now to mean she wanted to talk.

"I was thinking about George," he said. That was not entirely untrue. "He would be really proud of the way you've been sticking with your disguise."

Alessandra made a vague sound, focusing her attention on the scenery zipping past the window.

Oooh-kay. Hell, even if she didn't want to talk, he did. He was completely bored, the radio was bringing in only static, and this silent treatment thing was getting old.

"You know, I've been meaning to ask you, Al. Where'd you learn first aid? Not everyone would've known what to do when the person they were standing next to suddenly had blood pouring from a major vein."

She glanced at him. "Artery."

"Vein. Artery. Close enough."

"Arteries carry blood away from the heart. It's more life threatening to open an artery than a vein."

Harry glanced at her, but she was already staring back out the window. "So. Where'd you learn that? And if you tell me you went to medical school, I may faint. I'm not sure I can take many more surprises from you."

"Medical school?" She snorted. "Not in this lifetime."

"So where, then?"

She didn't answer right away. "I took a first-aid class in tenth grade and I really liked it, so I paid attention."

"And the fact that you liked it so much didn't make you think about studying medicine in college?"

Another pause and a long cool look. Harry watched

the road, but he could feel her studying him, as if deciding whether to answer his question.

"It never even crossed my mind," she finally said. "My mother would've been ecstatic if I'd married a doctor, but be one myself? Not a chance. But then again, I knew by the time I hit high school that I wasn't going to college. There wasn't any money. And there was no way I was getting a scholarship with my grades. They weren't really that bad, just relentlessly average."

Harry scratched the back of his hand with the three days of stubble on his chin. "I thought your father was in banking."

"That was only his day job," Alessandra told him. "In the evenings and on weekends—and probably on his lunch hour—he was a gambler. And that job didn't pay quite so well."

"Christ. I'm sorry. That must've sucked."

"Yes," she said. "It did." She laughed, but there wasn't any humor in it. "That's how I met Griffin, you know."

"What, at the racetrack?"

She gazed at him again for several long moments. "You must be really bored."

"I'm . . . interested in . . ." He took a deep breath. "The truth is, you've been handling all this shit really well, and I'm, well, curious about you. You're tougher than I thought—smarter, too. Frankly, I just don't get how someone like you got hooked up with Lamont and Trotta in the first place."

"Ah," she said. "There's that refreshing honesty again. It's very appealing, Harry, the way you put all the cards out on the table for everyone to see." Her voice hardened. "Except the last time you did that, you had an entire deck still up your sleeve. You can't blame me for wondering what you're hiding from me this time."

Alessandra was staring out the window again, her chin held self-righteously high. But it was just an act. She was working hard to hide her hurt. He could see it trembling in the corner of her mouth. It was there, too, lurking in her eyes.

I thought you were special.

"Jesus," Harry said, hating the guilt that pressed down on him. "You want complete honesty? Sweetheart, I'm more than happy to give it to you. No secrets, no tactful white lies, just the hard truth—is that really what you want?"

"Yes."

"Great," he said. "Let's see. We can start with the fact that I'm scared shitless about seeing my kids again. I don't know if Emily's going to recognize me—or worse, if I'm going to recognize her. I'm dreading talking to Marge, and I'm still worried about George. I knew a cop who was recovering nicely from a gunshot wound. One day he seemed fine. The next day he was back in the ICU with an infection. Day after, we were sitting shivah at his house. But I digress.

"When you sit that way, you look kind of like a beach ball with a head," he continued. "Your haircut is really, really bad, I'm probably going to lose my job for helping you this way, and I'm dying to fuck you."

He glanced at her. "That honest enough for you?"

Alessandra emerged from the bathroom in McDonalds to find Harry leaning against the wall, waiting for her. He straightened up, no expression on his face as he saw her, and she resisted the urge to touch her hair, to somehow try to fix the disaster that had looked back at her from the ladies' room mirror.

If she'd succeeded, it would have forever been known as the miracle of the McDonalds, because, quite frankly, nothing short of a miracle would make her look anything besides awful.

But that was the point. Looking awful was her disguise. It was her way of taking charge of her own destiny.

Some people might've gone out and bought a gun, learned to defend themselves. But Alessandra wasn't going to kid herself. No way would she ever be able to outshoot a mob hit man, even with years of training.

No, she was going to stay alive the way Harry suggested—by becoming invisible.

The biggest problem—aside from the fact that she was completely broke—was in figuring out exactly who she was now. Take away the beautiful face and hide the body, and what exactly was left?

Someone scared. Someone completely untrained to do anything useful. Someone who no longer knew how to communicate with other people.

Back when she was Alessandra, she knew how to respond to a statement such as "I'm dying to fuck you." While it was rarely said quite so bluntly, it was a message that she'd received more often than not, usually intimated with body language and subtle looks. As Alessandra, she might have dismissed it with little more than a pointed look. Or, she might've subtly flirted back, if there was something she wanted or needed.

But as Alice Plotkin, she simply did not know how to respond. First of all, she was uncertain how to read the statement. Did Harry actually mean what he said, or was there another underlying message? Did he mean "Wow, you are so completely unattractive, no other man could possibly be interested in you, so I'll take advantage of you by pretending to desire you. And maybe I'll get lucky and get laid while having a big laugh at your expense?"

Or did he mean "I'll tell you this to make you feel better because, even though it's not completely true, you don't repulse me, and if we do end up having sex, I'll just make sure all the lights are off."

"Look, Allie, I didn't mean to freak you out or anything," Harry said. "I mean, by saying what I said back in the car . . ."

Alessandra realized that she had blindly followed him and they were standing on one of the lines, waiting to order their daily indigestion. She had been staring sightlessly up at the menu.

"It's just . . . You wanted honesty," he continued, "and I . . ." He shrugged. "I took it a little too far, as usual. Some things probably just shouldn't be said."

"I don't know how to do this," Alessandra admitted. "Talking to men was easy when I was beautiful. But now . . ."

Harry was looking at her, studying her very naked, very plain face, his dark brown eyes so intense. It was as if the crowd around them had ceased to exist, as if they were the only two people standing in that fast-food lobby. He touched her hair, pushing a limp lock back behind her ear.

"The haircut really sucks," he told her.

She closed her eyes. "Yes, I believe you mentioned that once already today."

"But it's just hair."

"Spoken by the reigning king of bad hair days." She reached up and took off his baseball cap. His hair, as usual, was standing up in all directions.

He shrugged. "Maybe we should just get matching Mohawks."

Alessandra had to laugh.

He touched her again, his fingers warm and slightly rough against her cheek. "You're still beautiful," he said softly. "Too beautiful. It scares me, 'cause if someone looks at you too closely . . ." He shook his head.

And again, Alessandra didn't know how to respond. "And you're saying this," she finally said, "because you're dying to fuck me?"

Harry shouted with laughter. "Oh man," he gasped. "I have got to watch my mouth. If I have you saying the f-word, I must be using it far too often."

"I can't figure out what you want."

"Well, if you do figure it out, tell me. I'd love to find out myself."

"Friends," Alessandra said about a hundred miles west of the Mickey Ds where they'd stopped to get lunch. She turned to face him as he drove. "That's what I want, Harry. I want us to be friends."

Harry glanced at her. She was looking at him so intently, her face so serious—as if she were afraid he'd tell her no, no he didn't want to be her friend. "I thought, you know, that was kind of what we are. I mean, aside from the fact you still haven't forgiven me for using you as bait to catch Trotta."

She nodded, still so serious. "I'll forgive you, if you promise it won't happen again. Ever."

He held out his hand. "Deal."

She tentatively slipped her fingers into his, barely even shaking his hand before she pulled hers free.

She took a deep breath. "About what you said before," she started.

Harry knew exactly what she was talking about. "Al, I was way out of line. I'm really sorry if I made you uncomfortable."

"It would just be a lot easier for me right now, if we didn't make this too confusing. I'd like to—"

"I'm a grown-up," Harry told her. "You don't have to worry, I can—"

"Keep sex out of the picture."

"Keep my pants zipped."

"Good," she said.

"Good," he said, trying to find one single reason why the complete absence of sex in their relationship was, indeed, a good thing. Because Allie wanted it that way was the best he could come up with. And oddly enough, that was a good enough reason.

George swore softly and switched off the TV in disgust. "Figures the one week I'm in the hospital is the week before the baseball season starts. There's nothing on but stupid talk shows and dirt-bike racing. If I wanted to watch thirteen-year-olds ride dirt bikes, I'd have had a family of my own."

Kim looked up from the magazine she was flipping through. "Poor baby, you're bored."

"Bored and cranky and dying for a cigarette." He'd been weaned almost entirely from the pain medicine that had made him float comfortably above both the bed and his body. His leg alternately ached and stung. He was sick of hospital food and completely worn out by Stan coming in all hours of the night to take his blood pressure and check his bandage. Dude.

"Poor George." Kim put down her magazine and leaned forward, giving him a sympathetic smile and unobstructed view down the front of her blouse.

George felt a flash of guilt. She'd been nothing but sweet to him, spending every minute of the allotted visitors' hours by his side for three days straight. She'd gotten a motel room near the hospital, paying a price she probably couldn't afford just to be near him. And yet every time he looked at her, he wished she were Nicki.

Nicki—who didn't even care enough to call him on the phone.

"I know what I like to do when I'm bored," Kim told

him with a devilish smile. She pulled her chair closer, slipped her hand beneath the light cotton spread that covered him.

"Um," George said. Her fingers were cool against his thigh. He reached down to catch her hand before she found the edge of his hospital gown. "These doors don't have locks."

"So?"

"So these doors don't have locks."

"That makes it more exciting," she whispered. "Just think, we could be walked in on any minute."

"My point exactly."

"That wouldn't be boring."

"That's a good point, as well, but it's just . . . perhaps a little too nonboring for me."

Kim stood up and pulled the curtain around the bed. "How's that?"

She was serious. George laughed. "Kim! God, this is crazy."

"So I'm a little crazy. I thought you knew that about me already."

She sat down, this time on the edge of his bed. She pulled aside the blanket, careful of his injured leg.

"Kim . . ."

"You're not really going to tell me to stop, are you?" She leaned forward to kiss him, softly, lingeringly on his mouth, as she slowly pulled up his hospital gown.

She kissed him again. On the chin. On the throat. On the chest. On his stomach. She smiled up at him before she lowered her head once more.

George drew in a breath and closed his eyes. Kim had been right about one thing. He was definitely no longer bored.

*   *   *

Nicole went into the hospital, trepidation churning in her stomach.

George was going to live. She knew that. According to his doctors, he was doing remarkably well, healing nicely, no signs of infection, prognosis positive.

Still, she knew until she walked into his room, until she looked into his eyes and saw for herself that he really was okay, she wasn't going to be able to concentrate.

The past few days had been awful. It had taken her five times longer than usual to accomplish the mundane little tasks she had to get done. During her meetings in D.C., her concentration had been way off. Her mind had been several hundred miles north, in upstate New York.

Nicole forced herself not to pace as she got onto the elevator that would take her up to George's floor.

"Are you telling me that Griffin first came to your house as some kind of knee breaker?" Harry was eating Chee•tos from the bag, and the tips of his fingers were bright orange. "Christ, would you look at this? Forget dye packs. They should just throw these things in with the money during a bank heist. I'm marked for life."

"He wasn't exactly a knee breaker," Alessandra gave him a crooked smile. "More like, you know, a ball breaker."

"Griffin?" He shook his head. "I still can't see it."

"He was working for a law firm that assisted some of their clients in debt collection. When I first met him—I was still in high school—he was delivering papers for my father to sign, some kind of application for a second mortgage. The interest rate was a joke, it was so high, but it would pay off the people who wanted to break his knees. My father didn't have to sign, but if he didn't, the next man who came to the door would be carrying a baseball bat instead of a briefcase."

Harry looked almost as bad as she did. His chin was covered with more than stubble but far less than a beard, and his eyes were bloodshot. It had been more than twenty-four hours since they'd made their only motel stop, and while Alessandra had slept off and on since then, Harry hadn't. As they drew nearer to Colorado, she wondered if he intended to drive straight through.

"So Griffin set up a second mortgage," Harry guessed, "probably taking a percentage from both the mortgage company and the bookie, and ended up dating and then marrying the poor bastard's underage daughter. What a deal."

"Actually, my father didn't get the mortgage."

Harry glanced up from the road. "He didn't?"

"And Griffin didn't even ask me out until I was eighteen, even though I knew he wanted to. He was infatuated with me." She sighed. "At least he was at the start."

"We don't have to talk about this, if you don't want."

She looked over into Harry's eyes. "Really," he added. "If it's going to make you feel bad, let's not go there."

For a man whose default mode was irreverent humor, he could be remarkably sensitive, uncharacteristically gentle.

"There's not that much to tell," she told him. "Griffin paid off my father's debt. He signed me up for elocution lessons, enrolled me in a finishing school—"

"A finishing school?" Harry laughed. "God, I didn't know they still had those. You must've been bored out of your mind."

"I was flattered by Griffin's attention. He clearly thought highly of me."

"He was turning you into his little creation," Harry countered. "Pouring you into the trophy-wife mold."

"I didn't mind. At least not at the time. The day I

turned eighteen, Griffin took me to dinner and asked me to marry him."

"Did you, like . . ." He started again. "Did you have to marry him? I mean, Christ, the pressure had to be intense, if he'd spent all that money on you and your family."

"No," she said quickly. "No, I wanted to. I really did." At least that's what she'd managed to convince herself. "He was everything my mother had been telling me—for years—that I'd wanted. You hear something often enough, Harry, and you believe it. I'd been hearing that the only way I would get ahead in life was to use my looks. Marry a wealthy man. Be a perfect wife so he wouldn't ditch me when I got older. I wasn't smart enough to do anything else—I heard that enough times, too."

"You know now that they were wrong, right?" Harry asked. "You're one of the smartest people I know. You spend all your time reading. I've never met anyone who can read as fast as you."

Alessandra smiled. "It's funny how good that makes me feel—you know, hearing you say that. When I was in high school, if a teacher complimented me on a project that I'd done well, I was like 'Whatever, but hey, what do you think of this new color eyeshadow I'm wearing?' " She laughed. "I was stupid—because I didn't realize that I had other options, other choices. It never even occurred to me to go for this creative writing class at school, even though I loved to write—because only the kids who had straight As got into it. So I didn't even try. It never occurred to me to say, 'Wait, I don't want to marry Griffin,' not because I had anything against Griffin, but because I didn't want to get married. I'd just always assumed I would get married—I didn't think I had a choice about that. And he seemed so perfect—handsome, rich, connected . . . And I really did think I loved him. Of course, I was a child."

"He was so much older than you. That didn't bother you?"

"Not until later, until I realized that our entire relationship was built on him telling me what to do, and my doing it without question. I married him when I was nineteen, thinking that would instantly make me a real adult. After all, there I was. A married woman. But all it really did was extend my childhood another seven years. I made virtually no decisions during our marriage. I had no say in our life."

She sighed again. She'd tried so hard to make her marriage work—to the point that she'd neglected her own personal needs. "But back when I was eighteen, Griffin was my personal Prince Charming. He was so handsome and high-class, and he had money and a great job—or so I thought. I honestly didn't realize who he was working for, Harry." She corrected herself. "At least not at first."

"But eventually you knew."

"Yes," she said. "Eventually I knew."

Yet you didn't leave him. Harry didn't say the words aloud, but Alessandra heard them anyway.

"I loved him," she said quietly. "But you know what, Harry? He didn't love me. He just liked owning me, and when I turned out to be defective, he got rid of me."

"He was nuts." The tone of Harry's voice left no room for argument. "I mean, look at what he did. He makes bad investments left and right, and loses all of his liquid assets. He could have sold that mausoleum you called home and reduced his expenses, but instead, he keeps investing, and keeps losing his shirt. So what does he do next? What's the solution he comes to, financial genius that he is? He steals a million dollars from Michael Trotta. Now, not only is that biting the hand that feeds you, but it's also fucking insane. Is it any surprise that he would dump you? No. Because the man definitely had a screw loose."

"Our marriage hadn't been working for years," Alessandra told him. "If he hadn't left me, I would've left him. Not right away. But I like to think that, eventually, I would've been strong enough to walk away from him. But I wasn't ready to give up on him yet. I don't know, maybe I was scared. Or maybe I was just making another mistake, hanging on when there was no hope. Maybe I never should have let myself love him in the first place."

"You can't choose who you love or how much you love them. I learned that the hard way."

"With your ex-wife?"

"No." Harry moved into the right lane. "Look, let's stop and get something to eat that won't dye my intestines neon orange."

"No fair. After I told you about Griffin . . . ? You can't end the conversation just when it's getting interesting to me."

"Wanna bet?" He pulled the car onto the exit ramp, heading into the parking lot of another in a relentless string of McDonalds. "I need coffee. I'm starting to see double." He parked and turned to look at her. "You want to take a turn driving?"

Alessandra was surprised. "Do you trust me?"

He reached across her to open the glove compartment and take out his wallet. "Would I have asked you, if I didn't trust you?"

"No."

"No is correct." He handed her a ten-dollar bill. "The winner gets to buy the coffee, while the loser in the base-ball cap calls New York to check up on George."

"Harry. How can we really be friends, if you won't talk about yourself?"

Harry climbed out of the car. "How can I talk about myself when I'm so worried about poor George, lying in that hospital bed, probably in terrible pain . . . ?" He closed the door but then opened it right away. "Hey, get me one of those apple pie things, too, will you?"

Nicole took a deep breath outside George's room. She could hear the phone ringing inside. One ring, then two. Then three. And four.

If he was asleep, the phone surely would've woken him.

A nurse was breezing past, carrying a tray of medicine down the hall. She slowed. "Can I help you?"

The phone rang again.

"I'm here to see George Faulkner," Nicole said. "Is he out having tests or something?"

"No, he's in his room. You can just go on in."

The phone finally stopped ringing as Nicole opened the door, but the room was quiet. It was a double, but the first bed was empty. "Hello?"

There was a flurry of furtive movement from behind a thin curtain pulled around the bed on the far side of the room. Was the doctor back there? Or a nurse, changing his bandage? "George?"

A dark-haired woman emerged from behind the curtain, straightening her shirt and fixing her hair. "Gee, is it time for George's sponge bath already?" she asked.

The woman wasn't a doctor or nurse. Not even close. She was Kim. The stripper. Nicole's evil twin.

Kim was actually wearing a leopard-print blouse. Nicole didn't think she'd ever seen one outside of a cheap bar or nightclub. The thin fabric stretched tight across the woman's incredibly generous breasts, leaving little to the imagination. Her pants were so tight they might've been tattooed on, and her shoes had high, spiked heels. Fuck-me shoes, George used to call them.

How appropriate.

Nicole walked by her without a single word and pushed past the curtain. And there was George, sitting up in a hospital bed, intravenous tube still running into his arm, dressed in a hospital gown, a blanket pulled loosely up to his waist. His lean face was clean shaven, but his hair was uncharacteristically rumpled and perspiration beaded on his forehead and aristocratic upper lip.

It was so obvious what he and Miss Blow Job had been doing.

As Nicole watched, the stripper took her purse from the windowsill and reapplied her lipstick.

Nicole silently cursed herself for not expecting this, for letting herself stupidly fantasize that George would be waiting for her visit, that he would be glad to see her. She cursed herself for walking into a situation in which he'd managed to hurt her. Again.

"Well," she said. Years of practice hiding her emotions made her voice sound matter-of-fact. "Looks like you're feeling better."

He was honestly surprised to see her. Surprised, and dreadfully chagrined. He sat awkwardly, trying to hide the obvious physical evidence that she'd walked in on him being serviced, so to speak, in his hospital room, of all places. "Nicki. God, I wasn't expecting you."

"Obviously not."

Behind her, Kim cleared her throat.

George looked even more embarrassed. "Oh," he said. "Yes. Nic, this is Kim Monahan. Kim, Nicole Fenster. Nicki's my—"

"Boss," she interjected. "I'm George's boss." There was no way in hell she was going to give Suction Lips the satisfaction of knowing she was George's ex-wife.

"Nice to meet you." Kim stepped closer, starting to

hold out her hand, but Nicole backed away, turning to look at George.

She had no intention of shaking the other woman's hand. She knew only too well where it had recently been.

"What are you doing here?" George asked.

"I need to know where the hell Harry is." Thank God she had a good excuse. She turned to Kim. "You'll excuse us . . . ?"

"If I have to."

"I'm afraid you have to," Nicole told her as sweetly as she could manage.

Kim took her time getting her purse. She crossed to George and kissed him full on the mouth.

From the window, Nicole could see the interstate in the distance, all the tiny cars rushing past.

"Don't worry, honey, I'll be back," she heard Kim whisper.

And then Kim was gone, the door closing tightly behind her.

George's hand was shaking as he discreetly tried to wipe away a bead of sweat rolling down the side of his face.

"That physical therapy sure can be tough," Nicole said tartly.

"Look, Nic, I'm sorry, but I don't know where Harry is," George said quietly.

"He's your partner, George. Give a guess."

"I think—I don't know this for sure—that he went to see his kids. He was having some kind of hassle with them."

"Would he have taken Alessandra Lamont with him?" she asked. "Was there something going on between them?"

"No. I think she wanted to start something, but Harry

wouldn't let it happen. I don't know what was wrong with him. I know he liked her, though."

"I'll need you to give him a call."

"I don't have his phone number," George told her. "You don't have it either—it's not in his personnel file. He's a little paranoid about letting anyone know where his kids are."

"Someone must know."

"No, Nic, he's been really careful about this. Even when he calls them on the phone, he's got this special coded number that he uses. It bounces his call all over the place, makes it impossible to trace where he's calling or where he's calling from. I think it costs him about a million dollars a minute, but he says it's worth it. Jesus, I wish they would let me smoke."

"So we can't reach him." Nicole started to pace. "Shit."

George shifted painfully in the bed. "What's going on?"

"We need to find Alessandra Lamont," she told him. "An informant came in yesterday and told us the price on Mrs. Lamont's pretty head has gone up. Significantly. It's over two million dollars now."

"For her husband's one-million-dollar theft—which was paid back in full?" He gave a low whistle. "That doesn't sound right."

She stopped at the foot of his bed. "Yeah. There's something else going on here that we don't know about. This one's personal—and it rings of desperation. We can't let this opportunity get away from us. If Trotta's desperate, he'll make mistakes."

"So you think if we can set up Alessandra again, this time we'll get Trotta."

"It's worth a try." She started pacing again. "If Harry calls you, just find out where he is. I don't want him to know what's going on. If he has gotten involved with Mrs. Lamont . . ."

"Maybe it would be better to let Alessandra go," George said. "Just let her disappear."

"You don't think Trotta's going to 'just let her disappear,' do you?"

He sighed. "No."

He was watching her, his face serious, his light brown eyes somber. He looked good with his hair messed. He looked good sitting up in bed, with life in his eyes—much better than he would have looked laid out in a coffin. And Nicole knew in a flash of bitter realization that she'd far rather him be alive and having sex with someone else, than dead.

"I'm glad you're all right." She had to work hard to keep emotion from filling her voice.

His voice was husky. "Nic, I was hoping you'd come." His eyes were warm—too warm. As if he actually gave a damn. As if he hadn't been the one who'd left her. And as if the son of a bitch hadn't had his penis in someone else's mouth just a few minutes ago.

"Too bad I didn't wait ten minutes, though, so that you could've come first." She gave him her iciest smile as she breezed toward the door without even saying good-bye.

"Hey, I thought you were going to let me drive?"

Harry looked out of the window at Alessandra, who was standing next to the car, holding two large coffees. Her smile faded as she caught sight of his face.

"Oh, no," she said. "Is George . . . ?"

He reached through the open window and took the hot cups from her, placing them in the car's cup holders. "I didn't get through to George."

"Then . . . ?"

"Get in, okay?"

She crossed around the front of the car and climbed in the passenger's side, shutting the door behind her. Her eyes were about as big as he'd ever seen them, her mouth tight with anxiety. "What's the bad news, Harry? Just tell me."

Harry couldn't think of a single way to make it any easier for her to hear what he was going to say, so he just said it. "Baby Jane Doe's been adopted, Al."

She laughed. "Oh, my God!" She closed her eyes, and pressed her hand to her throat. "I was so sure you were going to tell me that she had died. But adopted . . . That's . . ." Tears sprang into her beautiful eyes. "That's good news." Her lower lip began to tremble. "Who got her? Do you know? Did they tell you?"

"They wouldn't give me a name, but the nurse I spoke to said they seemed very nice."

"I'm—I'm so glad." She was fighting her tears with such intense effort. Every muscle in her body was straining. Her shoulders were so tight that Harry's neck hurt.

He reached for her. "Al—"

"Don't!"

He put his hands on the steering wheel instead. "You know, Allie, it's okay for you to feel sad about this. I know how much you wanted her for yourself."

"Yeah," she said, her voice shaking. "As if I was ever going to be able to get her."

"I'm sorry."

"Yeah," she said again, looking away from him. "I know." She stared out the window, still blinking back her tears. "Do you mind if I don't drive right now?"

He wanted to hold her so badly his teeth hurt. "No, I don't mind."

Alessandra nodded. "Great."

Harry turned the key and started the car. He backed

out of the parking spot and drove out of the lot. Within forty-five seconds they were back on the highway.

He kicked it up to seventy, kept his eyes on the road, and pretended not to see that Allie's tears had won, that she was silently crying as she sat, turned away from him.

He ached to hold her, but she'd made it clear she didn't want that kind of comfort from him.

And that was a shame, because right about now he could have really used a hug, too.

Twelve

SHAUN OPENED THE front door, expecting the postal carrier or a UPS delivery, expecting anyone in the world besides Mindy MacGregor.

But it was. Mindy the Mountain, larger than life, standing on his front porch for the entire eighth-grade class to see.

She smiled. "Hi. Do you want to go over to the park, shoot some baskets?"

Mindy was forever determined to put her height to good use. She played basketball every day, even when it rained. She didn't seem to notice that no matter how often she practiced, she wasn't getting any better. She was way too clumsy and slow.

"I have a couple dollars," she added. "We could ride over to the 7-Eleven and get an ice cream after."

She smiled again, a little less certainly this time, and Shaun realized he was staring. He was standing there with his mouth all but hanging open, in complete shock.

He'd been nice to Mindy over the past few days. He'd run into her in the library and, in the back corner, where no one could see them, he had helped her sign on to the Internet to look up information on Civil War re-enactments of the Battle of Gettysburg. She knew barely nothing about the Net, and he'd taken time to explain search engines and Web sites. They'd talked about music, about his dancing, too.

He'd told her about the red-haired girl he'd met in California, making it sound as if she were his girlfriend. He'd even given her a name. Lisa. He talked about Lisa as if they were practically engaged.

He thought that would be that, but today she'd sought him out after chorus, lending him a CD of some a cappella group she thought he'd like. He hadn't even looked at the CD, let alone listened to it. He'd just stuffed it into his backpack and fled the scene.

But she'd followed him home.

She was standing on his front porch, her bike parked by the gate.

For all the world to see.

It was obvious she thought he was as lonely and pathetic and as desperate for a friend as she was. But he wasn't. He wasn't like Mindy. He didn't need any friends. He didn't want any friends. And he especially didn't want any friends like Mindy MacGregor, God help him.

"Grab your bike," she said. "Or we can walk, if you want . . ."

Now that she knew he wasn't potential boyfriend material, she was far more relaxed, more confident. That was good, but he wished she'd go be more confident somewhere else.

"I, uh," he said. "I'm sorry, I, uh . . . can't." Quick, think of a good reason. "I've got, um, homework and . . . and my father is coming to visit, so I have to clean my room." Brilliant. Sheer genius. A parental visit was an undeniable bona fide excuse.

She smiled again but with far less confidence now. "Well, I don't mind helping you clean your room. They say two heads are better than one. And when cleaning, four hands are better than two, right? Besides, I'm great at cleaning. My mom owns Merry Maids. I help her out all the time when her regular staff calls in sick."

If she came inside, her bike would be out front for anyone passing by to see. All it would take was Ricky or Josh or any of their asshole friends, and by tomorrow morning the entire school would know Mindy the Mountain had spent the afternoon at the Leprechaun's house.

God.

But if he turned down an offer for help, she'd know the cleaning thing was only an excuse, and her feelings would be hurt.

"Maybe." He cleared his throat. "Maybe you could put your bike in the back, behind the garage. Marge—my aunt—doesn't like it when we leave bikes out front."

Mindy turned around, and there was Emily's tricycle, right next to her ten-speed. And when she looked back at Shaun, he could tell from her big magnified eyes that she knew the reason he wanted her bike to go in the back had nothing to do with Marge. She knew why he didn't want to shoot hoops with her, too.

He didn't want to be seen with her. He didn't want anyone to know they were friends.

The flare of hurt in her eyes made him feel sick to his stomach. God, he was no better than Ricky or Josh.

No, he was worse. Ricky and Josh hadn't given her false hope by being nice to her, the way he had.

"I don't mind moving my bike," she said. She arranged her mouth into an empty smile. "I'll, um, meet you at the back door, okay?"

Now Shaun felt even worse. She knew the truth, but she was so eager for a friend, she was willing to be treated like shit. She should have punched him in the face, stomped him into the ground, and spit on his bloody remains, screaming her rage. Instead she silently moved her bike.

As she rounded the corner of the house he wanted to call to her, to tell her to wait, tell her it was okay to leave her bike out front. What the hell did he care what anyone thought? But he could see Andy Horton coming down the street on his Rollerblades, and he closed the door instead, praying that Mindy move her big butt a little faster.

And completely hating himself.

He was a complete coward, a total loser. No wonder his dad hated coming to see him.

"Tell me about your kids."

Alessandra drove with both hands on the wheel, just a little bit slower than Harry liked. He kept glancing behind them to see what was keeping her from pulling into the fast lane. There were never any cars there.

Her eyes were still bruised and tired-looking from her tears, her nose still faintly red, despite the fact that she'd slept for at least an hour after she'd cried herself out.

"You drive too slowly," he told her.

"Don't change the subject."

"Speed up. You're making me nuts."

"I will if you tell me about your kids."

Harry sighed. "All right. Jesus. Shaun's in eighth grade. He looks like his mother. Emily's in her second year of nursery school. She looks like me, poor thing, kind of dark and short."

Alessandra glanced at him. "You're not short."

"According to George I am. It's okay—I don't mind. You know what they say about short men?"

"No, and I don't want to know because it's going to be rude, isn't it?" She rolled her eyes. "But probably funny. Okay, tell me. What do they say about short men?"

"Got me. Damn, I was hoping you'd know."

Alessandra laughed. He loved making her laugh. It was a particularly nice victory now, since she was still so sad about Jane's adoption.

"I thought you were going to drive faster," he said. "Although I better warn you, the engine's souped up. If you don't pay attention, you'll be pushing ninety miles an hour before you know it."

"Thanks for the hot tip. But I thought you were going to tell me about your kids."

"Do you have to practice being so annoying," Harry asked, "or is it something that comes naturally?"

"It's a well-thought-out part of my cover. Alice Plotkin is definitely annoying. God knows she annoys me, it's only fair she should annoy you, too." She glanced at him again. "That's why I've decided to talk like this from now on," she added in a high-pitched squeaky, ear-jarring voice.

"Knock it off. You're not supposed to be the funny one. I'm the funny one."

"I'm not trying to be funny," she said in that same awful voice. "I'm just trying to be thorough, to completely be Alice Plotkin in every possible way."

"Stop," Harry said. "Dear Lord, help me. I feel like Dr. Frankenstein—'Oh, God, what have I created?' "

She was laughing again, and Harry realized with a jolt that he was having a good time. He was driving cross-country and enjoying himself. A completely impossible paradox.

He liked her. It was wild—he actually liked Mrs. Griffin Lamont. She was more than he'd thought. Far more. In fact, he couldn't remember the last time he'd been so wrong in his first impression of a woman.

Her world had ended. Her life had virtually been stolen from her. And yet she was moving ahead. She refused to be caught in the pain or mired in the complete unfairness of it all.

"Tell me about your children," she said in her normal voice. "We're getting close, I want to know what to expect."

Harry shrugged. "I'm not exactly sure what you want to know about them."

She chewed on her lower lip. She had beautiful lips, so full and gracefully shaped.

No sex. No thinking about sex. No thinking about gently capturing that lip with his own teeth and . . . Harry turned away, digging through the glove compartment for the map.

"Well," she said slowly. "What do they like to do? What kind of personalities do they have? Start with basics. Then we can move to the tougher issues. Like how have they dealt with the tragedy of losing first their mother and Kevin, and then you?"

Harry bristled. "They haven't lost me."

She didn't say anything, she just glanced at him.

"Okay," he said defensively. "So I haven't exactly been around, but it's not like I'm dead. It's not like I'm never coming back."

She still didn't say anything, so he went back to the easier questions. What do they like to do? He wasn't sure. Not anymore.

"Shaun's kind of quiet," he said, thinking aloud. "He always liked to read—in fact, he'd rather read. Kev and I used to be out in the yard, throwing a ball around, and Shaun would just sit on the deck with a book. He was a pretty good baseball player. I coached his Little League team a few years ago. He's really fast, but not much of a hitter, unfortunately. A good bunter, though, because of his speed."

"Does he still play?"

"I don't know," Harry admitted. "When I spoke to Marge last, she said he got one of the leads in the school musical." He laughed. "That completely blew me away— I had no idea the kid could sing. He was always so quiet. I mean, what's a shy kid like that doing up onstage? I was sorry I missed it."

She looked at him again. She didn't say a word, but he knew what she was thinking. His kid had a lead in the school musical, and he'd missed it? What kind of father was he?

A shitty one. There was no doubt about that.

"Quiet people aren't always shy. They might just be quiet because they can't get a word in edgewise," Alessandra said. "I had this great-uncle—he was about six and a half feet tall, and he was the biggest, loudest, funniest man I'd ever met. And he had this little tiny bird of a wife, Aunt Fran, who just kind of sat off to the side and smiled, never saying much of anything. She spent one Christmas at our house, a few years after Uncle Henry had died, and I remember being so surprised when I talked to her, because she was even funnier than my uncle had been. It was just when he was around, he took up so much space, she never felt the need to speak up."

"You think Shaun was quiet because both Kev and I were always so loud?" Harry shook his head, answering his own question. "Yes. Em was loud, too. She was only two, but I used to call her 'the Mouth.' She was like this little fierce space alien who was either scowling or laughing, nothing in between, and . . ." His stomach hurt. "I hate talking about this."

"You hate talking about your children?"

"No, I mean, talking about what it was like . . . before. Jesus. You know, I busted my ass to make the divorce be okay, to make us all be okay, to still be a family even though me and Sonya weren't together. We made it through some really bad shit and I remember thinking just days before . . . that the worst was behind us. But then I got the call to come ID the bodies and . . . Can we talk about something else?"

"That must've been so hard for you. I can't imagine losing a child. And Kevin was your favorite."

"What, is Alice Plotkin suddenly a psychoanalyst now, too? Let's just drop this, all right? Besides, parents aren't supposed to have favorites." He made a lot of noise unfolding the map. But even that didn't erase the fact that she was right. Kev had been his favorite, it was pretty damn obvious.

Harry had pretended that their bond had been special because Kev was the oldest, but it had been more than that. They had had the same sense of humor, the same love of the absurd, the same likes and dislikes. They'd both tried to include Shaun in the things they'd done together, but even though he tagged along, he always was just a little too young, a little too outside their loop.

It was so damn hard to face Shaun, because the kid had to have known Kev was Harry's favorite. He had to have known Kevin's death affected Harry in ways his own death never would have. And the guilt of that was almost too much for Harry to take.

"What was he like?" Allie asked. "Kevin, I mean. Do you ever get a chance to talk about him anymore?"

Harry shook his head. No. He tried not even to mention Kevin's name. It hurt too much. "You want to tell me about Jane?"

She glanced at him again. "I'd love to. She was barely a week old when I first met her. Her mother left the hospital a few hours after she was born and never came back. For the first two months, it was touch and go daily as to whether she'd survive. But then she started to get stronger, and I'd stop in the nursery and hold her, give her a bottle.

"Let's see. She has brown hair and brown eyes, and the kind of smile that makes you feel so good. I mean, she would just look at me as if I were the most wonderful person in the world." She paused. "I would have given anything to be able to take her home with me."

She glanced at him again. See? She could talk about Jane.

"Yeah, well, at least Jane's still alive," Harry said defensively. He regretted the words as soon as they were out of his mouth. It sounded as if he were saying "My pain is more valid than yours." And that wasn't what he'd meant. "I'm sorry," he said quickly. "I'm—"

"I kind of picture Kevin as a smaller version of you," Allie said, giving him a chance to redeem himself.

He took a deep breath. "No," he said. "No, he didn't really look like me. He had hair that was kind of the color yours is now. He wasn't a particularly good-looking kid. It was like he got the worst of both me and Sonya. My nose. Her chin. What a mess. But he was always smiling, and when he smiled, his face suddenly made sense. Then he was beautiful. He was one of those people who always saw the glass as half full, you know? An optimist."

God, now that he was talking, he couldn't seem to shut up. "He was an amazing athlete, too. He had this incredible pitching arm. He was a fourteen-year-old kid, and I was already dreaming of the majors. I mean, I wasn't like one of those psycho Little League dads, foaming at the mouth and calling in the recruiters, but when I let myself have my little fantasies, I could picture him playing for the Mets." Harry laughed. "He'd always been small for his age, but he was starting to grow, doing that awkward, gangly thing with his arms and legs. He was at that point when he was turning from a kid into a teenager, you know? His face wasn't a little boy's face anymore. You could start to see glimpses of the man he was going to become, and . . ." His voice shook. "Jesus, just like that he was dead."

Alessandra let the silence surround them, let him have a few long minutes to grieve and then regain his composure before she spoke. "He sounds as if he were the type of person who would be upset at the thought of you wasting the rest of your life, trying to get revenge."

Harry stared at her as if she'd just announced her intention to join a satanic cult.

"Don't look at me like that," Alessandra chastised him. "I bet you've never stopped to consider that, have you? The fact that Kevin would hate knowing you're obsessed with avenging his death to the point where you no longer have a life of your own?"

"Excuse me," Harry said. "Did I ask for your opinion? I somehow missed the part where I asked for your opinion."

"Are you going to give custody of Shaun and Emily to your stepsister?" she asked.

"Ah, Christ," he said. "How the hell did you . . . ?" He answered his own question. "George told you. I'm going to fucking kill him."

"They're the ones who need you, Harry. I know you probably don't want to hear this, but Kevin doesn't need you anymore."

He turned away, staring out the window the way she had done just hours before. After several long minutes of grim silence, Alessandra switched on the radio. She'd obviously said more than enough.

*   *   *

George turned on the light and reached for his cigarettes and the book on his bedside table. He tried not to disturb Kim, but she stirred.

"Can I get you something, baby?" she asked sleepily. "Are you hurting again?"

There was no "again." He was hurting, period. It made sense that his leg would hurt. After all, someone had put a hole in it. He simply hadn't anticipated it hurting so much, for such a long time, even now, after he was home from the hospital.

Still, there was nothing Kim could do.

"It's not time for another pill." He lit a cigarette and took a long drag, turning his head to blow the smoke away from her. "Why don't you go back to sleep? I'm going to read for awhile—as long as the light doesn't bother you?"

Kim raised herself up on one elbow, and the sheet fell away from her perfect, full breasts. "If you want, I could score you something stronger than that lousy prescription the doctor gave you."

"Excuse me, have you forgotten you're talking to a federal agent? I didn't just hear that." He reached for his ashtray.

"They should've at least given you Percodan."

"I don't need drugs. And especially not any illegal ones, thanks."

The window in his bedroom was open, and the night air was cool. As George watched, her body responded to the cold, her nipples tightening to rigid peaks.

She slowly pulled the sheet down even farther, giving him an unobstructed view. "Or we could try the . . . What did they call it on that infomercial? 'The holistic approach to controlling pain'?"

She reached for him, but he caught her wrist with one

hand and lifted her face back to eye level. "You know, it would be okay if we just talk."

She looked completely confused. "Talk?"

"Don't get me wrong," George told her. "I like it a lot, but everything we do doesn't have to be a lead-in to sex. In fact, it's killed a little bit of the anticipation, if you know what I mean."

She didn't know what he meant. "You don't like it when I go down on you?"

Now that was something no man would probably say he didn't like. "No, Kim, I just said I like it a lot. A whole lot."

"I do, too."

George laughed. "Well, that's good. I hope so. I mean, I figured you did, because why else would you do it, right?"

Kim looked away.

Well, wasn't that interesting?

"Have you noticed that except for once or twice early in our relationship, we've rarely had actual sex—you know, sexual intercourse? We always have oral sex, and I'm never on the giving end. I touch you, you pull away, and then you distract the hell out of me." He watched her closely. "Don't you think that's a little unfair?"

She still wasn't meeting his eyes. "Since you've been injured, it seems less likely I'll hurt you if . . ." She stopped herself and shrugged. "Honestly? I like it better."

"You like the fact that you've given me about four hundred orgasms, and I've given you only two?"

"You want to go down on me?" The way she said it, it sounded about as appealing an idea to her as torture.

"Right now, I want to talk."

Her face brightened. "If you want, you could talk, and I could—"

"I have to admit, it's completely outside my realm of

experience, turning down an offer like that," he said, not wanting to hear exactly what it was she could do while he talked. She was unusually creative when it came to oral sex, and he was already more than half aroused. Still, he knew next to nothing about this woman who had all but moved into his apartment.

"But it's nearly midnight," he continued. He put out his cigarette butt in the ashtray and set it back on the bedside table. "My leg aches like a bitch, and I just want to lie here with my arms around you and talk for a while. May we do that, please?"

Kim's brown eyes were enormous in her face. Silently, she slipped into the crook of his arm, resting her head on his shoulder, letting her hand lie somewhat stiffly on his chest. She was much too tense.

"I don't know much about you," George said, letting his cheek rest against the silky smoothness of her dark hair, running his fingers up and down her back in an attempt to relax her. What was she afraid of? "I don't even know where you grew up."

"In the city," she said. "I've always lived here in New York."

"And you've never wanted to live anywhere else?" he asked. "I'd have thought a dancer with your talent would've headed down to Atlantic City by now. Or even out to Las Vegas. I'm not criticizing, but the Fantasy Club is pretty low-rent."

She lifted her head. "God, I'd love to go to Vegas."

"So what's keeping you here?"

The tension that had been starting to flow out of her was instantly back. "Nothing. Everything. I don't know." She tucked her head against him again, tightly closing her eyes.

George felt a flash of alarm. "Kim . . ." He cleared his throat. "Uh, you're not sticking around New York because of me, are you? Because, I have to be honest with you, nothing's changed since that first night we got together. I'm still not ... There's no chance of ... Nothing's changed. We've got no real future."

"I know that." She lifted her head again, steadily meeting his gaze. "You're still hung up on your ex."

George had to laugh. "Of all the crazy . . . I never said that."

She gently pushed his hair back from his face. "You didn't have to."

He gazed back at her for several long moments, wondering what else she knew about him. "Okay," he finally said. "So you know my deep, dark secret. It's only fair you tell me yours. Why don't you ever want to do anything in bed besides, well, what you do?"

She chewed on her lip as she gazed at him, as if deciding exactly what to say. She opted for what had to be the truth. "I don't like, you know, doing . . . the other." She shrugged. "I just . . . don't like it."

"Why not? I mean, I'm . . . Wow. I don't think I've ever met anyone who didn't like sex."

"It doesn't have anything to do with you," she told him earnestly.

"Well, gee, that's good, I guess." George looked at her. She was lying next to him, nearly naked. She had one of the most incredible bodies he'd ever seen in his life. It was a body built for sex—all positions, all styles, all the time.

"It makes me feel like I can't breathe," she tried to explain. "Kind of panicky and scared. I don't like feeling like that, so I try not to do it. I don't . . . you know, climax. I just . . . fake it if I have to. But if you really want to—"

"No. God. If it makes you feel bad, that kind of takes the fun out of it for me."

"Some guys wouldn't care."

"Well, jeez, I'm not just some guy."

She smiled almost shyly. "Yeah, I guess not."

"So . . . about the other . . . You know, the, um, oral sex. Do you really like doing that, or is it just the least worst option?"

Kim didn't hesitate. "Oh, no, I like it."

"You sure you're being honest with me?"

"I like it," she said again. "I guess I like knowing that even though you're bigger than me, I'm the one with the . . . I don't know, power, I guess."

"So it's a control thing," George said. "You want to be the one in charge. That's . . . interesting."

"You think I'm interesting?"

"Yes, I do. And I also think something pretty awful must've happened to you, probably when you were a kid, huh?"

She didn't say anything, but he could see from the look in her eyes that he was dead on target.

"If you ever want to talk about it," he said quietly, "I'm here. I'm not going anywhere for a while."

She nodded.

"I have one more question for you," he said, pushing her hair back from her face so he could look into her eyes. "If you know I'm still hung up on my ex, why exactly are you here?"

She rested her head on his chest, listening to his heart beating. "I like that you need me," she told him. "And I really like that you don't need me too much."

"I should do it." Harry's voice broke through Alessandra's reverie. She turned away from the drops of rain that were beading on the window, glittering from the lights of the other cars on the road, and looked at him.

He'd slept some. Yesterday, while she was driving. He still looked awful, though. The bags under his eyes were dark and pronounced, his eyes themselves were bloodshot. And he was having a particularly bad hair day. His mouth was a grim line, surrounded by that more-than-stubble, not-quite-beard.

But, as if he felt her looking at him in the quiet darkness, he turned and gave her a very small, heartbreakingly rueful smile. "I mean, who am I kidding, you know? My kids need stability, and, well, if you read my personnel file, stability wouldn't be a word that comes up much."

He was talking about granting custody of his children to his stepsister. No, what was it he'd said? Marge wasn't even related to him by marriage. But sister or not, how could he even consider giving away his children?

"You probably shouldn't make any major decisions while you're so tired," Alessandra said diplomatically. "Why don't we just get there, get the bloody hell out of this car? That alone will make you feel better. You can hug your kids, and then you can sleep on it, see if you still feel the same way in the morning."

"Hell," Harry said. "You said hell. You said bloody hell." He laughed. "This is clearly another example of my bad influence."

"If it were an example of your bad influence," Alessandra informed him, "I would have suggested we arrive and get the fuck out of the car. Or perhaps, get out of the fucking car, which has a different meaning altogether, doesn't it?"

Harry shouted with laughter, just as she knew he would. "You know, when you say it, it sounds almost polite."

"You're going to have to watch your mouth around your kids."

"I will," he said. "I do. I know."

He was quiet again, his laughter fading far too quickly. The windshield wipers were moving with a rhythm that suddenly seemed too loud in the stillness.

"I'm scared to death," he said. They were approaching an exit, and he pulled across the highway, signaling to get off. "Allie, I'm sorry, but we have to stop. I can't show up at Marge's, looking like this, in the middle of the night. It'll be nearly one-thirty before we get to Hardy, and that's no good."

Hardy. The name of her new hometown was Hardy, Colorado.

The clock on the dash read a few minutes after twelve. They were close. Really close. God, she hoped Hardy was more sophisticated than some of the little clusters of mobile homes passing for towns that they'd driven past.

"I think it's a good idea to stop for the night," she agreed. "You'll feel better if you shave and change your clothes. If you want, I'll even cut your hair. I'm not really that good at it, but frankly, it can't get much worse."

Harry shot her a crooked smile. "When you put it like that, how could I turn you down?"

Thirteen

❧ ❧

"**H**EY," HARRY SAID. "You're supposed to cut my hair, not criticize my wardrobe."

Alessandra turned and gave him a look that was both disdainful and pitying. "What wardrobe? An extra pair of dirty jeans wadded into an unrecognizable mass, three wrinkled T-shirts, two pairs of socks—one with holes in the toes, one with holes in the heels—and two pairs of silk boxers do not form even the most basic foundation for a wardrobe."

Harry rubbed his head with his towel then carefully began rewrapping his ribs with the Ace bandage. "I'll bet you didn't know I was the silk boxer type."

She studiously ignored him, glaring down at his three clean T-shirts, all faded, all wrinkled, as if doing so would change them into something more presentable. "I think we should buy you something new to wear to-morrow morning. Something like khakis would be re-laxed, but not as relaxed as jeans. And a polo shirt, casual, but with a collar. That would be a good look for you. Something in red would—"

"It's a good idea," he interrupted. "In theory."

She stopped ignoring him. "Why is it only good in theory?"

"I'm nearly all out of cash. We need gas and breakfast, and unless you're too tired, I'd love to have a beer or two tonight." Even with the door tightly closed, Harry could hear the music from the bar attached to the motel office. Somebody was playing Travis Tritt through a sound system that was set all the way up to ten. "Once we're in Hardy, I can get money from the bank—I have an account in Marge's name I can access. But until then we can't afford much of anything."

Alessandra wouldn't give up. "So we'll go to the bank first, buy the clothes after we get to town, and—"

"Marge has my bank card."

She was only temporarily stopped. "Okay, so we go to a laundromat. We can afford to spend a few bucks to wash your jeans, can't we? You can wear clean jeans and one of my new T-shirts. They're all men's extra large. You won't look perfect, but you'll look all right. Particularly after we cut your hair."

"We? I thought you were cutting my hair. If you expect any help from me . . ."

"You can help by sitting here." Alessandra pulled out the rickety chair that sat in front of a desk beneath a mirror. She patted it invitingly.

Harry sat.

Alessandra was examining him from all angles, her eyes narrowed and her lower lip caught between her teeth.

He grimaced as he faced himself in the mirror. He looked better having shaved, but not a whole lot better. "I look like shit."

Her eyes met his in the mirror. "You better practice using a cleaner vocabulary."

"I look like crap."

She smiled. "That's not a whole lot better."

She was touching him now, combing his still-wet hair, running her fingers through it, checking the length. It felt unbelievably good.

"I don't know how else to say it. I look like some kind of ghoul from Night of the Living Dead."

Alessandra attempted to center his head, frowning as she concentrated. She leaned forward from behind him, and he could feel the softness of her breasts against the back of his head. If he was lucky, she'd stay right there, just like that, forever.

"You don't look that bad," she said. "Just tired. A little Visine, some cucumbers on your eyes in the morning . . ."

"Cucumbers?"

"Don't move." She backed away.

"Did you say cucumbers? On my eyes?" He tried to hold his head perfectly still, watching her in the mirror as she picked up the scissors they'd bought at a twenty-four-hour pharmacy.

She began to cut his hair, slowly at first. "It's an old beauty trick. It helps reduce swelling and bags under your eyes. Preparation H also works very well."

"Oh, ho—no way am I putting hemorrhoid ointment on my face! Or cucumbers. Jesus."

"Maybe getting a good night's sleep will help."

"Chances of that are slim to none," he said. "I shouldn't've slept in the car. Now I'll never fall asleep."

Particularly not with her sleeping in the bed next to him. That, combined with knowing he was going to have to face his kids in the morning . . . There was no doubt about it, this was going to be one of the longest nights of his life.

"We can go have a drink after this." She brushed off some of the hair that had fallen on his bare shoulders, her long, elegant fingers cool against his skin. Her fingernails were starting to grow back; she had stopped biting them, as if her anxiety had lessened some with her decision to completely disguise herself. They were very short, but neatly filed. "I don't mind. Maybe that'll help you relax."

Harry knew exactly the way he wanted to try to relax tonight—and it involved her touching him just like that, but all over. Unfortunately, that wasn't going to happen. Allie wanted to keep sex out of their relationship. She had been surprisingly right about a lot of things, but in this case, she was dead wrong.

Theirs could be the perfect sexual relationship. They were close, but not too close. They knew each other well enough to see their faults and recognize their differences, to know that anything they started could never be permanent. There'd be no false expectations, no future disappointments.

But he wasn't even going to bring up the possibility again. He'd promised no pressure, promised to be good. Unless she was the one who changed her mind, he wasn't going to have sex with Allie tonight.

Tomorrow, however, he'd have the opportunity to get into her shirt. Too bad she wasn't going to be the one wearing it, though.

"What are you smiling about?" she asked.

He shook his head.

"Don't move!" She leaned forward to position his head again.

Ah, yes. Harry closed his eyes.

Nobody noticed her.

As Alessandra followed Harry into the bar, slouching the way he'd taught her, a few people looked up, but they immediately looked away, dismissing her just like that. She was not worth a second look.

She tried to tell herself that was a good thing. She had achieved the anonymity necessary to stay alive.

Still, a part of her—a large part of her—felt like crying.

"You want a beer?" Harry shouted to be heard over the pounding music.

She hated beer. But plain Alice Plotkin wasn't the type to have a glass of white wine—if they even served such a thing at a place like this. She forced a smile and nodded.

Harry frowned at her and said something that she couldn't quite make out over the noise. She gave him a questioning look and he leaned closer.

"Don't smile," he said. He was so close, she could feel his breath warm against her ear.

"Why not?"

But he'd already moved away, toward the bar.

His haircut looked good. He looked good. A little tired, maybe, but very good. In fact, he'd caught the attention of more than one woman sitting at the bar. Now there was true irony.

She'd cut his hair short enough so that it didn't matter if it stood up straight. The new length gave an edge to his face. It made his eyes stand out, made him look a little bit dangerous.

The faded T-shirt he wore clung to his muscular back and shoulders, and his jeans . . . His jeans fit very nicely.

The woman next to him at the bar was a redhead who had obviously learned how to apply makeup at the Barnum and Bailey School for Clowns. She leaned toward Harry, smiling as she spoke to him.

He grinned back at her, and she glanced back at Alessandra as she spoke again, crossing two very unremarkable-looking legs, letting her short skirt ride up just a bit.

Alessandra turned away. She didn't want to watch Harry check out the redhead's legs.

Lord, this was harder than she'd anticipated.

It was much easier to be Alice Plotkin when she was alone with Harry. He didn't look at her differently now that she no longer wore nice clothes and makeup. In fact, she'd caught him watching her when he thought she wasn't looking more often now than before. And sitting in the car, talking about anything and everything, it didn't matter that she didn't look like a beauty-pageant winner. In the car, she'd often forgotten she had the haircut from hell. In the car, when Harry smiled at her as if he genuinely liked her, she didn't feel lost and afraid.

Something bumped her arm, and she turned around to see him standing behind her, holding two mugs of beer. She took one from him.

"Wanna find a table?" he shouted.

Alessandra nodded, miserably aware that the redhead's eyes followed them all the way across the room.

The floor was sticky. The decor consisted of rough wood and a few grimy mirrors here and there. The overall appearance was aided by the poor lighting. The tables were small and round, with uneven pedestals that made them tilt back and forth. Harry set his beer on one near the back exit, by the rest rooms, and pulled out a chair for her.

She sat down. "You shouldn't do that."

"What?" He pulled his own chair close to hers. Too close—but necessary if they were going to attempt to talk.

She shouted into his ear. "You shouldn't—"

He quickly pulled away, nearly knocking over his beer. Gesturing for her to move closer, he put his mouth next to her ear. "Don't shout," he told her. "If you get real close, you don't have to shout, okay?"

He was speaking in a quieter than normal voice, and it gave the illusion of intimacy. It was as if she were in his arms, as if he'd lifted his head from a kiss.

"Now what shouldn't I do?" he continued. He turned his head, giving her his ear.

He smelled incredibly good even though he wasn't

wearing aftershave. Come to think of it, she couldn't remember Harry ever wearing aftershave. He smelled like
the cheap soap that came with the motel room, like the
bargain shampoo he'd picked up so as not to use up her
more expensive brand. He smelled like Harry, clean and
honest.

"You shouldn't pull out the chair for me, or even open
doors for me," she told him.

He pulled back slightly to look at her, his face only
inches from hers. Even in the dim light, she could see that
his eyes were brown and only brown. There were no
flecks of gold or green, just one single, deep shade of
chocolate.

He studied her intensely then leaned toward her again,
his breath warm against her neck as he spoke. "You
don't think Alice Plotkin deserves that kind of respect?"

"She's supposed to be invisible."

"She's not invisible to me."

Again, he pulled back, and the warmth in his eyes
seemed to heat her from within. His gaze flicked down to
her mouth, and Alessandra knew with complete certainty that he was going to kiss her. In just a moment, he
was going to pull her toward him and kiss her. She
couldn't think of anything she wanted more.

Cutting his hair had been torture. He'd sat there, without a shirt on, Ace bandage around his ribs, obliviously
sexy. She'd touched the hard muscles of his shoulders
and back more than once, using the lame excuse of
brushing cut hair off him.

Sometimes—okay, more than sometimes—the hair had
been imaginary.

Touching Harry was like touching electricity. She
hadn't wanted to stop. His hair was so soft and thick, his
skin silk over steel.

Silk. Silk boxers. Dear Lord. The thought of Harry in his silk boxers was a dizzying one.

The fact that he wore silk boxers didn't really surprise her, though. It made sense that beneath his rumpled and rough exterior lay the delicate smoothness of silk.

She held his gaze for what seemed to be forever, remembering the way he'd kissed her before, nearly giddy with anticipation.

He moved then, but instead of moving toward her and catching her mouth with his own, he sat abruptly back in his chair.

He didn't kiss her.

And he didn't look at her. He looked around the room, looked at his beer, even drank some of it, tapping his fingers on the table in time to the blaring music.

What had just happened here?

Alessandra followed Harry's gaze, thinking something had distracted him and . . .

One of the mirrors on the wall was positioned just right—she stared into her own eyes, gazed into her own pale face. Oh God, her hair looked awful. Everything about her looked awful. No wonder he didn't want to kiss her.

But looking bad was a good thing, she reminded herself. Except, right now, it felt awful.

She had to remember Ivo. Remember that look in his eyes in the Stop and Shop. Remember the way he'd aimed his gun directly at her and fired. If it were up to Ivo, she'd be dead right now. He was out there, still, maybe looking for her right this very minute. Having him find her and kill her—now that was a bad thing. Looking awful was merely an inconvenience.

Harry knocked on the table, and she glanced at him, startled. He gestured to her untouched beer. "Aren't you going to drink that?"

He didn't move toward her—she read his lips across the table.

She shook her head, pushing the mug toward him. He took it by the handle, careful not to touch her hand.

Harry took a healthy slug of Alessandra's beer, cursing himself, cursing Allie, cursing the fact that he hadn't had enough money to get them separate motel rooms. They had been on the road long enough for him to relax. If Ivo had managed to follow them, he would have put in an appearance before this. And if he hadn't followed them, he wasn't going to find them now. Harry's car was as traceproof as possible. It was the most common make and model on the road. He'd switched plates from a collection he had in the trunk a number of times, even changed the color at a body shop when Alessandra had her hair done.

But it was all moot. He didn't have the money for separate motel rooms.

And Allie wasn't in danger from Ivo. The only person in danger here was Harry. He was in danger of making a complete fool of himself. Again.

The back door opened with a crash, and he spilled the beer down the front of his shirt as the rest-room lights glinted weakly off the barrel of not one, but three—no, four—rifles.

He'd been wrong. Allie wasn't out of danger. He'd made a mistake, and it was probably going to cost them their lives. He pushed her down onto the floor, thrusting himself in front of her as he drew his gun from the back waistband of his jeans.

Four to one, no six—shit, there were six gunmen! He might've been able to take four if he used up his life's allotment of miracles all at once, but six! He'd have to fire first and keep firing even after he was hit.

They were all heading directly for him, all carrying the same odd rifle and . . .

All carrying the rifle barrel down.

Harry hesitated, a heartbeat away from spraying the wall with the first man's brains, searching their faces for Ivo's pale eyes.

Ivo wasn't there. All of the men were young, in their early twenties. They weren't looking at him or Allie at all. They were laughing and . . .

They walked right past him, and he realized why the rifles seemed so odd.

They were the kind of rifles that fired paint balls.

These clowns weren't Trotta's men. They were ass-holes who didn't have the brains to know not to bring weapons into a bar, even if they were only for sport.

As Harry lowered his gun, he watched the bartender and several other men converge on the men with the paint-ball rifles. And the six of them were escorted right out the front door.

Allie was clinging to him. He'd pushed her back, against the wall, pinning her with his body. "My God," she breathed. "I thought . . ."

"I know. I did, too. Jesus, I almost killed them." He pulled away from her, aware that he was crushing her, aware how soft she felt against him. He winced as he re-holstered his weapon. Hitting the floor that way had definitely not been what the doctor had in mind when he'd told Harry to take it easy on his broken rib.

It was strange. No one had noticed. They'd made a dive onto the floor, he'd pulled a deadly weapon, and no one in this bar had given them a second glance.

Shit, maybe Allie was invisible.

Allie touched his chest, lightly at first, then harder, pressing her hand against the beer-drenched front of his shirt. "You're not wearing a bullet-proof vest this time."

She was shaking even more than he was.

Harry shook his head. "No, I'm not."

"From now on you wear one!" There was more than fear in her eyes now. There was anger. She was positively blazing mad, shouting loudly enough for him to hear her over the music.

Her eyes were brimming with tears, and she was nanoseconds from losing it. Maybe she was invisible and no one would notice, but he wasn't going to take that chance.

He stood up, pulling her with him toward the back door.

The night air was cool and fresh. The decibel level of noise dropped instantly as Harry closed the door tightly behind them.

"I didn't bring a vest," he told her. The back parking lot was dimly lit by a neon sign for the motel that sputtered and flashed.

"Then you better get one. Tomorrow."

He laughed at her vehemence. Bad mistake.

"Don't you laugh at me—I'm serious!"

"Al, it's not like I can just go out and pick one up at the grocery store."

"Don't you understand? If those men had been after me, you would have been killed!"

"But they weren't—"

"Don't you ever, ever do that again! Don't you dare die for me!"

She was serious. She was fighting her tears, willing them from escaping. "Promise me," she said fiercely. She all but stamped her foot. "You have to promise me, Harry!"

"Thing is, Al," he said carefully, "I could think of worse things. See, I'm kind of . . . kind of fond of you, and . . ." He shrugged.

The tears won, streaming silently down her face.

Her knees looked as if they were about to buckle, and Harry did the only thing he could possibly do. He pulled her into his arms. "Hey," he said. "Hey. Come on, Allie. It's okay. It was a false alarm. We're both okay, everyone's safe and—"

"I'm kind of fond of you, too," she whispered, and his heart nearly stopped. "I couldn't bear it if something happened to you. Your friendship means so much to me."

Harry laughed. Friendship. Right. For a moment he'd actually had the audacity to think—

Allie reached up around his neck and lifted her own face and . . .

For about three seconds, he stood there like an idiot, unable to react, unable to comprehend.

Then his synapses fired, and he realized that yes, she was kissing him.

Once comprehension dawned, reaction didn't take long to kick in. He pulled her hard against him in an embrace that had absolutely nothing to do with friendship and everything to do with the fact that he'd wanted to be inside her since that very first moment he'd gazed into her eyes.

He kissed her ravenously, angling his head to inhale her completely, meeting and matching her explosion of passion. The sensation of her tongue thrust boldly into his mouth was completely knee weakening, and he felt them both sway.

He pressed her more completely against him, his hands cupped around the soft roundness of her rear end, kissing her even harder, even deeper. She made a low sound in the back of her throat, a soft moan that accurately expressed everything he was feeling.

She tasted like fire, sweet and hot, like his idea of

heaven. Her hands slid up beneath the edge of his T-shirt, cool against his bare skin as she gripped his thigh with her legs, pressing herself even closer to him, her message unmistakable.

It wasn't a question, but he answered it anyway. "Oh, yeah," he breathed. Oh, impossibly fabulous, incredible, wonderful yeah. It was all the invitation he needed to run his own hands up under the edge of her shirt, to touch the amazing smoothness of her skin, to gently cup the fullness of her breasts.

She made that same soft, sexy noise, pressing herself more completely into his hand.

He pulled her back with him into the deeper shadows alongside the building, catching her already taut nipple between his forefinger and thumb with one hand and lifting her up against him with the other. She spread her legs, and he pressed himself between them, fitting the hardness of his arousal against her softness, pressing her back against the concrete blocks.

"Oh, Harry," she gasped. "Oh, please . . ."

She reached between them, unfastening the top button of his jeans, unzipping him before he could stop her.

Dear Christ, they were in the parking lot!

But then she touched him. Polite, refined, cool-as-ice Alessandra Lamont had her hand down his pants, fingers wrapped around him in the parking lot of a cheap bar. Someone wake him—he had to be dreaming.

But then as she stroked him, caressed him, he knew this was no dream.

It was, perhaps, the best reality he'd ever experienced.

She was unabashedly direct about just what she wanted, completely oblivious to the rest of the world.

When she released him, it was only to unfasten her own pants, and Harry pulled back slightly, catching her wrists in his hands. He was breathing hard, and he rested his forehead against hers. Jesus. Jesus.

"Harry," Alessandra whispered. "Can we go to our room? Because I'm dying to . . ." She pressed herself more tightly to him. "You know . . ."

Harry laughed. And swung her up into his arms.

Fourteen

ALESSANDRA CLOSED THE door by leaning on it, already tugging at Harry's shirt, well aware he was working hard to rid her of her own, which was nearly impossible to do while they kissed.

But she couldn't stop kissing him. She didn't want to stop kissing him.

He wanted her. Now.

She felt like laughing and crying, but she settled for kissing him.

Beer had never tasted so good as it did on Harry's lips.

He found the front clasp of her bra, unfastening it and groaning softly as he covered her with his hands. He touched her with just the right combination of gentle roughness, breaking free from their kiss to lean down and draw her hungrily into his mouth.

Her jeans were so loose they fell right off, but Harry's stuck to his thighs. It didn't matter. She pushed down the silk of his shorts even as she slipped off her own panties. And then she was touching him again.

The sensation of his lips and tongue drawing hard on her breast was exquisite, but it wasn't enough.

His hands skimmed her body, slightly rough against her skin, touching her everywhere except where she wanted to be touched, driving her completely insane.

She moved his hand directly between her thighs, and he lifted his head to look up at her.

She'd spent quite a bit of time looking into Harry's eyes over the past few days. Despite their rocky start, she knew him well, perhaps better than anyone else on earth. But she'd never seen anything remotely like the heat she now saw in his eyes. The intensity made him look a little scary, made him seem a little like a stranger. And for the first time since she'd started kissing him in the parking lot, Alessandra felt a flash of trepidation.

But then he smiled, and he was Harry again. He touched her, softly at first, then harder, deeper, stroking her with the very tip of his finger, his smile fading as he watched her eyes, as he looked down at her, naked, in his arms.

Again, his touch felt deliriously good, but it still wasn't what she wanted. She shifted her hips, driving him more completely inside of her as she tugged again at his pants.

"Please, Harry. Can we . . . ?"

"Oh, yeah. I have condoms in my backpack." He released her, struggling for a moment with his jeans around his ankles, hopping toward the bed and falling back onto it in an attempt to kick his legs free.

But Alessandra was done waiting. As Harry sat up to push his boxers and jeans off his feet, she straddled him, kissing him hard on the mouth. She couldn't get enough of his kisses. But she didn't want to think what that might mean.

He put his arms around her—it didn't seem possible that arms that big, with muscles that were so clearly defined, could hold her without hurting her. But hurting her was so not what he was doing.

She could feel him hard between them as she kissed him. His mouth was so soft as he kissed her lips, her neck, her breasts.

It only took the smallest adjustment of her body, and she pushed herself down to surround him completely, to fill herself with him. This was what she'd wanted.

"Whoa," Harry said. "Whoa, Allie, condom!"

Now that she was here, she wasn't going to stop. "We don't need a condom. I can't get pregnant, remember?" She began to move on top of him, pushing him deeply inside of her.

"Oh, God," he said, running his hands down her back, moving with her. "Safe sex. This is about safe sex. I need to get a condom."

"I was married for seven years." If he was trying at all to stop her, it wasn't going to be by moving that way. It felt so good, so right. "And you haven't had sex since 1996."

"Yeah, but between 1995 and 1996, I have absolutely no idea who my wife was sleeping with." He filled his hands with her breasts. "I mean, aside from me. And there was something of a list."

Oh, Lord. "She must have been a complete fool."

"I could say that about Griffin. I think I probably have said that about Griffin. Except I think I used the word asshole." He smiled crookedly. "Sonya and Griffin. What a pair of losers. What are we doing talking about them, anyway? You know, I think we owe it to them both to have truly incomparable sex tonight, just to prove what losers they were."

Alessandra pressed his shoulders down so he was lying back on the bed, pushing him impossibly, amazingly deeper inside her. She heard herself moan.

"Oh, yeah," he murmured. "Oh, God, do that again." She did. "That?"

"Oh, yeah. That definitely falls under the heading of incomparable. Although you better do it another twenty or say, fifty times, just to make sure."

Alessandra laughed. "Do you always talk the entire time you make love?"

"I promise you, if you let me get that condom, I'll use my mouth for far better things."

She lifted herself completely off him. "Go, but hurry."

Harry nearly vaulted across the room, fumbling and spilling everything out of his backpack in his haste.

As he tore open the foil packet and covered himself, Alessandra froze, catching sight of herself in the mirror.

Her hair. She'd forgotten about her awful hair. It hung limply around her unadorned face, making her look about as appealing as a wet cocker spaniel. And, Lord, she should have at least gone into the bathroom and put on a little makeup. She looked terrible.

She stood up, uncertain what to do. There was nothing wrong with her making herself look nice in the privacy of their room, was there? But the idea of spending fifteen minutes or more—she looked again at her hair, definitely more—in the bathroom right now was not a particularly good one. Still, she wasn't the one who had to look at her. Harry was.

But he was already coming back to her, grinning in that way that only Harry could grin. He grabbed her around the waist, throwing them both down on the bed. "My turn to be on top."

"Get the light," Alessandra said.

He was kissing her breasts, touching her with his tongue in a way that took her breath away. "What?"

She wiggled free. "I'll get it." The switch was by the door. She flipped it, and the room became pitch-black. The curtains completely blocked out any light from the parking lot.

"Isn't it a little late to suddenly be shy?" Harry's voice surrounded her in the darkness.

She stood by the door. "I'm just . . . I just . . ."

He let out a very loud, very disparaging breath of air. "Yeah, I know what 'you just.' " He turned on the light by the bed. "What is it with you? You look at yourself in the mirror, and I don't have a clue who you see looking back at you. It sure as hell isn't the woman I see."

"I look in the mirror, and the person I see is so . . ." She shook her head. "The way I look, I can't believe anyone would want me. Not the way you seem to want me."

"Seem to?" Harry looked down at himself. "This is only a seem to? You better come over here and check this out, because when it comes to wanting you, this rates a definitely."

Alessandra laughed softly in disbelief. "See, I just . . . I know you're nice, so—"

"Yeah, I'm always getting erections just to be nice. Come over here, and I'll be even nicer." Harry held out his hand. "Come on."

She went to him. "May we turn off the light?"

"No! Are you nuts?" It wasn't the answer she'd been expecting. Harry held tightly to her hand so she wouldn't pull away. "I want to look at you," he explained. "I love looking at you anyway, and I've just discovered that looking at you while you're naked is a special treat."

He drew her hand to his mouth and kissed it, turned it over and kissed her palm, her wrist, her arm. "A couple things to get straight here," he continued, between kissing the inside of her elbow, her arm, her shoulder. "I love your haircut because it's helping to hide you from Trotta. And whether you think so or not, I think you're even more beautiful without your makeup on. So, no, we may not turn off the light. I want to be able to watch your face while I make you come."

He'd reached her neck, and as she lifted her chin to give him better access, he knew he'd won. But sweet

Jesus, if this woman thought she shouldn't make love in the light because she didn't look good, she was nuts.

He kissed her lips as sweetly and gently as he possibly could, slowly pulling her back with him onto the bed.

He ached to be inside of her again, but he did no more than kiss her and run his hands lightly across her beautiful body. The fact that she'd wanted him so badly before, and had been so bold about it, had been the most incredible turn-on. He wanted to get back to that place.

It didn't take long for her to completely reignite. She deepened their kiss. She pulled him close, cradling him between her legs. She drew his head to her breast, arching her body up to him in a silent plea for more when he touched her lightly with his tongue.

She reached between them then, taking him in her hand, guiding him to her.

"Allie, look at me," he whispered, and she opened her eyes.

He slowly buried himself in her, slowly pushed himself home as he looked down into her eyes.

The soft noise she made was sexy as hell, her voice thick with pleasure as she sighed his name.

Harry couldn't remember the last time he'd felt so alive.

Her smile was tremulous, but it was a smile. As she reached up to touch his face, her eyes shone with tears. Of course, she fought them, blinking them back. By now, he would've expected no less than a good fight from Allie.

She was so amazing. Such a fascinating blend of hard and soft, of strength and sweetness. And insecurity. She wasn't perfect—it was ironic, really. Her relentless belief that she was imperfect was her biggest imperfection.

As he gazed down at her, his chest felt uncomfortably

tight, but it was from more than the dull ache of his broken rib.

He would do anything for her, anything to keep her safe.

Even die.

Still watching her eyes, he began to move, slowly at first, then faster, taking his cues from what she wanted.

She liked sex hard and fast.

That was good, because he liked it like that, too.

It was bad, because it didn't take him long before he was clinging rather desperately by his fingernails to the edge of the orgasm cliff.

She kissed him hard, pulling his mouth down to hers, attempting to enter him as completely as he entered her. It was a kiss of complete abandon, of complete surrender, of total passion. As she kissed him, he tried to fight his need for release, tried to cling tenaciously to that edge, to give her everything she wanted and more. He wanted to give Allie the most incredible sexual experience of her life, to watch her shatter beneath him, but when she kissed him like that, with her heart in her eyes, with complete passion in her soul, he was toast.

His release crashed on top of him like a tidal wave, lifting him up and knocking the breath clear out of his lungs with its force.

He felt her follow almost immediately, felt her grip him more tightly, heard her cry out his name.

He was too blown away to feel any kind of relief over the fact that he hadn't completely left her in the dust. He couldn't speak or even think coherently.

But slowly the roar around him subsided, and slowly he became aware that he was completely crushing Alessandra.

She didn't seem to mind.

As he lifted his head, she smiled at him.

The muscles in his face were among the few Harry still had control over, and he smiled, too. He would have rolled off her, but she held on to him, lifting her head to kiss him lightly on the lips.

And he knew. Right at that moment. Right when her lips brushed his, he realized he was in serious, serious trouble. Whatever had just happened here had been way, way more meaningful than the casual, everyday scenario in which the vacationing FBI agent did the nasty thing with the former chief eyewitness, simply to relieve boredom.

"Congratulations," Allie said, kissing him again.

"What? Why?"

She smiled up at him again, touching the side of his face. "I don't know—it just seemed like the right thing to say after three years of celibacy. Too bad we don't have a bottle of champagne to open." Her smile turned warmer. "I would make a toast. Something like 'Here's to it not taking another three years before you get some again.' "

Harry laughed as he rolled off her and pulled her into his arms.

"Just in case it's not blatantly obvious," Alessandra said as she snuggled against him, sighing as he ran his fingers up and down the smoothness of her bare back, "I'm in favor of you not waiting another three years."

Back away. Back away. Distant alarm bells started sounding in Harry's head. She was getting too close. She was assuming this was the beginning of an ongoing relationship. And God knows that would only be trouble.

She lifted her head and gave him another of her killer smiles. "In fact, I'm in favor of not even waiting three hours."

Harry kissed her. What was he supposed to do? After she said something like that, something that made his hair stand on end with anticipation? Was he really supposed to not kiss her?

"You know what's funny?" she asked, propping her head up on one elbow to look at him.

He shook his head, losing himself in the calm blue ocean of her eyes.

"Since this mess started, I've resigned myself to never having as good a life as I had before—you know, huge house, three cars, lots of money. I thought I was going to have to work hard to keep myself from making comparisons and always having things come up short." She touched the side of his face. "But all of a sudden, I'm in the best place I've ever been in my entire life."

Her words should have made him leap up and out of that bed and start running for the mountains. Those bells in his head should have been shaking his brains loose with the noise of their alarm. Instead they were nearly drowned out by the sound of his heartbeat, by the roar of the blood rushing through his body. And instead of wanting to run away, he wanted to kiss her again.

So he did.

He was assuredly in big trouble, but trouble had never tasted quite so sweet.

"He doesn't know where his partner is." Kim closed her eyes, trying to keep her voice even, almost matter-of-fact as she stood in the cool night air at the pay phone four blocks from George's apartment. "If you want, I'll stay close to him, but I think—"

"I'm not paying you to think." Michael Trotta's normally smooth voice was tight. "Just stick like glue to Faulkner. Become permanently joined at the hips. Use that vacuum cleaner you've got for a mouth on him, day and night, if you have to. Sooner or later, he's going to find out where O'Dell has Alessandra hidden, and I want you to be on top of him when he does."

With a click, Michael hung up the phone.

Kim was sweating. She'd soaked the underarms of her favorite silk blouse just from talking on the phone with him. She stood for a long moment, the phone still tucked against her ear, regaining her equilibrium.

Who was this woman that Michael was looking for? And why on earth was he so bound and determined to find her?

Kim had seen her photo in a file on George's desk. Alessandra Lamont was one of those beautiful, icy, frigid blondes. She was the type of woman Michael would really enjoy being seen with, never mind that she was someone else's wife. Never mind that she probably gave head with all the enthusiasm of a dead hamster.

Her husband had swiped a million dollars out from under Trotta's nose. Had he done that because he knew his wife was doing the mob boss? Was that what this was about? Jealousy and revenge?

Michael had had the husband killed, Kim had no doubt about that. Had that hit really been about the money, or had Michael simply grabbed an opportunity to have the blonde all for himself?

But now this Alessandra had run off with George's partner, perhaps triggering yet another round of jealousy and revenge.

Kim knew Michael well enough to know that running away was never an option. No one could ever run far enough. No one could hide forever.

Kim finally hung up the phone, fixing her hair as she headed back toward George's apartment. She had to remember to stop at the market and pick up some Häagen-Dazs ice cream. That was the excuse she'd given George for going out in the first place in the middle of the night. It would look very strange if she returned without it.

Her life was a mess, no question about it. She often wished she could be someone else, just magically take on their existence, their life. But today she was very glad she was Kim Monahan and not Alessandra Lamont.

Whoever she had been to Michael, wherever she was hiding, whatever the reason he wanted to find her, Alessandra Lamont was as good as dead.

Fifteen

⟳

"Allie? You still awake?"

Alessandra smiled. It was bizarre. She was starting to really like when Harry called her that. "Yes."

She was lying nestled against him, his hand cupped possessively on her breast, his leg thrown across hers.

"I've been thinking." His voice was rough from the lateness of the hour, and his breath was warm on the back of her neck.

Lord, all he had to do was breathe on her and she wanted him again. She could feel the tip of her breast tightening beneath his hand.

But it wasn't just her. The relentless attraction was mutual. She could feel the weight of his growing arousal against her leg. He shifted slightly, as if to try to hide it, but there was no way she could have missed it.

Harry took his hand from her breast and pulled his leg back onto his own side of the bed, shifting so that he was sitting up and not touching her at all.

She turned toward him, missing his warmth.

"I know this is a little bit after the fact," he told her. He'd turned on the bathroom light earlier and left the door open a crack so that it wasn't pitch-dark in the room. But the way he was sitting, his face was completely in shadow. "And I probably should have said this before we . . . um, did what we did . . ."

236

"Made love," she said.

"Yeah," he said, shifting slightly. "See, well, that's kind of what we need to talk about because the words that popped into my head were 'fucked our brains out,' and there's a big difference between those two definitions of the same event. Made love implies . . . certain promises that the other doesn't. I really don't want you to get the wrong idea about what's happening here. I can't make you any promises, Allie. And I'm sorry, I really should have told you that while we still had our clothes on."

He took a deep breath, and she just waited for him to continue. "I feel bad about saying this to you now, you know? But it wasn't an intentional oversight, I swear. I like you, I really like you—far too much to disrespect you that way. I just . . . I've wanted you for so long, and suddenly there you were, giving yourself to me. I wasn't thinking about what expectations you might have. I wasn't thinking at all."

He didn't love her. Harry was telling her he didn't love her, and Alessandra nearly laughed out loud.

Too many men had said those words to her. I love you. They'd used it to try to lure her into their arms for an hour or a night or even longer. She'd heard it so often, starting back when she was a young teenager, it hadn't taken her long to know it meant nothing. They loved the way she looked. They loved the idea of being seen with someone as beautiful as she had been. Even though they said the words, they didn't love her.

But in her entire life, no man, not even Griffin to whom she'd been married for seven very long years, had ever told her that he liked her.

Until now.

Harry really liked her. It had nothing to do with the

way she looked—how could it, the way she looked now? He liked her. He liked Allie, the person she was inside.

Her heart had never felt so full.

And she had never felt so uncertain and afraid. Had she found this potentially wonderful relationship with this impossibly honest, painfully attractive, down-to-earth man, only to have it taken away from her right away?

"I've known from the start that you've got to go back to New York sooner or later, so I guess my only expectations were that we'd end up in bed again during the week or so you stayed in town," she said, choosing her words carefully. She pulled the blanket up so that it covered her breasts, aware that he was looking at her, aware that she was not hidden by the shadows. "But if you don't want that—"

"Whoa," Harry interrupted. "That's not what I said. I'll be in your bed every night as long as I'm here, if you'll let me. I just didn't want you to, you know, start choosing the china pattern, because that's not where this is heading."

"Harry, believe me, I don't want to marry you." She didn't want to marry anybody. At least not within the next few years or so. It would be insane to get involved in a permanent relationship at this stage of her life. She didn't even really have an identity yet. She was smack at the start of discovering who she really was, who she was going to be for the rest of her life. She needed to learn about herself before she could be effective as half a couple. Didn't she? And on top of that, she was in hiding.

"I just spent seven years married," she continued. "And as much as I like you, too, I have a feeling our relationship would be a little bit too much like the one I just got out of. As tempting as it is to be taken care of, I don't want to be someone's possession again."

Harry was quiet for a moment. "Well, I'm a little insulted you think being with me would be anything like it was with Griffin. But it's stupid to feel insulted because it's a moot point, right? We're not going to go past this." He gestured to where they were on the bed.

"Maybe we shouldn't make any rules about what we are or aren't going to do," Alessandra said, still carefully. "Maybe we can just play it by ear. I like being with you— you make me laugh, and you're great in bed. And you said you like me, too, so . . ." She felt a flush of warmth as she said the words aloud. He liked her. "So let's spend the next week . . . Well, you can call it whatever you want to, I still prefer 'making love.' "

"No promises," Harry said again.

There was a lot she wouldn't promise him. She wouldn't promise that she wouldn't do something very foolish and fall in love with him. She wouldn't promise she wouldn't try to make him fall in love with her, too. Real love. True love. The kind that starts out as liking and grows from respect.

She loved that Harry respected her, nearly as much as she loved the fact that he liked her.

"I'll only make you one promise," she said as she straddled him, the sheet sliding off her. "And that's that I intend to let you sleep very little over the next week or so."

Harry laughed and pulled her up against him. "That's the kind of promise I can live with." Then he kissed her long and hard on the mouth.

"What the hell is this?" Kim stood in the dining-room doorway, holding her fake-fur coat closed, staring at the feast on the table.

"Wow, you got home fast." George smiled, spreading his hands. "I figured since I can't take you out to dinner, I'd get dinner to come to us."

"Dinner?" Kim said. "This is about dinner? Jesus, Mary, and Joseph, George!" She stormed down the hall toward the bedroom.

It wasn't the response he'd expected. He'd imagined she'd be surprised in a positive way, pleased that he'd gone to such lengths to make her happy. He slipped his crutches under his arms and followed her.

"It's Italian. From La Venitia. You love La Venitia."

She whirled to face him, and he realized that beneath her coat she was wearing only a red velvet thong and matching heels.

"You scared me to death. I get off stage, and Carol's standing there with a message that you called, that you needed me to get home quick, that it was urgent. Urgent, George! I'm having a heart attack, thinking you fell, thinking your stitches somehow opened up and you were bleeding to death, thinking something awful might've happened. I call you back, and the line's freakin' busy. I don't even bother to change. I just grab my coat and run. I couldn't find a cab—I ran all the way here." She pulled off her coat and threw it onto the bed. Her bare breasts were covered with the body glitter she wore to dance, and they sparkled with each ragged breath she took. She sat down, pulling off her shoes. "Now I'm sweating like a pig and I've got blisters on my heels the size of donuts."

George sat next to her on the bed, laying his crutches on the floor beside him. "Oh, God, babe. I'm so sorry. I had no idea you would be worried. I just wanted you to get home quick, while the food was still hot."

He reached down and took her foot into his hands. She'd only exaggerated a little bit about the blisters. While the skin hadn't broken, her heels looked red and sore.

"Let me get a wet washcloth to put on those," he said.

"And I think I have some ointment in the medicine cabinet."

"I'll get it." Her anger had vanished as soon as he'd touched her, and now she just sounded as if she were going to cry. She started to get up, but he pushed her back.

"No, I'll get it. I'm doing okay with the crutches. Besides, this is my fault. You sit. Let me take care of you for once, okay?"

She nodded silently, wiping away the tears that had flooded her eyes.

George avoided his reflection in the bathroom mirror as he wet a cloth with cool water. This evening was turning out exactly opposite from the way he'd planned. He'd wanted to do something nice for Kim, and instead he'd completely upset her. He'd wanted to sit separated by the dining-room table and talk to her, take their physical relationship as far out of the picture as possible. He wanted to continue to let her know that every single evening didn't have to end with her getting him off.

Instead, he was going to go back in there and sit on the bed, with her wearing only a pair of microscopic thong panties. God, he was already hard. It would take her about point oh-seven seconds to notice that, and then she'd be all over him.

And although she'd insisted otherwise, he still didn't quite believe she really liked any kind of sex at all.

He maneuvered clumsily out of the bathroom. Kim had flopped back on the bed and lay staring at the ceiling, her feet still on the floor. She turned her head to look at him as he came into the bedroom, her mascara smeared slightly underneath her eyes, making her look even more exotic and sexy than usual.

Of course the fact that she was nearly naked helped.

"Did I mention how completely, absolutely, incredibly

sorry I am?" he said as he sat next to her. "Scoot back, will you?"

She obediently moved back on the bed, and he took her feet into his lap, gently pressing the cool washcloth against her heels. "How's that?" he asked. "Better?"

She nodded. "I thought . . . something awful had happened," she said again in a very small voice. She was a performer, but this wasn't any kind of act. The tears came back to her eyes. "George, would you mind holding me?"

Well, now let's see. Would he mind touching all that smooth, sparkling skin? Would he mind pressing the softness of those goddess-quality breasts against his chest? Would he mind lightly kissing her full lips and breathing in the sweet scent of her perfume?

No, George didn't mind at all. He kissed her, unable to keep himself from running his hand down her back, all the way down past the soft curve of her bottom. God, what a body.

He took care always to touch her gently, always lightly. Now that he knew, he never held her tightly in his arms. He always made certain she could pull free if she wanted to.

He let Kim be the one who deepened their kiss.

He just kept caressing her. Running his hand down her back and then across to her front, lightly brushing the soft velvet V of her panties with the very tips of his fingers, sweeping up her soft stomach, barely touching her breast, leaving just a whisper of sensation against her nipple, then up to her neck, her shoulder, and down her back again. And again and again and again.

She sighed, relaxing against him. "That feels so nice."

"Mmmm. I could do this all night, if you want."

He felt her open her eyes, her lashes brushing his neck. "You would . . . do just this? All night?"

"And love every minute of it." He softly kissed her forehead.

As his fingers brushed her breast again, she made a soft sound of pleasure, pressing herself up toward him so that he actually touched her. But he didn't let himself fill his palm with her, didn't draw her nipple into his mouth, the way he was dying to do. What he wanted had to wait.

"You're in control, babe," he whispered, his hand sweeping down her back again. "You tell me or show me what you want, and I'll do it, just the way you want. And if you want to stop, we stop."

He let himself linger just a moment longer on the gentle mound beneath her velvet panties before moving up to touch her stomach. She didn't pull away, so he slid his hand back down and touched her again, still lightly, still through her panties.

She made a noise, deep in her throat, that might've been pain or fear, and he quickly withdrew back to her stomach, tracing circles around her belly button. "Did you want me to stop?" he asked. "Is that what you wanted?"

"No." She spoke so softly he almost didn't hear her.

He touched her breasts again, both of them this time, not quite as lightly, but still taking care to be gentle. Her nipples were taut with desire and he wet them with the very tip of his tongue as he slowly trailed his hand down to her panties. He traced the edge of them with one finger. "May I?"

She was trembling, drawing in one ragged breath after another.

"I'm just going to touch you like this." He demonstrated on the outside of her panties, just the same light, barely there caress. "Okay?"

He held his breath, both terrified and elated that she would trust him as much as she already had. He prayed that she wasn't doing this because she thought he wanted her to. He prayed that he could make her see that whatever had happened in her past wasn't about sex and pleasure, but rather violence and power. And that while they might seem similar on the surface, they were two entirely different acts.

George didn't have much he could give her, but he could give her that knowledge, that truth. If she'd only let him.

He kept touching her, and she opened her legs slightly for him. Just a little bit, and then just a little bit more.

"I'm going to take that as a yes," he whispered, slipping her panties down her thighs. She kicked them free—another sign of agreement—and then he touched her. Lightly. Gently. Just the way he'd promised.

Touching her was like touching satin, smooth and warm and perfect. And still she didn't pull away.

He kissed her breasts, tugging gently on her nipples with his lips. She moaned, lifting her hips to press herself against his fingers, surprising him and surprising herself even more.

Then she froze, and George lifted his head to look down into her eyes. She was still breathing hard, still trembling. As he gazed at her, she moistened her lips and gave him a shaky smile.

"Oh, my," she said.

He smiled, feeling a burst of pleasure so intense, it nearly brought tears to his eyes. It was amazing really. He had a hard-on the size of the space shuttle, yet it was his heart that seemed to explode in his chest. "More?"

She nodded.

He pressed his fingers more deeply inside of her, watching her eyes as he used his thumb to slowly caress her.

"Oh," she breathed. She moistened her lips again. "Can you . . ."

"Yes," he said. "Whatever you want, babe, absolutely, unequivocally yes."

She actually blushed. "Can you make it feel this good with your . . . you know?"

He did know. "Yes."

He rocked onto his back, grabbing for a condom from his bedside table drawer with one hand, while still touching her with the other. He had his pants open and pushed down and himself covered, all with one hand, in the blink of an eye.

"You say stop, we stop," he told her again as he rolled her onto her side and nestled himself behind her. This way he wasn't on top of her. This way she wouldn't feel pinned down and out of control.

And still he touched her, still gently, his arm around her. He pressed himself against her from behind, slowly entering her with just the tip of his arousal before just as slowly pulling back again. He did it again, going a little bit farther this time, careful not to move too fast.

She made a soft sound, and when he did it again, she moved with him.

She didn't tense up, she didn't pull away, she didn't tell him to stop. Slowly, impossibly slowly, he made love to her. Each stroke seemed to take a lifetime in which he lived and died and lived again.

Dear God, this was probably going to kill him—but what a way to go.

She began to climax with him deep inside her, and he felt his own release begin, but still he kept it slow, pulling back in a movement that felt so good, he was certain this was it. His brain was definitely going to explode. The next slow thrust pushed him over the edge as she continued to tremble around him, and he came in an eruption of pleasure so intense he saw lights and colors behind his closed eyes.

But his physical pleasure was nothing compared to the joy of the knowledge that he'd taken this woman to a place she'd never been before.

"Omigod," Kim was saying. "Omigod, omigod. I didn't know. I never knew."

She turned toward him, her beautiful brown eyes brimming with tears. She was shaking, and he held her, still gently, still making sure she knew she could pull free.

But she reached up and touched his face, surprise in her voice as she looked at him. "You're crying."

He was.

She kissed him. "Oh God, George," she whispered and her own tears overflowed. "What am I going to do? I don't want to be in love with you."

Shaun went into the playroom to find Mindy upside down on the couch, watching Gilligan's Island.

"I think this time they're really going to make it off the island," she told him. Her head was dangling off the front of the couch, her long legs stretched up against the wall behind it. Gravity was doing funny things to her breasts.

Shaun looked away, uncomfortable at the thought of Mindy having breasts. He didn't really think of her as a girl. Not the way he thought of the redhead from California.

"The Professor's built a radio out of coconuts," Mindy reported. "If he's smart, all he needs to do is use one of Ginger's underwire bras for an antennae."

Shaun walked to the window under the front eaves, bending slightly to keep from hitting his head. "I hate to break it to you, Mind, but they never get off the island."

"Well, why would they want to?" she asked. "They're

in paradise. You know, I used to wonder why the Professor didn't just choose Mary Ann. I mean, what was he waiting for? She was so obviously the nicest person on the island. But then I figured it out. The Professor's gay. All those years, he had a thing for Gilligan."

Shaun stood silently, looking down from the vantage point at the third-floor window, looking out at the street in front of the house. No traffic passed. No cars pulled up. Nothing moved.

"Well, jeez," Mindy said, turning right side up as she muted the TV with the remote control. "You must've left your sense of humor down in the kitchen."

He didn't look at her. "I don't think the idea of someone being gay is particularly funny."

Mindy was silent, and when he turned to look at her, her eyes were even more enormous than ever behind her glasses. It was strange. He rarely noticed the odd effect her glasses had on her eyes anymore. She'd spent every afternoon at his house for the past three days, and was here again, this Saturday morning. Instead of driving him completely insane, he'd found he liked her company. He liked turning around and finding her there. He even liked the really stupid jokes she made.

Most of the time.

"No," he said. "I'm not gay. Why do people always think I'm gay?" He answered his own question. "Because I like to dance? That's so stupid."

"It's okay if you are," she said softly. "I'll still be your friend."

Friend. She was his friend and would be no matter what, and he still made her hide her bike behind the house and sneak in through the back door. They'd talked about all kinds of deeply personal, private things, yet he never gave her more than a cursory nod when they passed in the hall at school. He never sat with her at lunch, even though they both often sat alone.

She may have been his friend, but he was no kind of real friend to her.

To his complete horror, his eyes filled with tears. He quickly turned back to the window.

"You're freaking out because your father's not here yet," Mindy said in that same quiet voice.

"I don't think he's coming." Shaun finally admitted it to himself. Oh, he'd played the game, telling himself that he was tough, he was able to face reality, that he wouldn't believe Harry was really going to visit until he got here. But the truth was, he'd hoped.

He'd even prayed.

He'd pretended it was for Emily's sake, when the truth was, he'd wanted Harry to come. He'd wanted his daddy to come and make everything right again.

But Harry wasn't coming.

Any minute now, the phone would ring, and Harry would apologize and—

"Mindy!" Em was standing right outside the play-room door, shouting loud enough to knock it off its hinges. "Are you in there?"

Even though Shaun was farther away, he was faster and he reached the door first, opening it. "Don't shout! Aunt Marge is working downstairs," he said. "God, how could someone so short be so loud?"

Emily stood outside, holding a box that was nearly as big as she was. "I'm here to see Mindy."

"Oh, Em, thanks." Mindy pushed past him and took the box. "You brought me the—"

"Photo albums?" Shaun couldn't believe it. All he needed to do now was to have to sit with his little sister and look at pictures taken back when his life was more than this unbearable mixture of sadness, fear, and hurt.

Pictures of his mother with her arms around him, laughter lighting both of their faces.

God, he missed her. He missed Kevin, too.

The tears that were never far from the surface these days clogged his throat.

There was no way he could do this today, no way he could sit with Em and make up more of his lies about why Harry didn't come see them more often. Daddy loved her, of course Daddy loved her, but he was just too busy with his goddamn important job. He was too busy saving the world. And that meant he couldn't spend even one lousy day with them out of three hundred and sixty-five.

His voice shook as he turned to look at Mindy. "You asked Em to bring up the photo albums?"

Mindy looked perplexed. "Is that bad?"

Shaun glared at his little sister. "You know you're supposed to ask Marge before you take these out."

"That was my fault," Mindy cut in. "I wanted to see what your father looks like."

So did he. He wanted desperately to see what his father looked like these days. Fat chance of that happening.

"I was curious," Mindy continued.

"Maybe you should mind your own goddamn business!" he spat, all of his frustration erupting into violent anger. "You're always over here. Always in the way. Always curious and sticking your big nose into everything. Fats MacBlubber, taking up twice the space on my couch. I didn't ask you to come here! Why don't you just go home and leave me alone?"

Em tugged on his shirt. "Don't say goddamn. Don't say goddamn."

He slapped at his sister's hand, harder than he should have. "Guess what, Em? Dad was supposed to visit us, but he's not coming. And it's not because his job is so important. It's because he doesn't love us. He's probably lying somewhere, too drunk to get out of bed. He doesn't work for the president. The reason he doesn't come here is because he's an asshole who doesn't give a shit about us!"

"Don't say shit," Em whispered, her eyes overflowing with tears as she clutched her slapped hand close to her chest.

"You're the asshole." Mindy pushed past him, scooping up Em into her arms as she ran from the room.

Shaun felt sick to his stomach, all his anger turning instantly to shame. Dear God, what had he just said? What had he done? His legs felt weak, and he lowered himself onto the couch.

The TV was still on, still muted, and in brilliantly garish 1960s-era color, Gilligan silently mugged for the cameras as the skipper hit him over the head with his hat.

Harry hadn't slept well.

When Alessandra woke up, she could tell just from looking that if he'd slept at all, it had been only fitful dozing.

This man had fearlessly thrown himself in front of her last night. He'd been prepared to use his body to stop bullets meant for her, hadn't batted an eye as he'd calmly faced death. He'd done the same when he'd leapt in front of Ivo's gun.

But when it came to facing his children, he was terrified.

"It's going to be okay," she told him.

"Maybe. But it's not going to be easy," he said quietly.

She touched his hair, admiring the way his new cut still managed to make him look sexy, even mussed from sleep. At least one of them was going to have a good hair day. "I think you should be honest with them about why you haven't been to visit. And I think you should all go in for grief counseling."

He sat up, swinging his legs over the side of the bed, his back to her. She could barely hear him when he spoke. "What if it's too late?"

"As long as you're alive, there's no such thing as too late." She believed that with all her heart.

He was silent, and she touched his back. "If you want," she said, "I'll hold your hand."

Harry closed his eyes, wishing he could just sit there forever. "Yeah, I might take you up on that."

This was completely stupid. His kids were kids. All he needed to do was explain. Well, try to explain. He wasn't sure he actually could explain. But they were kids—he was their father. They'd forgive him. And then they could start over.

He'd visit more often. Monthly, at least.

He'd be able to see Allie then, too. They could continue on in their current nonrelationship damn near indefinitely. He liked that idea.

She leaned over, holding him tightly from behind as she kissed his cheek. "Just let me know if you need me."

Harry watched as she walked naked into the bathroom, closing the door behind her. He hadn't been completely honest last night, not with her, not with himself.

Her vehement reaction to his suggestion that she might be interested in marriage had bothered him just a little too much. What kind of head case was he—that he should be disappointed when Allie gave him the response he was hoping for?

But he had been disappointed, and her absolute certainty that she did not want to marry him had stung.

He'd thought long and hard about it last night, between his long, hard thoughts of Shaun and Emily. Realistically, he knew there was no way in hell a woman like Alessandra Lamont would want more from a man like him than quick, hot sex. He was by no means a member of the millionaires' club—not even close. He hated his job, and his family life was about to detonate. With the exception of his newly awakened sex life, there was not one part of his existence that wasn't in complete shambles.

And his sex life was about to go up in smoke, too, from his own foolish stupidity. Yes, he was on the verge of fucking up the one good thing he had going.

He was falling in love with Alessandra Lamont. Of all the stupid-ass things he could do, he knew that would be the worst. It would completely sabotage his friendship with her.

Let me know if you need me, she'd said.

He needed her. Desperately. But there was no way in hell he was going to tell her that.

"I'm assuming there's been no word at all from Harry." Nicole sat on the edge of George's forest-green sofa. It had been their sofa, and this had been their living room, before the divorce. They'd made love right here, in front of the TV, more times than she could count.

George lit a cigarette and glanced in the direction of the kitchen, where Kim was fixing them all a cup of tea. Tea. It was absurd, the stripper making them tea in what used to be her kitchen. But Nicole would have agreed to a cup of arsenic just to get Kim out of the room.

"No," he said. He lowered his voice. "But I've been thinking, trying to remember anything he might've said. I don't know if this is going to help, but once, when he was completely plastered, he mentioned something about Colorado."

"Colorado's a pretty big state." Nicole waved his smoke away from her face.

George shrugged. "Best I can do."

"Keep thinking."

"I will. I haven't got much else to do—aside from the kinky sex, that is."

He was only saying that to piss her off. Nicole gave him a completely unperturbed, vaguely disinterested smile.

"Hey, did you see the new curtains?" George asked. "Can you believe I finally got curtains?"

In all the years that they'd lived here, Nicole had never gotten around to putting curtains up in the living room. Toward the end of their marriage, they'd argued about it bitterly. George had thrown it in her face as an example of her unwillingness to spend any time at all improving their life together. Of all the stupid arguments, that one had really taken the cake.

His new curtains were a swirl of green and off-white, complementing the couch almost perfectly. "They're very nice."

"Oh, do you like them?" Kim came in carrying three mugs on a tray. The tray had been a wedding gift from George's Aunt Jennifer; the mugs were the ones they'd picked up at a craft fair during their honeymoon. Kim gave George a smile, a softness coming into her eyes as she looked at him. "I had fun making them."

"You made them?" Nicole said, then mentally kicked herself for making more than a noncommittal noise of agreement.

George was getting far too much enjoyment from this.

"I like to sew. I also like to walk around naked at night," Kim explained, making an aren't-I-naughty face as she set down one of the mugs on the table next to George's lounger, "but I felt funny doing it with no curtains on the windows. It felt kind of like I was putting on a free show."

"Wouldn't want to do that," Nicole murmured.

Kim put Aunt Jennifer's tray in the center of the coffee table. There was a plate of home-baked cookies on it as well. "Please help yourself. I wasn't sure if you wanted lemon or sugar."

There was that softness again as she looked at George. It was as if he'd suddenly turned into Elvis or God or someone equivalent.

"Nic likes it plain," George said with an answering smile at Kim that implied shared secrets. "I think she thinks it'll put hair on her chest."

Kim was wide-eyed. "Why would you want hair on your chest?"

"I always wondered that, too," George mused. "Have one of the cookies," he told Nicole. "They are incredible. Kim is the absolute best cook." He turned to Kim. "Nic manages to burn water."

As Nicole stood up, she turned to Kim and lied. "I'm sorry, I'm going to have to skip the tea. It was . . . nice seeing you again. Will you do me a favor and give me another minute alone with George? All those FBI secrets, you know . . ."

"Why don't you order us Chinese for lunch, babe?" George suggested. "You can use the phone in the bedroom."

He actually patted her on the bottom as she passed his chair, and she actually seemed to like it.

Nicole sat back down on the couch, waiting until she heard the bedroom door close behind Kim before she turned to George. "Well, you really made me feel bad— she's obviously everything I never was. Except guess what, George? I don't feel bad. Big freaking deal. So you found yourself Trixie Homemaker. She cooks, she sews, she strips, she screws—all at the drop of a hat. I'm sure that's very lovely for you, but look into my eyes and read my lips. It means nothing to me. Congratulations, you really hurt someone this time—except the person who's getting hurt here isn't me. It's Kim."

George was just sitting there with no expression, his injured leg extended before him, cigarette held loosely between his fingers, watching her. "You done?"

"No. What's gonna happen when you're tired of this game? She's obviously crazy about you. She obviously expects you to marry her. Unless you're so twisted that you're ready to keep this farce going 'til death do you part, you are going to emotionally eviscerate this girl. And I hate to say it, George, but I think she's probably a nice girl—a stupid girl—but at her core I think she's nice. Be a man for once in your life and be honest about what you're doing here."

George smiled. "Be a man. That's funny. I never had an opportunity to be a man before—you were always snatching that role away from me."

Frustrated, she turned to leave.

"Nic."

She stopped but didn't turn around. She couldn't bear to look at him, couldn't bear to look at what they'd done to each other with all their anger and pain.

"I'm a shit," he said softly. "I hear myself saying things I know will hurt you, and I can't seem to stop. But this thing with Kim, it's not about you and me anymore. You were right, it started that way. But then, she, um . . . Well, these last few days have been . . . Jesus." He couldn't meet her eyes. "Damnit, I'm in trouble here, Nicki, and I need to talk to you about it."

Oh, God. He actually loved the stripper. Nicole felt her heart grow very, very still.

"She's dancing tonight," George continued. "Her shift starts at ten-thirty. Can you come over about ten minutes after that?"

He wanted to tell her he and Kim were getting married. That's what this was about. "I'll have to check my schedule," she said, heading for the door, keeping her voice cool, professional, as if her last hopes for a reconciliation with the only man she'd ever loved hadn't just been swept away.

"This is important."

"I'm sure you think it is," she said, letting herself out of the one place she'd ever thought of as home.

Sixteen

❧ ❧

TRUST GOOD OLD Marge to try to pretend the situation was completely normal.

Harry leaned against the porch railing, hands in his pockets, heart in his throat, unable to take his eyes off Emily.

She was sitting next to Marge, half hiding behind her aunt, silently staring at him as if he were the devil incarnate.

She was beautiful. She was still pretty tiny, but much of her babyness was gone. She was a little kid now, but, just as when she was a toddler, her default expression was fierce.

Her face was grubby, with clean streaks on it, made from recent tears. Very recent tears. She was still sniffling.

"It shouldn't be too hard to find an apartment this time of year," Marge was telling Allie. "There's a small college in town, and some of the students invariably don't return from spring break. The rest will be leaving next month, so the landlords who've got an empty place will be pretty desperate."

Harry gave Emily a tentative smile.

She retreated behind Marge's arm.

He knew it was too much to hope that she would leap into his arms, but this was ridiculous. Surely she hadn't forgotten him completely. Had she?

"Something tells me I'm going to need a job before I can find an apartment," Allie said. He was going to have to tell her to work on her voice. She enunciated too damn well. And the way she was sitting, so straight, with her legs crossed . . .

"What kind of work do you do?" Marge asked.

Harry glanced at his watch. "So what happened to Shaun?"

"Em, hon, run and see what's keeping your brother," Marge gently commanded the little girl.

"He said shit," Emily informed them. "And asshole." She looked at Harry as if to gauge his reaction. Or maybe to imply that he was one. Who could know with a kid that little?

He kept his face perfectly bland.

"Please go and get him," Marge told her.

"Is he in trouble?" Em asked, almost hopefully.

"No, he's not," Marge said with the kind of patience Harry himself had had at one time. "Just get him, please."

Em glanced back at Harry as she opened the screen door, letting it bang shut behind her.

He looked up to find Allie looking at him. She was unable to keep a smile from slipping out.

He would've smiled, too, but his stomach hurt too much. Emily probably didn't recognize him. There was nobody he could blame for that besides himself. He'd been gone for too long. Two years was an entire half of her life.

"I guess Shaun's your kid," Allie said.

"I don't know about that." He looked challengingly at his almost stepsister, gripping the railing behind him with both hands. "How 'bout it, Marge. Is Shaun still my kid?"

"I think you better ask Shaun that." Marge turned back to Allie, as if they were sitting together at a garden party. "I'm sorry, what is it you said you do?"

"Well, I—I'm not sure," Allie admitted. She looked at Harry, her concern for him clear in her eyes. "I'm kind of in a transition period, just getting out of a—a bad relationship. I'm afraid I don't have many skills, or education, and . . ." She forced a smile. "I guess I was thinking about some kind of retail sales. Or maybe waitressing . . ."

Jesus, what was taking Shaun so long? Didn't he care that Harry was here?

Allie was still watching him, aware that Marge's small talk was driving him mad. She put down her glass of lemonade and stood up, moving to stand next to him, slipping her hand into his, and squeezing it slightly.

So far this sucked. He didn't have to say the words aloud, he knew she saw it in his eyes.

She nodded slightly, holding his hand even tighter. She knew.

Marge knew, too, but the way she dealt with the tension was to play the scene as normal. And normal was making small talk with Allie.

"One of Shaun's friends' mom owns a company called Merry Maids," she said. "A housecleaning service. She's always looking for help. It's hard work, but the pay's much better than working retail or even waitressing. Most of the waitressing jobs are over by the college, and believe me, students don't tip well. I'm a professor at the college, in case Harry didn't tell you."

"Housecleaning, huh?" Harry laughed. The absurdity of Alessandra Lamont cleaning other people's houses for a living cut through his misery, and he glanced at Allie, expecting to see her amused at the idea as well.

Instead, she was nodding at Marge. "Actually, no,"

she said, clearly as much a pro at small talk as the other woman. "He said you were a writer."

"It's possible he didn't know," Marge replied. "I just got the teaching position last September. Of course, it has been nearly an entire school year."

"The name of that company looking to hire people was Merry Maids?" Allie asked, perhaps purposely trying to steer the conversation away from that barely disguised dig Marge had gotten in.

"You can't be serious," Harry cut in.

She looked at him, her eyes the exact same shade of blue as the sky. "Why not? I need a job. I have no money, Harry. I've got to do something."

"But cleaning houses?" He laughed. "I don't know, Al. You haven't even really seen the town. How do you know you even want to stay?"

"I thought the plan was for me to stay," she said quietly. "I know you have to leave soon, but—"

"You have to leave soon? Now why isn't that a surprise."

The kid who pushed open the screen door was nearly as tall as he was. Harry stared, and it took several long seconds for the fact to register. Shaun. This gangly teenager with the changing voice was Shaun.

Emily slipped back onto the swing, next to Marge, her eyes large and accusing.

Harry was speechless.

Shaun was not.

"Well, hey, Harry, how are you?" the kid said, his almost too-handsome face twisted in an expression of hostility, his green eyes—so much like Sonya's—hard behind his wire-rimmed glasses. Instead of holding out his hand to shake, he crossed his arms, purposely burying his hands in his armpits. "Nice of you to drop by." He made a big show of looking at his watch. "But, oh, gee, don't let me keep you. You've already been here for ten minutes—that's at least twice as long as you stayed the last time you came to visit. See you in a year, Dad."

He turned and walked away, down the porch steps.

Harry felt like throwing up. He deserved Shaun's fury. "I'm sorry," he said quietly. "I know I've made some mistakes in the past few years, but if you walk away from me, we don't have a prayer of dealing with any of it."

Shaun spun back to face him. "Some mistakes? You've made a shitload of mistakes—one for every goddamn day you weren't here—"

"Shaun, you will not speak to your father that way." Marge's voice rang with quiet authority. "Not around Emily, not around me."

The boy instantly fell silent, but he clearly had plenty more to say.

"Let him speak," Harry said.

"Not that way," Marge countered sternly. "Shaun, keep it clean or keep your mouth closed."

Harry's temper sparked. "I can deal with my own kid, thank you very much."

"Can you really, Harry?"

"Is that what this is all about?" he asked, mad as hell and wishing that Marge weren't looking at him with such concern, such gentleness, such goddamned love in her eyes. How could she love him—and still want to take his kids away from him? "You don't think I can handle my kids anymore so you want legal custody?" Allie put her hand on his arm, her fingers cool against the heat of his skin. He shook her off. "What is wrong with you? How the hell could you do this, Marge?"

"It was my idea."

Harry turned and stared at his son. His idea?

Shaun's smile was bitter. "Aunt Marge tried to talk

me out of it. I would have filed the petition for the name change six months ago, but she told me to wait, to talk to you first. But you didn't seem to want to talk to me, so . . ." He shrugged. "I went to see the lawyers on my own."

"Name change?" Harry repeated stupidly. "You want to change your name?"

"Emily doesn't even know her real name is O'Dell. We've been Shaun and Em Novick for so long, I figured we might as well make it legal. But the lawyers told me they couldn't file anything for me without your permission. That's when the issue of custody came up. I was told that even though I'm a minor, I could sue for transfer of custody, based on abandonment."

"Abandonment." Harry couldn't breathe. It wasn't Marge who'd filed those papers. It was Shaun. His own son.

"Ugly word, isn't it, Harry?" Shaun's eyes glinted with contempt. "But it pretty much describes the situation, doesn't it? Unless you've got a better word for being gone for two years."

Harry couldn't speak. What could he say? Behind him, on the swing, Emily had quietly started to cry. Her muffled sobs were an appropriate soundtrack to this scene as he stared into Shaun's unforgiving face.

"I'm—I'm sorry," he finally said, his voice little more than a whisper.

"Oh, that makes it all better," Shaun said sarcastically.

"Shaun, I don't know—"

"I do," his son told him. "I know it's too late. I know I don't want to be an O'Dell anymore. And I know I don't want you to be my father."

Too late. Despite what Allie had told him, Harry had come too late.

"So just go back to whatever rock you crawled out

from under and leave me and Em alone. We're better off without you."

We're better off without you.

It was the final knife blade to his already damaged heart. It was a truth Harry couldn't deny. They were better off without him, in every possible way.

He looked around, at the paint that was starting to peel on the railing. At the painful blue of the perfect spring sky. At Marge, holding Emily close, head down as they sat motionless together on the porch swing. At Allie, her face ashen, her eyes enormous in her face as she waited to see what he was going to say, what he was going to do.

There was nothing he could do. It was too late.

He walked down the stairs, past the hardened set of Shaun's face, down the path to the street, where the car was parked. He'd left the doors unlocked—in this part of town, it wasn't necessary to lock. He'd made sure of that before he'd bought Marge this house two years ago.

He took his pack from the backseat and opened the front zipper pocket, took out the custody papers, unfolded them, and signed his name on the dotted line.

"Harry." Allie started toward him, complete dismay in her eyes.

He tossed the signed papers down onto the front walk. "I'm gone," he said.

Neither Shaun, Marge, or Emily moved. All three of them could've been statues, they stayed so completely still.

Allie, on the other hand, was bearing down on him like a freight train.

He climbed into the car and started the engine, hoping he could put it into gear and pull away before she got in. Christ, he might as well leave her behind here, too.

But he wasn't fast enough, and she threw herself into

the car a fraction of a second before he jammed his foot on the gas.

He pealed out, leaving huge streaks of rubber on the street behind him, wanting only to get away.

"Lord, Harry!" Alessandra was thrown hard against him. She scrambled to get back into her seat, to get her seat belt fastened. "How could you do this?" She waved the custody papers she'd grabbed off the ground. "How could you just sign away your children?"

Harry didn't answer her. He just pushed the car into higher gear, moving dangerously fast on the residential streets.

"Harry, dammit, slow down!"

He didn't look at her, didn't slow down, didn't do anything but glare at the road, his eyes hard, his mouth a grim gash in his angry face.

"So that's it, then?" she asked. "You sign the papers, walk away, and don't look back?"

"That's right."

"I can't believe you're just going to give up without a fight!"

"Believe it." He took a hard left onto a main road and the back tires skidded, squealing noisily. Instead of slowing down, he pushed it even harder, taking the curves much too fast.

"Harry, please. The speed limit here is—"

"If you don't like it, you can get the fuck out of the car."

He skidded into the oncoming lane as they went around a curve, and a truck swerved wildly, going past them with its horn blaring.

"That's enough!" Alessandra shouted, furious at him for risking her life, furious at herself for thinking she could make him listen, that he would even care to listen.

"Stop this car right now! You can kill yourself if you want, but I want to live!"

If there was one thing she'd learned over the past few weeks, it was that she did truly, absolutely want to live.

Harry swerved into the parking lot of a restaurant on the side of the hill, skidding to a stop in the gravel. He stared straight ahead through the windshield, the muscles jumping in the side of his jaw. "You don't like the way I drive, like I said, get out."

He was ditching her. Just like that, he was going to leave her behind as surely as he'd left his own children.

"How can you do this?" Alessandra asked, her voice shaking. "How can you just walk away from your family?" How could he walk away from her, from what they'd just started? "How could you have spent two years—two years, Harry—away from those beautiful children, to work at a job I know you hate? Didn't you look at them back there? Didn't you realize how special they are? Do you even know how brave and strong Shaun had to be to stand up to you that way? Did you even look into Emily's eyes and see how badly she wanted you to just grab her and hug her? What is wrong with you?"

She was crying now. She couldn't keep herself from crying. "How can you not see that those kids should be at the absolute top of your priority list? God, I would sell my soul to the devil to have a child, and you've got two that you're willing to give away. Fight for them, Harry! How can you not fight for them? You've fought so hard and so long to avenge your dead son, yet you'll do nothing for your children who are still alive! You've got so much, but you don't see it. You only focus on what you don't have. I've got no one, I've got nothing—right now I literally have nothing—but you know what? I've still got more than you do, because I have hope. I look to the future, and I see the possibility of better things. I dream of better things. You've got those better things right there in your hands, and you're just throwing them away to chase ghosts from your past."

She only stopped to take a breath, ready to keep going. She was willing to talk until her face turned blue if she could only make him see what an awful mistake he was making.

But he cut her off. "What do you know about loss?" He turned and looked at her, and she saw a maelstrom of pain and anger in his eyes. "How dare you sit there and pretend to know what it feels like to have your child die?"

"You're right," she whispered. "I don't know anything about it. But I do know that I would make sure that losing one didn't mean I lost all three. I would make sure it didn't mean I'd spend the rest of my life throwing away everything—and everyone—good that came along."

Harry laughed harshly. "Hey, you were good, sweetheart, but you weren't that good."

She recoiled as if he had hit her.

Harry didn't know why his words should upset her so much—she'd just told him she had no one and nothing in her life, so she herself clearly didn't consider last night to be anything special or Harry to be someone who mattered.

She opened the door and as soon as she did, Harry knew without a doubt that, despite everything he'd just said, the dead-last thing he wanted right now was for her to get out of his car.

But it was too late for apologies, too late to halt the anger-tinged words that spilled out of him.

"What do you want me to do?" he asked. "Go back there and make Shaun accept my apologies? You heard what he said. Sorry's not good enough."

She searched her pockets for a tissue and came up empty. "So find out what is good enough." Her voice was quiet, as if that nasty lie he'd said about her not being that good had taken some of the fight out of her. "Get counseling. It'll hurt, and it'll take time, and it'll be much, much, harder than quitting, but my God, you'll walk away from it with your family intact instead of shattered like this!" She gave up and wiped her nose on the back of her hand.

He couldn't meet her gaze. "Yeah, maybe after I bring down Trotta—"

She got mad all over again, her voice rising. "And after Trotta, it'll be someone else, some other bad guy who might've been in the room, who might've known something about the conspiracy that ended up killing Kevin! When are you going to stop?"

"Allie, I need to get this guy."

She nearly spat at him. "Yes, I'm aware of how badly you need to get him. I was nearly a casualty of your last attempt. Now you're willing to sacrifice your family. Why that should surprise me, I don't know. I guess I just never learn. You know, at this point, it wouldn't surprise me at all if I found out you'd set me up for another hit in an attempt to catch Trotta again."

"I wouldn't do that. I promised you—"

"What about your promises to your children? Just by bringing them into this world, you made promises to them that you're not keeping."

"What about my promises to myself?"

Alessandra wrestled her bag from the backseat. "Those are always the first ones that should be compromised—those promises we make to ourselves. Because God knows our motivation isn't always pure."

"I have to go back to New York in a week or so."

She slipped the strap over her shoulder. "Why wait?

Leave today. Oh, and don't bother looking me up if you ever come back."

"What are you going to do, walk back to town from here?" he asked, unwilling just to leave her there, unwilling to face the ultimatum she'd delivered. He didn't want to never see her again. But he had to go back to New York.

"Yes."

"It's farther than you think."

"I'd walk to the moon before I got back into that car with you."

"I'm serious, Allie. It's at least three miles, and there's no sidewalk."

She gave him her ice-queen look. It didn't work so well with the teary eyes and the red nose. "So it might take me a while to get there. But I will get there. Unlike you, I don't just quit halfway when the going gets tough."

"Oh, for christsake—"

"Have a nice life, Harry."

She slammed the car door shut and started walking toward the restaurant. He put the car in gear, following as he leaned over and opened the window.

"So, what? You're going to get a job cleaning houses?"

"It's not as if I have a lot of choices here." Even though she was walking away, she was still talking to him.

Allie, wait. Don't walk away from me. But he couldn't say those words. It was too hard to do. It stripped him too bare. "You shouldn't be cleaning houses. You should be writing. You're a good writer."

She stopped and looked at him. "And you know this from reading two lines from my journal?"

Oh, shit. He tried to shrug, tried to hide the truth. "Well, yeah."

She wasn't fooled, not for one second. "You read my journal." It wasn't even a question.

"Just a little. Only ten pages."

"Ten pages?"

"That short story you wrote about Jane—"

"That was private!"

"It was good." He knew he was in the wrong here and it made him angry all over again—at her, at himself, at the entire goddamned world. He wanted her to stay, and he didn't want himself to want that. "You should be writing," he said again. "Cleaning houses—that's the stupidest thing I ever heard."

She was so angry she was shaking. "Yeah, I'm not known for being supersmart. Just look who I chose for a friend. I couldn't have been more wrong about you, Harry. I'm glad I found out the truth before I did something really stupid, like fall in love with you."

He couldn't respond to that. What could he possibly say? His anger instantly morphed into something colder, something harder. Something that hurt like hell.

"I was, um, planning to give you some money," he told her, amazed he could speak past the pain in his chest. "You know, to get started, to make first and last month's rent on an apartment . . ."

"I don't want your money," she said just as she began walking again. "I don't want anything from you."

"But—"

"I can sell my engagement and wedding rings. It's not like I need them anymore."

"No, Al, please. Don't do that. I'll get you the money."

She stopped walking and turned to face him. "I'm not your responsibility anymore," she told him. "Wow, that was easy, huh? You didn't even need to sign anything to get rid of me." She backed away from the car. "Just drive away, Harry. I don't need you. Just like Shaun said—I'm better off without you."

She walked away, and this time Harry let her go.

Seventeen

❧ ❧

"**I**T'S GETTING LATE. Don't you need to leave pretty soon?" George raised his voice so that Kim could hear him from the kitchen.

She stuck her head out the door. "I'm off tonight. I switched shifts with Paulette, so I'll be doing a double tomorrow."

"Oh, shit," George said. Tonight was the night he'd finally convinced Nicole to come over to talk. It had taken her nearly a week to get back to him, and several days more to pin down a date that she was available and Kim was scheduled to work.

She was due to arrive in a matter of minutes.

Kim stuck her head back. "What?"

"I hate it when you have to do double shifts," he covered quickly.

"Poor baby." She blew him a kiss. "I'm making popcorn—want some?"

"Uh, sure," George said, searching wildly through the papers and magazines on the coffee table for the cordless phone. He grabbed it quickly and punched in Nic's number, but her answering machine picked up after only two rings. He waited for the beep and then spoke as softly as he could into the phone. "It's me. Don't come here. Change in plans. Call me."

There was a chance—a slim chance—that Nicki would check her messages on her way over.

"Who're you calling this late?" Kim asked, carrying a microwave bag of popcorn and two bottles of beer from the kitchen.

"Just—one of the cases I was working on. I tried calling one of the other agents, but . . . he wasn't home."

Kim sat down next to him, handing him one of the beer bottles. "Is it the case you were working on when you got shot? The one about what's his name, the mob boss from the Island. Trotta?"

George smiled as he tossed the phone back into the clutter on the table. "You know I'm not allowed to talk about that."

"But it's so exciting. I mean, you could have been killed. Don't I deserve to know just a little bit about it?"

"You already know too much from snooping in my office."

Kim feigned insult. "I was not snooping! I just happened to see that file."

"Liar, liar, pants on fire."

She threw her leg over him and straddled his lap. "Pants on fire sounds like fun." She kissed him, and just like that, all playfulness was gone. When she pulled back to look at him, he knew exactly where they were heading.

And he was dying to go there—but for the fact Nicole was about to show up.

He touched Kim's face, trailing his fingers along the soft curve of her cheek. "Babe, you are wearing me out."

She smiled, a very young, very shy smile that made his chest feel tight. God, when she looked at him that way . . .

"Why are you so interested in Michael Trotta?" he asked.

She looked away from him, her smile fading. "I don't

know. I've heard stuff about him. He's dangerous. It scares me a little, thinking that he might somehow hurt you. Scares me more than a little."

"And that's really it," he said. "No other reason?"

She looked at him and took a breath as if she were about to speak.

The doorbell rang.

It was impossibly bad timing.

"Shit," George said.

"Are you expecting someone?" Kim asked.

"No." Liar . . . He helped her move off him and reached down for his crutches.

Kim ran for the door. "I'll get it."

"No!" he shouted, and she froze. At her surprised look, he cleared his throat. "I mean, let me. Please. I don't like you opening the door so late at night."

"God, George, you always make me feel so safe." She peeked out through the peephole then turned to face him, surprise creasing her brow. "It's your boss."

George made himself frown, made himself sound perplexed. "Nicole? What is she doing here?" Liar . . . He opened the door. "Nic, God, what a surprise." He raised his voice. "Yup, Kim, you were right. It's Nicole. What brings you out this way so late at night, Nic, when I wasn't expecting you at all?"

Nicki looked good. Wherever she had come from, she was dressed in going-out clothes, not just work clothes. A black dress that actually made her look feminine, showing off the trim, athletic body she normally hid beneath boxy suits. Her hair was fancier than usual, all pouffy and styled and hairsprayed, and she wore perfume—a scent he used to love.

She lifted one eyebrow lazily and shook her head in disgust. "Good thing I didn't use my key," she said barely audibly.

George made a face of pain. "I'm sorry," he mouthed silently.

Kim peeked cheerfully over George's shoulder. "Hi, Nicole. Good thing you didn't come five minutes from now, because we probably would have been naked."

And George wouldn't have answered the door—and Nicki would've let herself in with her key. The key she hadn't given back after she'd moved out. That would've been awful.

"Don't you look nice," Kim continued. "This can't be about work . . ."

"Actually, it can," Nicole fabricated quickly. "I was in the neighborhood, and I saw your light on. I have a computer file I wanted to drop off—it's too sensitive to send electronically." She drew a small disk box from her handbag and opened it, handing one of the disks to George with a cool smile. "When do you think you'll get a chance to look at this?"

"Tomorrow night," he told her. "Definitely. Kim's got a double shift that starts . . . What time, babe?"

"Six-thirty."

"Yeah, and goes until about two A.M."

"Well, I'm not sure what my schedule's like," Nicki said, "but if I'm free, I'll . . . give you a call."

"That'd be fine," George said. "Because, you know, as long as Kim's not home, I won't be having any wild sex, so you won't be interrupting anything." Now, why did he say that? He'd promised himself he was through tormenting Nicki. And he didn't want to alienate her—he wanted her to come over. He had to talk to her.

"Gee," Nic said dryly. "That's so much more than I ever wanted to know." She smiled tightly at Kim. "Good night. Sorry to have disturbed you."

George slipped the disk into the pocket of his shirt then closed and locked the door.

"Didn't that strike you as being just a little too coincidental?" Kim stood with her arms crossed, her eyes narrowed slightly.

"Um," George said. "No?" Pants on fire . . .

"She just happened to be in the neighborhood," Kim mused. "Just happened to be all snazzed up, and she decides now's the time to drop off some computer disk?"

George smiled weakly. "Yeah, well, you know . . . She works all the time. That's why she's the boss and I'm not."

"No," Kim said decisively. "This is more than that. You know what I think?"

George held out his hands in surrender. "What do you think?"

"I think she's hot for you."

George choked. "That's crazy."

"No, I'm serious. I think your boss wants to do you. I've seen the way she looks at you. And how many bosses would go all the way upstate just to visit one of their employees in the hospital?" She shook her head. "No, George, I'm pretty sure. You better watch out for her. She's dying to catch you alone in the elevator."

"I don't know," George said, using his crutches to maneuver his way back to the couch. Kim had absolutely no clue that at one time he and Nic had been married, and the sparks she thought she saw were from anger, not lust. Well, maybe a little from lust. He and Nic had always had their best time in bed right after a fight.

"I think she came over tonight hoping I would be out."

"And I think you're wrong," he lied.

She turned toward him suddenly. "Liar, liar, pants on fire!"

George started guiltily. "What? I'm not—"

"That's where we were before we were so rudely interrupted." Kim smiled sweetly, cluelessly, thank God. Her smile turned wicked. "I believe you were about to set my pants on fire?"

"There he is again!" Mrs. Gerty stood peering out her front window. "It's one of those little Japanese cars. Maroon. And the driver looks like a real hooligan."

Alessandra didn't have to go to the window to know who was sitting in the car outside Mrs. Gerty's house, but she looked anyway to appease the elderly woman. "That's just Harry."

He'd been following her around now for close to an entire week.

"He's stalking you," Mrs. Gerty insisted. "No, don't touch the curtains. He'll know we've spotted him."

"He's not a stalker. He's kind of like . . . a bodyguard." Harry never got out of his car. He just slouched behind the steering wheel, following her wherever she went.

Her days had fallen into a pattern. She woke up early, left her tiny furnished apartment above the Yurgens' garage, and walked over to the Merry Maid's office. The owner, Natalie MacGregor, had the good fortune of being overwhelmed by client requests, and the tiny office was in a permanent state of uproar.

Allie spent about half an hour each morning organizing the work orders by proximity, and making sure the trucks were stocked.

Then she went out in one of the trucks and worked her butt off, hustling from one assignment to the next until she went home at about seven, showered, and collapsed into bed with a book. And tried like crazy not to miss Harry.

In the past week, he hadn't approached her, hadn't said so much as a single word to her. He just followed her.

She was still furious with him. When she'd first spotted

him trailing her, she'd dared to hope that since he was still in town he was trying to work things out with his kids. But she'd run into Marge in the supermarket, who'd told her Harry wasn't staying with them. He hadn't stopped in, didn't call, didn't come by. He was staying at the motel up by the interstate.

Except Allie knew he wasn't really staying there, because he was sitting in his car outside her house when she went home in the evening, and he was still there, in the exact same place, when she woke up the next morning.

His single goal seemed to be to make absolutely certain that Alessandra was safe. He'd apparently been serious when he'd signed the papers giving up custody of his children.

As mad as she was at him, she missed him terribly. She missed his ceaseless conversations, his raunchy sense of humor. She even missed his foul language.

She spent most of her days and all of her nights completely alone. Except for the fact that she was working hard, the lack of company was much as it had been when she was married to Griffin. He'd been gone during the day, and when he was home at night, they talked very little. He spent much of his time reading or watching TV. If they spoke at all, it had been about social engagements and his work schedule.

Yes, she'd spent seven years with very little conversation, and certainly no debating or arguing. It was funny that after only such a short time, she should miss it so much, that she should miss Harry so much.

But she was not—was not—going to approach him. If he wanted to come to her and apologize, well, that would be one thing. But for her to go to him . . . No, she wasn't going to do that. She was strong enough not to do that, strong enough to know that as much as she missed him, she didn't need him in her life. She was better off without him. He had far too much emotional luggage attached—anything more than the most casual of friendships would be a complete disaster. And before she'd walked away from him, Allie had been well on the verge of blasting past all pretense of casualness.

She would not let herself love him. Absolutely not.

"I bought some butter cookies from the bakery." Mrs. Gerty opened a tin of cookies that was nearly as large as she was, as Alessandra finished washing her dishes. "You need to eat about forty of 'em—fatten you up a little."

"Oh, no, thanks," Allie said. "But I can't. I'm . . ." Allergic. She wasn't supposed to tell people she was allergic to milk and butter. "Not hungry," she finished lamely.

Mrs. Gerty didn't believe her. "I'll put some in a baggie for you to take. I can't talk you into coffee today, can I?"

"I'm sorry, no. But thank you anyway." Alessandra finished cleaning out the sink and took off the rubber gloves Mrs. Gerty insisted she wear to save her hands. She had to run to the next job and then to the next, or she wouldn't get home until after eight tonight.

She felt bad for not being able to stay and keep the elderly woman company, though. Clearly Mrs. Gerty wanted someone to talk to as much—or perhaps even more than—she wanted someone to clean her house. She paid for service four times a week. Allie had been there three times this week already, and the place was immaculate.

"I guess I also can't talk you into taking a walk with Hunter and me." Mrs. Gerty sighed.

"I'm sorry, no."

Mrs. Gerty was about eighty pounds, four feet eight and birdlike. Her enormous dog, Hunter, weighed nearly twenty pounds more. And while Allie didn't know his exact breed, he was definitely of the attack-dog variety.

She had to walk past his fenced-in yard to get to Mrs.

Gerty's door. The first time she'd come over, she'd stopped short at the sight of him. She would have turned around and had another of the Merry Maids assigned to this house, but she knew that Harry was watching her from his car.

She had to be strong and tough. She had to prove that she could do things that were difficult. She had to show him that she wasn't a quitter. Like some people she knew.

So she'd held her breath and she'd walked past Hunter, and she'd survived. She'd survived seven times now. Four trips into the house, and three trips out. And while she knew it wasn't the same as letting a dog lick her face, it was a major step for her.

"Mrs. Gerty, I'm going over to a friend's house for dinner tonight. Marge Novick, do you know her? She teaches English at the college. We were going to order pizza and salad and then maybe rent a movie. I bet she'd be thrilled if you joined us."

The elderly woman turned away, pretending to be completely engrossed in trimming imaginary dead leaves from her African violets. "Oh, I couldn't just . . ."

"Sure, you could." Alessandra knew what it was like to be lonely. "I'm not taking no for an answer. I'll pick you up around seven." She'd have to borrow the Merry Maids truck, but she'd done it last night to get groceries, and Natalie had had no problem with it. It meant walking home from the Merry Maids parking lot after dark, but with Harry following her, she'd be perfectly safe. "Is it a date?"

Mrs. Gerty actually had tears in her eyes. "It sounds . . . lovely. Thank you, Alice."

"My friends call me Allie," she said. "See you at seven."

She let herself out, and as she went past Hunter's yard, she forced herself to stop and look into the dog's eyes. They were deep brown and filled with intelligence and possibly . . . friendliness? He cocked his head inquisitively, trotting close to the fence and wagging his stubby tail.

He seemed to recognize her, even to like her.

But then he started to bark, and she jumped back, her heart pounding.

She ran down the driveway and climbed into the truck, slamming the door behind her. She dug for her keys in the front pocket of her jeans but then lifted her bottom off the seat as she realized she was sitting on something.

It was an envelope. A very thick envelope.

Inside was a Social Security card with Alice Plotkin's name on it and nearly four thousand dollars in crisp, new, big-headed hundred-dollar bills.

There was a note scribbled on the outside of the envelope. "Don't use your old Social Security number ever again." There was no "Dear Allie," no "Love, Harry."

But she knew it was from him.

She could see Harry in the side mirror, parked about forty feet back from the truck. She took the Social Security card and carefully put it in the glove compartment with her wallet, and then she climbed out of the truck and marched over to him.

She threw the envelope onto his lap through the open window. "I don't want your money."

He shrugged. "Suit yourself. I thought you might appreciate being able to get an apartment in a slightly better part of town."

"I happen to like my apartment, thank you very much." It was all hers, completely hers. She and she alone had picked it out, and she alone was responsible for paying the rent. That was a good feeling, an empowering feeling. So what if it wasn't the Taj Mahal.

"I'd feel better if you'd take a few bucks and put some locks on the windows, maybe a dead bolt on the door. That place is a security nightmare."

He looked awful. His eyes were rimmed with red and his face was nearly gray with fatigue. He looked as if he hadn't slept in a week. He certainly hadn't shaved in at least that long.

"Yeah, well, it's my nightmare," she told him tightly. "Not yours."

He looked up at her, looked at her oversize Merry Maids T-shirt, her dirty jeans, the bandanna she'd tied around her head to keep her hair out of her face. "You're working too hard. You look like shit."

"I look like shit, because that's my cover, remember? God, Harry, you just always know exactly what to say, don't you? As to whether I'm working too hard, that's none of your business." Allie crossed her arms. "It's been a week. When are you going to stop following me around?"

"Hey, it's not like I want to follow you. I just . . . I need to be sure that you're safe. Forgive me for being diligent and doing my job."

"I'm safe. Besides, I stopped being your 'job' when we left New York."

"New York." He ran his hand down his face, rubbing his eyes. "I've gotta get back there, but . . ." He shook his head and made a sound of complete, intense exasperation. "I don't know why I've got this weird sixth-sense thing happening—you know, like somehow I know something bad is going to go down. It's driving me fucking nuts. There's no way Trotta could track you here now. I know that, but still . . ."

He rubbed his forehead with one hand, as if he had a massive headache, and Allie's anger softened.

"Maybe the sixth-sense thing isn't about me," she

said. "Maybe it's because you know if you leave, you'll never patch things up with Shaun. Look, Harry, I'm having dinner at Marge's house tonight. Why don't you—"

He held up his hand. "Don't start," he said. "Just . . . go back to work, Allie. You can't save me. You were smart to walk away when you did. I'm going to . . . Yeah, I'm definitely going to leave on Monday. You're going to be fine. I'm just going to give it a few more days."

Monday. Monday was in four days.

"Will you . . ." She swallowed and had to start over. "I hope you'll come back sometime soon, to see your kids." And me. She couldn't say the words aloud. She had far too much pride, too much self-respect.

Harry smiled, but it was a smile filled with pain. "That's one of the things I like best about you, Al. Even when a situation is utterly hopeless, you still find a way to hope."

"Harry, your situation is not—"

"I'm going to say good-bye now," he said. "I think it's probably easier that way."

Kim paced the living room while George took a nap.

He'd gone into the bedroom to lie down more than three hours ago, and he was still sound asleep.

She wanted to wake him up. She was going to wake him up. Soon. She had only a few hours before she had to go to work, and she had to talk to him.

She had to tell him about Michael Trotta.

She would be honest. She would tell him how Michael made her approach George at the Fantasy Club. She would tell him that at first she was only doing a job. But she would make him understand how that all changed when she'd fallen in love with him.

George would understand. She knew he would. He

would kiss her gently, the way he always did, and he would smile at her and for the first time in her life, everything would be all right. He would figure out a way to keep her safe from Michael. If anyone could do it, George could.

She made another circuit around the living room, slowing as she approached George's bookshelf. He had tons of books, more than twenty times the number of books she'd read in her entire life, maybe. He had books on every subject—medical books, books about guns, books about World War II. They were neatly arranged in groups according to subject. She smiled. George had an entire shelf of books about Star Trek. He was a science-fiction nerd. She should have known.

Another shelf was devoted to what looked like a collection of photo albums, yet another to fitness and diet books. One of the titles caught her eye. Better Buns in Thirty Days. Now, had George bought that book simply to look at the pictures of women's butts, or did he have a secret wish for self-improvement?

She pulled out the book and flipped it open.

It was definitely a book written for women, and the pictures were nothing special. Any Victoria's Secret catalog had far better thrills.

But then she saw handwriting on the cover page—a note, written right on the book.

She angled it toward the light.

"To Nic, the best piece of ass in the agency. Happy Anniversary. Your husband, G."

Kim stared at the words, wishing they didn't make quite so much sense.

Nic. Nicole. G. George. Anniversary. Husband.

Oh, God.

She could be wrong. She might be wrong. Although suddenly things started to click into place.

Nicole dropping over at all times of the day and night. The barbed comments they both made, the simmering tension between them.

And last night . . .

Last night Nicole had come over expecting that Kim wouldn't be home, because George had told her Kim wouldn't be home.

George was cheating on Kim with his ex—the woman he'd all but confessed to being still hung up on. The woman he still loved.

Maybe she was wrong.

She reached for the photo albums, hoping to find a clue.

The first held pictures from a vacation. Scenery. Mountains and valleys. Who the hell bothered to take pictures of only scenery?

She snapped it shut, fighting tears she refused to let come—after all she could be wrong. She put it back, drawing out the album with the white cover. White, wedding . . .

It was a professional album, with thin paper protecting the photographs. She pulled the paper back, and . . .

George and Nicole. Gazing into each other's eyes. George looking heartbreakingly handsome in a black tuxedo, Nicole, the bitch, in a white dress and veil.

Oh, God. George was still in love with Nicole. Except their relationship was so perverse and twisted, he had to use her to make Nicole jealous enough to want him back. He didn't love Kim, he'd never loved her, he would never love her.

As Kim stared at the photo, all of her hopes of everything finally being all right crashed and burned.

Shaun found Mindy at the basketball courts by the high school.

She was playing Around the World, all alone, and to his surprise, she was sinking most of the shots.

He knew exactly when she spotted him—she started missing.

He'd said some awful things to her. It had been over a week, and she still hadn't shown up back in his playroom. She was the one who now avoided him at school, running if she saw him coming.

He knew he'd killed their friendship. He'd pushed past the point of forgiveness with the things he'd said. He knew it was possible—no, it was probable—that there was nothing he could say to make things right again.

But he had to apologize. He couldn't bear the thought of Mindy going through the rest of her life actually believing he'd meant what he'd said.

She kept shooting, kept missing, as he parked his bike and walked out onto the court.

"Better watch out," she said, shooting over his head. "Someone might see you talking to me."

"I don't care."

"Yeah, well maybe I care if someone sees a loser like you talking to me."

What could he say to that? "I . . ."

"What do you want?" she asked, holding tightly to the ball, as if she were keeping herself from throwing it at his head—but just barely. "Spit it out. If you're here to say you're sorry, get it over with, so I can tell you to go to hell and get back to my practice."

"I brought some pictures of my father to show you."

It wasn't what she'd expected him to say, and she blinked her enormous eyes, temporarily silenced.

Shaun held out the photo album as if to prove his point and she actually moved closer. He opened the cover, and she sidled slightly behind him, to look over his shoulder.

"These were from Em's second birthday," he told her. "Harry and my mom were divorced by then, but they were both at the party. They were really nice to each other, but I knew there wasn't any chance of them getting back together because my mom was already spending lots of time with this other guy, Tim—he, you know, stayed overnight a lot."

Mindy touched the clear plastic that protected the photographs, pointing to a picture of Harry holding Emily in one arm, his other arm locked around Kevin's neck. Shaun, nearly twelve years old and still tiny, stood nearby.

"That's your dad?" she asked.

He nodded. In the picture, Harry was laughing. They all were laughing—all except Shaun. He just looked wistful.

"And here's my mother." There was another picture beneath it—Sonya holding Shaun in her arms. Shaun had never fought to get away, not like other nearly twelve-year-old boys. He'd loved her so much.

"That's you." Mindy ran her finger across his face. "Wow, you were short. You're, like, twice as big now." She turned the page, looking at the other photographs, all taken during that same party.

Shaun and Kevin, playing ball with Emily. Everyone mugging in front of the birthday cake they'd all helped decorate. Harry giving Kevin a piggyback ride. Em and Shaun hanging on to his legs.

"Who's this?" she asked, pointing to Kevin. "A cousin?"

"He was my brother. Kevin." Shaun didn't look up, but he could feel the change in Mindy. She'd gone very, very still at his words. Was. Past tense. It said it all without having to say the awful words, the ugly words like died. He knew she wouldn't ask for the details—no one ever did. It was as if now that Kevin was gone, no one wanted to speak his name.

Everyone wanted to back away from death, to keep their distance. Problem was, death had come and set up permanent camp in Shaun's yard. There was no avoiding it. It was there for him, every day, right in his face from the moment he woke up in the morning and realized painfully once again that Kev and his mom were dead.

Dead. Not gone, not passed away, not quietly past tense, but horribly, violently dead.

"He and my mother were killed when a truck hit their car," he told her. "It was just a few months after these pictures were taken."

"I didn't know," Mindy whispered.

"How could you know?" he asked. "I didn't tell you."

"Oh, Shaun." Her gigantic eyes were filled with enormous tears.

He forced himself to hold her gaze. "It doesn't excuse the things I said to you." It didn't excuse Harry's actions either. Em had needed him. Shaun had needed him. But he'd left them to struggle through on their own.

"Maybe not," Mindy told him, "but it makes it much easier to forgive you."

"So how is Harry?" Marge asked. "He looked awful. Is he drinking? His mother was a terrible drunk."

"The entire time I've known him, he's only had a couple of glasses of beer." Allie toyed with the crust of her pizza. Marge, bless her, was lactose intolerant, and had ordered one of the pizzas without cheese, thus saving Allie from a dinner of only salad. "He doesn't sleep well, though. He's . . . haunted."

"I worry about him," Marge said. "The few times I've seen him around town, he's looked as if he's just barely holding on. If you see him, do me a favor and let him know I've taken to leaving the answering machine on at night and turning off the ringers on the phone. I've been getting these awful prank phone calls in the middle of the night. Students, I think. I'm pretty sure I'm not going to teach again next year. Anyway, just let him know, will you?"

"I haven't really talked with him lately myself," Allie said.

Marge glanced toward the living room, toward the sound of Emily's laughter. The little girl had taken an instant liking to Mrs. Gerty. Annarose Gerty. They were all on a first-name basis here.

Shaun and Mindy had gone upstairs to the attic playroom and were watching TV. Shaun had been terse all throughout dinner, Mindy anxious.

Harry's son was a dancer, of all things. Marge was taking him and Emily into Denver that weekend for an audition with a summer dance company that would be based here at the college in Hardy. According to Shaun's teachers, he was almost guaranteed to win a spot.

"Feel free to tell me to mind my own business," Marge said, "but it seems kind of strange, you coming all the way out here with Harry, and then him leaving, and you staying behind. Particularly since it's so obvious that he's as crazy in love with you as you are with him."

"Oh," Allie said. "Oh, no." She laughed. "You're wrong, we're . . . we were just friends."

"Ah," Marge said. "My mistake."

Eighteen

~ ~

Harry sat in the dark, with the car window open, listening to the quiet sounds of the warm spring night.

The light in Allie's apartment had gone out hours ago and everything was completely still.

He knew he should go back to the motel, get some sleep. He knew he'd reached the point where he was physically exhausted. He'd be asleep the second he hit the bed.

Or he would be if he could only shake this feeling of dread he'd been carrying around for the past week.

Something was wrong. The feeling hovered around him relentlessly. It was the same feeling he'd get if he ever accidentally left the house with the stove on. The threat of impending disaster would niggle at him until he went back to check. Somehow part of his brain knew that something had been left undone, that something had slipped past him.

Allie's life depended on the fact that nothing had slipped past him now. He knew he'd done everything right. He knew she was completely hidden from Trotta. So why couldn't he shake this feeling?

Fatigue could play a part. And the fact that he missed her so goddamn much might have something to do with it, too. Add in a barrel of shame from knowing his son's accusations had been right on the nose. He may have taken care of Shaun and Emily's financial needs—he'd made sure they were housed and fed and cared for—but he'd abandoned his children on the most basic, emotional level.

And there was nothing he could do to change the past, no way he could take a do-over.

So instead, he'd walked away from his kids for good.

He knew if he could do that, leaving Allie would be a piece of cake.

Harry got out of the car, taking care to close the door silently behind him. He made a slow circuit of the garage. Allie's place was on the second floor of that outbuilding. The apartment door was cheaply made, the lock ridiculous. Anyone could kick it open with one well-placed push. And if they wanted their entrance to be a silent one, they could easily climb to any one of the apartment windows—none of which had locks.

He should've insisted she get an apartment with some kind of security system. He should've insisted she take that money today.

He should've told her the truth—that once he left, he wasn't coming back, not ever. He should've told her to stop hoping.

But expecting Allie to stop hoping was as ridiculous as thinking she could stop breathing. If there was one thing she had plenty of—too much of—it was hope.

His own hope was gone. He'd used it all up that day he got the call to come identify Sonya and Kevin's bodies. All the way to the hospital, he'd hoped it was a mistake, hoped it was someone else's ex-wife and kid who'd been brought in, DOA.

But he'd hoped in vain.

So he no longer wasted his time on hope. He factored it out of the equation. He didn't hope he wouldn't hurt Shaun and Emily anymore—he'd completely handled that by pulling himself out of the picture. In the same way, he'd removed himself from Allie's life. He shouldn't have to hope Trotta wouldn't find her. He should know that wasn't going to happen.

But that little niggling doubt remained, and as he stared up at her open bedroom window, he found himself hoping—fervently—that he was simply overtired, and that somewhere, somehow, he hadn't left some burner unattended, about to explode into flames.

"Lemon-pepper linguine," Harry said with a smile, his warm gaze dropping to her lips right before he bent to kiss her.

Alessandra knew she shouldn't melt against him. She knew she should warn him, tell him they had to run.

They were back in the Super Stop and Shop, and any minute now George was going to get shot.

But then the sharp sound of the gunfire rang out, and it was Harry who jerked, Harry who was hit.

Harry whose life she was trying so desperately to save.

"Don't do this," she begged him as the life drained out of him through a gaping hole in his chest. She was covered with his blood. There was no way to stop it, no way to save him. "Don't leave me, don't you leave me!"

"I'm going to say good-bye now," he told her. "I think it's probably easier that way."

He pointed up toward the ceiling, and Allie lifted her head.

Mrs. Gerty's dog, Hunter, was perched on top of the shelves, balanced on the stacks of canned goods. He wagged his tail and seemed to smile. But then his face changed, and he wasn't friendly Hunter anymore. He was Pinky, Michael Trotta's dog.

He snarled and barked, glaring down at her with his devil's eyes, tensing his body and leaping, teeth bared.

And Alessandra screamed and screamed and screamed.

"Nightmare! Allie, come on, wake up. You're having a nightmare."

She opened her eyes, and Harry was there, really there, safe and whole, leaning over her bed in the moonlight. She reached for him, and he pulled her into his arms, holding her tightly.

"It's okay," he murmured. "You're okay. Jesus, you scared me to death. I heard you screaming from the street."

His arms were so warm, his chest so solid, Allie couldn't speak. She could do nothing but cling to him and hope he'd never let her go.

"That dog spooked you today, huh?" he asked. "I saw the way you ran."

He pushed her hair back from her face, running his fingers through it again and again. The sensation was dizzying. He smelled so familiar, and his arms felt so much like being home. How could he leave her? How could he even consider leaving her? She wanted to cry.

"You're shaking," he said. "It must've been a bad one, huh?"

She nodded.

"Can I get you something?" he asked. "A glass of water, or . . . ?"

Or what?

"Stay with me." Her voice broke as she asked him— no, not asked, begged. She was strong, she knew she was strong. She'd spent the entire past week being strong, proving to herself and to Harry that she would be fine without him. And she would be. But it didn't make her want him any less. And so she would beg if she had to. "Stay with me tonight."

Tonight and forever. But she didn't dare say that aloud.

But even the softness of the moonlight couldn't hide the despair etched onto his face. "Is that smart?" he asked, searching her eyes.

"No," she said and kissed him.

He made a noise like the air deflating from a tire but then he kissed her back, taking her mouth as if he, too, had spent the week lying awake all night, remembering their lovemaking, intimate detail by achingly intimate detail.

"I've got to close the screen," he whispered, pulling back from her and crossing to the window. That must've been the way he'd gotten inside. Somehow he'd climbed all the way up to the second floor. "I think I broke it," he told her. "I wasn't very careful when I came in."

"Just close the window," she told him, but he stood there, as if considering leaving, now, the way he'd come in.

"Harry," Allie whispered. "Please?"

The moonlight made her bedroom silvery and bright. She could see his face from across the room, and she knew he could see her just as clearly—the light from the window above her bed shone down like a spotlight upon her.

She unfastened the buttons of her pajama top, and for once, he was completely silent. She slipped it off her shoulders, slipped her legs out of her pants, pushing her pajamas off the bed and onto the floor.

She was banking on the fact that he'd told her the truth. She was depending on the fact that he found her irresistible, because there she was. Right there in the light. No hiding, no excuses. She may not like what she saw when she looked into the mirror, but she liked what she saw reflected in Harry's eyes. He liked her, bad hair and all.

He closed the window.

It seemed to take forever for him to walk back across the tiny room. And then he sat down on the edge of the bed, just looking at her, touching her only with the heat of his gaze.

And silent. Still so silent.

She took a condom from her bedside table and held it out to him. At his quizzical look, she explained, "I was hoping you'd be back."

He touched her then, just one finger against her cheek. "You never give up hope, do you? Even when something's completely hopeless."

"But you did come back, didn't you?"

He laughed in amazement. "I should go—if only to prove you wrong."

"I hope you don't go." She moved then, straddling his lap, pushing him down onto the bed. "Of course, it's always good to give hope a little help whenever possible."

Alessandra kissed him hard, tugging at his T-shirt, pressing herself against him. And she knew that it had taken every ounce of his control to sit there without touching her for so long. He exploded, pulling her against him, touching her everywhere, skimming his hands across her body, groaning as he filled his palms with her breasts.

"Yeah, this is definitely helping." He pulled his shirt over his head then reached down to help her unfasten his belt.

He covered himself with the condom in an instant then held her hips, pulling her down onto him.

His quiet "Oh, yeah" echoed her wonder at their joining so perfectly—it brought tears to her eyes. He was leaving on Monday. He was going to walk away from something so impossibly right.

She kissed him again as she moved on top of him,

awash in the simplicity of the truth she'd been denying
for so long.

She loved Harry. She loved him unlike she'd ever loved
anyone before. He was her friend, her lover, her one true
love. He filled her heart and lightened her soul. She was
okay without him, but how could she settle for only
okay, knowing she could have this irreplaceable pleasure, this one-of-a-kind sense of contentment with him in
her life?

The sheer strength of her emotion should have frightened her—love had always been an imprisoning thing.
She'd loved Griffin, at least she had at first, and he'd
locked her away from the world. But he'd taken her love
and given her only material things in return, and he'd
treated her like a possession.

She knew that she wasn't Harry's possession. He'd
never treat her that way. He respected her too much.
And—perhaps unfortunately—he wasn't her possession,
either.

Because she had no chains with which to hold him, he
was bound and determined to walk away.

Harry groaned as he moved beneath her, as close to his
release as she was to hers. As she looked down into his
eyes, as she watched his emotions play across his face,
she knew another truth. A far harder truth to face.

It simply wasn't a matter of making him fall in love
with her. Because even if he did love her, he wouldn't
stay. He loved his kids, she knew he did, yet he was leaving them, too.

It was as hopeless a situation as she'd ever encountered.

Harry reached between them, touching her, sending
her over the edge as he gazed into her eyes. She kept her
eyes open and let him see everything she was feeling, the
sweet intensity of the pleasure he gave her, the limitless
passion she had for him, the strength of her love. She'd

never dare to say the words aloud, but if he wanted to, it was there for him to see in her eyes.

His own release followed immediately, and although he, too, held her gaze, Allie closed her eyes.

She didn't want to see his truth—that despite all she was willing to give him, that despite the fact that neither of them would ever find such perfection again, he was already gone.

Still, as long as she kept her eyes closed, she could hope he was going to stay.

It was a little before two-thirty in the morning when Kim let herself into George's apartment. It was raining, she hadn't been able to flag down a cab, her feet hurt, and she'd been touched inappropriately by patrons not just once tonight but twice. The bouncer had had to intervene, and it had gotten ugly for awhile.

The living room was dark, and she moved quietly, thinking that George had already gone to bed. But as she hung her raincoat in the front closet, she heard his voice from the bedroom.

He was talking on the phone. "No, she's not home yet. And I'm not going to ask where you were, babe, out this late." He laughed, the sound low and intimate, and Kim's heart broke. Babe. He was talking to her. To Nicole. She headed for the bedroom, intending to tell George exactly what she thought of him, the two-timing son of a bitch.

"Yeah, you were working," he said. "What a surprise. Anyway, thanks for calling me back, Nic. I think I figured out a way to find Harry."

Harry. George's partner. The one who'd run off with Alessandra Lamont. This was it. This was the information she'd been waiting all these weeks to hear. Kim froze, standing there outside the bedroom door.

She didn't want to listen, didn't want to know. She

didn't want to have to betray George, even if he was a two-timing son of a bitch.

"I was watching some stupid late-night movie about this child-custody battle, and I suddenly remembered. Right before we went up to Paul's River, Harry got this letter in the mail from some lawyers, telling him that a petition had been filed with the court challenging his custody of his kids. Something about a name change, too. That petition would be a matter of public record, wouldn't it? The kids' real names would've been used—Shaun and Emily O'Dell—and their address would be on the petition, right? That's got to be easy to find—I mean, it's just a matter of checking the county records. I know Colorado's a big state, but the records are probably on computer . . . And once we find Harry . . ."

George was silent for a moment, and when he spoke again, his voice was unnaturally grim. "This better get me a promotion, boss." He laughed, but there was no humor in it. "Yeah, right. Let me know what turns up."

He hung up the phone, and Kim scrambled back, away from the door, as silently as possible. She went into the kitchen, opened the refrigerator, and stared inside as if she were looking for a late-night snack.

George stopped short at the sight of her, balancing precariously on his crutches. "Kim. God, when did you get home?"

She glanced up at him. "Oh, hi, baby. I just got in. I'm starving."

He was silent, just looking at her.

"I'm thinking about running out for some donuts."

"Oh," he said. "Really? Isn't it raining? And we've got some of those good cookies you like . . ."

Kim frowned into the fridge. "No, I think I want a donut." There was a pay phone in front of the twenty-four-hour Frosty Donuts. She could call one of Trotta's men while the information was still fresh in her mind. Shaun and Emily O'Dell. Petition to the court. Name change, custody. Colorado. She couldn't let herself think about what that phone call would mean for Alessandra Lamont. She could only focus on what Michael would do to Kim if he found out she knew and didn't tell him. And he would find out. He always found out.

George sat down heavily at the kitchen table, as if his leg was really hurting him again. "So, you're going to, like, go back out at this time of night? In the rain? For a donut?"

She closed the refrigerator. "Want one?"

"No," he said quietly. He stared down at the table, and when he looked up at her, she could swear for just an instant that he was going to cry.

There was no way he could know she'd overheard that phone call—that phone call to his ex-wife, Nicole, whom he was still in love with, whom he spoke to and got together with, every chance he could. The bastard. He deserved to be betrayed, didn't he?

"I'll be back before you know it," she said.

She hurried to the closet and got her raincoat, took her keys from the table by the door, and let herself out of the apartment.

The stairway down from the fourth floor was brightly lit, as was the glistening street outside. The rain had slowed to a gentle drizzle, and as Kim headed for the pay phone, she glanced back up at the windows to George's apartment.

She could see him standing there, just a shadowy silhouette, watching her go. He lifted one hand in what might've been a wave, but she turned quickly away, pulling her collar around her neck, pretending not to see, pretending not to care.

*   *   *

Alessandra kept her eyes tightly closed when she woke up, keeping reality at bay for as long as she could.

Harry was not going to be there, still in her bed, still lying beside her. But as long as she kept her eyes closed, she could pretend that he was.

She listened for a moment, but her apartment was silent. The water didn't run in the bathroom, the kitchen stove didn't make that odd ticking sound as it heated the water under the kettle, no one stirred and sighed beside her.

She opened her eyes.

Just as she'd expected, Harry was gone.

There was no note, no sign he'd ever been there at all. Just the slightest burn from his unshaven face on her chin. Just his scent and the warm memory of his touch, lingering on her skin.

She'd lost. If he could leave after last night, she'd lost for good.

And soon Harry would be leaving for New York, and he wasn't going to come back.

Maybe not ever.

Unable to stop her tears, Alessandra stepped into her shower and washed herself clean, wishing it were as easy to wash Harry from her heart.

Harry knew exactly when Allie spotted him.

She was approaching the intersection of Gulch and Main when he caught up with her, and she hit the brakes of the Merry Maids truck just a little too hard.

Her next stop was a sprawling stucco ranch on Killingworth Lane. She sat in the truck for a long time, as if she was waiting for him to approach her.

But he didn't move.

He couldn't move. It would entirely defeat the point of this kind of surveillance if he approached her. Besides, what could he possibly say? Thanks for another of the greatest sexual experiences of my life?

Glancing back at his car, Allie finally took the cleaning cart to the front door and disappeared inside. It was at least an hour and a half before she came out, again looking over at him hesitantly, as if hoping he'd get out of his car, stroll over, and chat.

He still didn't move.

He could tell from the way she climbed into the truck and from the jerky way she pulled out into the street that she was mad.

Her next stop was right around the corner. This time, instead of unhooking the cleaning cart from the back, she climbed down from the cab of the truck and marched toward Harry's car.

Ah, shit.

"You're just going to pretend last night didn't happen?" Her words were clipped, her face tight as she gazed down into his open car window. "Just like that, we're back to so-called normal? You keep your distance, we don't talk unless you're . . . you're . . . fucking me?" The words came out a whisper. She looked so completely upset, so devastated, Harry had to close his eyes. He hoped it would shield him from the guilt, but he knew it wouldn't help. He knew he shouldn't have stayed last night. He knew it would be a terrible mistake.

"Look, you were the one who asked me to stay. It was your idea." But he should have walked away. He should have, but he'd been completely unable to. All of his willpower was completely gone when it came to this woman, and that still scared the shit out of him.

"Were you just going to follow me around until Monday and then leave?" she asked, both tears and hope in her eyes, as if she actually thought he might tell her no. No, he was going to come over to her place for dinner tonight and what? Confess that he was completely in love with her, and that despite that—or hell, maybe because of it, he was still going to go to New York? And—as long as he was taking the complete fantasy route here—then he'd gently explain his obsessive need to fill the awful emptiness Kevin's death had carved inside of him with his pursuit of Michael Trotta, and he'd explain it so that she'd understand.

But Allie wouldn't understand. No one could. He didn't understand it himself.

As he gazed up into her pale, pinched face, he knew if he didn't get pissed, he was going to start to cry.

"I'm not sure what you want me to do," he told her roughly. "Send flowers? Not my style. Propose marriage maybe? Lie and pledge my undying love? I don't see the point in playing those games. I'm out of here on Monday, and I've already said good-bye."

He saw the complete and total death of hope in Allie's eyes, and he knew without a doubt that he'd pushed too far. He'd finally killed whatever it was she felt for him.

She turned away, her movements wooden, and he knew that although she'd told him not to bother to come back before, this time if she said it, she would mean it.

And sure enough, she turned back. "There'll be locks on my windows tonight," she said, then walked toward her truck, not looking back again.

Nineteen

"SHALL I LEAVE room for you to put cream in your coffee?"

"No, thanks," Harry said, "but if you've got any extra caffeine you can throw in, maybe some spare No-Doz lying around . . ."

The girl behind the counter was looking at him as if he were an escaped serial killer, about to pull his collection of human ears from his jacket pocket.

"Joke," Harry said. "That was just a joke."

He paid for the coffee, found a plastic top and a cardboard sleeve so he didn't burn his fingers, and went out into the glaring brilliance of the noon sunshine.

He caught sight of his reflection in the glass door. Christ, he looked like crap. He hadn't shaved in more than a week, hadn't showered or changed his clothes since early yesterday morning. His hair was already outgrowing the cut Allie had given him, standing up straight and making him look as if he'd permanently caught his finger in an electric socket.

He looked as if he might actually have a collection of human ears in his jacket pocket.

Allie's truck was parked in front of Renny Miller's Garage. She'd been cleaning the back office and now stood talking to Renny out by the big bay doors.

Renny's body language was unmistakable. He just

kept moving closer, leaning his tall, lanky frame against the wall, doing damn near everything but wrapping his arms around her.

Allie was looking extremely uncomfortable, and she did her best to inch away, but Renny just kept coming.

It was all Harry could do not to go over there and smack him.

But Allie had been acting as if Harry were invisible all day long, and he suspected if he did go over there, he'd be the one who'd end up getting smacked. And rightly so. He couldn't have it both ways.

He leaned against his car and took a sip of his coffee, letting it burn all the way down. He couldn't remember the last time he'd eaten. He'd been on a liquid caffeine diet for much too long.

"Daddy! Daddy!"

Harry turned, and there, coming down the sidewalk, running toward him with an enormous smile on her face, was Emily.

Emily.

He couldn't believe it. Scowling little hostile Emily was smiling at him. Somehow she'd remembered him, somehow she'd made the connection that he was the guy who'd played ball with her out in their backyard in New York. He was the guy who'd been up for all those late-night feedings and diaper changes. He was the guy who'd sung her that lullaby that hadn't quite managed to put her to sleep because they were both laughing too hard.

"Look at my cowboy boots!" Emily shouted. Her dark brown hair was falling out of her ponytail and into her eyes, exactly the way it had when she was two.

Harry stood up, setting his coffee cup down on the roof of his car, moving toward her, ready to catch her when she leapt up and into his arms, the way she used to greet him when he came for his daily visits after the divorce.

Except she didn't do it. She ran past him, dodging him like a professional linebacker, and he realized she hadn't been calling to him. In fact, she didn't even recognize him. Her smile faded, and for an instant, as she looked back at him, he saw a flicker of fear and mistrust in her eyes.

He stood there, staring after her as she ran toward the bay doors of Miller's Garage. She called out again, "Allie! Allie! Marge let me ride the giantest horsey!"

She'd said Allie, not Daddy. Christ, his brain had played one mother of a trick on him. As he stood gaping like a complete idiot, his daughter launched herself up and into Allie's arms.

And Allie knew. She looked at him over Emily's shoulder as she hugged his little girl, and she knew he'd thought his daughter had been running toward him for a hug.

But Em didn't know him from Adam. He was just another weird stranger on the street, just another potential danger. He was someone to run from, not run to.

And, oh, Jesus, that hurt more than he would have believed. It drove home for the very first time just exactly what these past two years had cost him.

He'd brought down Frank Riposa and Thomas Huang, one dead, the other facing criminal charges that would put him away for the rest of his life. But Allie had been right from the start. Although he hadn't fired the bullet that did the job, he'd watched Riposa die, watched the man's life gurgle away from him on a New York City sidewalk. But it hadn't brought Kevin back. It had only made Harry feel sick.

He'd let himself believe it would hurt too much even to look at Shaun and Emily. He was afraid that just by seeing them he would be reminded of all that he'd lost.

In his mind, he'd superimposed Kevin's face over theirs, and he'd thought he'd do the same when he was with them, thought they'd all just pretend that Shaun would step up and fill Kevin's shoes—an impossibility from everyone's angle. Shaun wasn't Kevin, but Kevin had never been anything like Shaun. For the past week, Harry had been haunted not by Kevin, but by the image of Shaun, standing there and looking him in the eye, strong enough and tough enough to tell him to go to hell, to tell him he'd had enough of Harry's shit.

Kevin never would've done that, not in a million years, had their roles been reversed. He wouldn't have had the guts.

It had been the fault of men like Riposa, Huang, and Trotta that Kev and Sonya's lives had been lost, but Harry alone was responsible for the loss of his other two children.

All along he'd blamed the mob bosses for the disaster his entire life had become, but in truth, his own inability to cope with tragedy, his refusal to move forward, his obsession with revenge, and his total loss of hope had injured him far more deeply.

He alone had to bear the responsibility for the complete devastation of his life.

A son who hated his guts.

A daughter who didn't recognize him on the street.

A woman who might've loved him, who might've been showing him how much she loved him last night, who might've been offering him the most precious of gifts—a gift he'd refused to see, let alone accept.

She was looking at him now, but only with pity in her eyes. The love was gone. He'd killed that completely today.

He turned away, afraid that he was going to be sick right there in the street.

Marge was standing behind him, and she, too, had seen everything. He backed away from her, aware that she was speaking, but unable to hear her over the roaring in his ears.

He unlocked his car door and got in, starting the engine. He had to get out of there. Now.

He backed out of the parking spot, and his cup fell forward, hitting the front hood and breaking apart like a water balloon, spraying the windshield with coffee.

Harry didn't stop. He couldn't stop. He just turned on the wipers and kept going.

The walk home from the Merry Maids office was a particularly long one that evening. Allie was exhausted, both physically and emotionally, and the bag of groceries she was carrying got heavier and heavier with every step she took.

Harry was gone.

She hadn't seen him once that entire afternoon. Not after that incident in front of Renny Miller's Garage. Dear Lord, the look on his face had been enough to make her want to weep for a week.

She'd thought maybe he'd approach them, that maybe he'd sit down right there and introduce himself to Emily, start to rebuild all that he'd lost.

But instead he'd run away.

This time she was certain he was gone for good.

She refused to let herself care. She would not care. She . . .

Harry's car was parked crookedly at the curb in front of her apartment.

Her heart skipped a beat, and her pulse surged. She stopped for a minute, briefly closing her eyes and forcing herself to remember. Big deal. So what if he was still here. She didn't care.

But as she got closer, she saw that the car was empty. Harry wasn't slouched in front of the steering wheel.

She refused to care, but she couldn't stop her steps from quickening as she walked down the Yurgens' driveway. She didn't care, but she was running by the time she turned the corner.

And Harry sat on the wooden steps that led to her apartment door. He was leaning back against the railing, as if he were too exhausted to hold himself up. Still, he straightened when he saw her.

Allie stopped short.

He looked awful. Worse even than he'd looked when she saw him downtown a few hours ago.

His face was gray and his eyes were swollen and red—he'd been crying. He tried to hide it, but his hands were shaking.

"Hey, Allie," he said, as if his being there was an everyday, run-of-the-mill occurrence, instead of the major miracle that it was.

She set down the groceries. "Harry."

With anyone else, she would have read the desperation in his eyes as an invitation to go to him and pull him into her arms. But with Harry, she couldn't assume anything. She couldn't risk waking up tomorrow and finding out that she'd been wrong. Again.

So she stood there and looked at him.

He wouldn't hold her gaze. He looked around, only occasionally meeting her eyes, and a few times he opened his mouth as if he were going to speak.

Allie just waited, hoping, God help her, that he wouldn't get up and walk away. Daring to hope . . .

He rocked back and forth very slightly, like a runner getting into position to start a breakneck sprint, cleared his throat, and finally spoke. "You once told me . . ." His voice broke, and he cleared his throat again, the muscles in his jaw working furiously as he clenched his teeth. "You told me to, um, just to . . ."

His gaze met hers, and for the briefest split second she could see beyond his flip facade, his tough guy, foul-mouthed, don't-care attitude, to the very naked, very lost man inside.

"Just to let you know if I needed you," he finished in a barely audible whisper.

He forced his gaze up again, forced himself to look her directly in the eye despite the fact that now more than just his hands were shaking, despite the fact that tears were brimming in his eyes. "I need you, Al," he whispered. "I really, really need you."

Allie set the bowl of soup in front of him and Harry picked up the spoon. But it wasn't because he was hungry. It was only because she seemed to want him to eat something.

She was silent, just sitting across her kitchen table from him, waiting for him to talk to her.

That's why he was here, wasn't it? To talk to her, to be with her, to have her hold him.

God, he wanted her to hold him.

But she'd been careful not to touch him, careful not to get too close as she'd unlocked her apartment door and let him into her home.

Her home. And this tiny apartment was a home. She'd only been here a little more than a week, and the furniture was all secondhand, but she'd somehow managed to make this place her own.

There were books everywhere. The posters on the wall exuded color and warmth. The very air smelled like her.

He put down his spoon then picked it up again, needing desperately to hold on to something.

"I'm glad you came here," Allie said quietly, saving

him from the responsibility of having to speak first. "But I have to be honest with you, Harry. What you really need is a professional counselor. You and Shaun and Emily. And Marge. She's part of this, too. You've got to figure out what you want—"

"I know what I want." He looked up at her, gripping the spoon so hard his hand shook. "I want my life back."

"You can't have it," she said, her blue eyes filled with compassion. "But you can start over. It's not so bad to start over, you know."

He didn't know, but she did. She'd done it. She was impossibly strong, impossibly brave, impossibly tough.

Far tougher than he was.

"You're never going to have the same relationships with Shaun and Emily that you had two years ago," Allie continued, "but you can have something new. Something that might even be better than what you had to start with.

"You know, I have friends here in Hardy," she told him, as if that fact still surprised her. "Marge and Natalie and Annarose Gerty. And I'm—I'm writing a book. I'm only up to page ten because I've been so busy with work, but . . ." She smiled self-consciously, unable to hold his gaze. "I figure, why not try, right?"

"That's so great, Al," he said, feeling tears pressing against his eyelids. Please God, don't let him start to cry. "I think that's really great."

She looked at him again, and it was as if she'd made a conscious choice to let him see deep inside her. "Griffin would've laughed at me," she told him. "If I'd ever told him anything like that, he would've laughed, and maybe patted my hand."

"If I ever pat your hand," Harry told her, "you have my permission to shoot me."

On the surface, what he'd said had been mostly in

jest, but the things his words implied were terrifying. If I ever . . . The implication was that there would, indeed, be an ever.

He knew Allie had caught the implication, too. She sat very, very still for a moment. But then she looked up at him.

"What are you going to do, Harry?" she asked him quietly.

"Do you . . ." He had to stop and clear his throat, blink back the tears that still threatened to escape. He tried to sound noncommittal, tried to sound as if the answer to this question didn't have the power to rip out his heart. But even though he tried, his voice shook when he spoke. "Do you think Shaun and Em will ever forgive me?" Would she, Allie, ever forgive him? He couldn't ask that, too. He just couldn't risk hearing her tell him no.

Allie reached across the table and took his hand. "I know they will," she said. "They're your kids, Harry. It's going to be hard, and it's going to take time, but they will. Especially if you don't give them any choice in the matter." Her smile was decidedly watery. "I think you should move in with them. It's your house, they're your kids—just move in." She faltered. "I mean, if . . . you've decided to stay."

"I want Trotta," he said, needing to be honest even though she couldn't possibly understand. "I want him, Allie, so bad it hurts."

He was holding on to her hand so tightly her fingers must've hurt, too. But she didn't try to pull free.

"Do you want him more than you want your kids back?" she asked.

"No. But it's close," he admitted. "I know that's really screwed up, but . . ." He'd been running so long with anger and revenge as his fuel, he couldn't just shut it off. He wanted Trotta. He burned to bring the bastard down.

But Allie didn't condemn him. She just kept letting him hold her hand. "So what are you going to do?" she asked again.

"I'm good at what I do," he told her. "I hate it, though, working for the Bureau. But I'm good at it, I know it, so it's really hard to think about quitting. Isn't that fucked up?"

"No," she said.

"Yeah, it is." He was the one who finally pulled his hand free. "I suck at relationships. I always have. So what am I thinking about doing? Quitting the thing I know I'm good at to go do the thing I've never really gotten right."

"You don't suck at relationships—"

"I do. Look at my track record. Sonya. Christ. My entire marriage was a joke. You know, I didn't know if Em was even my kid until after she was born and we ran paternity tests. Sonya told me it was my fault she started sleeping around—that she was looking for the kind of connection I didn't give her."

Allie was quiet, just letting him talk.

"I don't know what she wanted," he told her, his anger keeping his tears at bay. "I mean, I honestly don't have a fucking clue what it was I didn't give her, and that scares me to death because it means I'm just going to keep on making the same mistake over and over again with anybody I ever try to have any kind of relationship with, you know? Kevin was the only person I could ever just be with, the only person I didn't have to work at being around."

It had been that way with Allie, too, but he didn't dare say that aloud.

"Maybe it was her fault," she said softly. "Maybe all this time you've been great at relationships, and Sonya was the one with the problems. Or maybe it was something in between. Part your fault, part hers. It sure seems as if it was at least part hers, because in my experience, the way to strengthen a relationship is not to jump in bed with someone else."

"I feel like I'm unraveling," Harry said. He'd never talked about any of this with anyone ever before.

"You once told me maybe it was time to get rid of Alessandra Lamont. Well, maybe it's time to let Harry O'Dell unravel a little bit."

He shook his head. He wasn't sure he could do this.

"What do you want to do?" she asked him. "What do you really want, Harry? It's your life, your choice. Either stay or go. But if you're going, please, do me a favor and leave now."

Harry looked at her, sitting there across from him. Her hair drooped in her eyes, and she wasn't wearing even the least little bit of makeup. Her T-shirt hid her body, and her jeans came from the bargain bin at Target.

She didn't want him to leave. He could tell from the I-don't-care angle to chin that she did, in fact, care.

What did he want? He wanted her to care, that much he knew.

"I want to stay," he said, and the sheer truth of his words unraveled him a whole lot more. "Please." His voice shook like a four-year-old's. "Can I stay?"

"I think he's finally sleeping now," Allie told Marge. "He took a shower and shaved, and I made him something to eat. He wanted to go right over there tonight and talk to Shaun, but I told him I didn't think you were leaving for Denver tomorrow until about noon. I don't think he's slept in more than a week, and frankly, he looks awful. I told him I was afraid he'd scare Shaun to death. He has a better chance of looking human in the morning."

Marge was silent for a moment on the other end of the phone.

"We talked for about five hours," Allie told her. "He knows Shaun needs more than an apology, and he seems open to doing whatever it takes. If you know any counselors, maybe someone over at the college, that Shaun might be comfortable going to with Harry . . . ?"

She and Harry had talked for a long time about all the different ways he could rebuild his relationship with his kids, but they'd both completely skirted the issue of exactly what his remaining in Hardy would mean to the two of them.

"I can't promise that Shaun is going to greet him with open arms," Marge finally said. "But I will make sure he's home in the morning. Bless you, Allie. Can you get Harry over here by ten?"

"I'm not responsible for this," Allie told her new friend. "Harry will be there because he wants to be there. And . . . brace yourself, Marge, because he's planning to move in."

"Oh, thank God." Marge's voice was thick with tears. "And thank you. You may not think you're responsible, but you're a good friend to him."

A good friend. As Allie hung up the phone, she knew she had to take care not to be too good a friend to Harry. He was asleep in her bed, and—for her own sake—she had to camp tonight on the couch. She would not climb in with him. She couldn't risk hurting herself that way again.

She took Harry's clothes from the washing machine in the kitchen and put them in the dryer.

She put on her pajamas in the bathroom, scrubbed her face, and brushed her teeth.

Then she went into the bedroom to get an extra blanket from the closet and to take one of the pillows from the bed. She moved quietly, even though he'd been completely exhausted and she didn't think anything would disturb him.

She was wrong.

He stirred, rolling over, as if he'd been forcing himself to stay at least half awake, listening for her, waiting for her.

"Allie, can I hold you?"

His words from just last night echoed in her head. Is that smart? Again, the answer was a resounding no. But sometimes the right thing to do wasn't smart.

She slipped into the bed beside him, needing to feel his arms around her as much as he needed to hold her.

As he held her close, she heard him sigh.

And without another word, Harry slept.

And Allie lay in the dark and loved him, even though she knew it wasn't the smartest thing to do.

Twenty

CHRIST, HE SHOULDN'T still be here.

Harry's face was buried in Allie's hair, his legs intertwined with hers, his arms still tightly wrapped around her as the morning light brightened her bedroom walls.

What the hell was he doing here?

But then he remembered. He'd come to her last night, a complete wreck. She'd brought him inside, fed him and cleaned him up, and let him rant and rave for hours and hours.

She'd listened, asked questions, and helped him sort through his options, helped him make a battle plan for the beginning of the rest of his life.

She'd done all that for him—including climb into bed with him when he'd asked. She done it even though she didn't owe him anything—except maybe a big kick in the pants.

She stirred, turning toward him as she opened her eyes then froze, as if he were the last person in the world she'd expect to find in her bed ever again.

"Hi," he said. A brilliant opening. Witty, yet concise.

She was wearing those silly flannel pajamas she seemed to like so much, but his hand had slipped between the top and the bottom to rest against the smoothness of her back. At this proximity, the freckles scattered across her cheeks and nose were so adorable his heart nearly stopped, the blue of her eyes the closest thing to perfection he'd ever seen.

She gazed into his eyes for a long moment, searching, then shook her head slightly. "Harry, I don't want—"

He kissed her, unwilling to hear what it was she didn't want. She resisted for all of one one-hundredth of a second before she melted against him. And when he deepened the kiss, she was right there with him.

It was wrong of him to do this, wrong of him to rid her of all that flannel so he could feel the smoothness of her skin against him. It was wrong of him to touch her the way he was touching her, to kiss her harder, deeper, to settle between her legs and to enter her with one smooth thrust as she raised her hips, inviting him to do just that.

He pulled out right away. What was he doing? When it came to this woman, he was completely out of control. "Condom," he said.

"Top drawer," she answered.

If there was a Guinness World Speed Record for that sort of thing, he would have broken it, no question.

Still, she pulled him back to her as if he'd taken ten years instead of ten seconds, and within moments she had him exactly where he'd been before sanity had taken over. She began to move beneath him, slowly, languorously. It was delicious, the perfect sleepy pace for the early-morning hour. He moved with her, pushing himself hard and deep, but still so slowly, inside her, and her arms tightened around him.

"Yes," she whispered.

One thing about Allie, when it came to sex, she knew what she wanted, and she wasn't shy about getting it. Still, he'd cut her off before. She'd been about to speak.

"What don't you want?" Harry asked, lifting his head to look down at her. "Tell me what you were going to say."

Her eyes were half closed, and she made a soft sound of pleasure as he slowly filled her again.

"I was going to say I don't want to make love to you right now," she told him. She smiled crookedly. "I think it's safe to assume I wasn't being quite honest."

He hesitated. "Are you sure, Al? Because . . ."

Because what? Because he cared more about her than he'd let her believe? Because this wasn't just mindless sex, it was making love—it had been right from the start. He'd just been too damn blind to see.

He was in love with this woman, completely, hopelessly in love with her.

He'd sat there last night, talking about staying in town, talking about how hard it was for him to give up his hunt for Michael Trotta, talking about the best way to regain Shaun and Emily's trust and love. But he'd been too chicken to bring up his feelings for Allie. Too scared to ask what he could do to regain her trust and maybe, dear God, gain her love. Too afraid to tell her that he loved her, afraid to mention marriage, afraid she'd look at him again with that pity in her eyes.

So he'd said nothing at all.

Allie pressed him even more deeply inside of her and he felt like crying, it was so good. "Kiss me, Harry," she murmured.

He did, as sweetly and as tenderly as he possibly could, hoping she'd know from his kiss just how much he truly loved her.

Shaun stopped short as he went into the kitchen.

"Good morning," Harry said.

Out of all the people he expected to see sitting at the kitchen table, his father was probably one hundred and forty-two on the list.

His knee-jerk reaction was to turn around and walk out of the room. Go back upstairs.

Instead, he went to the cabinet and opened it, pretending he was taking his time to choose between Cheerios, Raisin Bran, and Frosted Flakes, when in truth he never had anything but Cheerios for breakfast. "Who let you in?" he asked, his back still turned.

He heard Harry shift in his seat. "Actually, I have a key." He cleared his throat. "Which is good, seeing as how I'm going to be moving in."

"Here?" Shaun turned to face him.

"Yeah." Harry had obviously made an effort to clean himself up before coming over. His hair was freshly cut, his chin clean shaven, his jeans slightly stiff from the wash.

"You're going to live here?"

"Yeah."

"You mean . . . when you're in town?"

"Yeah."

Shaun turned back to the cereal. Of course that's what he'd meant. And of course, Harry was in town only once a year. "Yeah, right."

"Which is going to be all the time from now on," Harry added, "seeing as how I'm going to be faxing my boss a letter of resignation on Monday."

All the time. Hope raced through him, but Shaun ruthlessly crushed it back. If he'd learned anything over the past two years, it was that hope only made the disappointment hurt worse.

He took down the Cheerios from the cabinet, his movements jerky as he opened the box and poured some into a bowl. "You're quitting your job, and that's supposed to just make it all better? You move back, and we're one big happy family? Just like that, you're den dad for Em's Brownie troop, and oh, hey, maybe you could help coach my baseball team."

"I will if that's what you want."

Shaun slammed his bowl onto the table and the Cheerios went flying. "No, Dad, it's not what I want because I don't have a goddamn baseball team. Kevin was into baseball. I'm sorry to disappoint you, but I'm not Kevin. I'm a dancer. I happen to love to dance." He took the milk from the fridge and poured some into his bowl, sloshing it over the side. "And no, before you even ask, just because I'm a dancer doesn't mean I'm gay, all right?" He sat down at the table and began shoveling cereal into his mouth.

"Slow down," Harry said. "That's a good way to get a stomachache. I know you're a dancer, and I guess I assumed that since you're only fourteen, questions about your sexual preferences wouldn't really be an issue yet. But maybe I'm wrong—I'm the first to admit I'm way out of touch."

Shaun snorted. "Understatement of the year."

Harry cleared his throat, as if maybe this wasn't as easy for him as he was pretending. "I understand you've got an audition down in Denver today for a summer dance troupe."

Shaun stared across the table at him. "You know about that?"

Harry nodded. "I know you're not Kevin. I don't want you to be Kevin. He was . . ." He cleared his throat and forced a smile. "He was one of those people who just always had it easy, you know? All his life. Everything was a piece of cake for him—school, sports, the social scene. He never had to fight for anything, and because of that, he was never particularly good at anything. If there was one thing I'd've wished for him, it was that he'd have had a little friction in his life. It's easy to just drift along when everything goes your way. But when you've got to stand up and fight—that's when you become a man."

He paused, waiting until Shaun looked up, until Shaun met his gaze.

"I see that in you, kid," he continued. "You're not afraid to look me in the eye. Hell, you're not afraid to spit in my eye. And that's good. I'm proud of you for that. I wish I'd been around to help with the fights, but you did more than okay on your own. And I hear you're one of the best dancers in northern Colorado. I'm proud of that, too."

Shaun pushed his chair back from the table and tossed his cereal bowl in the sink. He took a sponge and mopped up the mess on the table, stalling for time, afraid his voice would break, afraid of letting his father know how much his words had mattered. "Well, that was heart stirring, Harry, but two years is too long for you to be able to buy your way back in with one moving speech."

"I know that," Harry said quietly. "I know it's not going to be that easy. But I'm a fighter, too, Shaun. And I'm telling you, we're going in for counseling. I'll contest the shit out of your petition for change in name and custody if I have to. I'm home, I'm sorry, and we will work this out, even if it kills us."

Shaun fought the tears that came to his eyes, fought the hope that kept trying to grow inside him. "You don't know how badly I want to believe you."

"You don't have to believe me. I'm here. I'm not going anywhere."

"Don't do this halfway," Shaun told him, his voice shaking despite his attempts to hold it steady. "If you're going to do it halfway, if you're going to go back to New York next week or next month or even next year, just go now, okay?"

"I'm telling you, I'm not—"

"Right after the accident, right after Mommy and Kevin died, after we moved here with Marge, I couldn't sleep at night," Shaun told his father. "I knew you were in New York, hunting down the men who killed Mommy and Kevin. And I was so scared. I would just lie awake at night, making myself sick with worry that you were going to get yourself killed, too. I spent about a year nearly throwing up every time the phone rang, because I was so sure it was going to be the call telling us you were dead.

"But then I realized," he continued, "that it really didn't matter. Because you were already gone. The part of you that was Dad was killed along with Kev and Mom." His voice broke again, and he stopped to take a deep breath and to clear his throat. "I still can't shake this séance feeling I get every time I see you. It's kind of like a scheduled haunting—a yearly sighting of a ghost from the past."

"Ouch," Harry said. He didn't bother to hide the tears that were glistening in his eyes.

"Yeah," Shaun said tightly. "It still really hurts me, too." He rinsed out his cereal bowl. "So. If you're going to exhume yourself and stick around, you better plan to stay until Em's high school graduation. If you can't do that, leave now."

"I'll be here when you get back from Denver," Harry told him.

"I'll believe that when I see it." Shaun headed for the door. "Excuse me, I've got to go pack my overnight bag."

"Break a leg, kid," Harry said. "I love you."

Shaun paused but didn't look back. "The jury's still out on that one."

*   *   *

"Harry, wait!" He was getting into his car when Marge came out onto the porch. She came down the steps and along the concrete path. "I think you better come inside and hear this."

"Can't it wait? I was just going to get my stuff and check out of the motel and—"

"There're about two dozen messages for you on the answering machine. I turned the phone off last night and let the machine pick it up because I've been getting prank calls from some of my students. I didn't turn it on again until just now, and—"

Her words didn't make sense. "Messages? For me? No one knows this number. No one knows I'm here."

"It was someone calling from the Farthing FBI office. You should listen to the messages, Harry."

The implications of her words literally rocked him back on his heels. Good thing his car was there or he would've fallen on his ass. Somehow, someone from the Bureau had tracked him here. But how? He pushed himself forward and ran toward the house.

"There were calls for you every half hour," Marge continued, following him. "The last was just a few minutes ago. They say it's urgent."

Christ, how they'd found him didn't matter. What mattered was that if the FBI had managed to track him here, Michael Trotta wouldn't be far behind. Jesus, he had to find Allie.

"Get Shaun and Emily into the car right now. Don't pack, don't do anything. Just get into the car and go." Harry shouted up the stairs. "Shaun! Emily! Get down here right now! Time to go." He took the wad of cash he always carried from his pocket and handed it to Marge. "Buy whatever you need, but don't use a credit card. Don't stay in the hotel where you've got reservations. Don't go to Shaun's audition—"

"What?" Shaun said, coming down the stairs. Emily was right behind him, still in her pajamas, her hair tangled around her wary face.

"Just go to Denver, go to the FBI headquarters there," Harry continued. "Demand protection—tell them who you are and that I'm afraid Michael Trotta might try to use you to get to Allie. Her real name's Alessandra Lamont, and Trotta wants her dead. He's got a two-million-dollar contract on her head." He turned to Shaun. "I'm so sorry, kid."

"You said you were quitting!"

"I am," Harry said, "but someone forgot to tell Michael Trotta that."

"I don't goddamn believe this!"

Harry caught Shaun's arm, pulling him out to Marge's car. "Please," he said. "I need you to help me. Trotta will grab you and Em and kill Marge without blinking just to prove to me that the threat is real. You need to go now. Don't stop, go straight to Denver—do you understand?"

Shaun nodded, his face pale as Marge helped Em with her seat belt.

Harry pulled his son into his arms for a quick hug. "I'll be right behind you with Allie, and I'll explain everything when we get there, okay?"

Shaun's arms tightened around him. "Be careful, Dad."

"I will." He leaned into the car and briefly touched Em's hair. She looked up at him, her eyes wide.

"Is Allie the president?" she asked.

Harry didn't get a chance to answer, didn't get a chance to even guess why the hell Em had asked that.

Marge pulled out of the driveway, and he ran into the house to call the Farthing office and find out what the hell was going on.

Allie walked into town, hoping she'd find Annarose Gerty before she left the supermarket. She'd gone to

Mrs. Gerty's house to tell her she was going to have to cancel their tentative plans for dinner tonight, but the elderly woman wasn't home.

Under normal circumstances, Allie wouldn't change her plans, but this was hardly normal. She suspected that after his conversation with Shaun, Harry was going to need the company of a friend. Badly. Mrs. Gerty would understand.

And Allie—fool that she was—would end up back in bed with him tonight, redefining the word friend. She sighed.

She was going to have to tell him. She was going to have to just say it. I love you. And then he could help her deal with it. But not yet. Not until he got his relationship with his kids under control. It would be cruel to drop yet another emotional neutron bomb on him now.

She briefly closed her eyes, praying that Shaun wasn't tearing Harry into completely unrecognizable pieces.

She spotted Hunter lying calmly on the sidewalk outside the market, loosely tied to a parking meter. Good. That meant Mrs. Gerty was inside and—

Allie's blood ran cold.

Whenever she'd heard that expression in the past, she'd assumed it was an exaggeration.

It wasn't.

Her hands and her feet actually tingled from the sensation, but somehow, somehow she didn't stop dead in her tracks. Somehow she kept walking even though Ivo was there, across the street, in front of the dry cleaners.

Ivo. Michael Trotta's hired gun. Unmistakably tall, with unmistakable cheekbones and completely unforgettable eyes. He was getting out of a black luxury sedan with four other men. They split up, each going in a different direction, Ivo heading directly toward her.

* * *

"Oh, sweet Christ," George said. "Are you telling me that this is the first you've heard of this? That no one from the Farthing office notified you before this?"

"They still haven't notified me," Harry ground into the phone. "I tried calling the number they left on the machine, but the fucking line's fucking busy. I have to find Allie. Just tell me—fast—how bad is it?"

"Bad," George told him. "We tracked you down through—"

"The court records," Harry supplied. "The petitions that Shaun's lawyers filed. They're all public record. Shit, I knew it. I knew there was something wrong, something I should've realized. Goddamn it!"

"The Colorado team was supposed to set up protection," George told him. "Surveillance. The whole thing. Another trap with Alessandra Lamont as bait. Jesus, I'm going to kill Nicki. Harry, we already leaked your location to Trotta. The son of a bitch is completely out of control. It doesn't make any sense, but he just raised Alessandra's snuff price to three million. If his guys aren't already there, they'll be there soon enough. Christ, the agents from the Farthing office were supposed to be ready for them."

Harry didn't say good-bye. He just hung up and ran.

Allie's heart was pounding so loudly, she couldn't hear the sounds of the cars going past in the street.

From the corner of her eye, she could see Ivo pause, waiting for the traffic before he crossed.

He was heading toward her.

She put her head down and hunched her shoulders, the way Harry had taught her.

Oh, Lord, how could he have found her here? Harry had been so convinced that they were safe.

From the corner of her eye, she saw him look directly

at her. She saw him look again, harder, his eyes narrowing slightly.

The sky was a deeper and darker shade of blue than she'd ever seen in New York. The morning sunshine was hot on her face, the air fresh and clean, the spring day beautiful. It was a perfect day and she drew in one breath after another, well aware that each could be her last.

Dear Lord, she didn't want to die.

Ivo pivoted slightly so that he was heading directly for her, his hand reaching beneath his jacket, probably for his gun.

No, she didn't want to die.

And she saw him.

Hunter.

Tied to a parking meter directly in front of her.

He stood up when he saw her coming, tugging at his leash. He only barked once, but once was enough to expose the razor sharpness of his teeth.

Still Allie didn't let herself shy away. She fought all her instincts to flee and went toward the dog, knowing that this animal, the object of her most terrifying childhood nightmares, had the power to save her life.

And dear Lord, she wanted to live.

She knelt next to Hunter, wrapping her arms around the big dog's neck, closing her eyes as he brought his enormous mouth with his enormous teeth toward her face.

He licked her. His tongue felt funny and rough, and as she opened her eyes, he seemed to be smiling at her.

From the corner of her eye, she saw Ivo turn away. He knew Alessandra Lamont was more afraid of dogs than anything in the world.

What he didn't know was that Alessandra was more afraid of him than she was afraid of dogs.

She hugged Hunter more tightly. "Thank you," she whispered.

He licked her ear.

She stood up and gave him one last pat on the head, trying to make it look casual, trying to make it look as if she patted dogs' heads every day of her life. And then, moving slowly, using Alice Plotkin's hunch-shouldered, shuffling walk, she headed in the opposite direction from Ivo.

She made it down past Renny Miller's Garage, down almost all the way to the corner of MacDouglas Street.

She would've kept going, would've been free and clear, but then—

"Yoo-hoo!"

Oh, Lord, no. Not Mrs. Gerty.

Allie didn't turn around. She dropped her head lower and shuffled a little faster.

"Yoo-hoo! Alice!"

This was why Harry had wanted her to take a name like Barbara. Barbara didn't sound anything like Alessandra. Barbara was completely different. Barbara was safe.

Allie stopped at the corner, praying that the light would change so that she could cross. Promising God that if He let her live, she would change her name to Barbara.

"Yoo-hoo! Allie!"

She saw her blurred reflection in the big glass window of Bodeen's Pharmacy, saw Mrs. Gerty waving, saw there was no one on the sidewalk between them. Allie.

She saw that Ivo had turned, saw him now start toward her, reaching again beneath his jacket, moving at a trot.

And Allie didn't wait for the traffic light. She turned down MacDouglas Street and ran for her life.

Harry saw Ivo first.

He was running down Main Street, gesturing, and

Harry quickly spotted at least two other men across the road. Ivo was telling them to get the car, and Harry knew he had to move fast.

Then he spotted her.

Allie, running down MacDouglas as if she were going for Olympic gold.

Harry turned the corner just as Ivo did.

Ivo drew his gun, stopping short to balance it with both hands and draw a bead on Allie.

Harry did the only thing he could. He went for the intercept, driving his car right up onto the sidewalk, blocking Ivo's aim.

The bullet hit his car with a thunk, and Allie looked over her shoulder in alarm. But her alarm quickly turned to relief as she saw it was Harry behind the wheel.

He squealed to a stop, pushed open the door, and she threw herself inside. He had the pedal to the floor before she even closed the door.

"Oh, God," she was saying. "Oh, God. Oh, Harry. It's Ivo!"

"I know." He had to make a choice. Head for the local police station or the highway to the FBI office in Farthing. The local station was tiny—with never more than two officers on duty. There was no way they were equipped to hold their own against Ivo and two of his men. Or more. It was possible Ivo had more than two men with him. "Did you see how many shooters he had with him?"

"There were four other men."

Four. Jesus. Okay, the highway. He had a head start. He knew these roads better than they did. He could make it to the Bureau office in Farthing in just under three hours.

"How did you know?" Allie asked. She had a very odd

look on her face. "I said, 'It's Ivo,' and you said, 'I know.' How did you know?"

"Shit," Harry said as a large black car appeared in his rearview mirror, moving far too fast to be just anyone. "Al, you didn't happen to see the kind of car Ivo was driving, did you?"

She turned and looked out the back. "That one," she said.

"Hold on." Harry pushed his little car into higher gear, moving on the residential street as if they were already on the interstate. The subcompact had the definite advantage—he could pass other cars, even when facing oncoming traffic, just managing to squeak by. It wasn't any fun for the people he was passing, but it put the two of them farther and farther ahead of Ivo's black cruise ship on wheels.

Still, it wouldn't take a genius to figure out where they were heading. Of course, there was a 50 percent chance Ivo would think they'd headed toward Denver instead of east to Farthing.

They took the exit ramp onto the highway on two wheels, squeezing past a pickup truck already there, brushing against the guard rail.

Allie clung to the handgrips, her face pale.

Once on the highway, Harry opened it up. His car could move, putting them miles and miles ahead of Ivo. His souped-up engine guzzled gas, but it was well worth it in times like this. He could do ninety-five without even blinking and—

"Shit."

Allie briefly closed her eyes as she shook her head. "I hate it when you say that. That never means anything good."

"I had a full tank of gas this morning," he told her. "But now my gauge shows nearly empty and the gas light's on. That bullet I took must've hit low in the tank. We've been leaking gas for the past ten miles."

And they were continuing to leak, way too fast.

He looked around. They were in the middle of no-where. Moving farther into the foothills of the Rocky fucking Mountains, God help them. The next exit east of Hardy was at least another fourteen miles away. He wasn't going to make fourteen miles, not going ninety-five the way he was. And he wasn't going to make four-teen miles going anything less than ninety-five—not if he wanted to keep Ivo's bullets out of his and Allie's heads.

"So where's the backup?" Allie asked, her voice tight. "Isn't this where backup is supposed to come and save the day?"

"I wish. I'm afraid we're on our own."

"There's no backup?" She was furious. Totally pissed. He didn't blame her.

"No. We're going to have to lose 'em in the—"

"You're telling me you set me up again, you son of a bitch, and you didn't arrange for backup?"

Jesus, did she think . . . ? "Allie, I swear, I had nothing to do with—"

"And I'm supposed to just believe you? You're not be-hind it this time—even though it's exactly the same thing that happened before?"

The gas alarm went off, a series of much too pleasant tones considering the direness of their situation. What-ever they were going to do, however they were going to handle this, they had to do it now.

"Okay, Allie," Harry said. "We're going off-road. I need you to hold that thought and hold on tight."

"God, I hate you! I can't believe I trusted you!"

There was a particularly large hill, a baby Rocky Mountain, coming up on the left. Harry approached it still going ninety-five, searching for a split in the highway, one of those places where state troopers turned around. He saw one, but he didn't slow soon enough and left a healthy trail of rubber on the road. He threw the car into reverse and backed up, the engine whining. There wasn't any traffic on the other side of the highway—even if there were, he would've kicked his car out into it. Any minute now Ivo's black boat could appear over the rise, and then they'd be dead.

He crossed both lanes, heading off the shoulder of the road, skidding down a soft patch of grass, and taking the car as far into the woods as he possibly could.

If they were really, really lucky, Ivo and his shooters would head toward Denver and wouldn't stop until they got there.

If they were only mostly lucky, Ivo and his goons would head east, but just zip on past them. They'd be halfway to Farthing before they realized they weren't catching up to Harry because Harry wasn't in front of them anymore.

But Harry had to bank on the worst-case scenario—that Ivo would somehow figure out they'd pulled a U-turn and would see the tracks leading into the woods and find the car. He and Allie had to start up the mountain, moving as far away from the car as they possibly could.

He got out and opened his trunk, jamming a supply of ammunition into the pockets of his jacket, grabbing his binoculars and a fanny pack he kept loaded with energy bars and caffeine gum.

"There's a map in the glove compartment. Take it," he ordered Allie. Allie, who hated him. He didn't blame her. Right now he hated himself. He should have known. As soon as he'd seen that letter from those lawyers, read the words "petition the court," he should have realized anyone—including Michael Trotta—could now find his kids, thus finding him, thus finding Allie.

There were two extra sweaters in his trunk. He threw one to Allie and tied the other around his waist. It got cold out here at night, and it was conceivable that they'd still be here come sundown. Provided they weren't dead.

Allie silently put the sweater on. Grimly held out the map for him to put in his pocket. Silently, grimly hated him.

"I didn't set you up."

Her expression didn't change.

This may have been his fault, but it was going to be a job to convince her that he hadn't set her up. And right now he needed to focus on another job—keeping them alive.

He checked his gun. "Let's go." He headed up the mountain, holding out his hand to help her along.

She didn't take it.

He hadn't really thought she would.

Twenty-one

$\sim \! \! \! \! \! \! \! \!$

TREE BRANCHES SWATTED Allie in the face as she tried to keep up with Harry.

He was effortlessly heading up the side of the steep hill, as if mountain climbing were something he did everyday. As if setting up his lover were something he did everyday.

She couldn't believe she was back at the beginning, stripped of the life she'd been trying to rebuild for herself, once again running for her life.

She couldn't believe she'd been stupid enough to make the same mistake twice.

He paused at the top of a rise, waiting for her to catch up, training his binoculars down on the highway below.

"At this point, I'm guessing they headed toward Denver first," he told her as she drew near. "My gut feeling is that they'll turn around after about fifteen miles, after they don't catch up with us. Ivo doesn't know my car has warp engines—well, at least it does with an intact gas tank."

He was talking as if nothing had changed between them. As if they were friends out for a day hike in the woods. As if she weren't a fraction of a second from going postal, slapping him hard across the face, pushing him down the mountain, and bursting into tears.

"He'll be thinking it's a subcompact piece of shit," Harry told her. "That we probably can't do more than sixty without shaking apart. So he'll turn around and head toward Farthing. I just want to watch him go past, and then we can hike back down to Hardy."

"And then what?" she asked, unable to keep her voice from shaking.

He looked up from his binoculars to glance at her. "I know you're not going to like this, but I think we'll need to get you back into protective custody. At least for a little while—"

"No. I'll take that money now," she told him. "That money you wanted to give me? I'll just take it and disappear." She could do it now. She knew how to do it.

He looked up at her again. "Allie, if they found you once—"

"They found you Harry. Although I'm sure they had help doing that, didn't they?"

"Not from me—hang on, here they come." Harry brought the binoculars back up to his face.

Allie could see the black car approaching, the only traffic on the road in either direction. It was moving fast in the right-hand lane, and it sailed past.

Thank God. She and Harry were safe, at least for now. Allie slumped down onto the rotting trunk of a fallen tree.

"Shit."

Allie closed her eyes. "No," she said. "Don't say that."

"They're stopping," Harry told her. "And, damn, they're backing up."

She stood up. They were. They were backing up to the place in the road where she and Harry had turned around. "How did they know?"

"The tire tracks." Harry's voice was tight. When he'd hit the brakes to turn around, he'd left streaks of fresh rubber on the road, gleaming like signal beacons. "They're like freaking arrows, pointing this way." He secured the binoculars.

"They might not see the car."

"And aliens might erase their memories with their stun guns." Harry grabbed her arm and pulled her with him up the hill. "Come on, we've got to move!"

"Goddamn it! Goddamn it!"

Kim let herself into the apartment warily, but George was alone. He was in the living room, shouting into the telephone.

"I don't give a damn if Nicole's in an important meeting—it wouldn't matter if she were having a private conference with God. Interrupt her. Page her. Get her on this phone now!"

He paced back and forth in front of the windows, using only one crutch but limping heavily. He didn't see her, didn't know she was there.

He was far too upset. He wanted to speak to Nicole.

"No, she may not call me back. If you hang up this phone or put me on hold, I'm going to come down there. And believe me, friend, you don't want me to come down there."

He was silent then, either listening to someone on the other end of the phone or waiting.

Kim waited, too. She stood glued in place by a sick desire to hear just what it was George needed so badly to say to his ex-wife.

As she watched, George's shoulders tightened, and he seemed to grip the telephone more tightly. "You bitch," he said, his voice harshly unfamiliar in its intensity. "You told me everything was taken care of on the Colorado end. You promised me—you swore this wouldn't go wrong again—but Harry just called me. Nothing's set up. There was a completely halfhearted, half-assed attempt to get in touch with him that failed, and now he's on his own."

His words were so different than what Kim had expected to hear, it took her several moments before they made any sense.

"What were you thinking?" he spat. "Was the plan to just let Alessandra Lamont die? Did you think you'd gain more notoriety from this case if the charge was murder one instead of just conspiracy to commit? God, I am so over you! I know you were willing to sacrifice our relationship for your career, but I had no clue you'd be willing to just let someone die—Jesus, not just one person but two. Because you know as well as I do that Harry's with her. And he's not going to run to safety when the bullets start flying."

He paused, listening only briefly before he interrupted. "Bullshit. I know why I'm not out there, but why aren't you? How could you do this?" His voice broke and he paused. "You didn't know. That's not good enough, Nic. This was your case. You're supposed to know." Another pause. "If I find out you knew about this—and I will find out—you're history, babe. Listen closely, because I'm not going to say this twice. If you were part of this, you better just pack up your office right now. Transfer out while you still can. And go very, very far away. Because I won't want to see your face ever again."

He pushed the button to cut the connection, then turned and threw the telephone across the room.

It hit the wall mere feet from where Kim was standing.

The look on his face was terrible. She'd never seen him so upset. He didn't apologize for throwing the phone. He didn't say anything. He just stood there, breathing hard and staring at her.

Kim didn't know what to say. She was afraid to speak,

afraid she'd somehow reveal that she knew far too much about this case, about poor, doomed Alessandra Lamont.

"I think I might've helped kill my partner," he told her. "And Alessandra, too . . ." He laughed, but it sounded more like a sob. "Nice way for me to pay her back, huh? She saves my life, and I make absolutely certain that she'll die."

He turned away, and Kim stepped toward him. She knew it wasn't the right time, but she had to know. "George . . . You told her that you were . . . over her?"

He turned back, both his eyes and his voice curiously flat. "Yeah," he said. "Sure. Why not spread around some of the pain? I kind of failed to tell you, babe, that Nic is my ex-wife. You know—the one I wasn't quite over? Except I have been over her for a while." He laughed again, another pain-filled expulsion of air. "Now I've just got to figure out a way to get over you."

This was insane. Harry was literally dragging Allie up the side of a mountain, with five professional killers hot on their heels.

It was true that this was a big mountain and these were vast woods, but Harry knew it wouldn't take much to track them, considering they were leaving an elephant-size trail through the underbrush.

And that was if Ivo hadn't signed a local tracker onto his team. He probably had. Both Ivo and Michael Trotta were meticulous. They wouldn't have overlooked the possibility of their hunt for Alessandra ending up in the Colorado wilderness. And if one of those other four men was indeed a tracker, he would be able to follow them no matter how careful they were.

"What are we going to do?" Allie asked, panting as they pushed farther up the hill. "You don't really think we can outrun them, do you? And there's five of them. They're bound to split up."

"We don't have a lot of options." He helped her up and over a fallen tree. She no longer refused his hand. That was either a good sign or a bad sign. Harry didn't know which. Probably a bad sign, since she'd spoken of taking his money and vanishing—if they survived this.

Please God, let them survive this.

"We could hide," she said.

"They'd find us," Harry told her.

"Well, we could find a place—I don't know, a cave or something—where we could hold them off with your gun."

"And hope that the FBI finds us before they go back to their car and get a grenade thrower out of the trunk?"

Allie was silent for a moment, just pushing forward, using both hands to scramble up the ever-steepening hill. "So what exactly are our options?"

"We keep moving."

"That's it?" Her anger wasn't far from the surface, and it bubbled up again. "Do you screw up all your cases this way, or is there just something about me that brings out this incompetent side of you?"

"I didn't set this up," he told her for the four thousandth time. "If I did, there would have been backup. Believe me."

"I'm done believing you. I believed you twice—and you know that old saying? 'Fool me once, shame on you. Fool me twice, shame on me.' I'm making up a third part to that saying. Fool me three times, just shoot me now."

Harry laughed. It was the wrong thing to do.

"You think this is funny? We're probably going to die, and you think this is funny?" She was furious. "You said I'd be safe here, and I trusted you. I did more than trust you, I slept with you, over and over again! Oh, God, the whole time you were probably laughing and—"

"Allie, you gotta believe me—I didn't set this up. George did. George knew about that letter I got from the lawyers. He probably figured out there were court records with Shaun and Em's names and address on it. And this snafu stinks of Nicole Fenster, too. But I swear to you, I didn't know. There's no way in hell I would've set you up. And I didn't mean to sleep with you. I mean, it wasn't something I planned and . . ."

Yeah, and that wasn't exactly helping. Making it sound as if the lovemaking they'd shared had been some kind of an accident, like Whoops, golly, how'd my penis get in there?

There probably wasn't anything he could say to make her believe him. But he wanted her to. They were probably going to die, and he didn't want her to die hating him.

As they crested the top of the mountain, Harry saw a flash of blue below them.

A river.

There was a river down there.

Maybe, just maybe, Allie at least wouldn't have to die.

"Can you swim?" Harry asked her.

"What? Why?"

"Damnit, Al, just answer the fucking question."

She flinched, and he felt a surge of remorse. He'd meant to clean up his language, but he'd never gotten around to it. He probably wouldn't get a chance to now.

"I'm sorry," he said quietly. "Allie, I'm so sorry about all of this. I honestly thought we were safe here. I told you, I wouldn't risk my kids' lives that way. And I wouldn't risk your life either. Because I . . ."

She was looking at him, and he could see that familiar flicker of hope in her eyes. Hope that he'd say the words that were sticking in his throat. Despite everything she'd said, she wanted to believe him. And he knew that all he had to do was say it.

"I wouldn't set you up that way," he said again, squeezing the words out, hoping the verbal running start would give him the necessary momentum, "because I'm in love with you."

Harry loved her.

Harry loved her.

Allie nodded, looking back the way they'd come, back down the mountain, to where Ivo and his men were bound to appear any minute.

"Yeah, I know," Harry said, taking her hand and pulling her with him down the other side of the mountain. "My timing needs a little work. But I just thought there wouldn't be—"

"No." She refused to let him continue. "We're not going to die. Don't you dare give up on me, Harry. We're going to make it. We have to. Because I love you, too."

He pulled her close and kissed her, sweetly but far too briefly. "I'm sorry," he said again, "but we've got to keep moving."

Allie nodded. She wanted to cling to him, to kiss him deeply, to feel his arms around her. But that was going to have to wait. Still, this was better than fighting. Much better. God help her, she believed him.

As Harry glanced back at her, she saw he had tears in his eyes. "You know, I hate to sound like a doomsayer, but sometimes love's not enough, Al. I wish it was all we needed, but—"

"We can do this." Her voice trembled with the power of her hope.

"Yeah." Harry took a deep breath. "Maybe we can." He released her hand and took the map from his pocket, unfolding it, still moving down the hill. "So can you swim?"

"Yes," she told him. "I can swim. It's not pretty, but I stay afloat."

"We've got a new option." He slowed as he pointed to a thin blue line on the map and then down the mountain. "We head for this little river. See it on the map? It's nothing major, but it'll go all the way into Hardy if you take it heading east. And if you walk in the water, there'll be no trail for them to follow. Swim if you have to. When you get to Hardy, go straight to the police."

"Wait. You keep saying you as if I'm doing this alone. Aren't you going to come with me?"

"I'll go farther west, up into those mountains, leaving a trail for these bozos to follow."

"But . . . they'll kill you if they find you!"

"Maybe, but they won't kill you, and that's my priority right now." He skidded again on the dried leaves. "Christ, going down is nearly as tough as going up." He pocketed the map and took her hand again. "Look, Al, if I don't leave another trail, they'll assume we followed the river. This way at least you get a chance to get away."

She worked hard to keep her voice calm and in control. "Yes, but it's me they're after. You're the one who should follow the river."

Harry's feet slipped out beneath him, and he nearly pulled Allie down the mountain with him before he caught himself. "Sorry, that's not an option."

She threw calm and control out the window. How could they possibly be discussing this? "Well, I say it is."

"There's no way I'm going to let you die for me," he told her. "Christ."

"Oh, and what? I'm supposed to just let you die for me? Forget it, Harry. We do it together, or we don't do it at all."

Harry slipped again, and this time they both went down. He held on to Alessandra, trying to protect her from the branches slapping past them and the bruising rocks that littered the forest floor as they skidded down the steep mountainside. He grabbed at a thin tree, but it was dead—it uprooted, spraying them with dirt instead of stopping them.

He caught another tree, a bigger tree, directly in the ribs, and through the haze of pain managed to throw his free arm around it. Jesus, his ribs again. Same rib. Of course. It had just started to feel better. But then he remembered. Allie loved him. The pain was inconsequential.

"You all right?" he asked Allie. Her hair was in his eyes, her arms tight around his neck.

She gasped, he struggled to sit up and . . .

"Oh, shit."

Another three feet, and they would have gone over the side of a cliff. Harry held on to both the tree and Allie as he looked over the edge.

Sheer rock went down about forty feet to the river that sparkled directly below. It was not some little narrow river you'd only get your feet wet walking across. The thin blue line on the map had been deceptive. It was wide and deep and running much too fast, with white water as far as the eye could see.

It was the kind of river you could drown in. The kind where the water could wash over your head and pull you under . . .

Allie tugged at his arm. "Come on," she said. "We've got to find another way down."

It was amazing, really. It was crazy, but Harry loved her even more for it. She could look at the river and still have hope. She didn't see it as the end of the line, the end of their options—the way he did.

She didn't see it for what he knew it to be—the end of their lives.

George sat on the sofa, his head in the palms of his hands.

Kim knew she had no choice. She had to tell him. He had to know that what happened to his partner and Alessandra Lamont wasn't entirely his fault. It was mostly her fault.

The irony was incredible. She had been prepared to tell George about Michael Trotta's demands, but she hadn't because she'd believed he still loved Nicole. She'd been jealous—bottom line—and she'd betrayed him.

She sat down next to him, but he didn't look up.

"I have to tell you about something I've done," she said quietly. "It's something I'm ashamed of."

He still didn't look up. It was better that way. It would be hard enough telling him without having to look into his eyes.

"I overheard your conversation with Nicki," she said. "The one where you told her how to find your partner."

He lifted his head, and she was the one who now gazed down at the floor. "I gave Trotta that information," she told him. "He told me if I didn't tell him everything I overheard, he'd make me wish I was dead. I know I should have gone to you and asked for help, but . . . I didn't. I was too afraid, and too jealous. I thought you were seeing Nicole again and . . ."

Tears rolled down her cheeks, and she finally found the nerve to look up at him, hoping to see compassion and understanding in his eyes.

Instead she saw nothing. No emotion, no light, no warmth, no nothing.

"I know," he said. "I knew all along that you were

working for Trotta. Why do you think I let you move in here?"

Kim was speechless. He . . . knew?

George smiled, but it didn't touch his eyes. "Surprise, babe. Here, all this time, you thought you were using me, but in fact, I was using you. That phone call you over-heard? That was a setup. We were feeding that informa-tion to Trotta, through you. I knew you were home, and I knew why you wanted a donut so goddamn badly. You did just what I expected you to do. I hope he paid you well."

He knew . . .

"Pack your things and get out," George told her flatly. "You better take whatever money you made from Trotta and leave town. Disappear. I should cuff you and bring you in. And if I see you again, I'll do just that." He stood up. "I'm giving you five minutes, and then I'm getting the handcuffs."

She couldn't believe it. Couldn't believe that this was happening. "But . . . I love you. And you love me. I know you love me."

"Yeah," George said, slipping his crutches under his arms and walking out of the room. "Ain't life a bitch?"

"Now what?" Allie asked.

Harry shook his head. He couldn't believe they'd got-ten this far.

They'd worked their way down to a narrow ledge about twenty feet above the rushing water, and there was, without a doubt, nowhere left to go.

"We'll have to go back," he told her. "Try a different route."

This hope thing was contagious, and far more pleasant than the alternative, which was lying down and waiting for Ivo and his buddies to put bullets in their brains.

With a little hope, he could pretend that he and Allie actually had a future. A little more hope, and he could see his days and nights filled with her warmth and beauty. And love. God, she loved him. How could he not hope to live happily ever after for longer than the forty minutes he'd originally estimated Ivo would take to catch up with them?

With hope, he could pretend it was just a matter of time before they could return to Hardy. He'd move into Marge's house with Em and Shaun, and he'd let his relationship with Allie grow. They'd take their time, and maybe in a year or so, when Allie was ready, they'd get married.

God, he hoped she'd want to marry him. He hoped he would spend the rest of his life with her at his side.

The truth was, if they did survive, they'd have to leave town. Trotta knew about Hardy, so they'd have to hide again, someplace new. Shaun and Emily would be angry— Marge probably would be, too. It would be harder than ever to regain their trust. And as for Allie . . . She'd already told him—no question—that she didn't want to marry him.

Still, he could hope.

But then it happened. A gunshot. A bullet plowed into the ledge.

Harry pulled Allie back against the cliff, shielding her from flying bits of rock. A piece hit his leg and it stung. But the sting was nothing compared to the sharp pain he felt as all his hope was deflated.

There was no way out. He'd failed her. They were temporarily shielded by the cliff that jutted out above them, and he had enough ammunition to temporarily hold off anyone climbing down onto their ledge, but it was only a matter of time before Ivo sent a sharpshooter to the mountain on the other side of the river. From there, a man with a high-powered rifle would be able to pick Harry and Allie off like targets in a shooting gallery.

There was no hope. They were dead. Still, he pulled out his gun and fired a warning shot down the narrow path that led to their ledge.

"I guess we can't go back," Allie said, almost matter-of-factly. "So we'll have to go forward."

Forward? There was no forward.

She must've seen the skepticism in his eyes because she kissed him. "We can jump into the river."

"Into that river? No sane human being would jump into that river." He fired again.

"That's the point. They won't follow us. Certainly not by jumping from up where they are."

"We'll drown."

"No, we won't," she countered. "Not necessarily. I'm a good enough swimmer. I'll stay with you."

"No," Harry said. "Nuh-uh, no way."

"At least we'll have a chance. If we stay here, we will be shot." She kissed him again. "I know it scares you, and you're right, we might die. But I'll take might die over will die, any day. At least if we jump, there's hope."

Hope.

At least there was hope.

True, it was completely insane hope. An impossible long-shot hope.

They jump off this cliff into that river, and maybe, just maybe, they'd survive.

As Harry gazed down into Allie's eyes, he could see that crazy hope. And as long as he was going to buy into it, he might as well go big. "Marry me."

She looked at him as if he'd spoken in Chinese.

"I'll jump with you," he told her, "if you'll marry me."

Allie laughed, covering her mouth with one hand, as if

they weren't standing at the edge of an impossible situation, as if she truly thought there was a chance of them someday standing in a church and exchanging vows.

Ivo had stopped shooting at them, probably saving his ammunition. Harry knew it was only a matter of time now before he sent one of his men across the river. And then there'd be no way for him to shield Allie, nowhere for them to hide. No hope.

"You really want that?" she asked.

"Yes," he told her, and damned if that hope didn't lodge in his chest and make him feel like it truly were possible.

She nodded. "I'd love to marry you." There were tears in her eyes as she smiled at him.

Harry kissed her hard. They could do this. They could do this. He holstered his gun, and breathing hard, he took her hand.

She smiled.

He nodded.

And together they jumped.

Twenty-two

ALLIE WRAPPED THE blanket more tightly around her as she sat in the interview room in the Farthing FBI headquarters and stared at the wanted posters on the walls.

One of the faces looked familiar, but she couldn't remember where she'd seen the man before. He had short dark hair, dark eyes, and cheekbones to die for. Definitely of Hispanic heritage. Was he one of the men she'd seen with Ivo in Hardy?

Lord, that was just what she needed—the guilt and responsibility for bringing public enemy number four into a sleepy little town like Hardy, Colorado.

She shivered. She was cold, she was tired, she was hungry—and the flat eyes of America's Most Wanted gave her the creeps—but as Harry came back into the room and smiled at her, she was happier than she could ever remember being.

He looked about as bad as she felt. Completely bedraggled and half drowned. His clothes were wet and his sneakers squooshed when he walked.

He looked beautiful.

Another man intercepted him, pulling him aside and speaking quietly into his ear. Harry's smile faded.

Allie couldn't hear what Harry said, but she could read his lips. Shit.

Oh, Lord, what now?

"Ivo and his boys got away," Harry told her point-blank as he sat down beside her at the table. "A fuc—Excuse me. A frigging statewide manhunt, and we don't even turn up the car Ivo was driving." He took her hand. "This means it's not over. We don't have Trotta, and he's still after you."

He looked down at their intertwined fingers, and when he looked back up, his dark eyes were serious. "I need to ask you something," he said. "But before I ask you, I want you to know that no matter what your answer is, it doesn't have anything to do with you and me, and it's not going to change the way I feel about you. I just need you to answer it honestly, okay?"

Allie nodded.

"There's a lot of speculation about why Trotta hasn't given up on whacking you," he said, obviously choosing his words carefully. "We just got word from a New York informant that the price on your head is up to five million."

She couldn't believe it. "Five million? Dollars?"

Harry nodded. "This doesn't read as your everyday, average punishment kind of hit. There's something else happening here, and people are thinking that there must be some kind of personal connection between you and Michael Trotta. Some kind of intimate connection."

"No, Harry," Allie said, understanding what he was asking. "There's not. There wasn't. I didn't have any kind of personal relationship with him. I couldn't. I wouldn't. He was married. I was married."

He squeezed her hand. "I'm sorry I had to ask you that."

"It's a valid question. Why would he spend five million dollars to see me dead?"

Harry shook his head. "Is it possible Griffin had some information that he somehow passed on to you? But no, that wouldn't stand up in court, it'd be hearsay. Was there something you saw or heard, or some documents or tapes Griffin might've had—"

It hit her in a flash, and Allie stood up. "Enrique. Enrique something."

"Who?"

She pointed to the wanted posters, to the face of the Hispanic man. "That's where I've seen him before." Add a pencil-thin mustache, grow his hair to chin length. Yes. Yes, definitely. "In Michael Trotta's office. As I was leaving, he was trying to get away. He was handcuffed and bleeding. I think he'd been shot as well as beaten. His face was . . ." She shook her head. "He got blood on my blouse and pants. He told me his name was Enrique something. Montone? Montoy?"

Harry crossed to the wall, to the posters that overlapped each other there. "Enrique Montoya?" He took the flyer from the wall and handed it to Allie. "Are you telling me that Enrique Montoya was in Michael Trotta's office while you were there?"

Allie nodded, quickly skimming the printing on the flyer. One-hundred-thousand-dollar reward leading to the arrest and conviction of the person or persons responsible for the death of FBI Agent Enrique Montoya. Montoya disappeared mid-March in Florida and turned up dead several weeks later in New York. Autopsy reports place his date of death on . . .

She looked up at Harry. "He died the same day I was in Michael's office."

He was already on the phone. "I need Christine McFall. Yeah, hi, Chris. It's Harry O'Dell. Yeah, I'm still kicking." He paused. "No, please don't call me sir. Okay, fine, call me sir, but just answer this question for me, all right?" Another pause. "I need to know about Alessandra Lamont's

personal possessions. Was anything left in the Farmingdale house after the fire? Any clothes in the closets that
might've retained pieces of explosive material and been
saved for evidence?" He nodded. "I'm looking for a pair
of pants and a blouse that have bloodstains and . . ." He
looked at Allie. "What color?"

"No," she said, suddenly understanding why he was
asking. "They weren't in the house. I had so few clothes
I couldn't just throw them out, so I took them to the
dry cleaners. Although the woman there told me she
wouldn't be able to get the stains completely out. It's
been weeks, but they're probably still there."

"Which dry cleaners?"

"Huff's. On Main Street, near the old movie theater?"

"Chris," Harry said into the phone. "Go to Huff's on
Main Street in Farmingdale, and pick up Alessandra Lamont's dry cleaning order—a blouse and a pair of ladies'
pants. Bag it as evidence and take it to the lab. Have them
run DNA tests on whatever bloodstains you can find.
We're pretty sure the blood's Enrique Montoya's. Yeah,
you heard me. Montoya's. Let me know what you find."
He hung up the phone and turned to Allie. "With that
evidence and your testimony, we've finally got Trotta."

George threw the file down on Nicole's desk. "Kim
Monahan. Drop the conspiracy charges against her.
Now."

She looked up at him coolly. "Give me one good
reason why I should."

"Because I'm asking you to."

"Well, well. This girl actually matters to you."

"Just do it, Nicki. If you don't, I'll never let you live
down the Alessandra Lamont snafu."

Nicole only managed to look bored. "It wasn't my
fault. Andrew Bell in the Washington office thought we'd

benefit from the publicity of getting Trotta on a murder charge. Of course, he claims he made the decision to withhold protection based on the fact that Lamont had refused protection in the past."

"It was a setup. We leaked information because we believed a task force would be in place to intercept the hit attempt. You should have followed up on the case, and you know it. You're damned lucky Alessandra and Harry O'Dell weren't killed. And you're lucky, too, that Harry's leaving the FBI. If he came back here, he'd have every right to kick your ass across the street and back— in front of everyone in this office."

She finally had the decency to look embarrassed. "Yes, well, I certainly am lucky, aren't I? I tell that to myself all the time."

She sounded bitter. But George didn't care. Whatever she regretted about her life—including losing him— she'd done to herself. He adjusted his crutches and turned to go.

"George."

He turned back.

"Consider the charges against Kim dropped," Nicki said quietly. "You can bring her out from wherever you've been hiding her."

He shook his head. "No, she's gone. I . . . told her to leave." And she had. Just like Nicole, Kim had given him up and left without a fight.

"I'm sorry," Nicki said. "I thought you and she . . . Well, the night that you asked me to come over—the night you told me you thought Kim was connected to Trotta . . . Before you told me that, I was sure you were going to say you were getting married again. You know, you and Kim. I mean, you both just seemed so happy together."

"Trotta was paying her to be there with me. I pretty

352 Suzanne Brockmann

much suspected that from the start. It was all just an act." Yeah, and maybe if he said it enough, he'd start to believe it, too.

"But you seemed—"

"Happy?" George snorted. "Come on, Nic. I was living with a gorgeous woman who would go down on me at the drop of a hat, and someone else was footing the bill. Why shouldn't I seem happy?"

"I think you were hoping she wouldn't pass that information to Trotta."

She was dead right. He'd prayed that when it came down to it, Kim wouldn't betray him. But instead of confronting her about her connection to Trotta, he'd tested her. He'd waited until he heard her come in, and then he'd pretended to be on the phone with Nicole, letting Kim overhear information they'd wanted leaked to Trotta. And sure enough, she'd gone right out and passed on the information. They had tape recordings of her phone conversation with one of Trotta's assistants.

He had hoped Kim would come to him. He had thought that she loved him. But he'd never admit that. Especially not to Nicole.

"I think this girl managed to hurt you," Nicole told him. Her eyes looked so sad, as if she honestly cared. Must've been just a trick of the lighting. "Is it possible you have a heart after all?"

"Who, me?" George asked. He started out of the office. "Not a chance. You and me both, babe. Totally heartless."

Harry was still on the phone when Allie got out of the shower.

It was a weird déjà vu—someone had left pajamas for her on the bed, just like the first time. She put them on and went out into the living room, drying her hair with a towel.

"No," Harry was saying, "Shaun, it's not your fault. You had no idea that filing that petition would—" He paused. "Yeah, I know it sucks, and I'm sorry you'll have to leave your friends. But maybe we can all sit down together and figure out where we want to live and—" He sighed and rubbed his forehead. "Yeah, Marge, too. Okay. Okay, yeah, I'll see you tomorrow." He hung up the phone with a sigh. "Shaun's pissed. He doesn't want to start over in a new town."

"I'm having trouble with that, too."

"I'm sorry," Harry said.

"That's not your fault."

"Yeah, I know, but I'm still sorry. George called. He's sorry, too."

"How is he?" she asked, glancing at herself in the mirror. Her hair was growing out. She was actually starting to look human. And that meant it was time to get another cut. Maybe a shag this time. She'd looked terrible that time she'd gotten her hair cut in a shag when she was little.

"His leg's much better. I told him that was good because I was going to come out there and break his other one. He seemed to think that would be okay."

She looked up at him. "You're not really going to New York . . . ?"

"No," he said quickly. "No, I was just, you know, getting on his case. Letting him know that I forgave him."

"By telling him you were going to break his leg?"

"He was really upset. I was afraid if we got too touchy-feely he might start to cry. Or maybe I might start to cry." He just stood there, gazing at her for several long moments. He smiled crookedly. "Of course, I might start to cry anyway. I'm still amazed that we really made it."

"I'm not. I didn't doubt it for a minute." Allie thought for a second, reconsidering, remembering the fear she'd felt in the cold river, knowing Harry wasn't a strong swimmer. "Well, except maybe when we first hit the water."

Harry cleared his throat and turned away slightly. "You know, Al, I just want you to know, I won't hold you to that promise you made me on that ledge. I mean, I seriously thought we were going to die, and it was just this kind of fantasy thing, you know?"

It took Allie a moment to realize that he was talking about his marriage proposal. "Oh," she said. "No. I meant it when I said I wanted to marry you." Realization dawned. "Oh, but if you didn't mean it . . ." She took a deep breath. "I can't have babies, remember, so if you wanted—"

"No," Harry said. "Jesus. That wasn't what I meant at all. I'm—I'm dying to marry you, but my life is pretty much a wreck. I'm unemployed as of about an hour ago, and my home life's a circus. One kid hates me, the other doesn't recognize me on the street."

"Shaun doesn't hate you."

"He's not happy about leaving Hardy. He was counting on getting into that dance troupe and—" He shook his head interrupting himself. "I guess what I'm trying to say is that I'm not exactly any kind of prize."

"I'm not a prize, either," Allie told him. "And good thing. I've done that before—been someone's prize. It wasn't any fun." She crossed to the self-service bar and opened a bottle of seltzer. "As far as the baby thing goes, you know I've always hoped that someday I could adopt . . ."

"Hey, that's perfect, because my kids seem to want to be adopted."

"I meant, a baby."

"I know, I was just making a bad joke."

"I can't joke about this, Harry. Maybe I'm hypersensitive because of what happened with Griffin, but I couldn't stand it if something like that happened again."

"Allie."

She turned to find he hadn't moved. He was standing there, by the phone, in his soggy jeans and almost-dry T-shirt, with his hair a mess and his heart and soul there for her to see in his beautiful dark brown eyes.

"I want you to marry me because I love you," he said, "not because I'm looking for some kind of baby-making machine. I want you to be my lover and my friend, not some trophy on the shelf, and I desperately want you to help me with this mess I'm in with my kids. I want them to be our kids. And if you decide you want a baby in a year or five or ten, I will help you adopt one, and I will love him or her as much as I love Shaun and Emily." He smiled. "And, for the record, I personally am truly looking forward to never having to use birth control ever again, for the rest of our very, very long lives."

Allie waited to see if he was finished.

He wasn't. "It's going to be hard work. I don't want to gloss that over. I'm not easy to live with. And I know that right now Shaun's not easy to live with and—"

"You sound as if you're trying to talk me out of it," Allie said.

He was silent for a moment, and when he looked up at her, he didn't try to hide the uncertainty in his eyes. "I'm scared I'm going to let you down."

She held her hand out to him. "You already jumped off one cliff with me today. Come on, Harry. Let's go two for two."

Harry laughed.

And took her hand.

And kissed her.

Free fall had never felt so good.

Epilogue

S<small>HAUN LOOKED FOR</small> Harry and Allie in the crowd backstage, after the performance.

He couldn't see Harry, but across the room he could see eight-year-old Emily, who was still small enough to ride on their father's shoulders. She waved to him, giving him a double thumbs-up.

He'd danced particularly well tonight.

Maybe it was knowing his family was in the audience. Or maybe it was something about being back in Hardy for the first time in more than four years.

He'd always wanted to dance on the big college stage, now he finally had.

He hadn't seen much of the town when the Tap Masters tour bus pulled in late last night. And he'd spent most of today in rehearsal. It was good—they'd worked out some kinks in the opening number. But he'd wanted to walk past the old house, maybe go down to the basketball courts . . .

"Shaun Novick?"

He turned around.

"Oh my God, it is you."

The young woman standing behind him was nearly as tall as his own six feet three inches. She had long, thick brown hair that cascaded around her shoulders, a body like a goddess, and the most incredibly beautiful eyes he'd ever seen in his eighteen years of life.

"O'Dell," he said. "My name's O'Dell."

"But it was Novick, wasn't it? There couldn't be two Shauns who look just like you, who dance just like you . . ." She smiled, and his mouth went dry. She had the most amazing smile. "You got contact lenses. I did, too."

He looked into her eyes. Looked closer and . . . "Mindy?"

"I got your letter," she told him. "I would've written back, but you didn't give me your new address."

"I couldn't," he said. "I'm sorry."

"I know. You explained about that man who was after your father and . . . I just . . . wished I could've written back, that's all." She gave him a searching look. "Am I blowing your cover by recognizing you here today?"

Shaun smiled. "Michael Trotta, the mob guy, was killed about three months after he went to prison. We've pretty much used our real names since then." He paused. "How about you? What are you doing here? Do you still live in Hardy?"

"Yeah. I'm home for Christmas break—at least I was. I've got to catch a flight back to school in about two hours. I got a scholarship to UCLA." She gave him another of those amazing smiles. "I'm on the women's basketball team."

"That's so great." He couldn't stop smiling at her. "Only two hours, huh? Too bad."

"Actually, my mom's in the parking lot getting the car. I've got to go." She held out her hand. "I'm so glad I got a chance to see you. It was a great show."

There was no way in hell he was only going to shake her hand. He pulled her into his arms.

It was the right thing to do—she hugged him just as

tightly, and when she pulled back, she was laughing. "God, I had such a crush on you in eighth grade. I would've died and gone to heaven if you'd ever hugged me like that then."

"I was awful to you. I can't believe you don't hate me."

She touched his face. "I forgave you. Remember?"

He didn't want to let go of her. "Yeah, I remember."

"Did you work things out with your dad?"

He nodded. "Yeah, we're cool. Harry's doing great— he's here today. So are Allie and Emily and Sam, my brand-new brother. Harry and Allie just adopted a baby."

"Allie?"

"My stepmom. You met her—she used to work for your mother, cleaning houses."

Mindy nodded. "Okay, right."

"She's a writer now. Her second book's out in June. This one's going to be big. I can feel it, you know?"

"So Allie married your dad? That's great."

"Four years ago," he told her. "Right after we left town. She's incredible. I'm crazy about her. Sometimes I wish Harry hadn't married her so that I could."

"Hmmm," Mindy said, narrowing her eyes as she looked at him. "Does that mean you're still not gay?"

Shaun had to laugh. He gave her a very pointed once-over. "What do you think?"

Her cheeks were pink, but she took his left hand and wrote her phone number on his palm. "I think I'd love to see you again. Call me if you're ever in L.A.?"

"I will definitely be in L.A., I will definitely call you, and I'm definitely still not gay."

"And I definitely still have a crush on you." She gave him another of her million-dollar smiles as she disappeared into the crowd.

Shaun watched her until she reached the doors. She turned and waved. Hot damn. Mindy MacGregor.

"Did you get her number?" Harry asked from behind him.

Shaun held up his left hand.

Harry high-fived him. "You were so good." He pulled Shaun in for a hug. "I am so proud of you." He stepped back and looked up at him. "Does that happen often? Women chasing you down and writing their phone numbers on your various body parts?"

Shaun laughed as he lifted Emily into his arms for a hug. "I usually don't let them write on me."

"This one was different, huh?"

"Harry," Allie said, shifting Sam to her other shoulder. "Didn't you recognize her? That was Mindy MacGregor."

Harry looked from Allie to Shaun. "That was your friend Mindy, with the glasses?"

"I remember Mindy," Em said. "She always smelled so good."

"Yeah, she still smells good," Shaun told his sister.

"Is she still playing basketball?" Allie asked.

"UCLA."

"Go Mindy. I always knew she'd grow out of her awkward phase." Allie turned to Harry. "You never really knew her, but she was a kid who refused to quit. She was the world's worst basketball player, but she practiced hard and never gave up hope." She kissed Shaun on the cheek. "Call her right away and ask her to marry you."

Shaun laughed. "Yes, Mother."

Harry had put his arm around Allie. Even after four years, he couldn't stand next to her without touching her. They made being in love look really, really good.

"Thanks for coming," Shaun told them. "I know it wasn't easy to get here with the baby and Harry's crazy schedule."

Harry's security consulting business was finally taking off.

"This was good for me," Harry said. "I'm working on learning to delegate."

Allie just smiled.

"You were incredible," Harry told Shaun. "As if you didn't know. Still, we wouldn't have missed this for the world."

Shaun smiled and hugged his father again. "I know."

Read on for an exciting preview of

FLASHPOINT
by Suzanne Brockmann

Published by Ballantine Books
in April 2004.

Before tonight, the closest Tess Bailey had come to a strip
club was on TV, where beautiful women danced seductively in
G-strings, taut young body parts bouncing and gleaming from
a stage that sparkled and flashed.

In the Gentlemen's Den, thousands of miles from
Hollywood in a rundown neighborhood north of Washington,
D.C., the mirror ball was broken, and the aging stripper on the
sagging makeshift stage looked tired and cold.

"Whoops." Nash turned his back to the noisy room, carefully keeping his face in the shadows. "That's Gus Mondelay
sitting with Decker," he told Tess.

Diego Nash had the kind of face that stood out in a crowd.
And Nash obviously didn't want Mondelay—whoever he was
—to see him.

Tess followed him back toward the bar, away from the table
where Lawrence Decker, Nash's long-time Agency partner,
was working undercover.

She bumped into someone. "Excuse me—"

Oh my God! The waitresses weren't wearing any shirts.
The Gentlemen's Den wasn't just a strip club, it was also a
topless bar. She grabbed Nash's hand and dragged him down
the passageway that led to the pay phone and the restrooms. It
was dark back there, with the added bonus of nary a half-
naked woman in sight.

She had to say it. "This *was* just a rumor—"

He pinned her up against the wall and nuzzled her neck, his
arms braced on either side of her. She was only stunned for
about two seconds before she realized that two men had staggered out of the men's room. This was just another way for
Nash to hide his face.

She pretended that she was only pretending to melt as he kissed her throat and jawline, as he waited until Drunk and Drunker pushed past them before he spoke, his breath warm against her ear. "There were at least four shooters set up and waiting out front in the parking lot. And those were just the ones I spotted as we were walking in."

The light in the parking lot had been dismal. Tess's concentration had alternated between her attempts not to catch her foot in a pothole and fall on her face, the two biker types who appeared to be having, quite literally, a pissing contest, and the unbelievable fact that she was out in the real world with the legendary Diego Nash.

They were now alone in the hallway, but Nash hadn't moved out of whispering range. He was standing so close that Tess's nose was inches from the collar of his expensive shirt. He smelled outrageously good. "Who's Gus Mondelay?" she asked.

"An informant," he said tersely, the muscle jumping in the side of his perfect jaw. "He's on the Agency payroll, but lately I've been wondering . . . " He shook his head. "It fits that he's here, now. He'd enjoy watching Deck get gunned down." The smile he gave her was grim. "Thanks for having the presence of mind to call me."

Tess still couldn't believe the conversation she'd overheard just over an hour ago at Agency Headquarters.

A rumor had come in that Lawrence Decker's cover had been blown, and that there was an ambush being set to kill him. The Agency's night-shift support staff had attempted to contact him, but had been able to do little more than leave a message on his voice mail.

No one in the office had bothered to get in touch with Diego Nash.

"Nash isn't working this case with Decker," Suellen Foster had informed Tess. "Besides, it's just a rumor."

Nash was more than Decker's partner. He was Decker's friend. Tess had called him even as she ran for the parking lot.

"So what do we do?" Tess asked now, looking up at Nash.

He had eyes the color of melted chocolate—warm eyes that held a perpetual glint of amusement whenever he came into the office in HQ and flirted with the mostly female support staff. He liked to perch on the edge of Tess's desk in particular, and the other Agency analysts and staffers teased her about his attention. They also warned her of the dangers of dating a field agent, particularly one like Diego Nash, who had a serious 007 complex.

As if she needed their warning.

Nash sat on her desk because he liked her little bowl of lemon mints, and because she called him "tall, dark, and egotistical" right to his perfect cheekbones, and refused to take him seriously.

Right now, though, she was in his world, and she was taking him extremely seriously.

Right now his usually warm eyes were cold and almost flat-looking, as if part of him were a million miles away.

"*We* do nothing," Nash told Tess now. "*You* go home."

"I can help."

He'd already dismissed her. "You'll help more by leaving."

"I've done the training," she informed him, blocking his route back to the bar. "I've got an application in for a field agent position. It's just a matter of time before—"

Nash shook his head. "They're not going to take you. They're never going to take you. Look, Bailey, thanks for the ride, but—"

"Tess," she said. He had a habit of calling the support staff by their last names, but tonight she was here, in the field. "And they are too going to take me. Brian Underwood told me—"

"Brian Underwood was stringing you along because he was afraid you would quit and he needs you on support. You'll excuse me if I table this discussion on your lack of promotability and start focusing on the fact that my partner is about to—"

"I can get a message to Decker," Tess pointed out. "No one in that bar has ever seen me before."

Nash laughed in her face. "Yeah, what? Are you going to walk over to him with your freckles and your Sunday church picnic clothes . . . ?"

"These aren't Sunday church picnic clothes!" They were

running-into-work-on-a-Friday-night-at-10:30-to-pick-up-a-file clothes. Jeans. Sneakers. T-shirt.

T-shirt . . .

Tess looked back down the hall toward the bar, toward the ordering station where the waitresses came to pick up drinks and drop off empty glasses.

"You stand out in this shithole as much as I do wearing this suit," Nash told her. "More. If you walk up to Decker looking the way you're looking . . . "

There was a stack of small serving trays, right there, by the bartender's cash register.

"He's my friend, too," Tess said. "He needs to be warned, and I can do it."

"No." Finality rang in his voice. "Just walk out the front door, Bailey, get back into your car and—"

Tess took off her T-shirt, unhooked her bra, peeled it down her arms, and handed them both to him.

"What message should I give him?" she asked.

Nash looked at her, looked at the shirt and wispy lace of bra dangling from his hand, looked at her again.

Looked at her. "Jeez, Bailey."

Tess felt the heat in her cheeks as clearly as she felt the coolness from the air conditioning against her bare back and shoulders.

"What should I tell him?" she asked Nash again.

"Damn," he said, laughing a little bit. "Okay. O-*kay.*" He stuffed her clothes into his jacket pocket. "Except you still look like a Sunday school teacher."

Tess gave him a disbelieving look and an outraged noise. "I do *not.*" For God's sake, she was standing here half naked—

But he reached for her, unfastening the top button of her jeans and unzipping them.

"Hey!" She tried to pull back, but he caught her.

"Don't you watch MTV?" he asked, folding her pants down so that they were more like hip huggers, his fingers warm against her skin.

Her belly button was showing now, as well as the top of her panties, the zipper of her jeans precariously half-pulled down. "Yeah, in all my limitless free time."

"You could use some lipstick." Nash stepped back and looked at her critically, then, with both hands, completely messed up her short hair. He stepped back and looked again. "That's a little better."

Gee, thanks. "Message?" she said.

"Just tell him to stay put for now. They're not going to hit him inside," Nash said. "Don't tell him that, he knows. That's what I'm telling *you,* you understand?"

Tess nodded.

"I'm going to make a perimeter circuit of this place," he continued. "I'll meet you right back here—no, in the ladies' room—in ten minutes. Give the message to Deck, be brief, don't blow it by trying to tell him too much, then get your ass in the ladies' room, and stay there until I'm back. Is that clear?"

Tess nodded again. She'd never seen this Nash before—this order-barking, cold-bloodedly decisive commander. She'd never seen the Nash he'd become in the car, on the way over here, before either. After she'd made that first phone call, she'd picked him up downtown. She'd told him again as they'd headed to the Gentlemen's Den, in greater detail, all that she'd overheard. He'd gotten very quiet, very grim, when his attempts to reach Decker on his cell phone had failed.

He'd been scared, she'd realized as she'd glanced at him. He had been genuinely frightened that they were too late, that the hit had already gone down, that his partner—his friend—was already dead.

When they got here and the parking lot was quiet, when they walked inside and spotted Decker still alive and breathing, there had been a fraction of a second in which Tess had been sure Nash was going to faint from relief.

It was eye-opening. It was possible that Diego Nash was human after all.

Tess gave him one last smile, then headed down that hall, toward one of those little serving trays on the bar. God, she was about to walk into a room filled with drunken men, with her breasts bare and her pants halfway down her butt. Still, it couldn't possibly be worse than that supercritical once-over Nash had given her.

"Tess." He caught her arm, and she looked back at him. "Be careful," he said.

She nodded again. "You, too."

He smiled then—a flash of straight white teeth. "Deck's going to shit monkeys when he sees you."

With that, he was gone.

Tess grabbed the tray from the bar and pushed her way out into the crowd.

Something was wrong.

Decker read it in Gus Mondelay's eyes, in the way the heavyset man was sitting across from him at the table.

Mondelay gestured for Decker to come closer—it was the only way to be heard over the loud music. "Tim must be running late."

Jesus, Mondelay had a worse than usual case of dog breath tonight.

"I'm in no hurry," Decker said, leaning back again in his seat. Air. Please God, give him some air.

Gus Mondelay had come into contact with the Freedom Network while serving eighteen months in Wallens Ridge Prison for possession of an illegal firearm. The group's name made them sound brave and flag-wavingly patriotic, but they were really just more bubbas—the Agency nickname for homegrown terrorists with racist, neo-Nazi leanings and a fierce hatred for the federal government. And for all agents of the federal government.

Such as Decker.

Even though Deck's speciality was with terrorist cells of the foreign persuasion, he'd been introduced to informant Gus Mondelay when the man had coughed up what seemed to be evidence that these particular bubbas and al-Qaeda were working in tandem.

Those insane-sounding allegations could not be taken lightly, even though Deck himself couldn't make sense of the scenario. If there was anyone the bubbas hated more than the federal agents, it was foreigners. Although the two groups certainly may have found common ground in their hatred of Israel.

Dougie Brendon, the newly appointed Agency director,

had assigned Decker to Gus Mondelay. Deck was to use Mondelay to try to work his way deeper into the Freedom Network, with the goal of being present at one of the meetings with members of the alleged al-Qaeda cell.

So far all Mondelay had provided him with were leads that had gone nowhere.

Mondelay made the come-closer-to-talk gesture again. "I'm going to give Tim a call, see what's holding him up," he said as he pried his cell phone out of his pants pocket.

Decker watched as the other man keyed in a speed-dial number, then held his phone to his face, plugging his other ear with one knockwurst-size finger. Yeah, that would help him hear over the music.

Mondelay sat back in his chair as whoever he was calling picked up. Decker couldn't hear him, but he could read lips. He turned his head so that Mondelay was right at the edge of his field of vision.

What the fuck is taking so long? Pause, then, *No way, asshole, you were supposeda call me. I bin sitting here for almost an hour now waiting for the fucking goat head.*

Huh?

Fuck you, too, douchebag. Mondelay hung up his phone, leaned toward Decker. "I got the locale wrong," he said. "Tim and the others are over at the Bull Run. It was my mistake. Tim says we should come on over. Join them there."

No. There was no way in hell that Mondelay had been talking to Tim Ebersole, Freedom Network leader. Decker had heard him on the phone with Tim in the past, and it had been all "Yes, sir," and "Right away, sir." "Let me kiss your ass, sir," not "Fuck you, too, douchebag."

Something was rotten in the Gentlemen's Den—something besides Mondelay's toxic breath, that was.

Mondelay wasn't waiting on any goat head. He was waiting for the *go ahead.* The son of a bitch was setting Decker up.

Mondelay began the lengthy process of pushing his huge frame up and out of the seat.

"You boys aren't leaving, are you?"

Decker looked up and directly into the eyes of Tess Bailey, the pretty young computer specialist from the Agency support office.

But okay, no. Truth be told, the first place he looked wasn't into her eyes.

She'd moved to D.C. a few years ago, from somewhere in the Midwest. Kansas, maybe. A small town, she'd told them once when Nash had asked. Her father was a librarian.

Funny he should remember that fact about her right now.

Because, holy crap, Toto, Tess Bailey didn't look like she was in small-town Kansas anymore.

"There's a lady over at the bar who wants to buy your next round," Tess told him, as she shouted to be heard over the music, as he struggled to drag his eyes up to her face.

Nash. The fact that she was here and half-naked—no, forget the half-naked part, although, Jesus, that was kind of hard to do when she was standing there half-fricking-naked —had to mean that Nash was here, too. And if Nash was here, that meant Decker was right, and he was about to be executed. Or kidnapped.

He glanced at Mondelay, at the nervous energy that seemed to surround the big man. No, he got it right the first time. Mondelay was setting him up to be hit.

Son of a bitch.

"She said you were cute," Tess was shouting at Decker, trying desperately for eye contact. He gave it to her. Mostly. "She's over there, in the back." She pointed toward the bar with one arm, using the other to hold her tray up against her chest, which made it a little bit easier to pay attention to what she was saying, despite the fact that it still didn't make any sense. Cute? *Who* was in the back of the bar?

Nash, obviously.

"So what can I get you?" Tess asked, all cheery smile and adorable freckled nose, and extremely bare breasts beneath that tray she was clutching to herself.

"We're on our way out," Mondelay informed her.

"Free drinks," Tess said enticingly. "You should sit back down and stay a while." She looked pointedly at Deck.

A message from Nash. "I'll have another beer," Decker shouted up at her with a nod of confirmation.

Mondelay laughed his disbelief. "I thought you wanted to meet Tim."

Decker made himself smile up at the man who'd set him

up to be killed. Two pals, out making the rounds of the strip clubs. "Yeah, I do."

"Well, they're waiting for us now."

"That's good," Decker said. "We don't want to look too eager, right?" He looked at Tess again. "Make it imported."

Mondelay looked at her, too, narrowing his eyes slightly —a sign that he was probably thinking. "You're new here, aren't you?"

"He'll have another beer, too," Decker dismissed Tess, hoping she'd take the hint and disappear, fast.

Mondelay was in one hell of a hurry to leave, but he was never in too much of a hurry not to harass a waitress when he had the chance. He caught the bottom of her tray. Pulled it down. "You need to work on your all-over tan."

"Yeah," she said, cool as could be. "I know."

"Let her get those beers," Decker said.

"I'd throw her a bang," Mondelay said as if Tess weren't even standing there. "Wouldn't you?"

Deck had been trying to pretend that a woman who was pole-dancing on the other side of the bar had caught his full attention, but now he was forced to look up and appraise Tess, whom he knew had a photo of her two little nieces in a frame on her desk along with a plastic action figure of Buffy the Vampire Slayer. Nash had asked her about it once, and she'd told them Buffy represented both female empowerment and the fact that most people had inner depths not obviously apparent to the casual observer.

Decker felt a hot rush of anger at Nash, who, no doubt, had been taking his flirtation with Tess to the next level when the call came in that Decker needed assistance. He wasn't sure what pissed him off more—the fact that Nash had sent Tess in here without her shirt, or that Nash was sleeping with her.

"Yeah," he said now to Mondelay, since they'd been talking about the waitresses in these bars like this all week. He gave Tess a smile that he hoped she'd read as an apology for the entire male population. "I would also send her flowers, afterward."

"Tell me, hon, do women really go for that sentimental bullshit?" Mondelay asked Tess.

"Nah," she said. "What we really love is being objectified, used, and cast aside. Why else would I have gotten a job here? I mean, aside from the incredible health plan and the awesome 401K."

Decker laughed as she tugged her tray free, and headed toward the bar.

He watched her go, aware of the attention she was getting from the other lowlifes in the bar, noting the soft curve of her waist, and the way that, although she wasn't very tall, she carried herself as if she stood head and shoulders above the crowd. He was also aware that it had been a very long time since he'd sent a woman flowers.

They were in some serious shit here. Whoever set up this ambush had paramilitary training.

There were too many shooters set in position around the building. He couldn't take them all out.

Well, he could. The setup was professional, but the shooters were all amateurs. He could take them all out, one by one by one. And like the first two on the roof, most of them wouldn't even hear him coming.

But Jimmy Nash's hands were already shaking from clearing that roof. A cigarette would've helped, but last time he'd quit, he'd sworn it was for good.

He washed his hands in the sink in the men's, trying, through sheer force of will, to make them stop trembling.

It was that awful picture he had in his head of Decker gunned down in the parking lot that steadied him and made his heart stop hammering damn near out of his chest.

He'd do anything for Deck.

They'd been Agency partners longer than most marriages lasted these days. Seven years. Who'd have believed *that* was possible? Two fucked-up, angry men, one of them—him—accustomed to working alone, first cousin to the devil, and the other a freaking Boy Scout, a former Navy SEAL . . .

When Tess had called him tonight and told him what she'd overheard, that HQ essentially knew Decker was being targeted and that they weren't busting their asses to keep it from happening . . .

The new Agency director, Doug-the-Prick Brendon, hadn't tried to hide his intense dislike of "Diego" Nash, and therefore Decker by association. But this was going too far.

Jimmy used his wet hands to push his hair back from his face, forcing himself to meet his eyes in the mirror.

Murderous eyes.

After he got Decker safely out of here, he was going to hunt down Dougie Brendon, and . . .

"And spend the rest of your life in jail?" Jimmy could practically hear Deck's even voice.

"First they'd have to catch me," he pointed out. And they wouldn't. He'd made a vow, a long time ago, to do whatever he had to do never to get locked up again.

"There are other ways to blow off steam." How many times had Decker said those exact words to him?

Other ways . . .

Like Tess Bailey.

Who was waiting for him in the ladies' room. Who was unbelievably hot. Who liked him—really liked him—he'd seen it in her eyes. She pretended to have a cold-day-in-July attitude when he flirted with her in the office. But Jimmy saw beyond it, and he knew with just a little more charm, and a little bit of well-placed pressure, she'd be giving him a very brightly lit green light.

Tonight.

He'd let Decker handle Doug Brendon.

Jimmy would handle Tess.

He smiled at the pun as he opened the men's room door and went out into the hallway. He pushed open the ladies' room door, expecting to see her, live and in person. But she wasn't there. *Shit.* He checked the stalls—all empty.

It sobered him fast and he stopped thinking about the latter part of the evening, instead focusing on here and now, on finding Tess.

He spotted her right away as he went back into the hall. She was standing at the bar. What the Jesus God was she doing there? But then he knew. Decker and Mondelay had ordered drinks.

And he hadn't been specific enough in his instructions, assuming "get your ass in the ladies' room" meant just that, not "get your ass in the ladies' room after you fill their drink order."

The biggest problem with her standing at the bar was not the fact that she was bare-breasted and surrounded by drunken and leering men.

No, the biggest problem was that she was surrounded by other bare-breasted women—i.e. the real waitstaff of the Gentlemen's Den. Who were going to wonder what Tess was doing cheating them out of their hard-earned tips.

And sure enough, as Jimmy watched, an older woman with long golden curls, who looked an awful lot like the masthead of an old sailing ship—those things had to be implants—tapped Tess on the shoulder.

He couldn't possibly hear U.S.S. Bitch-on-Wheels from this distance. Her face was at the wrong angle for him to read her lips, but her body language was clear. "Who the hell are *you*?"

Time for a little secondary rescue.

He took off his jacket and tossed it into the corner. No one in this dive so much as owned a suit, and his was ruined anyway. He snatched off his tie, too, loosened his collar, and rolled up his sleeves as he pushed his way through the crowd and over to the bar.

"Oh, here he is now," Tess was saying to Miss Masthead as he moved into earshot. She smiled at him, which was distracting as hell, because, like most hetero men, he'd been trained to pick up a strong, positive message from the glorious combination of naked breasts and a warm, welcoming smile. He forced himself to focus on what she was saying.

"I was just telling Crystal about the practical joke, you know," Tess said, crossing her arms in front of her, "that we're playing on your cousin?"

Well, how about that? She didn't need rescuing. The Masthead—Crystal—didn't look like the type to swallow, but she'd done just that with Tess's story.

"Honey, give her a little something extra," Tess told him, "because she did, you know, lose that tip she would have gotten."

Jimmy dug into his pocket for his billfold, and pulled out two twenty-dollar bills.

Tess reached for a third, taking the money from his hands and handing it to her brand-new best friend. "Will you get those two beers for me?" she asked Crystal.

The waitress did better than that—she went back behind the bar to fetch 'em herself.

Tess turned to Jimmy, who took the opportunity to put his arm around her—she had, after all, called him honey. He was just being a good team player and following her lead, letting that smooth skin slide beneath his fingers.

"Thanks." She lowered her voice, turning in closer to him, using him as a way to hide herself—from the rest of the crowd at least. "May I have my shirt back?"

"Whoops," he said. Her shirt was in the pocket of his jacket, which was somewhere on the floor by the rest rooms. That is, if someone hadn't already found it and taken it home.

"Whoops?" she repeated, looking up at him, fire in her eyes.

As Jimmy stared down at her, she pressed even closer. Which might've kept him from looking, but sure as hell sent his other senses into a dance of joy. It was as if they shared the same shirt—she was so soft and warm and alive. He wanted her with a sudden sharpness that triggered an equally powerful realization. It was so strong it nearly made him stagger.

He didn't deserve her.

He had no right even to touch her. Not with these hands.

"Are you all right?" Tess whispered.

Caught in a weird time warp, Jimmy looked down into her eyes. They were light brown—a nothing-special color as far as eyes went—but he'd always been drawn to the intelligence and warmth he could see in them. He realized now, in this odd, lingering moment of clarity, that Tess's eyes were beautiful. *She* was beautiful.

An angel come to save him . . .

"I'm fine," he said, because she was looking at him as if he'd lost it. Crap, maybe he had for a minute there. "Really. Sorry." He kissed her, just a quick press of his lips against hers, because he didn't know how else to erase the worry from her eyes.

It worked to distract her—God knows it did a similar trick on him.

He wanted to kiss her again, longer, deeper—a real touch-the-tonsils, full firework-inducing event, but he didn't. He'd save that for later.

And Decker always said he had no willpower.

He looked out at the crowd, trying to get a read on who was shit-faced drunk—who would best serve as a catalyst for part two of tonight's fun.

"Did you find a way to get Decker out of here?" Tess asked. He could see that he'd managed completely to confuse her. She was back to folding her arms across her chest.

"Yeah, I cleared the roof." He wondered if she had any idea what that meant. He glanced back at the room. There was a man in a green T-shirt who was so tanked his own buddies' laughter was starting to piss him off.

But Tess obviously didn't understand any of what he'd said. "The roof? How . . . ?"

"I called for some help with our extraction." Jimmy explained the easy part. "We'll be flying Deck out of here—a chopper's coming to pick us up, but first we need a little diversion. Have you ever been in a bar fight?"

Tess shook her head.

"Well, you're about to be. If we get separated, keep to the edge of the room. Keep your back to the wall, watch for flying objects and be ready to duck. Work your way around to that exit sign, and . . . Heads up," he interrupted himself.

Because here came ol' Gus, right on cue, searching for Tess, wondering what the fuck was taking so long with their beers, impatient to send Decker to the parking lot where he'd be filled with holes, where he'd gasp out the last breath of his life in the gravel.

And here came Deck, right behind him, the only real gentleman in this den of bottom feeders, ready to jump on Gus's back if he so much as looked cross-eyed at cute little Tess Bailey from support.

"When I knock over that guy sitting there with the black T-shirt that says 'Badass,' " Nash instructed her, meeting his partner's gaze from across the room just as Gus spotted him with Tess. Gus reacted, reaching inside of his baseball jacket either for his cell phone or a weapon—it didn't really matter which because he was so slo-o-o-w, and Deck was already on top of both it and him. "Lean over the bar and shout to your girlfriend Crystal that she should call 911, that someone in the crowd has a gun. On your mark, get set . . ."

Fifteen feet away, Decker brought Gus Mondelay to his knees and then to the floor, which was a damn good thing, because if it had been Nash taking him down, he would have snapped the motherfucker's neck.

". . . Go!"